For Charlotte

Rebekah Hagglund

KRAUT

Based on a True Story

AUSTIN MACAULEY PUBLISHERS™
LONDON * CAMBRIDGE * NEW YORK * SHARJAH

Copyright © Rebekah Hagglund 2023

All rights reserved. No part of this publication may be reproduced, distributed, or transmitted in any form or by any means, including photocopying, recording, or other electronic or mechanical methods, without the prior written permission of the publisher, except in the case of brief quotations embodied in critical reviews and certain other non-commercial uses permitted by copyright law. For permission requests, write to the publisher.

Any person who commits any unauthorized act in relation to this publication may be liable to criminal prosecution and civil claims for damages.

This is a work of fiction. Names, characters, businesses, places, events, locales, and incidents are either the products of the author's imagination or used in a fictitious manner. Any resemblance to actual persons, living or dead, or actual events is purely coincidental.

Ordering Information
Quantity sales: Special discounts are available on quantity purchases by corporations, associations, and others. For details, contact the publisher at the address below.

Publisher's Cataloging-in-Publication data
Hagglund, Rebekah
Kraut

ISBN 9781685620127 (Paperback)
ISBN 9781685620134 (ePub e-book)

Library of Congress Control Number: 2023906743

www.austinmacauley.com/us

First Published 2023
Austin Macauley Publishers LLC
40 Wall Street, 33rd Floor, Suite 3302
New York, NY 10005
USA

mail-usa@austinmacauley.com
+1 (646) 5125767

First I must thank my husband, Kevin Groombridge, for the many lively hours of discussion and for his creative suggestions. Without his belief in the story and me, I would not have brought the manuscript to completion.

I am also grateful to my sister, Barb Clegg, who offered insightful advice and boundless encouragement throughout the writing of the novel.

Ruth Hagglund's knowledge of history made me aware of the complex and enduring issues surrounding World War II and helped me begin my research.

Finally, it is with great affection that I extend my appreciation to Gail Chapple, Deb Buset, Della Cryderman, Jen Edwards, Norm Clegg, Liz Murray, and Patti Bain for their contributions and enthusiastic support.

Table of Contents

Chapter One: Roots — 9

Chapter Two: Reconciliation — 16

Chapter Three: The Advent of Hitler — 25

Chapter Four: Disillusionment — 34

Chapter Five: Friendship — 43

Chapter Six: The Golden Pheasant — 49

Chapter Seven: The Apprentice — 56

Chapter Eight: The Fledgling — 66

Chapter Nine: Violence Unleashed — 78

Chapter Ten: Luminal Moments — 85

Chapter Eleven: Madness — 99

Chapter Twelve: Karl — 113

Chapter Thirteen: Retribution — 122

Chapter Fourteen: A Different Time and Place — 135

Chapter Fifteen: Home — 151

Chapter Sixteen: Shell Shocked — 158

Chapter Seventeen: Concealment — 167

Chapter Eighteen: Ultimatums — 181

Chapter Nineteen: Under Siege — 194

Chapter Twenty: The Spoils of War — 202

Chapter Twenty-One: Returning	211
Chapter Twenty-Two: Head West	224
Chapter Twenty-Three: Cataclysm	233
Chapter Twenty-Four: Nocturne	246
References	253

Chapter One
Roots

It was hot. Too hot even for July. The air in the log house was stifling. Anna picked up her towel and opened the screen door. The lake was completely placid, reflecting the cliffs on the opposite shore with absolute precision. The scratching of crickets in the tall grass and the cry of seagulls over the water were all she heard. The forest was resting in the noonday sun. Barefoot, she walked down the path to the wooden dock.

Years ago, she would have broken into a run and leapt into a dive off the end of the dock. Today, she draped her towel neatly over the wooden bench and lowered herself into the water carefully by way of a solid ladder. She made it. Her feet were firmly planted on the bottom. Instead of the initial shock of cold northern Ontario water, she felt pleasant relief as she quietly dove under and swam out past the dock. Swimming upward, Anna reached that point where she could see the trees and sky through the watery lens of the surface. She felt the sense of being alive between water and air, part of both worlds, merging somehow…

Breaking the calm surface, she took a deep breath of air and then rolled onto her back. She floated weightless in the clear water. The color of the lake reminded her of emeralds. "I need this—the silence, the freedom of Canada," she thought. Anna climbed out of the water and reached for her towel. She was seldom comfortable when her hair was wet or disheveled in any way, and yet today, she didn't care. "I can relax here in the heat. No one will be visiting. In fact, even Niels and Erich will likely be fishing all day."

After fetching a glass of Riesling, her cigarettes and sunglasses, Anna returned to the dock and eased into an Adirondack chair to absorb the sun's rays. As she lit a cigarette, she gazed at the towering red pines beside the cabin. The needles that had fallen last year had changed color from deep green to burnt orange, and with the heat, the blanket of needles released a simultaneously sweet and bitter scent. Anna turned her face to the sun, inhaling. The afternoon passed undisturbed.

Begrudgingly, she left the dock for the cabin where she changed into tan linen pants and a white sleeveless blouse. Her gold anklet, necklace, rings, and earrings were permanent accessories to her wardrobe, even in the wilderness. Once her ash-blonde hair was styled and a bit of makeup applied, she poured another glass of wine and was about to set out appetizers for her sons' return when she heard the slamming of the screen door. "*Mutti*, we are back but no fish. They just aren't biting today. Maybe it's too hot. What can we have for supper instead?" asked Erich.

"Ah, that's too bad about the fish, boys, but we'll be fine. We have steak. We'll eat," Anna joked. Just then Niels came up from behind her and threw out his arms on either side of her body with a very large and slippery fish suspended from each of his hands. Shrugging her shoulders and wincing with revulsion, Anna shrieked, "Oh Niels! Take them outside and filet them. Don't show me those fish again until they are chunks of clean meat on a plate ready for me to prepare for our fish fry!" She enjoyed cooking and eating the fish but wanted nothing to do with the blood and guts.

Anna chopped half of the pickerel into small pieces and covered them in a thick batter made with pancake flour and beer. She then slowly lowered each piece into a pot of hot oil. Once they were puffy and golden, she transferred them onto a platter and served them with lemon slices and tartar sauce. "Did you see any signs of young bald eagles in the nest at Pine Point?" Anna asked.

"Yes, we saw two babies, and the mother returned from hunting long enough for us to get a picture of her feeding them. Check out the photos on my camera. We also saw an otter where that slide is on the bank at the river mouth, but it ducked under water before we could get a picture," Niels explained.

Anna returned to the kitchen island and dipped the remaining filets in a bath of egg, dredged them in her special mix of flour, corn flake crumbs and spices; then into the frying pan. She tossed the coleslaw with a vinegar dressing and took the potato wedges out of the oven. Her sons were talking about the recent Blue Jays' game they had attended in Toronto and about the real estate market in the big city.

The boys had lived in Toronto all of their adult lives but they headed north on the long weekend in July. The vacation had become an annual tradition set aside for Anna and her sons regardless of what was happening in their lives. The wives and children rarely joined them anymore. The wives seemed bored and uncomfortable in the wilderness, and the teenagers preferred to be in Toronto with their friends.

Niels and Erich, however, were born in Thunder Bay and looked forward to the change of pace, time with their mother, and sharing memories about their father. On the sofa table was a photo of him with the boys by their log home—all smiling as they held the catch of the day up for Anna to photograph.

"Niels, I made your favorite dessert, buttercream layer cake!" Anna announced as she carried the cake to the dining room table. Niels expressed boyish delight in his eyes as he hugged his mother, rocking her back and forth. Niels had the sturdy build of his father.

They took coffee to the dock to watch the sunset. The sky had turned a deep turquoise with pale, pink clouds when Erich broke the comfortable silence with, "It is 10:30 already so enjoy the view. We don't have much more time before they're upon us." As predicted, by eleven o'clock, the mosquitoes had descended. The family made a hasty retreat to the house, complaining loudly and slapping various parts of their bodies in an attempt to kill the voracious bugs.

"That's it for me, boys. Goodnight," Anna said as she made for her room with a book in hand.

She sunk into the deep mattress but covered herself with only a sheet. It was still far too hot for the duvet. From the open window, she could hear the mechanical humming of hundreds of mosquitoes against the screen. "The veil is really quite thin between ourselves and that which we dread," she thought, incongruously solemn after such a sparkling summer day.

The soft lamplight warmed the log walls of the bedroom and her mood. "The construction of this spacious log home was an enormous job for him and the log builders. He was so consumed with perfection—impossible with logs as far as I am concerned. I guess he wanted his building to reach the standards in Germany," Anna thought proudly.

In the Scandinavian tradition, the center of each log had been scribed and then cut out with a chainsaw to fit exactly onto the contour of the log below. Once the walls were constructed, the logs were cleaned and sanded. The men coated each one with a sealer that gave a low luster to the walls. They constructed the mason fireplace in the living room out of local granite rocks, and finally, the mantle, hewn from a cedar log, had been placed above the massive firebox. The undertaking took three summers.

"I hate to admit it, but neither of my sons became the man he was. I still worry about my middle-aged boys, and yet I would never have been concerned about their father when he was half their age. Times have changed," Anna mused.

She looked at the photo on the dresser and remembered, "This was taken in 1950. *Mein Gott*, we were such a happy couple. He was muscular and handsome, but my, his serious expression. Always so strong. No one ever guessed how depression tormented him after the war even after we immigrated here to Ontario."

"Surprisingly, *Vater* had managed to return to life after the war—not the same man we had known—Mother and I. But they couldn't kill him, no not Olav! Olav and Mari Muller, a son-of-a-bitch and a saint! How I miss my parents," she smiled to herself.

As Anna lay sleepless, unable to focus on reading her novel, her mind drifted back to Germany. She thought of Leipzig where she was born, a city with so much history and culture—contrasting with the almost frontier towns in northern Ontario.

Gracious architecture lined the avenues of Leipzig. Art, theatre, and music thrived. Venerated composers such as Bach, Schumann, Mendelssohn, and Wagner made Leipzig one of the music centers of Europe. It was this tradition that was the wellspring for her father Olav's passion for music.

After his graduation, Olav had taught music at the conservatory and in their home, and also played clubs and special events, including the Industrial Exhibition in Cologne. Anna had a poignant memory of that period when she was the only child in their family. "Yes, it must have been before the exhibition when we went to the park," Anna reflected.

Leipzig

As Mari spread a blanket on the grass for their picnic, she glanced at her husband, Olav. How she loved to spend time with him. He was knowledgeable, talkative and so attractive to her—his black eyes and thick dark hair, his sensual lips. Although six feet tall, Olav did not seem intimidating because of a constant, subtle slouch that made him appear relaxed. But she knew how when threatened, his lean body would respond with a speed and fury that inspired respect, and sometimes fear, in many powerful men. But for now, Olav seemed to curve into his saxophone, eyes shut, completely involved in the music he was playing for her. She smiled as she listened to the last refrain of "After You're Gone."

"Come and have some lunch, *lottchen*," Mari called to Anna, and to her husband, "That sounds wonderful, Olav, *meine guteliebe*, but you must eat too. Look we have cheese, smoked salmon, rye bread and cake!"

Anna, who had been picking flowers, presented her mother with a slightly mangled and drooping bouquet of daisies and clover that had been unable to withstand the tight grip of her little hands. She then turned and reached her arms upward to Olav who swept his daughter into the air and spun her in a circle, legs outstretched.

"Anna is flying," Olav sang out. Anna giggled until they fell onto the blanket.

She clung to her father's neck and begged, "*Vati* again, please *Vati!*" Olav flashed a smile and in a moment was spinning her wildly around. Then for the finale he threw her up in the air and caught her firmly on the way down.

"My *lottchen* is so brave," he said as he kissed her flushed cheek. "And now, let's eat what *Mutti* has prepared for us."

They ate hungrily, not needing to say much, cocooned in the warmth of the summer sun and a sense of family. After a large piece of cake, Olav rolled up his shirt sleeves and lit a cigarette. Mari poured them each a glass of Mosel and began to pack up the remains of their lunch. Anna was splashing in all directions as she ran through the shallow water along the bank.

Then Mari lay on her side with her head supported on one hand, facing her husband. She began, "Frieda says the Baumanns can barely make a living on the farm anymore. Many of the farmers are meeting together in protest…and, she says a man has been loitering around the hair salon lately, asking questions about all kinds of things. He asks for her opinion about the problems in Germany, what she wants to see changed. She says nothing to the stranger because she thinks he is a spy for Adolf and his thugs."

After a pause, Olav responded, "Like me, Adolf fought in WWI. In fact, I think he reached corporal and received the Iron Cross for bravery so he has shown his courage and dedication to Germany. Who knows, maybe someone like Adolf can make the changes we need. We had a great economy once.

Didn't they call us the industrial heartland of Europe? …We need those jobs back.

Even if we produced the goods, high tariffs are restricting our exports. And you know how the Armistice saddled the government with unfair reparations after the war. Look how Britain has blocked our food supply! We have been forced into an impossible position. Something must be done sooner or later. This can't go on."

Mari nodded in agreement.

"You say the farmers are protesting, but when are they ever satisfied? You know, I think that maybe your friend, Frieda, is overreacting," Olav concluded emphatically and then drew on his cigarette and took another sip of wine.

Mari sighed, "Yes, we want more self-sufficiency, but remember that the Social Democratic Party was committed to democracy, freedom for women, and the ending of racial discrimination as well. Adolf's party does not value these things.

I think Adolf admires Mussolini, the way he and his 'black shirts' seized power six years ago. Mussolini and his secret police—ruling elite! That is where I think Adolf is going. Ah! Adolf is a dangerous lunatic the way he rants on street corners and in beer halls. And Olav, what he says about the Jews upsets me terribly. I have read *Mein Kampf*!"

"Well Mari, I seriously doubt that we will have anything to worry about. It is unlikely that Adolf will even garner enough votes to win this regional election anyway. The communists will offset the vote. He will never become the *Fuhrer* as he likes to call himself? And the Jewish issue? Well, I tell you, my darling, it is sad to say, but most of Europe shares his view. It is prejudice, just human nature. Many resent the financial success of the Jews," Olav explained.

"Anna, Anna that is far enough *puppe*. Come in closer to shore," Olav called to his daughter.

"What of this man at Frieda's salon though?" Mari asked once more. "Frieda is concerned because his questions do not seem normal for salon conversation. And, I tell you, I have never seen Frieda overreact as you say. Maybe there is more to this…"

Unexpectedly, Olav shot his finger into Mari's face. "That is enough! I have told you the way it is, and you keep pressing me. Enough!" Olav hissed with unwarranted fury. "I came here to enjoy some peace with my family and you keep pushing me. I should go to the conservatory with Mr. Wolfe instead of trying to have a reasonable conversation with you!"

The day had changed drastically. Mari's hands trembled slightly as she rolled up the blanket, but her kind face remained calm, hazel eyes expressionless. She knew how to mask her feelings. She rationalized meekly, "I know Olav doesn't intend to hurt me. What did I say to upset him so? It is my fault for bringing up the topic of Frieda's salon. After all, I know he does not like some of Frieda's views or her independent nature. I will have to be quiet, less forthright with my opinions."

Olav stood poised, glaring at her, his face hard. "Well? What do you have to say for yourself now that YOU have ruined our day?" But Mari could not speak.

Anna heard her father's aggressive shouting and saw his threatening stance. She immediately stopped playing in the water, and quickly crept up behind her father and dripping wet, she hugged his legs, "I love you, *Vati*." Olav swung around angrily, but when he saw Anna's damp blonde curls and laughing blue eyes, he smiled and said, "Now I don't have to swim, do I? I am soaked. Watch out; I will catch you and give you a spanking!" Olav joked.

"You can't catch me, *Vati*," Anna squealed and off she ran with her father in pursuit, feigning a Herculean effort.

On their way home completely forgetting the outburst, Olav held Mari's hand and carried Anna on his hip. "What a fine day, my lovely ladies," he said.

Chapter Two
Reconciliation

Olav raised his collar and pulled the brim of his hat lower on his forehead as he left the conservatory and stepped into sleet. It was April of 1933. By the time he approached his home, rain had turned to ice pellets in the wind and the sky was dark and heavy, more like late evening than five in the afternoon. "Spring hmmpf! Well, weather is the least of our problems these days. Too many have been out of work since the depression—bankruptcies, starvation. That fool, Von Schleicher, reduced unemployment assistance and increased our taxes. How much more can we take?

Adolf was sworn in as chancellor last month and with the communists in check maybe Germany will see a return of jobs. Surely the new party won't be as ineffective as the Social Democrats," Olav thought.

Olav entered the house quietly, hung his wet coat and scarf on the carved wooden coat tree and placed his hat on the three-legged table that his mother had given them as a wedding gift. He made his way from the foyer, down the hallway where the stairs led up to the bedrooms, passing the living room to the left and dining room on the right and into the kitchen.

Mari was humming while she peeled potatoes for dinner. "You're home!" she said with a smile. "I am putting the potatoes on."

Olav had always admired Mari's composure. Being near her settled his stormy emotions. He placed his hands around her waist and pulled her close. He leaned over to kiss her, but was interrupted when Leo their four-year old son ran into the kitchen shouting, "Help, *Mutti,* Anna is tickling me. Help!" Mari lifted him up for a hug and then passed him over to Olav so she could feed baby Rita in the high chair. Later Anna, now twelve years old, set the table and Mari served dinner. Olav felt very content within the walls of his home.

The next morning Mari prepared a breakfast of boiled eggs, buns and jam as well as herring strips and coffee. Leo played with his spoon while he ate a bun smothered with strawberry jam. Mari fed Rita on her lap. Olav commented on the rainy weather as he smoked a cigarette and drank the remains of his coffee.

Then Olav noticed that Anna hadn't eaten. He looked at her with inquiring, gentle eyes. Anna returned a worried gaze and explained, "Yesterday we heard shooting in the street outside of the school again. Who do they kill? Do you think they will return today, *Vati*?"

Olav didn't answer his daughter, but Mari consoled her with, "Only bad people have to worry, not a lovely girl like you. I'll walk with you to school as soon as I take Leo and Rita next door to the Hoffmans."

That morning Anna didn't link arms with Mari as they walked down the street. She stood straight and held her head high, long wavy blonde hair reaching her lower back. Anna was slim and tall for her age and walked with controlled, determined steps. Today she was uncharacteristically quiet, her mouth firmly set. Mari finally asked, "Is something else troubling you, *mein liebe*? Talk to *Mutter*."

"Some girls at school tease me unfairly. They think I am the favorite of our teacher. I do not want problems, *Mutti*, so I complete my assignments carefully and do not talk to others during class. At break time, these girls won't play with me and my best friend, Klara. They whisper to each other and laugh at us when we pass by. They are stupid! They tell the teacher I do not sing *Deutschland* with the rest of the class just to make trouble for me. Why?" Anna exclaimed in almost a whisper.

"Oh they are probably jealous of you. Girls can be quite cruel if they feel another is superior in some way. Do not let them speak disrespectfully to you. You must stand up for yourself. Oh, here we are, my darling. I will come for you when school ends," Mari promised.

The day passed by without conflict, but just as the students were being dismissed for the day, Emily, the instigator, began to chime, "Anna loves teacher, Anna loves teacher."

To that Anna commanded, "Shut your mouth you stupid girl!"

But again Emily taunted, "Anna loves teacher, Anna loves teacher."

Anna pushed Emily in the chest, "You are stupid and so is *Herr Richter*! I don't love him."

By now the teacher, *Herr Richter*, was in the foray. He clamped on to Anna's arm, "Stop this right now! You come with me."

But Anna struggled free and faced him. "*Blode!*" she challenged. "I am not the one to punish!"

Without hesitation, the teacher slapped her face so hard, her nose and lip began to bleed. Anna held her position and didn't cry. Instead she warned, "*Vater* will teach YOU a lesson, teacher!" Then she turned and ran out of the school to where Mari waited. After one look at her daughter, Mari took her by the arm and rushed away from the school to their home.

Mari controlled the bleeding from Anna's nose and disinfected her lip, but her cheek was already beginning to bruise badly. They sat together at the kitchen table feeling tired and numb, worried about the consequences that would surely follow. Mari didn't press Anna about her injuries; instead, they sat quietly and sipped coffee. Leo played with tin soldiers on the floor. Rita was still napping. All was quiet for now.

Finally, Olav arrived home from work. When he saw his daughter's face, he demanded to know what had happened. After he heard the story, he sat down with them and stared out the window. His face darkened. Slowly he rose and without a word, he took the bat for cleaning rugs out of the broom cupboard and left the house.

When he arrived at the school, *Herr Richter* was preparing lessons in the classroom. It was over quickly. With precision and force, Olav bludgeoned the teacher, "Don't you EVER touch my daughter again or I WILL kill you!"

The following morning Klara was waiting at her desk for Anna. When she saw Anna, her eyes widened in shock. Then she quickly concealed her expression of fear and concern and whispered across the aisle to her friend, "He should never have done this to you!"

"He won't hit me again," replied Anna with fire in her eyes. She motioned with her chin to the front of the class. The headmaster was introducing a new teacher to the students.

At break the girls went outside and began skipping rope. They were surprised when Emily approached them. "May I play with you?" she asked politely. With a smile Klara made a motion with her arm to include Emily.

Anna interrupted firmly, "No, you may not!"

Emily stared at Anna and then turned away. Klara's cheeks flushed and her blue eyes were momentarily sad.

After Emily had rejoined her friends, Anna said, "Stupid girl."

To which Klara agreed, "Stupid girl." They both began to giggle as they resumed skipping rope.

Klara was much better than Anna at skipping and most other school sports for that matter. She was physically balanced and strong with her long torso proportionate to strong legs. Instead of being competitive with Anna though, Klara tried to help Anna when she tripped or fell while skipping. As far as Anna was concerned Klara was the only friend she needed.

Mari was planting a vegetable garden in the backyard, thinking about how to tell Olav that she was pregnant again when her husband came through the gate talking breathlessly. Apparently, he had been accepted to the Industrial Exhibition in Cologne again. He mentioned the money he would earn while taking his vacation from the conservatory and also assured Mari that he would not be gone for long. Mari had not seen him so exuberant for many months, and since the last time he had performed at the exhibition was in 1928, she encouraged him to go. The news of her pregnancy could wait for his return.

When Olav boarded the train for Cologne, the *brown shirts*, Hitler's private army, were creating confusion with their aggressive gestures and loud, coarse speech. While Olav pretended to doze, he noted that the situation on the train was quite ordinary, hardly warranting the behavior of the soldiers. They seemed to be searching for something or someone. As the passengers disembarked in Cologne, the *brown shirts* bullied what must have been one hundred people onto the platform and were checking their identification papers. Other soldiers were beating men and women viciously. Stifled screams filled the air and blood spatters covered the landing, but Olav passed unnoticed with his instruments.

When he arrived at the exhibition grounds, Olav drove the disturbing scene on the train from his mind. The smell of food, the noise of machinery, the rides, and orchestras rehearsing sent a wave of excitement through his body. Olav reached the organizers with ease and on his way to his assigned accommodations, met the boisterous drummer from his former band, who greeted him with, "Say, I haven't seen you since the show in '28! We left that crowd wanting more, yes, *Herr Muller*? Will you have a drink later?"

Along with Horst on stand-up bass, Cora on piano, and Olav on either clarinet or saxophone, the band had entertained audiences with jazz tunes from the United States. "Yes please, come over around 5:00," Olav invited.

A bottle of vodka later along with the obligatory toasts, and the men were well on their way to forgetting the angst in the air of Germany.

The next day, Olav and Horst were setting up for a rehearsal, alternating between lively banter and conversations about how to improve their repertoire when they were interrupted by a guttural, feminine voice uncomfortably familiar to Olav.

He turned around to see the pianist Cora. "Olav, darling," she said flamboyantly as she embraced him. "Will we be able to perform some songs together again? Perhaps *Ain't Misbehavin'* to shake things up?"

Olav was noncommittal as he gently backed a safe distance away from Cora. "Possibly, but let's see what the others have to say." He began to play his saxophone and other musicians joined him, including Cora.

That evening, Cora, determined to be with Olav, knocked at his door. As she entered the room, she asked in a low voice, "Do you remember 1928, Olav? You played words on your tongue that made my soul dance! I never forgot you." He hesitated, glaring at her. He couldn't get enough of her tiny body, deep voice and wild sexuality. The attraction overpowered him. He pushed her against the closed door and angrily kissed her mouth. In the days that followed, Olav was in a constant state of arousal, not only because of Cora.

He was addicted to the musician's life. With each performance the audience applauded and begged for an encore. Olav responded to the adrenalin sensation that the crowds evoked. He fed on the fusion of his passion for music and desire for recognition. He wasn't ready to leave Cologne just yet.

In Leipzig the family had been concerned about what had delayed Olav. Mari pacified the children with plausible explanations that remained invalidated with each passing day. After another week of worry combined with gestational toxemia, Mari was feeling quite ill. She called upon her mother-in-law, Beatrice, to help with the care of the children for a couple of days while she took some rest at Frieda's.

After a visit to the doctor for medication, Mari stayed in Frieda's apartment behind the hair salon sleeping and enjoying simple meals of broth and rye bread. She tried not to succumb to her raging thoughts. "Has Olav met someone in Cologne? Will he leave our family? How will I manage? How could he abandon us?"

Although Frieda worked in her salon in the daytime, during the evening the friends talked for hours and Frieda trimmed and arranged Mari's hair and polished her nails. Mari soon felt better under her care. "Life will be fine as long as I have my children and my friend. I can survive without him," she thought. She didn't know that Olav was, in fact, on his way home.

As Olav stepped off the street car in Leipzig and began to walk the remaining blocks home, his heart quickened. He longed for the company of his wife and the spontaneous affection of his children. He yearned for the familiar smells of cooking and cleaning, of the fresh linen on their bed, his wife's skin. He had stayed away too long and jeopardized the trust of his family over Cora and the orchestra. Olav closed his eyes as the scorch of shame struck him. He braced himself and opened the front door to his home.

Instead of his wife, his mother, Beatrice, greeted him sarcastically with, "Well Son, I hope you enjoyed your holiday while I have been caring for your children. Mari is staying with Frieda. She has not been feeling well."

"What is wrong with her? I must see her now!"

"She will be fine. You stay here and give her until tomorrow to rest. It is too late to fetch her now. I will take the children to the Hoffmans' in the morning and then see how Mari is," Beatrice ordered above Leo's screams.

Anna was trying unsuccessfully to calm her brother. Beatrice impatiently told her to leave him be, "*Grosmutter* will put Leo to bed, *naseweiss*."

The moment Beatrice left with Leo, Anna, now very frustrated, shook her head and thought, "*Grosmutter* thinks I am difficult! I can't do anything right in her eyes. She doesn't know how we like to do things in our house. Now that *Vati* is home maybe she will leave."

"Don't you have a hug for me, Anna?" asked Olav. But instead of returning his affection, Anna demanded angrily, "Where have you been? You never came home when you said you would. We have all been very frightened. How could you do this to us? …YOU made *Mutti* sick!" Anna was fearless as she confronted her father.

He listened with an expression of genuine pain. "Forgive me, *lottchen*, I was wrong. I should never have left you so long without word!"

Her anger vanished and she was once again a worried, young girl needing the protection of her father. She pressed her head against Olav's chest. "I am so glad you are home."

"Dinner is ready in the kitchen if you are hungry, Son," said the shrill voice from the stairs.

"Thank you, Mother," Olav answered formally while Anna stepped back from her father and wiped away her tears. She knew her grandmother couldn't bear demonstrations of love or weakness.

"What about me," Anna thought. "I haven't eaten either. It is our food not yours." In defiance, Anna marched into the foyer and took an apple from the bowl on the three-legged table. This was not allowed without her grandmother's permission.

"Put that apple back immediately!" Beatrice commanded.

She believed it her duty to discipline this willful grandchild and assumed she would have the support of her son, but instead he argued firmly, "Mother, Anna can have an apple if she wants. In fact, she can have as many apples as she pleases and some dinner too."

Anna, sullen through dinner, asked to be excused from the table and left the kitchen to go upstairs. As she placed her foot on the first step, her grandmother caught up with her and threatened in a low voice, "You'll mind me next time, or I'll give you a beating."

After taking another four steps up the stairs, Anna turned, now higher than her grandmother, and retorted confidently, "Mind your own business. We don't want you here anyway. We don't like you." She heard no reply as she climbed the remaining stairs to her room.

In the kitchen, Olav noticed his mother's crimson face and hard jaw. He attempted to change her mood with talk about recent political pamphlets and a bit of local gossip. He moved on to some anecdotes about the exhibition in an attempt to cheer her but was highly unsuccessful.

Finally, Beatrice said goodnight to her son, her posture remaining rigid and her face like stone. Olav closed the living room doors and thought:

"*Mein Gott*! *Mutter* is unbearable,
  my children are unhappy,
  my wife is unreachable,
  and I am...unfaithful." He had a cigarette and then reached for a brandy.

The following morning, Mari was having a coffee while helping Frieda clean the salon when suddenly Beatrice barged in announcing Olav's return. Mari put her coffee cup down and stared at Frieda. She was about to thank Beatrice for her help when the domineering mother-in-law truncated her sentence to complain, "I am appalled by the state of your home, Mari, you must be better organized... The windows could use a proper cleaning. I am too exhausted chasing after your disobedient children to possibly clean your house too. You have made me ill. I may need medical attention now. And YOU, You should be home to take care of the needs of your husband. What kind of a wife..." Mari, who had not had a chance to say a word, simply nodded. Beatrice abruptly turned and exited the salon seething with disgust.

After a brief conversation with Frieda, Mari left for the trolley car weakened by the confrontation. She was grateful that it was still morning. In the afternoon, violence often erupted in the streets among the *brown shirts* and later escalated in the bars and dance clubs during the evening. "Aggression in a void of intelligent thought..." Mari thought.

Mari brought the children home from the Hoffmans' next door and then put Rita down for a nap. She sat with Leo on her lap. He placed his head on her chest and told her stories that were partly true and mostly fantasy. Then she took the hand of Leo and climbed the stairs to put him to bed for a nap as well. The chill of Beatrice was gone and instead she had sweet Leo. She thought, "Four years of warmth transfers through your tiny hand. I love you so."

Mari was still weak but cleaning and cooking in her familiar surroundings made her feel better. Her anger gave her some energy as she thought, "He is so selfish! Cologne always Cologne! What will happen when I see him?" Mari wondered. She had finished making soup and dumplings when she heard the door open. It was too early for her husband or Anna to be home. "Hello, hello?" she called out.

The response was music from Olav's saxophone. He was playing "Yours is My Heart Alone." Never before had he played her favorite song with such feeling. As he entered the kitchen, he laid the saxophone on a kitchen chair. He walked slowly over to where she was standing and raised his hand to touch her face, but she blocked his forearm. They stood still, not touching, their eyes locked. Then Olav reached out and cradled her face in his hands. He kissed her gently at first and then deeply. Mari slowly responded but then began kissing his lips and face frantically. He lifted her onto the kitchen counter and raised her dress, stroking her thighs while he kissed her face. Then he took out the hair pins that held her long, dark blonde hair. He kissed her neck and opened the top buttons to expose her breasts. They didn't leave the kitchen.

Olav was overcome with relief when he realized that not only was his family still intact, but Mari was pregnant with their fourth child.

Olav's decision to put his family first was put to the test not long after the reconciliation.

The following week, the Mullers received a visit from an American promoter, Mr. Roth, whose family had emigrated from Germany. Olav had only met the man briefly at the exhibition and wasn't quite sure what the purpose of his visit might be.

Mari did not care for the man, too showy for her. But Anna and Leo thought he was fascinating. Mr. Roth wore a white Stetson cowboy hat, pale suit and bola tie. Leo was particularly taken with the Texan's leather cowboy boots.

"Olav, come to the States," Roth said. "You'll make a fortune. In my orchestra you will be a star. Y'all, have talent, sir!" and to Mari, "Mrs. Muller, you will love the States; the country is vast. You could own acres. Imagine raising your family on a big spread, or, if city life is your thing, the music scene is in New York. We are moving our orchestra to be among the greats like Duke Ellington and Paul Whiteman, Fletcher Henderson…"

Olav interrupted him in the midst of his spiel. "I am sorry, Mr. Roth that you have wasted your time coming all the way here to make such a proposition. My wife and I appreciate your offer and flattering words about my potential as a musician, but the answer is no."

Relief filled Mari's being. She would not lose Olav to the entertainer's life.

Pride filled Olav's heart. He had chosen to remain in Germany with his family for the rest of his life.

Disappointment filled Anna's heart. She would have liked to see the States.

Chapter Three
The Advent of Hitler

"The *Fuhrer* is delayed," the loud speaker blared. "Continue to enjoy the music and dancing." Olav bought another beer and read the pamphlet that had been distributed to everyone entering the beer hall. Hitler had been flying to halls across Germany oftentimes speaking in two different cities in one day. He never ceased campaigning in person as well as on the radio.

Tonight the people were wildly hopeful to hear the words of their leader who had a vision for a united and flourishing Germany. The music stopped. "The *Fuhrer* has landed! It won't be much longer until you will see him with your own eyes!" the Nazi officer announced over the loud speaker and then went on to denounce the current Weimar Republic.

"The cavalcade has arrived! He is entering the hall—Your leader!" The hall which was filled beyond capacity vibrated with the cheers of supporters. Tension mounted as Hitler took the podium.

He waited until the room fell silent then slowly began to talk about the people's party as he liked to refer to the National Socialist German Worker's Party—or more simply—the Nazi Party. His voice rose up an octave higher and increased in volume as he began to talk about the humiliation of Germany following WWI and the widely hated Treaty of Versailles. He vehemently gesticulated as he described a racially pure German people and superior industrial economy. His crescendo was an assertion that Germany's enemies would soon know the power of the Nazi party. The pride of the German people would be restored.

Hitler left an emotionally charged crowd for his cavalcade where he was swept away in a powerful display of roaring engines and heavily armed and uniformed soldiers. The national pride that Hitler's speech evoked was contagious. As the hall emptied, Olav heard people damning the Hindenburg government and its feudal ways and shouting for change.

Through this constant campaigning, the Nazi party had been gaining momentum in the regional elections and by 1933 the timing was ideal for Hitler to move to a position of power. President Paul Von Hindenburg of the Weimar Republic appointed Hitler as chancellor. At first Hitler retained most of the administration in the government so he didn't appear to be the leader of a coup. He also wanted the government to appear stable. In reality he was moving with lightning speed to secure his position.

By April the first concentration camp was established at *Dachau* to imprison political opposition. In May labor unions and associations were banned. By July, he eliminated all parties except the Nazis, and even the Communist Party did not revolt. However, for Hitler to gain complete control, he had to gain the loyalty of the military.

On one hand, the *brown shirts or Sturmabteilung (SA)*, led by Ernst Roehm were becoming mutinous even though they began as Hitler's private army. Mistrust of Hitler had been growing rapidly among officers.

On the other hand, Hitler had the challenge of winning the support of the traditional German army of 100,000 led by Prussian aristocrats who were typically opposed to the methods and ideology of the *brown shirts*.

To begin the unification of his forces, Hitler chose Heinrich Himmler, the head of the *Schutzstaffel* (SS), a Nazi elite bodyguard unit, to investigate Roehm. Also, Hermann Goering was appointed to create the *Gestapo*, the secret state police.

By June of 1934 the *Blood Purge* began. In Munich, 3,000 *brown shirts* were rampaging in the streets and denouncing Hitler and the German army. Hitler himself confronted the leaders in a rage, ripping off epaulettes with his bare hands and sending the leaders off to prison. He went on to the Hanselbauer Hotel to capture homosexual leaders who were sleeping off the night before. With a whip in hand, Hitler called for the arrest of the leaders as they emerged from their rooms.

Rudolph Hess, commandant of Dachau concentration camp, volunteered to shoot the traitors. Heines who had led an uprising against the Nazi Party in Berlin was shot along with Roehm and three others and the rest were sent to Dachau. The SS then arrested other leading *brown shirts* arriving at Munich's railway station en route to a secret meeting.

Hermann Goering ordered the storming of the Vice Chancellery. General von Schleicher, Hitler's predecessor as Reich Chancellor, a man who once described Hitler as unfit to hold office, was shot dead in his home with his wife. Gregor Strasser, a personal enemy of Goering and Himmler and open critic of the Party leadership, was taken to police headquarters and shot.

In Munich the *brown shirts* were the target while in Berlin, the Nazis aimed at the conservatives. The leaders were driven to the forest and shot in the middle of the night. In the region of Bavaria, former Minister Gustav Ritter von Kahr, who had played a key part in the quelling of the Hitler Beer Putch in 1923, was cut to pieces by the SS. At Nazi Party Headquarters, Hitler ranted:

"Undisciplined and disobedient characters and asocial or diseased elements will be annihilated."

Over the radio, Propaganda Minister Dr. Joseph Goebbels immediately condoned the torture and murder of hundreds of opponents during this *Blood Purge* with rationalizations that they must clean-up dangerous and degenerate elements to the Nazi movement. He broadcasted:

"If a mutiny broke out on board a ship, the captain was not only entitled but also obliged to crush the mutiny right away."

Hitler's actions received no criticism from judicial authorities. The people saw the events as decisive. Hitler made his position clear:

"I gave the order to shoot those parties mainly responsible for this treason… And every person should know for all time that if he raises his hand to strike out at the State, certain death will follow."

In August 1934, President Hindenburg died. Hitler assumed the office of both president and chancellor combined. He had become the sole leader, *Fuhrer,* of the Nazi Party and Germany.

The Weimar Republic was over and the Third Reich had begun.

These events were unknown to many Germans. Daily life continued. As Mari nursed Ralfie, Anna took Leo and little Rita outside to play in the backyard. Once she saw that they were playing well together, Anna went inside to the kitchen to prepare dinner. She watched her brother and sister carefully through the kitchen window as she put the *porkwurstchen* and potatoes on to boil. The coffee was made and bread sliced.

When the family was gathered around the table, Olav told them that he had been called up by the military to manage one of the *Erla Maschinenwerk* aircraft manufacturing plants.

"I will have an increase in pay!" He stood and with his hands on his chest boasted comically, "And, I will be *Oberleutnant*. You will think me very handsome in my new uniform!"

"*Vati* handsome? All the girls will like you," joked Leo.

"*Mutti* is the only girl for me," reassured Olav. "You, young man, will have to polish my tall leather boots!" Olav teased.

They were all smiling as Anna cleared away the plates.

Later when Olav was alone with Mari he urged, "Now you won't have to work so hard—take fewer sewing jobs."

"Olav, you are concerned, but don't worry. I enjoy my sewing and Anna helps with the housework and little ones. And, if we are both working we can afford extra food and household necessities."

To say Mari did some sewing was an understatement. Her fine costumes, dresses, suits and coats were in demand among the upper middle class in Leipzig. Not only was Mari a precise seamstress but her sense of style, creative designs, and color choices flattered her customer's body type. This customized quality guaranteed regular and loyal customers.

The couple agreed that the extra work would only be temporary and were convinced that the difficult times were behind them.

Olav had decided to continue music classes in the home with one student, a lawyer and long-time friend. He told Mari, "Tomorrow evening I will enjoy a violin session with *Herr Wolfe*."

"Ah good, darling, Frieda is coming by as well tomorrow," said Mari.

The following evening, Olav heard Mr. Wolfe's deep voice at the door. "May I come in, friends? I can't wait to be out of this merciless autumn cold." Although the Mullers had to ration coal, the house felt warm to Mr. Wolfe. The men retreated into the living room and closed the glass doors.

Mr. Wolfe smiled as they ended the first movement of a challenging double violin concerto by Bach. "Now let us play it at my tempo, Olav!" They both chuckled as they reverently placed the instruments in their cases. Olav reached for two glasses and the brandy and asked gravely, "So my friend, I hear terrible things. What has happened?"

"As you know, he has excluded Jews from civil service and universities, but now doctors and lawyers are barred from practice. Who could have imagined?

Remember the campaign against Woolworth's last year? We thought they couldn't be serious, considering the number of Jews Woolworth's employs, but Adolf's *brown shirts* completely destroyed the store.

Also, a colleague of mine on business from Hamburg said an ad in the newspaper read, 'Whoever buys Nivea articles is helping to support a Jewish company.' Is Nivea next?

A staggering number of Jews have already been arrested. He says the boycott of small Jewish businesses is occurring all across Germany. The humiliation to these German citizens is intolerable. Thousands are immigrating to avoid future harassment. Some have no choice. Their businesses have been ruined, homes vandalized, and families beaten," Mr. Wolfe exclaimed under his breath even though they would never be overheard in the Muller living room.

"Yes, and hundreds have left the universities," added Olav. "What will you do?"

"The men in coats were at the office today. And, the slogan they wrote on the window…" Mr. Wolfe's dark eyes revealed despair changing to anger. "I must act quickly, but Olav, I am German. I will not leave!" Mr. Wolfe growled.

He offered a cigarette to Olav and then lit one for himself. "Now that Adolf is in power, he will stop at nothing to fulfill his ambitions, he continued. No, I will not allow these Nazi fascists to drive me from my homeland."

Olav nodded. They drank in silence before continuing to discuss the growing military presence in Leipzig and the ubiquitous Nazi propaganda. As the men parted, they cheerfully talked about another music lesson, but when they shook hands good humor was replaced with grave concern in their eyes.

Olav watched while his friend disappeared into the night. When he returned to the living room, he thought, "Surely Adolf's racial policy is based on finance and will be more subdued when Germany's economy recovers."

While the men were in the living room with their music, Frieda had arrived. Anna came into the kitchen to say goodnight to her mother; but when she saw

Frieda, she rushed over and hugged her tightly around the shoulders. "*Tante Frieda*! When did you arrive? You look so beautiful! *Mutti*, look at her pink nail polish."

"Yes, it is very pretty but, please, go to bed now," pleaded Mari.

Frieda walked Anna to her room. "Anna, you must visit the salon soon, and I will paint your nails the same color as mine," Anna nodded eagerly.

"Let's say prayers." They both knelt beside the bed. "Now goodnight, my darling," Frieda whispered as she hugged Anna.

Mari and Frieda enjoyed listening to the violin music drifting in from the living room, but the music had the added benefit of protecting their frank conversation from the ears of the men.

Frieda told hilarious anecdotes about her clientele in the salon and some juicy but harmless stories that Katia, a Nazi call girl, had told her. Frieda had dyed the woman's hair platinum blonde and colored her nails while being entertained by Katia's bawdy language about the sexual habits of a few of her regular businessmen and nameless Nazi officers.

"Frieda stop! My side aches!" Mari laughed holding her side. She wiped the tears from her eyes. Frieda smiled broadly and shook her head back and forth at the thought of Katia.

Mari's mood became serious. "What is it, Mari? Did I say something that offended you?"

"Oh no, of course not! It is Anna… Frieda, I have been thinking about her future lately. Anna does not want to continue her education in university… The school requests that students make apprenticeship choices before Christmas. What will suit her?

She doesn't care much for sewing and doesn't seem to have the natural ability for it anyway. She won't consider nursing either. She says the thought of blood and broken limbs makes her nauseated. She has no idea about what job to pursue and the alternative?… I don't want her to marry and start a family before she is ready. She must learn to be independent…"

Mari paused and then wrinkled her forehead and pleaded, "I'm wondering if you would be willing to take her on as an apprentice at the salon. Anna worships you and is always eager to visit the salon. She has a sense of style and learns quickly. Once she knows what is expected, she will reliably complete her duties. Also, she is very polite unless…well you know."

"Yes, yes," replied Frieda without hesitation, "I will gladly take her on. You know I would do anything for you."

When Frieda Portner left the Mullers', her mind was full of questions about the apprenticeship. She made only one brief stop to talk with a friend before safely boarding the streetcar home. She was relieved to open the salon door and the world of beauty-making.

The salon was shaped in a rectangle with six dryers along the wall beside the entry and three styling chairs situated in front of mirrors on the opposite wall. A table for manicures was on one side of the entry and the cash register and chairs for waiting customers on the other. Three sinks and a doorway to Frieda's apartment were along the back wall.

Frieda's apartment had one bedroom with a dresser, bedside table, double bed, and ladder-back chair. There was no living room, but the kitchen was spacious, holding a sofa, antique dining room table and six chairs, and against the wall, a narrow table with a sink in the center. A tall cabinet contained a few dishes, pots, and a kettle and beside it a counter supported a small gas stove on which soup was almost always simmering.

At the rear of the kitchen was a hallway leading to a storage room that accommodated a narrow single bed on one side and a bathroom and toilet on the other. The back door led to a yard with a wash house, clothesline, and vegetable garden. The building had no cellar or underground foundation.

Frieda walked through the salon to her apartment, took a glass from the cupboard, and sat down at the kitchen table. She reached for the brandy and poured herself a generous drink. With her elbows on the table she took a long sip and then slowly placed the glass down. She lowered her head into her hands and shook her head as she considered the consequences of her conversation with Mari. Her mind was racing.

"How can I possibly apprentice Anna? She will live here most of the time. How can I conceal my work from her?... Anna is very astute so perhaps she could be of use.

I have no choice anyway. I owe Mari. Her parents took me in after mother and father were killed. What of my obligation to the others though? Our cause is most important. People need my help!" she inwardly debated.

Life in the underground movement was bred into Frieda. As a small child she had listened to her parents and their friends debating politics and economics. They discussed the Russian Revolution of 1917 and WWI and struggles prior to the war.

For most of their adult lives, the Portners had been part of the communist underground movement reaching back to Bismarck's Antisocialism Law from 1878 to 1890 when the labor movement was forced underground. These networks were still active forty years later.

The Portners were members of the Communist Workers' Party of Germany and lived and worked in the industrial heartland of the Ruhr Valley. They were also union members and following WW1 advocated for turning ownership of industry over to the workers as a solution to economic problems—a highly unpopular notion for the conservative industrialists needless-to-say.

So in 1920 the government called for a general strike. In response, an uprising of over 50,000 armed workers occurred in the Ruhr Region. Included in the Red Ruhr Army were several left-wing groups—the Communist Party of Germany, the Communist Workers' Party of Germany, the Independent Social Democratic Party of Germany, and the Free Workers Union of Germany.

At first the Red Ruhr army was successful in defeating the opposition whose goal was to overpower what they saw as the rising proletariat.

Eventually the government troops sent in to crush the uprising outnumbered the Red Ruhr army of workers and defeated them with brutality and mass executions. Among the dead were Frieda's parents and most of their friends. Frieda was only ten years old when she was swept out of harm's way to the safety of a farm outside of Leipzig.

The Baumanns who owned and lived on the farm had underground connections and were friends of her parents. They took care of the Portner estate and ensured that the money was held in trust for Frieda.

Later, Mari's parents, also friends of the Baumanns agreed to take Frieda in while she apprenticed to become a beautician. At only eighteen years old she bought the salon in Leipzig that would become her permanent home.

Since the time spent on the Baumann farm, Frieda was part of clandestine groups that organized and sprang into action during the rise of Hitler and the Nazi Party. On her bicycle she had distributed pamphlets and newspapers among sympathizers whose ideology was rooted in Marxist theory. When she was older, Frieda ran passports and reported on spies and the movements of the Nazis.

However, by 1933 the Gestapo had crippled the communist movement. Double agent, Wilhelm Gather turned in influential leaders. Over 100,000 communists and trade unionists were in concentration camps.

Since then her small operation had assisted communists, Jews, and other Germans who had been targeted unfairly by the Nazi Regime. She and her contacts had supplied forged papers, a temporary place to hide, or transportation to the border.

Frieda offered sanctuary in a hidden cellar under her apartment. She had been careful when making the room. It was under her bed. She had taken weeks to complete the task, always late at night. First, she skillfully removed the wooden floor boards but ensured that they could be quickly replaced, blending with the rest of the floor. She transported pails of dirt to the back yard where she then blended the dirt with the earth in her vegetable garden. She salvaged and stole pieces of wood to support the sides of the 10×8 space. Each night after her routine of digging, she would return the floorboards carefully, and drag the carpet with the bed on top into position. Once completed, blankets, a mattress, candles, a flashlight and a slop pail furnished the dugout.

After the nights of work, Frieda checked that no dirt had penetrated her gloves and got under her nails. Her nail polish must not be chipped, her filthy clothes could never be seen—there must be no suspicion about her nocturnal activities.

Frieda's impeccable looks belied this secret life. She was 5'4" with thick, shoulder-length black hair that had a styled wave but if left alone would form large curls around her face. Her brown eyes were set in flawless pale skin. Frieda always seemed to be wearing fresh red lipstick on her full lips though no one ever saw her apply it. The rest of her makeup gave her a softly feminine look. Mari designed Frieda's form-fitting dresses and coat—all haute couture.

Frieda knew her appearance was important not only because she was in the salon business, but also because her looks distracted Nazi observers from any lines of investigation. No one suspected her clandestine war against Hitler and his Nazis.

Chapter Four
Disillusionment

During their last school year Anna and Klara befriended an academic loner named Nathalie. She was an outstanding student, excelling in all subjects. Other high-achieving students envied Nathalie and treated her with disdain even though she tried to avoid attention and recognition of any kind. The teacher disciplined Nathalie for day-dreaming on more than one occasion; yet, Nathalie was only pre-occupied with her thoughts. She had moved far beyond the rudimentary content in the teacher's lesson.

With the rise of Hitler Youth, students were becoming increasingly competitive as they sought awards or hid certain unacceptable behaviors to escape punishment. Corporal punishment was common for children who, for instance, did not show upright posture while seated or stand at attention during the singing of *Deutschland*.

Anna had taken Nathalie under her wing and made sure she said *Heil Hitler* and complied with any other mandatory responses on cue. The girls also kept watch in case other students tried to harm her.

As the friendships developed, the three girls would often go to the Mullers' and sometimes Klara Kalbfleisch's after school. They had not been invited to Nathalie's home and Anna was full of curiosity.

Nathalie was an only child and lived in an apartment with her mother, Lena Lenz, an actress who had performed at the *Altes Theater*. They lived in the artist's section of Leipzig.

When Anna or Klara inquired about her mother, Nathalie was reticent about divulging any details and was slightly embarrassed about her mother's fame. Anna just attributed this to Nathalie's more academic bent and reserved nature.

Finally, one evening when the girls were on their way to the cinema, Nathalie asked if they would like to have coffee at the apartment after the movie. "Sure," both girls chimed immediately. Anna couldn't wait.

They watched, "The Scarlet Empress," starring Marlena Dietrich. On the way to Nathalie's, Klara remarked, "Imagine a German woman becoming Catherine the Great of Russia. A woman can reach great heights if she marries the right man."

"Maybe a woman can reach great heights on her own," countered Nathalie.

"Or…is it possible for a woman to marry the right man AND succeed on her own merit?" questioned Anna.

They entered a door beside a book store called the *Gut Buch*, and climbed the stairs to a landing. When they opened the door to the apartment, Anna was struck by how exotic the apartment seemed. She could smell incense. The sofa, actually a day bed, was surrounded by oversized cushions covered with Indian fabric of rich burgundy, green, and gold tones. The large coffee table served as the dining table with cushions on the floor for seating. Two large armchairs in plush burgundy were situated in front of an oak side cabinet that held an assortment of bottles of alcohol and four glasses. A gramophone was in the corner beside a lamp with a fringed shade.

The pieces of art that hung behind the sofa involved splashes of color and others featured distorted figures that made no sense to Anna. Photographs of Lena in a variety of costumes on stage as well as individual portraits filled most of the remaining wall space. A small kitchen, two bedrooms, and a bathroom were in the back of the apartment.

Nathalie had tidied the apartment before leaving for school that morning just in case her friends came by. Her mother and stepfather were to be home late, but evidently plans had changed.

"Darling, I am home," her mother announced as she made her entrance.

"But you told me you would be late, Lena!" protested Nathalie.

Anna could detect no family resemblance in Lena and Nathalie Lenz, not in their physical appearance, mannerisms, or personalities.

Nathalie had deep auburn hair, blue eyes and almost white skin and was thin like a ballerina. Unlike a ballerina, though, she was physically fragile. Nathalie was withdrawn and her voice was soft.

Lena, on the other hand, had dark hair and eyes and a voluptuous body that she revealed proudly in her scarlet dress with low cut bodice and slit up the side. She had a large mouth and full lips accentuated by lipstick that matched her dress. Her deep voice filled the apartment as she walked with confidence to where the girls were standing.

With one hand on her hip and the other under her chin she said, "You are clearly Anna, the brave one, and you must be Klara the sensible one—well my young beauties have a seat while I get a drink. Nat where did I put my cigarettes? Darling, get your friends a coffee, will you?" Nathalie left for the kitchen while Lena fitted a cigarette into a long holder and with an exaggerated movement of her hand inhaled deeply. She blew the smoke out slowly as she studied the young girls.

Unexpectedly, Lena asked, "So, none of you has a boyfriend yet?" They shook their heads. "Anna, tell me, what type of boy do you want?" Anna had never discussed such a question with an adult before, but answered without hesitation and plainly.

"I want a boy that is dark-haired—definitely NOT blonde—and handsome. I want a boy that does not always follow rules. He must be strong and smart. What type of man do you want *Frau Lenz?*" Anna asked boldly.

Lena threw her head back and laughed a long, rolling chuckle that was oddly devoid of mirth. Then suddenly she stood up to refill her glass. "Anna, YOU may call me Lena…the boy you desire is not Aryan. Is that not too great a risk? As for me, the man I desire is one who can take care of me. He must enjoy the arts and…be good in bed, of course!"

Nathalie rolled her eyes as she gave her friends their coffee. Klara's naturally rosy cheeks blushed deeper as she suppressed a nervous smile. Anna pursued the conversation further, partly out of curiosity but mostly to respond to the challenge. "Lena, what if he is ugly or fat, what then?"

"Yes, well then the whole thing is impossible!" Lena exclaimed as she threw out her arms and shook her head.

They were still laughing when Nathalie interjected with, "Lena, you already have a husband, remember?"

"Oh yes, RUPERT!" Lena replied with an exaggerated look of surprise. "In fact, Rupert will be home soon so on your way my darlings and visit again soon."

When Anna and Klara left for home, they realized how very different their friend Nathalie's life was from theirs. She lived in a glamorous apartment, called her mother by her first name, and had a stepfather, Rupert. Her life seemed to have so much mystery and excitement compared to family life at the Mullers or the Kalbfleisch butcher shop where Klara's family lived and worked.

Anna longed to tell *Mutti* all about her experience but feared that she would not be allowed back to the Lenz apartment; so instead, when Anna arrived home she held the Mullers' newest addition to the family, Otto, while Leo boasted about how he was the best swimmer in the physical education program at school, Rita held her doll that Mari had made for her, and Ralfie played on the floor with his soldiers.

Starved for company, Mari looked forward to talking with Anna now that Olav was away. He had been moved from the aircraft manufacturing plant to a location outside of Munich to train new recruits for Hitler's ever expanding army. He returned only when on leave. Mari relied on Anna not only for help with the chores and children but also for conversation.

However, she would not let Anna know this. Instead, Mari began, "Soon you will begin your apprenticeship with *Tante Frieda*. I want to take your measurements so I can make you a new dress, skirt and blouse. What do you think?"

"Oh *Mutti,* that is too much. And maybe I should wait another year to start my apprenticeship. Don't you need me at home? I would have to live downtown at the salon during the week wouldn't I?" asked Anna.

"You must learn a trade," Mari said firmly. "You must have a job so that you don't have to rush to be married. Adolf would have every German woman pregnant and at home if he could! Have you seen the latest posters of the blonde pregnant woman with her muscular blonde husband?

Screened Aryan couples have been receiving interest free loans if the wife gives up her job by the time of the wedding. They even receive reductions in their loan for each child born and qualify for vouchers for furniture and household equipment.

No, Anna, I don't want you pressured into marriage before you are ready. You like the salon and will learn from *Tante Frieda*."

"I think I could become a good beautician with *Tante Frieda* as my teacher. I am excited to be given such an opportunity. My only reservation is that I will miss you. How often may I come home?" asked Anna breathlessly.

"You should be free to come home most weekends and Frieda has a telephone you can use with her permission. You must be careful downtown, though Anna. Follow Frieda's curfew. She tells me of the violence when men leave the bars. You will only be fifteen, my child, when you move to Frieda's," Mari said as she ran her hand gently down the side of Anna's face. "You must be very careful. We will speak more of this tomorrow."

"Thank you *Mutti*! I can't wait!" When Anna went to bed that night her thoughts alternated between her future at the salon and the mysterious Lenz family.

The next time the three friends went to the apartment, Nathalie's stepfather was in a heated argument with Lena. The girls waited in the doorway staring.

"You must take the part, Lena, we need the money and besides you may not have another chance."

"What are you saying, you bastard, that I am getting too old for another part? Is that what you really think?" Lena shouted.

Rupert tried to reason with her when he said more calmly, "No, of course not! God, you are so insecure and obstinate. The Nazi group—Fighting League of German Culture—I think they call themselves, is taking the theatre under its control. They want to replace European plays and other modern pieces with those German pseudo Nordic plays. *Brown shirts* have even attacked actors who oppose the plays and others who simply lead our bohemian lifestyle."

"How can they destroy our culture? The German public will demand a return to true art. This barbarian movement can't last," Lena protested, sweeping the air in front of her with her arm.

When they saw the three girls, Lena changed her demeanor instantly. With the flash of a smile she welcomed them. "Come in girls. We were just having a discussion about the theatre. You know how passionate we actors can be. Let us forget such things."

Lena turned with a flourish and put a 78 recording on the gramophone. "The Man I Love" reached their ears:

"When the mellow moon begins to beam, every night I dream a little dream…"

She poured herself a drink and raised it to her husband in a defiant salute as he left the apartment. The mood in the apartment changed immediately in his absence.

Lena lit a cigarette and then began swaying her hips slowly to the music. "Do you girls know how to dance? You don't; am I right? Well, it is time you learned!" The girls took turns dancing the foxtrot, waltz and Charleston with Lena. Although awkward at first, they caught on with Lena's expert guidance and insistence.

Suddenly, Klara tripped and almost fell to the floor which resulted in laughter and a break in their impromptu dance class. Klara began mimicking the goose-stepping of the Nazi march and kicked Anna in the backside. They all joined in a dance of mockery that at another time and place would have landed them in a concentration camp.

Anna couldn't wait for visits to Nathalie's to have a break from her daily routine. She now thought her life quite boring. She liked the way Lena treated them as adults and talked about important matters. Sometimes Lena would go into character and recite lines to them, her adoring audience. Her charisma filled the room.

On other occasions, they would debate a recent outrage or the blaring propaganda piped through the loud speakers in the streets. Lena encouraged the girls to think for themselves and debate issues that seemed to be deliberately ignored or censored by most citizens. Anna admired Lena's passion for life and courage to voice her opinions.

On a Saturday afternoon, returning home from helping Frieda, Anna stopped at the apartment to see Nathalie and Lena. She knocked on the door, but nobody answered. As she was about to leave, she heard Lena's plaintive cry from inside. She sounded far away. "Anna, is that you? Come in, please come in," she pleaded.

Lena was slouched in an armchair with mascara smeared over her cheeks. Her hair was a mess of tangles and her robe hung open. She was staring blankly at Anna. In a glance, Anna saw the empty vodka bottle and a pill box on the table.

"Is Nathalie at home, Lena?" Anna ventured, but there was no reply.

Anna didn't require an answer; instead, she quickly entered the kitchen for a glass of water and found a damp cloth and comb in the bathroom. She tightened Lena's robe and offered the water. She slowly combed her hair and cleaned the mascara from her face.

Lena continued to stare but finally slurred. "You are a good girl Anna… My daughter is disgusted with me. She is at the library. Will you find her and bring her home? I don't want to be alone. I don't want to be alone," Lena repeated in a raspy whisper.

When Anna and Nathalie returned, Lena was asleep in the chair. Nathalie said, "Anna, you can go home now. She will sleep until tomorrow." Nathalie looked frail as she laid a blanket over her mother and then to Anna she whispered, "Please, we will be fine."

Anna's mind was filled with images of her recent experience at the Lenz apartment and she was still confused when she arrived home. Her mother was listening to the "Hour of the Nation" aired promptly at 7:00 o'clock. The Nazis constantly broadcasted good news propaganda—the growth in jobs—Aryan mothers creating the pure race—healthy youth—the growing military strength. They were preparing the psyche of the people for war.

"We must eliminate the threat. Heaven help anyone who stands in our way!" screamed the voice on the radio.

Mari found the messages a disturbing mix of hope and terror.

Anna was immune to the propaganda because she was thinking of Lena. Although she didn't fully understand what was wrong with Lena, Anna was certain this was not the first time Nathalie had seen her mother in such a state. She felt chilled by the knowledge that she didn't really know much about Lena at all.

Lena had a turbulent past. She had parted from Nathalie's father before her daughter was born and supported herself on the income of an aspiring actress. Then her break came when she was cast in a play at the *Max Reinhardt Deutches Theater* in Berlin. Her success made her popular with artistic social circles that thrived in Berlin. This meant attending parties and frequenting clubs.

She became caught up in the Berlin clubs that were quite different from what Lena had known. Unlike many western countries where homosexuality was illegal, clubs in Berlin, from which there were hundreds to choose, were tolerant of gays, lesbians, and transvestites. The open eroticism had influenced the theatre and changed serious acting to a new form of burlesque.

Lena despised the move away from the true artistry she had known at the theatre and struggled, against her will, to keep up with the demands of her director. Finally, to create a strong image and cope with the pressure, Lena began taking cocaine at parties and before performances on stage; then, tranquilizers were necessary to come down when she became too erratic.

Eventually, Lena realized her lifestyle was destroying not only herself but also Nathalie. She knew she had to leave Berlin to survive in her career and to make a better life for her daughter. She chose Leipzig.

Once in Leipzig, Lena married Rupert, a mediocre actor who had followed her from Berlin. She had hoped he would become a father figure for Nathalie and that they could enjoy some semblance of family life.

Rupert was fifteen years younger than Lena. He idolized Lena which made her feel young and beautiful. Although a devoted lover for the first three years of their relationship, Rupert became restless, missing the social life in Berlin. Lena, now forty, was insecure about her relationship with Rupert.

Lena was also plagued with doubt about her future as an actress. Granted the Nazis were censoring the plays in which she typically performed, but she also suspected that her popularity was waning.

Only her love for Nathalie had given her life purpose and now she clung to her daughter's friends.

The three friends completed their final school year. Nathalie would be apprenticing to be a baker, Klara training to be a nurse, and Anna apprenticing to be a beautician. To celebrate, they had planned supper at the Mullers' and then the cinema to see "Roberta" with Fred Astaire and Ginger Rogers.

Nathalie said she had to make a quick stop at the apartment before the movie but Anna and Klara were pleased. They were all excited to tell Lena their good news.

When they threw open the door of the apartment, they cried, "Lena, you wouldn't believe…" but they were muted by the scene in front of them. Clothes were strewn across the furniture, empty bottles on the floor. Lena was lying naked on the sofa. She was voraciously kissing a young woman on the mouth while she fondled the girl between the legs. Rupert was moaning, kneeling over them, his penis erect.

Anna grabbed Nathalie's hand, turned her abruptly, and the three girls rushed out of the apartment to the street below. They ran a block before slowing to a walk. Tears ran down Nathalie's cheeks but no sound left her mouth. Anna and Klara stayed close, on either side of her.

Anna chattered, "I heard that this movie is only black and white but the music and dancing are superlative… Can you believe we are finished school.

We are fifteen and going to work… It is hard to believe isn't it…" She was unsuccessful in changing the mood.

The girls were too appalled to appreciate the film. When it was over, Anna and Klara took Nathalie home to be sure she would be all right. Lena was dressed, sober, and alone. As Nathalie turned to close the door on her friends, she nodded reassuringly.

Anna and Klara quickly descended the stairs and walked out onto the street sucking in a large breath of fresh air. They caught the same trolley car and sat beside one another in heavy silence.

Klara finally said empathetically, "Poor Nat! She carries such a burden. Her only relief is at the library… She must be so disappointed that she cannot go to university."

"I know," agreed Anna, "I can't imagine what she has been through and cannot see her happy as a baker." The girls gave up talking. The evening had been too disturbing.

"Here is my stop Anna, *Gute Nacht*." Klara left with a heavy heart.

Safely home and in the kitchen, Anna looked at her mother with renewed respect. "I will never again consider my home life boring," she thought. "My family is strong and decent. We have love in our home… *Mutti* is so beautiful."

Controlling her emotions, Anna said, "Soon *Vati* will be home on leave!"

"Yes, it will be good to have your father back," Mari smiled kindly. "Is something troubling you?"

Anna shook her head and then said, "I wonder what news he will have. Do you think we will be going to war?"

"I hope not, dear, I hope not. *Vater* will know," her mother replied. "Let's not talk of such matters now. It is late. Let's get some sleep."

The day had left Anna feeling stunned and repulsed. "I didn't really know Lena at all. I don't want to see her ever again," thought Anna angrily.

She felt naive and frightened of growing up, pursuing her apprenticeship, war. She wanted the security of home and family. "Soon *Vati* will be home," Anna repeated as she pulled the covers up around her neck.

Chapter Five
Friendship

Through the train window, Olav saw clean, neat cities, no slums. People were well dressed and they appeared well fed. The overall impression was of order and prosperity. Beautiful summer fields were laid out with precision so that no square foot of land was wasted.

When he arrived in Leipzig, he noted that similar to other German cities, guns and uniforms were highly visible in the streets. The railway station was a hub of soldiers in green uniforms and full war-kit. Camouflaged tanks, cannon and war trucks were lashed to the railway flat cars and freight depots were lined with trucks hooded with brown canvas. Rearmament was in full throttle by 1936.

Leipzig looked like a garrison with every fourth man in uniform. Traffic was interrupted frequently by cavalcades of huge machines, manned by steel-helmeted men roaring through the streets on maneuvers.

He knew he was a military man and that he would soon be fighting again as he had in WWI; but when he approached his home, Olav's only desire was to be a family man and musician.

They were all there. Mari had prepared a meal of schnitzel, potatoes and fried cabbage. Around the table the children interrupted one another excitedly to gain the attention of their father.

Born in his absence, Otto was a stranger to Olav. Olav alternated between holding the baby on his lap and lifting him in the air to examine his face. "He looks more like your side of the family, Mari, but he seems a bit ornery like me." Olav laughed.

"Oh Olav, he is such a contented baby. He is hungry not ornery," Mari said.

Later Olav noticed how Anna had matured, not just that her body was developing, but her expression had lost some of her girlish innocence and she rarely giggled as she had before.

Talkative Leo at seven years old was irresistible to everyone with his curly, dark hair and large, round, brown eyes. Ralfie listened and laughed. Rita preferred to play with her dolls close by.

"*Vati* and *Mutti*, may we have a music day with our friends to celebrate?" asked Leo enthusiastically. "We have not heard you play for so long."

Mari looked at Olav before answering. Families had to be very cautious about whom they invited for musical gatherings because so much of the German music had been banned, and American jazz was particularly hard hit by the Nazis. The propaganda said that jazz was the music of inferior African-Americans and that it was associated with decadence. The Nazis referred to jazz as *Nigger Music* in the newspaper and banned it from radio. The SS confiscated music, broke records, and raided jazz clubs.

Olav nodded. "We can trust our friends, the Hoffmans, Mr. Wolfe's family, and Frieda."

The next Sunday afternoon the Muller home resounded with jazz, Bach, and children's sing-along songs. Frieda had brought a mouth organ for the children's songs and they took turns playing the new instrument. After much needed laughter and dance, and a savory meal, the gathering reluctantly broke up. The Nazis couldn't break the spine of a long tradition of music among some German families and friends.

Despite the military presence, Anna was surprisingly carefree that summer. She had the sense of optimism that secure relationships and sunny weather bring. Anna, Klara, and Nathalie were inseparable—coffee at the Mullers, the movies, cycling, and swimming.

One particularly hot afternoon they rode their bicycles to the park for a swim. The water was warm, and so they were able to leisurely swim and float on their backs talking.

"Can you see that dog in the cloud?" asked Nat.

"That isn't a dog," said Anna. "It looks like a horse."

"You are both daft! It is a cloud, only a cloud."

"Look over there. You must see the angel," insisted Anna.

"Cloud," stated Klara clearly, "It is a CLOUD!"

"You have no imagination," teased Anna.

"I am a realist," Klara announced as she splashed Anna. The water fight had begun.

"Stop, I'm hungry," cried Anna as she walked onto the beach dripping wet. Soon they were untying the string that held the waxed paper wrapping around their sandwiches. They rolled over and lay on their stomachs to dry and doze in the warmth. When they rose to leave for home, Klara and Anna covered their mouths and were wide-eyed as they looked at Nathalie.

"Oh no, Nat you are lobster red," shrieked Anna.

Nathalie was sunburned on her back and absolutely alabaster on her front. She poked her arm and winced.

"Nat, as soon as you are home, ask Lena to pat vinegar all over your back. Do it several times and the pain and itch will subside," suggested Klara.
A brief silence followed as the three girls realized simultaneously that they had not spoken Lena's name since that shocking night.

"I guess we should be leaving. I must be home for supper," said Anna. Anna was sad thinking of how Nat would have no dinner waiting for her. She would likely be taking care of her mother. To dispel the sadness, Anna began singing a favorite song from school and soon the girls were pedaling along happily.

All too quickly summer came to an end for the three girls as did their childhood. Nathalie began her apprenticeship at the bakery which was close to her home. This was convenient since she could live at home and walk to work rather than live with the baker's family. She preferred to be near her mother. They needed the money that Nathalie earned, since Rupert worked only sporadically. The remainder of her time, Nathalie studied at the library.

Anna routinely stopped at the bakery to see Nathalie. She checked in to ascertain that her friend was all right or to pick up free bread to bring home. The bakers *Herr and Frau Becker* liked Anna's maturity and cheerful disposition but also appreciated that she helped with sweeping or washing up to show her appreciation for the free baking.

Anna had invited Nathalie to spend an evening with her family since Anna had only one more week before she began her apprenticeship at the salon. But, Nathalie was late. When the telephone finally rang, Mari and Anna were waiting for her call explaining what had happened. Instead, *Herr Becker* was asking about Nathalie.

Apparently, she had not been in to work or answered the phone when *Herr Becker* rang the apartment. Anna said she would check into it and immediately called the Lenz apartment. No answer. She knew instinctively that something was wrong.

When she arrived at the *Gut Buch*, Anna rushed up the stairs two at a time. Nathalie was sitting motionless in the large armchair staring at Lena. Lena's hair was done up and held with golden combs. Her cheek was bruised. She wore a long, pale green gown that was covered with blood near her waist. One of her gold sandals was still on her foot and the other had fallen to the floor. Lena lay on the sofa on her side with her right arm extended. A pill bottle lay beside her on the floor. Lena was dead.

Anna did not hesitate to act. She reached for the telephone and called *Tante Frieda.* In a serious, calm voice she reported the facts. Anna then wrapped Nathalie in a blanket and sat beside her, speaking gently, but Nathalie did not respond and rarely even blinked. She seemed not to hear, was completely unaware of Anna's presence. When Frieda arrived they were able to bring Nathalie to her feet and take her from the apartment to the salon.

Once there, Frieda immediately made a brief call to Father Engel who said he would take care of Lena's body and make arrangements for burial immediately.

Then she turned to Anna and said crisply, "Anna prepare the small room, please. Nathalie must stay here. Telephone Mari and tell her you will stay here with us, and that I will explain as soon as I can."

Frieda gave Nathalie a bowl of hot broth and a chunk of rye bread and sat down beside her. Frieda took the spoon and brought the broth to Nathalie's lips. "Come now darling, just a bit—sip a bit of the warm broth," Nathalie cooperated robotically. "Nathalie, do you make this type of bread at the bakery?" Nathalie looked at her and nodded once. "It is delicious isn't it? There now take another big bite," Frieda soothed.

The next day Frieda instructed, "Nathalie, you will stay with me until you are ready to return to the bakery. For now, girls, we must go to the apartment and gather Nathalie's things. Perhaps Rupert will be there… I will close the shop. Get ready. We will leave in ten minutes."

They arrived at the apartment to find nothing, absolutely nothing. No one was there and the apartment had been stripped. Even Nathalie's books were gone. Nathalie stood in the center of the living room staring at the spot where the sofa had been.

She moved around slowly shaking her head in disbelief as if it were a nightmare and in a moment Lena would be singing or talking to her about…and then she spotted something that had been missed behind the entry door. It was a portrait of Lena.

Nathalie dropped to her knees, held the photo to her chest, and rocked back and forth. She stared ahead at something not visible to Anna and Frieda. After a few minutes Anna said firmly, "Stand up Nathalie. We must leave. It is not safe. We will take the picture with us. NOW Nathalie, please." Anna reached down and helped her thin friend stand. "There, shoulders up, we must move." She laced her arm through Nathalie's. When they left, Anna breathed in the faint scent of incense as they closed the door of the apartment for the last time.

Only Frieda and Nathalie attended the brief funeral for Lena. Following the ceremony, Father Engel said, "Please sit down. We need to talk. Nathalie, my child, you must not return to your neighborhood or the theatre. Do not seek out any of your mother's friends. You see there can be no investigation, no inquiries of any kind. This is the work of the Gestapo. They will come for you too. You will be safe with Frieda. Now let us pray for God's protection and blessing."

Frieda did not allow much time for grieving. Her philosophy was that one must move on or perish. Grieving was a luxury that Nathalie could not afford, especially with her fragile body and complex mind. Frieda's fear was that Nathalie would retreat into a remote part of her brain—insane.

"Anna, I want you to call Klara and explain briefly what has occurred. We all must stay close to Nathalie and keep her involved in life."

Klara came to the salon as soon as she could. Nathalie was slumped in a chair at the table, but when she saw Klara enter the kitchen, she jumped to her feet and rushed to her. Klara held her tightly.

The girls settled at the table drinking coffee as they had on so many other occasions. No one talked about Lena or the circumstances surrounding the incident. Nathalie was comforted by her friends' voices and kind smiles, by an inappropriate laugh.

Before Klara left, she suggested, "Let's go to the library on Saturday, Nat?"

Nathalie instantly brightened and nodded. Klara knew that learning and the library were familiar to Nathalie and something to cling to for stability.

Frieda urged Nathalie to return to work at the bakery but kept a close eye on the girl so swiftly orphaned, so alone. Frieda thought, "The Gestapo may have killed Lena but they will not get to Nathalie if I have anything to do with it. Perhaps I can arrange for papers that show her as my relative… She will have a new family with me and the girls."

Anna had most weekends off from the salon and took Nathalie home with her. This was a balm for her friend. She was comforted by the solid warmth of Mari and the activity in the busy household. Ralfie especially took to her, constantly touching her red hair and smiling up at her with his pale blue eyes. He called her Nattie. She held on to him as if she were holding on to life itself, drinking in the baby smell of his blonde hair and perfect skin. She came out of the darkness during those moments.

Chapter Six
The Golden Pheasant

In 1936, Adolf Hitler descended on Leipzig. Crowds of people of all ages waved banners under a canopy of swastika pennants in anticipation of seeing Hitler in person. Anna, Klara, and Nathalie felt the cavalcade long before they saw it. Thousands of men in uniform stamping in unison created a vibration that travelled up through their bodies into their hearts.

Motorcycles revved their motors as they sped up and down from grey staff cars in the front to those in the rear. Soldiers were as far as the eye could see with the occasional motorized anti-aircraft guns nosing up to the sky.

The volume of the marching songs rattled the windows and filled the girls with awe. Men were mounted proudly on perfectly groomed horses that pranced across the cobblestones. The power of the military was tangible and intoxicating. And then he was in front of them standing in the open, black limousine. Adolf waved to the throngs with an expression of grim benevolence.

Tears of rapture ran down *Grossmutter Beatrice Muller's* uplifted face. She was seeing Germany's savior with her own eyes. "Soon decency will be restored," she thought, "and the immoral and rebellious punished. He will take Germany to glory."

Anna, Klara and Nathalie were smiling ecstatically, their cheeks flushed from the sheer magnitude of the event. They really weren't thinking about the politics or the implications of this great army. Their attention was drawn to the good-looking young *soldats*.

Mari, however, was solemn as she looked on. She thought, "These men have switched off their individuality to become a united war machine. They have an automatic reflex to commands, moving without thinking. Where will this war machine take us?" She stared transfixed as they snapped to attention, presented arms, goose-stepped left leg high.

Frieda's face was impassive. She knew this army was not only a threat to enemy countries but also to German citizens that the Nazis deemed enemies. She identified a particularly loathsome Nazi named *Herr Kaufer* scrutinizing the responses of the crowd. He was their community's cunning *block warden.*

Frieda never underestimated him, "Look how he watches us all. He relishes the hunt, salivates when he has a grip on the prey; raises his head to howl in victory when he sends another to the work camp or has grounds for a direct hit," she thought.

As the crowds dispersed, *Herr Kaufer* caught up with Frieda. "Excuse me *Fraulein Portner,* I would like a moment of your time."

"Yes, of course, what a memorable day for Leipzig to be honored by a visit from the *Fuhrer, Herr Kaufer!*" replied Frieda formally.

"I see you are still in the salon business. I hope that you are grooming your customers in the traditions that have been approved? We do not want to see the styles from Paris in Germany, do you understand?" *Herr Kaufer* said in that threatening and suggestive manner that Frieda despised. She nodded with the hope that he was finished.

But he wasn't. "Instead of dedicating your life to business, maybe you should consider marriage and family."

"I may be blessed soon, but, *Herr Kaufer,* your comments are so personal today when I am only thinking of the bright future for all Germans under the protection of the Nazi Party and our great leader—*Heil Hitler!*" Frieda said pleasantly enough.

"*Heil Hitler!* I will visit you soon, *Fraulein,*" he promised.

"I will look forward to that, *auf Wiedersehen,*" Frieda lied respectfully and then turned and strolled calmly away. He made her skin crawl.

Block wardens were low level officials in the Nazi hierarchy. They were responsible for a cell of about 50 city blocks. The wardens were nicknamed "golden pheasants" because of their brown/gold uniforms with red collar epaulettes. Their job was to promote enthusiasm for Nazi ideology and to act as informants to the Party. They hung flags, attended parades and rallies and passed names and other information to the *Gestapo.* Often their actions were punitive; for instance, they had the authority to stop state benefits or welfare payments to anyone who opposed the Reich or was labeled asocial.

Although lacking in intelligence, Bruno Kaufer thrived under the Third Reich. In his mind, he was the man ordinary people respected and feared. Bruno's superiors rewarded actions that would have resulted in severe punishment during his youth so his true self could be unleashed without fear of reprisal. He had been liberated from the control of his parents, the Church, and school.

Bruno's father had beaten him almost daily and demeaned his mother constantly. His mother, a devote Catholic, had turned to her religion for strength to cope with her wretched life. She brought Bruno to church so that he could benefit from the same support, but instead, introduced him to another form of hell.

During the years he was an altar boy, Bruno was molested by the priest. The ornate cross screamed from the chain hanging from the priest's neck as he forced him to have sex. Bruno assumed that his mother would suspect him of lying and his father would somehow blame him for the abuse. He guessed that the beatings would become more severe. He had no recourse but to succumb to the man's urges.

One day when Bruno was inspecting a school in his jurisdiction, his thoughts turned to religion. He held nothing but contempt for the rules of the Church. "I was shown no mercy or compassion. I don't have to endure the guilt, shame, or lies anymore and neither will the Hitler Youth. They will know freedom under the Nazis." He smiled to hear the children singing:

"We are the jolly Hitler Youth
We don't need any Christian truth
For Adolf Hitler, our Leader
Always is our interceder.

Whatever the Papist priests may try
We're Hitler children until we die;
We follow not Christ but Horst Wessel.
Away with incense and holy water vessel!

As sons of our forebears from time gone by
We march as we sing with banners held high.
I'm not a Christian, nor a Catholic,

I'm SA through the thin and the thick."

Bruno clenched his jaw and narrowed his eyes as he rejoiced to see the swastika on the wall where once a cross had hung.

The Nazi fervor and the power of his position were an aphrodisiac for depraved Bruno. His appetite could now be sated in so many unusual ways.

"Anna, would you wash *Frau Fischer's* hair, please," asked Frieda.

"Of course. I will be right there." Anna gently massaged the woman's scalp with the warm, almond-scented, soapy water and rinsed it thoroughly. "How have you been *Frau Fischer?*"

"I have been very tired since my housekeeper left. My husband works longer hours at the factory now, but makes less money, so I rely on my mother for help. My oldest son is ten years old and then four more boys. I hope that this one is a girl. Of course, we are happy that he is working, and I am pleased to have such a large, healthy family," the women added hastily.

"At least he comes home each day," interrupted another customer. "My husband was called up to the *Wehrmacht*. I receive money regularly while he is in the army, but we have only been married one year. I wish he was in Leipzig."

"Well, he must join the Party. It is the only way to be promoted or land a better job in Leipzig. My husband is supervisor at the office now that he is a Party member," added a diminutive woman at the next sink.

Frieda had clamped a few rods for a perm when the door opened and let in a cold draft of snowy air and Bruno Kaufer. "*Guten Morgen*, ladies. Forgive me for intruding, but I must speak to *Fraulein Portner,*" he said with insincere manners.

Frieda quickly moved toward the front of the salon to intercept Bruno. "Yes, *Herr Kaufer*, how may I help you?"

"It seems that a Jewess and her daughter were seen entering your salon, but they were not seen leaving," Bruno stated while staring into Frieda's eyes for her reaction.

"Hmm, I cannot recall who that might have been. When was this supposed to have occurred?" she inquired confidently.

"Last Friday afternoon, *Fraulein,*" he replied curtly.

"Oh yes, I cut her hair and the child's, but I am surprised that your source did not see them leave. Of course it grows dark so much earlier now…I did not catch their names but let me check our appointment book," Frieda offered. "No, nothing here. She must have walked in without an appointment, *Herr Kaufer*."

"Do you make it a habit to cater to Jews, *Fraulein Portner*?" Bruno raised the pitch of his voice and his level of aggression.

"I am unable to distinguish a Jew from my other customers, and of course, I cannot check papers since I am only a beautician not a person of authority like you, *Herr Kaufer*," Frieda responded humbly in an attempt to pacify Bruno.

Unaffected, Bruno demanded sharply, "I will inspect your apartment NOW."

"Of course, please this way." With grace Frieda led Bruno through her small apartment. He marched slowly, his eyes darting about each room for any sign of occupancy by others.

"Do you have an attic?"

"A small one."

"Show me."

Frieda pointed to the trap door in the ceiling of the back room. He roughly pulled the kitchen chair over and climbed up on it to peer into the attic. Nothing significant.

When they entered Frieda's bedroom, her heart rate quickened. Bruno's heart rate quickened as well but for a very different reason. He became aroused as he imagined himself in bed with Frieda. He saw her night gown hanging on the wardrobe and his penis became hard.

"May I return to my customers now *Herr Kaufer*?" Frieda asked deliberately seeking permission respectfully to avoid further scrutiny.

"Be more careful about who your customers are in the future. I do not wish to report that you are collaborating with Jews!" Bruno reprimanded loudly. "Yes, you may return to work for now."

The women were quiet as Bruno marched through the salon to the door. Cigarettes had been extinguished during the inspection. They were filled with apprehension.

"What nonsense, he was just looking for an excuse to see some pretty women," Frieda said lightly. The chatter returned and a few of the women lit cigarettes hastily. The room breathed a collective sigh of relief.

During the winter months Anna's grandmother, Beatrice Muller, had spent a large portion of her day spying from her upstairs apartment window at the house across the street. She followed the movements of a blonde, attractive woman named Katia.

"That whore! How many men can she see in one day? She doesn't belong here among us decent Germans," Beatrice hissed scornfully as she made an entry in her log. "I will be notifying that fine young man, *Herr Kaufer*, about that asocial young woman across the street and also about those irritating people upstairs. I cannot bear their sanctimonious attitude or their smelly, dreadful cat! They all belong in the camps."

The neighbors on the second floor were Jehovah Witnesses and she knew the Nazis did not approve of their brand of religion. Conveniently, she could rid herself of both the cat and the Jehovah Witnesses. "The block warden will be impressed with the work I am doing for *Mein Fuhrer*," the old woman rationalized.

Once informed, Bruno hastened to pay Katia a visit. "*Hure nude*," he shouted as he broke into her home. "The respectable people of this neighborhood have been complaining about the men coming and going from your home at all hours."

"What are you doing here? Get out!" Katia shrank back from Bruno's advance.

"I am here to teach you a lesson you filthy whore. You will listen very carefully. The *Fuhrer* does not approve of peroxide hair OR prostitutes," he sneered as he grabbed a fist of her hair and pulled her face to his. "This is how it will be. I can send you away to the camps or you can move to an address of my choosing. You will see me whenever I want and do whatever I desire. Are we clear?" He struck her face with force and then punched her in the stomach.

"Yes, *Herr Kaufer*," she moaned.

It was an evening in March of 1937 when Anna turned the salon sign around to "Closed" and reached up to shut the blind. She shouted urgently, "Frieda, it's Katia!" Anna threw open the door and the two women helped their regular customer into the apartment. She had been beaten severely. Removing her coat, they were shocked to see that she was half naked.

Katia lay on Frieda's bed shivering from the cold unable to talk coherently. Frieda wrapped her in blankets. "Anna, quickly now, get a basin of boiled water with salt and boil a cloth." Frieda poured Katia a brandy to stop the chill.

She raised her head gently and fed it to her. Katia's lip was so swollen she had difficulty sipping the drink. Anna appeared with the sterile cloth and water and Frieda began to clean the wounds.

"Oh no!" Frieda exclaimed in despair. "Who did this to you?" Blood was smeared across Katia's thighs and the bruising was extensive. He had used an instrument. No response came from Katia. "We must get you to a hospital in case of infection or hemorrhaging," insisted Frieda.

"No, that is not possible! I must hide. He will kill me next time." Katia pleaded.

Anna telephoned Klara for help. Klara unquestioningly responded, "I will stop by the hospital for an antibiotic and supplies. I will be there as soon as I can, Anna."

When Klara arrived, she treated the injuries efficiently and then insisted that Katia sleep. She feared hemorrhaging but the bleeding had stopped. Without lingering, Klara packed up. Little was said among the women and when Anna walked Klara to the door, Klara left with a nod and never mentioned the incident again.

As Katia slept, Frieda thought with sadness of the atrocities that had been dealt Katia from the time she was a girl. She survived the only way she knew. The next morning Frieda asked haltingly and with controlled fury, "Who did this to you?... A Nazi? ...or was it one of those rich businessmen?"

Katia was emphatic, "No, no...they can be managed. It was that pig—the pheasant, Bruno Kaufer. I know what he likes now and will keep him in line. I will be fine on my own again… These times are unpredictable, though. Will you hide some money for me?"

Frieda nodded. And then with gratitude Katia said, "How can I repay you?"

"No need. You are one of my best customers!" Frieda smiled.

"I must leave soon, Frieda, before I put you and Anna in danger," Katia said.

"You cannot leave unnoticed right now so rest and eat until I give you the word." Frieda was immoveable.

When Frieda gave her the signal, Katia left the safety of the salon reluctantly. She had experienced so little kindness in her life.

Chapter Seven
The Apprentice

March 1938 saw the German troops cross over the Austrian border. They met with no resistance. As they drove and marched through Austria's main towns, they were greeted by cheering crowds. Hitler was driven in an open-topped car, accompanied by a motorized column of his SS bodyguards to his birthplace, *Braunau am Inn.* Austria was now part of the Third Reich.

This was not a surprise to many since two years previously an agreement with the Austrian government had accepted that Austria was a German state. Many Nazis already lived in Austria. This strong presence along with mass unemployment and disillusionment with the Austrian government created a situation where most Austrians saw the German takeover as a solution to their problems.

A huge new Hermann Goering Works was set up for iron and petroleum production and Austria's gold and foreign currency reserves helped to bolster Germany's war fund. To relieve the manpower shortage in Germany due to conscription, over 100,000 Austrian workers were employed in the "Old Reich."

For the most part, people thought that the Reich had given them steady jobs and had overcome the hardships of the Weimar years. With the barrage of media promoting German national pride and economic recovery, most of the common German and Austrian citizens saw Hitler's mobilization of the troops as something to applaud.

"Look what I have, Anna, hair pins with swastikas on them. These should keep the block warden happy! I even saw toothpaste with a swastika on the label," Frieda announced as they prepared to open the salon for business.

The salon was busy all day. Maybe it was because of the warm spring air. The winter's cold could be forgotten for a time and the tanks and soldiers ignored in favor of the new life emerging from the earth.

Anna's first customer was boasting about her husband's job. "Anna, you cannot imagine our vacation! My husband works for the Heinkel aircraft works and through the 'Strength through Joy' program we were rewarded with a special vacation on a cruise ship to Finland. I swear my husband is feeling so much better now that he is back to work. We have already enjoyed the opera and plays. I deserve to be experiencing this life! You know, Anna, we have even learned to play tennis. And we have Adolf to thank."

"Yes, I have heard from others that the 'Strength through Joy' program offers a 75 percent discount on rail passes and 50 percent on hotel rooms. Affordable prices at resorts too," Anna added.

Another customer who was receiving a manicure broke in, "My husband says that his factory has changed because of the 'Beauty of Labor' program. Now the plant has proper washing facilities and toilets, changing rooms, lockers, and showers. They have work clothing and even a recreation area. Last month they saw a concert performed at work! Can you believe this?"

Anna agreed with her customer to avoid tension or conflict, "Yes, Adolf has given us jobs and made the workplace so much better. Who knows what the future will hold for us all."

Previously, Frieda had told Anna that in reality many of the workers had to complete the "Beauty of Labor" jobs with no wage. Whether they were employed in the aircraft works, the railway, or munitions, workers were ordered to work unreasonable hours. Employers planted Gestapo spies to ferret out any slackers or opponents of the regime. Any offenders were sent to work on the West Wall or were sent to the concentration camps.

Some employees had organized work stoppages—informal strikes—to improve wages and hours worked. Some called in sick or worked at a slower pace but the passive resistance was met with punishment by Gestapo spies.

Those who resisted were generally sent to the West Wall where construction was carried out around the clock in twelve-hour shifts. Living conditions were primitive, the pay poor, safety non-existent; and if targets were not met, laborers were forced to work double or triple shifts to catch up. Breaks were only after twelve hours of work. If the laborers resisted, they were accused of sabotage and sentenced to six months imprisonment in the camps.

The combined effect of employment programs extolled over the media and the secretive terror tactics of the Reich was creating a blind and mute workforce.

This silencing of the German populace was observed even in the salon; so when Anna saw a steady customer named *Frau Ada Von Brandt* enter, she was delighted. Ada was interesting. She had lost her husband in the Blood Purge in Berlin in 1934 and could not risk returning to her home in Prussia. She had escaped with her son, Oskar, to Leipzig.

When they first met, Anna had noted Ada's formal German accent and her aristocratic bearing even though she tried to disguise her heritage. To avoid unwanted attention, Ada had changed her name to Brandt since Von preceding a surname denoted aristocracy.

Ada's appointments had always been after hours so she could have open conversations with Frieda and now Anna. Most people were too afraid to voice their opinions, even minor objections, about what was occurring around them. Spies seemed to be everywhere. Compliance to the Nazi ideology was required among all age groups and genders.

Anna was interested in Ada's extensive knowledge on a variety of topics. While Anna set Ada's chestnut hair, they discussed recent changes in the direction of art under the Reich. "Anna, when I gazed upon Claude Monet's work and the Renoirs in Paris, I was struck by the stillness of the compositions, and yet the entire painting vibrated with complex shades of color applied with small, textured brush strokes. The impressionists were indeed the masters of colored light. It appears that the precise shape of objects or people was not important in their art.

I don't quite know if I can bear the art of Adolf Ziegler who conveniently happens to be the head of the Reich Chamber of Visual Arts. He paints his Aryan nudes in pedantic realism—devoid of any life, beauty or meaning. Always it is the Aryan race… How is it conceivable that another can dictate what one appreciates in art?" she said under her breath. Suddenly the door opened, but the women could relax. It was Ada's son.

"Hello *Fraulein Portner* and *Fraulein Muller.* How are you today?" beamed Oskar with the joyous energy of a child. "May I stay with *Mutter* if I behave."

"You are always welcome at the salon," assured Frieda.

"*Mutti,* I must attend Hitler Youth gymnastics at 8:00 tonight," said Oskar as he entered the salon smiling. "It is Wednesday, remember?"

"Oh I remember, Son. I am acquainted with their rules, and I do not wish to see you punished," Ada replied frowning.

Frieda locked the door and pulled down the blinds to prevent any late customers or undesirable visitors. "Have some cake, Oskar," offered Frieda.

"Thank you, *Fraulein Portner,*" the boy said politely.

Ada turned to the women as she remarked, "It seems to me that sports for children are not fun anymore. They have become militarized. On Sundays, Oskar begins a walk that can last most of the day. I swear this is to keep children out of our churches!

Last winter the Nazi coaches plunged the boys into ice water to teach physical endurance. Even the younger ones were forced to hike during the bitter cold of winter without warm jackets and hats—to toughen them. They are being trained to be the future soldiers. How long would Adolf have us at war? These are only young children! In fact, I have little confidence left in our teachers and coaches."

"Why are you not protesting?" Anna asked.

"First of all, I do not know to whom I could voice my concern. Secondly, I fear for our safety, Anna. My son could end up being humiliated in some way. For example, errant boys are forced to run the gauntlet as punishment.

The coach might talk to the golden pheasant. He would make our lives miserable." Ada was visibly concerned.

"Do not worry, *Mutter*. I am becoming very strong to protect you! Look at my muscles already," boasted Oskar as he rolled up his shirt sleeves and flexed his muscles.

"Ohhhhh my, look at you, young man," admired Frieda light-heartedly. "I have just the job for you. Come with me to the kitchen."

"You have made me look presentable again, dear Anna! I like it very much indeed," praised Ada as she looked in the mirror.

"I have learned much from Frieda. She is a wonderful teacher, Ada," Anna said sincerely. "How is Oskar managing in his classes at school?"

"I must constantly remind him to repress his views and frustrated feelings. Oskar is very much like his deceased father. He has an innate sense of right and wrong—of justice—and unfortunately he has a brave heart to motivate him to action. I worry about repercussions.

It is a struggle trying to raise one's child to follow moral principles. A parent can teach principles in the home but the child sees something quite different in the outside world. How can he correct wrongs or stand up for his beliefs with a threat always present? We have no freedom of speech. We have no freedom! Surely, we will see a revolt. The Third Reich cannot last much longer," Ada sighed.

Anna felt she could speak freely with Ada. She began, "I am not certain that everyone agrees, at least from what our customers say. My guess is that some people are scared and others are unaware. Or else…they are simply coping with the challenges of each day.

They are preoccupied with raising and feeding their children, whether or not their husbands are cheating on them or are drunk in the beer hall—work, money—you know. They don't really care what is happening outside of their homes or neighborhoods because they are tired from so much work."

Frieda and Oskar were back. Frieda interjected, "Meanwhile people see that we will inevitably go to war. The soldiers and tanks cannot go unnoticed. Men are working in the armament factories. The radio shouts at us daily about regaining the lost German lands. Look at Austria."

"Perhaps we secretly hope Adolf can make a better Germany and we have blinders on when it comes to how he will accomplish this. All of this can make one quite mad wouldn't you agree?" Ada smiled as she was leaving.

"*Auf Wiedersehen*, Oskar," sang out Anna and Frieda. With a wink, Oskar bowed and then opened the door for his mother to pass through.

Ada did not return until later that summer for her routine cut and set. She had been on a trip to an art show. "Six hundred and fifty pieces were selected from German galleries and museums and taken on tour." Many works were from foreign artists such as Pablo Picasso, Henri Matisse, Paul Klee and Vassily Kandinsky.

They were spectacular even though the Reich tried to diminish the grandeur of the collection. The rooms were poorly lit and paintings hung at odd angles, jammed together.

Anna, I had the impression that I would never see any of the paintings again… I was also very intimidated by the soldiers and curators. During the exhibition, Adolf was heard over the radio raging about the art saying:

"We must wage a war of cleansing against the last elements of subversion of our culture!"

Ada shuddered.

After a thoughtful silence Ada continued, "I met an American journalist there. His name is Franz, Franz Neumann. He is a foreign correspondent based in Berlin and covering the art tour. We were both observing a Matisse when he turned to me and said, 'The expression! How can the Nazis say this is degenerate?'

I, of course, was extremely guarded about how I should respond given the Gestapo spies that seemed to be everywhere. He was so direct, open, and disarmingly handsome. When he invited me to have coffee, I heard myself agree. I was not unwilling to learn more about him." She paused to smile as if picturing the moment in her mind.

"It was all quite extraordinary. As we left the exhibition he took a red card out of his pocket held it out in view of the cars and in a moment a taxi pulled over and we were transported free of charge to the cafe. He explained that the Nazis treat American journalists very well so they will report a rosy picture of an orderly and prosperous Germany. He was remarkably frank about the relationship between the Nazis and journalists.

In the cafe, Franz told me about covering the story of when the London Philharmonic Orchestra visited Leipzig, at the *Gewandhaus*. Was that two years ago, Frieda? You must recall when the Nazis destroyed Mendelssohn's statue during the night. Frieda nodded.

We discussed so many different things—life in the United States, the general attitude in Britain and France toward Adolf. For us news from abroad is almost impossible to access anymore. Franz was both humorous and philosophical." Ada glanced down for a moment and then, "He speaks fluent English, of course, but German is his first language. He was born in Berlin."

"Will you see him again, Ada?" asked Anna. But Ada could not reply. Someone was pounding on the locked salon door.

Frieda stood, hesitated, and then walked confidently to the door. She looked through the blind. "Thank God," she said, "Oskar."

Oskar rushed over to his mother and sat beside her. "Son, I thought you were at gymnastics until 6:30 tonight," Ada said as she touched his arm. "Is everything all right?"

"Yes, *Mutter,* we were permitted to leave early if the coach was happy with our drill."

"Well, Anna has almost completed her masterpiece anyway so you can wait here with me," said Ada unnecessarily. Oskar had no intention of leaving her side.

After mother and son left, Anna said to Frieda, "I am so pleased that Ada met Franz. Do you suppose they will see each other again when such a distance separates them?"

"Perhaps…" Frieda said in an abrupt and disinterested manner. "Anna, would you like to join me at the race track one Sunday?" asked Frieda, changing the topic. Anna nodded but was a bit surprised by Frieda's lack of interest in Franz or in Ada's happiness.

"You finish up in the salon, and I will prepare our meal; then let us have a brandy and talk about the race track further," said Frieda.

Frieda had already taught her far more over the last two years than the arts of the beautician, and Anna knew she was ready for more. She had observed much and at seventeen felt she was invincible. "Brandy? Hmm."

The day had definitely taken a turn. Anna felt privileged and mature as Frieda disclosed some of her past. Frieda explained, "Anna, my parents were killed when I was 10 years old and I was moved to the Baumann farm in the mountains. When I was fifteen, your mother's parents took me in so I could begin my apprenticeship. I'll never forget such kindness.

Helping you learn the skills of a beautician is one small way I can return the favor. Now I would like to help by teaching you other skills that may save your life someday."

"So to begin my young Anna, you do not know the beauty you possess. You must learn how to use it to your advantage," Frieda praised her. "You are seventeen so we must change your hairstyle so you look more womanly. Your long, thick blonde braid should be done up or cut.

Next your body is lovely, but you must always remember your posture. Stand up straight darling. You are strong. You must have good posture to give others the impression of strength and quality. See when I bring your shoulders back and place my hand in the small of your back. Can you feel it? There—always keep your back straight."

Although Anna was listening very carefully, she asked, "When will we have the brandy?"

"All right, you are eager, but this will be a difficult lesson to follow. Come have a sip. NO darling, this is how you hold the glass and you sip slowly—watch. How does it feel? We will keep drinking until you are drunk."

Anna's body felt an odd warm sensation.

"Anna, the irony with alcohol is that the very thing that enlivens you and gives you confidence will also make you very ill and vulnerable. Once you learn to control how much you drink, you can be impervious to those who may wish to take advantage of you. Do you understand what I mean?" Frieda tested.

"Of course," *Tante Frieda*, "Men will want to take me to bed."

"Yes. Your ability to control your alcohol, and at times, encourage others to drink more will be an enormous asset to you not only at the race track but clubs and parties." Anna wasn't sure what Frieda meant but enjoyed the attention.

"Again my apprentice, cheers! Let us sing." They sang, they danced, and they drank. When it was quite late and Anna had clearly had enough, Frieda urged, "Drink, drink some more."

"Drink, drink no more…" Anna blurted as she rushed to the bathroom to vomit."

The next morning Frieda brought Anna a glass of water and told her to get up and wash her face. After a dreadfully long day contending with thirst and nausea, she joined Frieda for dinner. The meal of sausages and potatoes was oddly unappealing to Anna, but she ate.

Frieda asked, "Tell me about last night."

"At first I felt fantastic, that I could do anything. I had so much fun…but then I lost control of my body and was unable to regain it. I don't remember how I got into bed," Anna confessed.

"That is what I mean by our vulnerability if we drink too much," Frieda reminded. "It is wise to sip your drink slowly or get a drink with no alcohol so it appears that you are drinking." Anna nodded.

"Another effect of drinking, Anna—and this is important—most people talk more freely than when they are sober. This can be very useful should you ever require information."

"What information? Who do I know with that sort of information?" Anna asked innocently.

"We don't know what the future holds for us, my darling," answered Frieda. "I want you to understand so you can take care of yourself in difficult situations if necessary. And…maybe you can help me too. Are you ready to listen to some more advice from your *Tante Frieda*?"

"Why yes, of course! Please tell me more."

"All right then. Stand up. Good, your posture is straight. You remembered. Now walk around the kitchen." Anna, somewhat embarrassed, walked slowly around the room.

"Yes that is it. Even when you feel rushed or frightened, appear to be calm. Don't let another detect any weakness from your demeanor. Try moving your hips just a bit more when you walk—good—not too much."

Now let us talk about our clothing. We may not be wealthy, but we must look it! You are very fortunate to have such a talented mother to design your clothing. Remember a few key points to discuss with her. Keep the lines of your clothing and the pattern of the fabric simple and the colors soft. Loud colors will draw the wrong kind of attention. Be subtle in your femininity, not overly sexy. Discuss with Mari. You are a woman now and your clothing should enhance that fact.

"Your hair, makeup, and nails must also be maintained—this should not be too difficult in our occupation, yes? Do not allow your nails to become chipped or ragged.

Now your hair—what do you think about a new style? Something more mature?" Frieda asked.

"Oh yes, I would like my hair to look like Marlena Dietrich's—shoulder length with the wave—pin curls?" Anna requested without hesitation.

"I like your choice. We will tend to that soon, as well as, dining etiquette and appropriate conversations for social situations," assured Frieda.

"Tonight let us talk about conversations with men. How do you respond to a boy or young man who approaches you, Anna?"

"If I don't like him, I pretend that I have a commitment and turn or walk away," Anna replied. "I guess I ignore them. I'm not really interested."

"All right, but now that you are a woman, older men may approach you. The man could be SS or Gestapo and a rebuff could be dangerous for you," Frieda emphasized seriously. "You must always be polite—show respect even when rejecting his attention. Outwit him"

"Just as you outwit *Herr Kaufer*?" asked Anna. "I have watched you and learned—sometimes we must even lie or conceal information?"

"Exactly, Anna. *Herr Kaufer* is a wicked and cruel man."

"I know, *Tante Frieda*. He boldly enters the homes of struggling families and demands money for 'Winter Aid.' Many give only because they fear what he will do to their children or relatives. He keeps some of the money for himself.

I also saw him take money from a businessman on the street. He keeps some of that money too doesn't he?"

Frieda nodded, "Bruno is involved in extortion. He receives information about the community from a number of informants, as well.

Now Anna, listen to what I am about to say… Your grandmother, Beatrice, is one such spy. Katia lived across the street from her."

Anna's body became cold as the implications of this information raced through her mind, as she envisioned her bitter, arrogant grandmother performing her murderous duty for the *Fuhrer*.

Frieda reached out and held Anna's hand but Anna was distant. The young woman across from her sat rigidly in the chair, her face expressionless, eyes narrowed.

Chapter Eight
The Fledgling

His nostrils flaring, the thoroughbred stud snorted and reared high above the handler's head. His blood red coat reflected the sunlight; raven tail brushed the ground; and rear hooves dug into the dirt as he backed up on his hind legs. The handler snapped the line and the horse dropped his front end to the ground. He was restless, dancing on the spot while the exercise boy tried to clip onto the stud's headstall to pony him around the track behind the shed row.

Anna walked over to the stalls where a favorite gelding, Frozen Fire, was stabled. The groom was walking him slowly, cooling him down after the last race. Sweat was drying where the cinch had been and along his chest and flank. The groom slipped a blanket over the horse's fine sorrel coat. The jockey took off his green and gold jacket while he discussed the race feverishly with the trainer.

Anna inhaled the scent of the horses deeply and listened for the rhythm of the horses' hooves as they were led to the washing stations, to a stall, or maybe the starting line. She drank in the scene of the track people busy on a range of tasks, their lives centered on the health, appearance, performance, and mind of the horse, oblivious to the mundane affairs of most Germans. Intuitively, she understood the intensity of their passion and their commitment.

"Anna, would you like to pet Fire today?" asked Stefan, the groom.

"Would it be all right if I give him this carrot I brought?" Anna replied as she took the carrot from her purse. The gelding took the treat with his velvety lips. Just then the gun fired to signal the start of another race. Anna waved good-bye to the groom and made her way to the club house. She strutted across the grounds since she couldn't run in her high-heeled, open-toed shoes. Anna felt feminine in her pale blue, fitted dress with matching hat and veil. Although the day was hot and sunny, like the social elite, Anna flaunted her grey fur stole. "I may not have money in my pocket but I sure look like I do!" she smiled to herself.

Anna was flushed when she finally located Frieda who was calmly surveying the crowd. Frieda conducted her business in the bustle of the track crowds and often used Anna as a decoy. Mostly Anna diverted attention through harmless conversations and flirting. Today Frieda suspected a car salesman of being a Gestapo spy. She wanted Anna to remove him from the track so she could complete her business and confirm the man's involvement with the Gestapo. Frieda worried, though, that this time she was taking too great a risk with Anna's life.

"You were looking at the horses in the back again, yes? That is fine, my darling. I have been managing." With the sweet, confidential look of women exchanging gossip, Frieda then delivered her staccato instructions.

"The man standing beside the far end of the refreshment table—wearing a grey suit—dark hair, graying at his temples. His name is *Herr Krausse* and I want you to go for a drive with him while I complete my business here. Find out if he is Gestapo. Return within an hour. Walk with me now, and we will strike up a conversation. Then I will leave."

"Of course, *Tante Frieda*, I will do this," Anna replied feeling the weight of her responsibility. The women stopped close to where *Herr Krausse* was standing and began talking and glancing around as though looking for a man to meet. He smiled and separated himself from a group who were animated about their winnings in the previous race. He saw other men in the room admiring the beauty of the women. He was interested.

Over the din of post-race analysis and laughter, *Herr Krausse* and the women exchanged small talk. Frieda excused herself and moved away, waving to a woman across the room, ostensibly an old friend. Anna was alone with him.

"So Anna, do you enjoy the race track?" asked *Herr Krausse*.

"Oh yes, I adore the horses. It is more than their exquisite beauty and movement that captivates me though *Herr Krausse*, it is the horse's immense power." Anna was quick to smile and held the man's gaze until they were interrupted.

En route to the refreshments, a heavy woman cradling a Dachshund knocked Anna's shoulder. "Excuse me," the woman said loudly.

"Would you care to get out of here—take a ride in my Porsche before the next race," *Herr Krausse* asked. "You might enjoy the power of the engine."

"I'd love to if you will allow me to drive," Anna challenged playfully.

"This way, Anna." *Herr Krausse* placed the palm of his hand in the curve of Anna's back and guided her out to the parking lot. The Porsche was a flawless silver color. The top was down. *Herr Krausse* opened the passenger door for Anna, looking at her thigh when her blue dress crept up as she lowered herself onto the leather seat. She could hear the motor rev as they drove down the busy road leaving the track.

They attracted the attention of many passers-by who couldn't help but admire the car, the distinguished man in his expensive suit and the stunning young blonde woman in the pale blue dress and fur stole. Anna had to admit she was exhilarated with her importance and privilege but also by the danger that might lie ahead.

"What line of work are you in *Herr Krausse*?" Anna began.

"Please call me Albert. I am in the car business. I sell mainly Opel and Ford products. The small American cars have become very popular here."

"And yet you drive a Porsche, Albert. What does your boss think about your lack of loyalty?" Anna challenged with a smile.

Albert's head turned sharply to face Anna, and then back to the road ahead. He was laughing. He liked her saucy attitude but also her intelligent observation. "You seem to be a bit of a handful young lady. How would you like to take the steering wheel?" Anna had ridden her father's motorcycle so she had an idea of how to shift gears but had never applied that to an automobile before. "I will pull over to the side road ahead where there is less traffic."

Albert helped Anna with shifting gears while she concentrated on steering, acceleration, and the clutch and brakes. They still couldn't get out of third gear. Laughing they pulled over to the side of the road to switch seats. Albert leaned over and stifled Anna's laugh with a kiss. "Let's get out of the car and walk for a while," he suggested.

He opened her door and they walked along a nearby stream. "So tell me more about your automobile business," ventured Anna.

"Well, our vision is to see the motor car as part of life for all Germans. The *Autobahn* has been an enormous success of scale and engineering. Our motorways will connect all of the major cities and people can travel with speed to any destination including the scenic areas of Germany. We have already completed 3,500 kilometers.

Although the railway is still the largest employer here and transports the bulk of passengers and freight, the motorization of Germany is coming."

Anna nodded, giving Albert her full attention. "How fascinating to think of a future where I might drive my own car all the way to Berlin!"

"Oh, my *schissen*, we will make a better future in every way," Albert exclaimed.

"What do you mean, Albert?" Anna asked innocently. "Who is 'we'—your company?"

Albert was preaching from the podium now. "The Nazi Party is what I am talking about, and of course, the *Fuhrer*. He is a brilliant leader. He has even designed a small car for our people. *Volkswagen* will be sold for under 1,000 reichsmark.

But more than that, we will have the living space to produce more food and products. The people will have great prosperity as Germany makes our appliances, our aircraft, our motorways, and our future. We cannot let anyone stop us on our path to *autarky*, Anna."

"I do not understand, Albert," Anna said honestly.

"We will become self-sufficient. Soon Germany will rely on no other countries for trade," he explained passionately.

"You are so brilliant, Albert."

He smiled and reached for her, but she went on. "Who would ever want to stop the *Fuhrer* on this path? We must do something to help!"

Albert's expression became grave when he said. "Sit down, *schissen*. You have no idea where traitors hide to undermine the great work of Nazis. And why? What can be gained by such futile opposition? But I will uncover them. You can count on that. I will punish them as they deserve."

"You are in the automobile business. What power do you have to arrest traitors?" Anna probed.

Assuming that Anna was harmless, certainly no risk to him, Albert boasted frankly, "I am *Gestapo* and I have friends in very high places to back me."

Albert was feeling powerful after impressing Anna and flattered by her overt admiration. He wanted her.

Anna held his gaze steadily and respectfully. She shook her head slowly from side to side. "And here I am with you. I am so fortunate to be with such an important man."

That was all he needed. Albert reached for her breast, squeezed it hard and quickly pulled her close to him. He brushed back her hair and bit her neck. He quickly moved to her lips as though he would devour her.

Anna squirmed out from underneath him while pushing his chest away with all her strength. She had to divert his advance before she was overpowered.

Controlling her sense of panic, she played the annoying adolescent. In a high-pitched voice she spoke rapidly. "I would like you to meet my father, Albert. In fact, I would like you to meet my whole family. *Vati* is on leave right now. He is *Oberleutnant* for the *Fuhrer*. He has been training the troops. He was a corporal in World War I just like the Fuhrer. I am sure *Vati* would love to meet you."

Her performance had the desired effect on Albert. He withdrew and became more subdued by the change in her behavior and the military status of her father. He was rethinking his next move on Anna. Was she worth it?

Anna helped him make his decision, "Albert would you drive me back to the track now? I can't wait to tell *Vati* all about you and the important work you are doing for Germany. Then you can take me to your car dealership."

Albert knew that Olav would do anything but agree to let his young daughter go out with a 43-year-old man. This could have consequences that Albert did not want at this stage in his career.

On their return to the track, Anna chattered on obnoxiously while Albert changed gears. "Yes, let us return to the track so you can catch the final race," Albert said agreeably but thought, "I will rid myself of her at the entrance and move on. I didn't see any suspicious activities this afternoon anyway."

When they reached the club house, Albert opened the door for Anna and touched her shoulder lightly before returning to the driver's seat.

"Call me please, Bertie," Anna cried with a deliberately annoying girlish giggle and wave. She spun on her heel and walked in measured steps toward the club house, her heart still pounding. Anna acknowledged what she had done, "I am only seventeen years old and I duped a Gestapo agent." A sense of relief and power filled her chest.

She greeted an elegant woman with two gray Weimaraners on leashes and had completely composed herself by the time she opened the door of the club house. She remembered her posture as she looked calmly about the room for Frieda. Anna spotted her talking with a large man who was lighting her cigarette (Frieda didn't smoke). Frieda put her hand lightly on his as she inhaled the flame from the match. Then he spoke into her ear and Anna caught the slightest movement as he dropped something into Frieda's pocket. They stood apart again and smiled and talked like old friends.

An older woman approached them and they began what appeared to be a friendly conversation. She looked exhausted or ill, too frail. The man took his leave and the two women continued to speak, their expressions polite and friendly. An onlooker would think they were chatting about the race track news or mutual acquaintances, their families or some other innocuous topic.

Anna made her way to the wall opposite Frieda so she could make eye contact. She knew not to interrupt Frieda's business. Frieda met Anna's eyes and gave her an almost imperceptible nod. As Anna walked over to the women, she could hear Frieda giving the recipe.

"What did it mean," Anna wondered.

"Cream the butter and sugar and add the eggs one at a time. Add the milk alternately with dry ingredients in small amounts and then beat until the batter slides smoothly off spoon… Oh Anna, where have you been? I would like you to meet an old friend of mine, *Frau Schwarz*." The noise ended her introductions.

People were on their feet outside in the bleachers and men were shaking their fists and yelling as they stared intensely through the windows of the club house. And then the final roar of the crowd. The winning horse was a full length in the lead. Frieda went to the booth to collect—what, she could only guess. Was it really money or a message?

"May I offer you a ride home?" asked *Frau Schwarz*.

"Thank you. That would be lovely," said Frieda.

When *Frau Schwarz* dropped them off at the salon, she declined the offer of a drink, and instead asked Frieda to confirm, "Was that 4 eggs and 1 bottle of rum in the pound cake, Frieda?"

"Yes precisely, and until next time, good health my friend!"

"When they entered the apartment," Frieda simply said, "Well?"

Anna's reply was brief, "Yes, he is Gestapo."

"Good work, my apprentice," Frieda said.

It was the end of September when Frieda suggested that Anna take time off to spend with her family. "My darling you have been working very hard and you deserve a break."

"Thank you *Tante Frieda*. I haven't seen them for over two months. Maybe I can see Nat and Klara too," said Anna enthusiastically.

Anna threw open the door. "I am home," she sang out. Mari came down the hallway to meet her while wiping her hands on her apron. "Oh *Mutti*, I've missed you," Anna exclaimed as she embraced her mother. "It is so good to be home."

Rita came down the stairs with a doll under one arm, "Anna, Anna, Anna." Anna hugged her sister, but when she tried to break away, the young girl would not let go of her neck. "Come little one, look at me." When she lifted her chin, Anna saw that Rita was crying. "Let's sit together in the kitchen for a while and talk to *Mutti*. Where are the boys?"

"Leo will be home soon from his sports program. Hitler Youth keeps them busy you know, and Ralfie is in the back yard playing with Axel and Rosa and some of the other neighborhood children. Just then they heard a wail. "And that is an unhappy Otto. He is hungry! Let's go have a coffee," suggested Mari as she put her arm around Anna's waist and walked with her down the hall.

"Is that chicken soup and dumplings I smell?" Anna asked. "Ahhhh."

As they sat at the kitchen table discussing their news, Rita sat on Anna's lap clutching her doll. During the conversation with her mother, Anna smoothed her sister's brow and kissed her cheek.

Otto demanded the attention of Mari but was not particularly interested in Anna at all. "*Mutti*, he is such a big baby! He looks like a little butcher—no mistaking him for a girl. Look how he eats. Otto is so content in his high chair with his food in front of him. This is a boy who does not play with his food or throw it around. No, into his mouth it goes."

Leo came in the back door with Ralfie asking, "Mutti, what is for supper? Anna, you are home!"

"Yes handsome, come over here and give me a hug." He hugged her neck from behind the chair since Rita would not relinquish her position.

Ralfie asked Anna, "Where is Nattie?" He was shy and stood beside Mari to watch his sisters and brothers from a safe distance.

"She isn't with me this time, Ralfie. But she will visit you soon," Anna assured her little brother.

Later that evening when the younger children were in bed and Anna had finished washing the dishes and sweeping the floor, Mari and Anna sat down at the table.

"I like your haircut, Anna. You look very fashionable. How is your work coming along at the salon?"

"I have learned so much from *Tante Frieda*. Many of our customers say I have a special flair for choosing a haircut that suits them. I love working at the salon, *Mutti*.

We hear a bit of gossip too. Women who would never consider speaking to me on the street, talk openly about their lives. Strange isn't it…

Mutti, may I see your latest creations?"

Her mother pointed at the doorway. There was Rita in her flannel nightgown holding the doll close to her chest. "Rita come sit on my lap for a while," Anna pleaded to Mari with her eyes. "Is that all right, *Mutti*?"

"Yes, this is a special night." However, it wasn't long before Rita was asleep. Anna carried her sister up to the bedroom that had once been hers. She could hear the heavy breathing of the three sleeping boys in the other room as she walked by.

Back in the kitchen, Anna began, "Is Rita struggling at school? I worry about how the other children and teachers treat her."

"Leo watches out for Rita, but still she is having many difficulties with her school work and the other students. Her one close friend is Axel from next door, and they keep to themselves. She is learning but at a lower level than the other children in the class.

And yet, Anna, her recent art work! *Vati* sent a watercolor set and charcoal pencils for Rita and she has created astonishing pieces. She stays indoors and draws or paints. I believe her art will be in a gallery someday… Anna, I wish I could send her to an art school; but regrettably, the art school has been closed."

"Tomorrow I will spend time with her and ask about each of the pictures… Does *Grossmutter Muller* ever visit?" asked Anna solemnly.

"No, we seldom see her anymore. She stays downtown where she can get around easier. I don't think she likes to visit us anymore and with *Vati* away, well… Why do you ask?"

"I am relieved to hear this, *Mutti*. I am about to tell you something that must remain a secret." Mari tilted her head to the side and raised her eyebrows. "Grandmother is an informant of the golden pheasant, *Herr Kaufer*. Yes, I know it is a shock, but I have proof," Anna said in a serious tone.

Mari looked down into her coffee cup and when she lifted her eyes, she said firmly, "Beatrice will never come here again. I never really trusted her. Rita may not be safe. I have heard of block wardens sending simple children, mentally ill, or the disabled away to be sterilized or admitted to institutions. They must never touch our Rita, Anna. She is such a sweet child."

"No one will harm Rita. I will not allow it," Anna uttered in a menacing way that Mari had never heard before. She believed her daughter.

When Anna went to her bed that night she lay beside Rita and looked at her angelic face, her long eyelashes and thick brown braids. "I will keep you safe, little sister," she thought as she slipped off to sleep.

The next evening Mari called, "Quickly, Anna, come and listen! They have invaded Czechoslovakia." Mari was sitting beside the radio while the news poured in during the Hour of the Nation. It was October, 1938.

"Oh no, this will not be like the takeover of Austria. The Czechs are against Adolf and Nazism. Czechoslovakia is still a democracy. This will lead to another world war! How can the English and French stand by? I must write to your father."

Family needs trumped her fears about the invasion of Czechoslovakia.-The children had to be fed and dressed. Mari had housework and customer orders to complete.

Later in the week, Anna suggested, "Since I am home, why don't you take a break? Maybe you could visit *Frau Wolfe* or *Tante Frieda* after mass. Klara and Nat are able to come over tomorrow so we can take care of everything while you are gone." Mari agreed.

The next day the young friends bundled the children in warm sweaters, mittens, and scarves that Mari had knitted. After a game of hide-and-go-seek, they took an autumn walk. Nathalie claimed Ralfie, Klara pushed Otto in the carriage, and Anna held Rita's left hand because her right was clasping a doll. When they returned home, they put the children down for their afternoon nap. Leo would not be home until dinner, and Mari was visiting the Wolfes so they had time to catch up over coffee.

"The invasion of Czechoslovakia is very troubling. I don't know what to think. How are the Beckers feeling about the invasion, Nathalie?" asked Anna.

"Well, they are pleased. They believe that Adolf is winning back our lands and people. After all he freed the Sudeten Germans," replied Nathalie.

Klara added, "My parents think that Adolf should have left the Czechs alone. *Mutter and Vater* know where this can all lead having lived through WW1. They are against the invasion, but they certainly like the restrictions that have been placed on the Jews. Business has never been better in the *Kalbfleisch* butcher shop with the local competition gone.

As far as I am concerned, I am against any more invasions. I see enough suffering in the hospital as it is and do not want to see a flood of wounded soldiers too."

"I agree, Klara. Like you I want to help. I want to become a doctor," announced Nathalie, "and work in the battle fields or in medical research. I want to do something more important than baking bread."

"How can you gain admittance to the university? The Nazi policy prohibits women from attending universities… and how will you meet their qualifications?" asked Klara.

"*Frau Weber*, the head librarian, whom I have known since school days, has been following my studies and is recommending me to a friend at the university. I will have to write an entrance examination, but I am prepared.

Doctors are in demand for surgeries and treatments but also research. Many new drugs such as methadone and Demerol, sulfa, and the nerve gas, sarin, are being tested on animals and patients.

And, the Nazi Physicians' Chamber and Rudolph Hess support herbal medicine and other natural remedies. They call it the 'New German Healing.' They need doctors to train others and administer this form of medicine."

After a pause she went on to a more sensitive topic. "The Nazis are committed to our Aryan race. Many doctors are also responsible for examining ethnic groups. 'Racial cleansing' is paramount," explained Nathalie.

Klara interrupted, "I know something of this. They do not want some groups of people to have children. They only want Aryans to multiply. Nat, we are busy nursing those who have had the sterilization surgeries. I have cared for adults as well as children in the hospitals. One of them was only twelve years old! And gypsies! We have seen so many gypsies in for sterilization lately. And there are others!"

The young women looked into their coffee cups, sickened by the magnitude of the information. Anna decided to change the mood with, "I hope they have not harmed our gypsy fortune-teller Mitza. I hear she is still in her secret apartment. Why don't we do something fun—find out what the future holds for us! Let's go to Mitza soon," suggested Anna. "Frieda will know where she is."

"I am glad to have you back at the salon, girls," welcomed Frieda. "Nat and Klara tell me your news. It has been many weeks since I have seen you. So much has happened."

The apartment smelled of the soup simmering on the stove. Nathalie brought bread so they all sat down to share a meal and talk. Anna thought that Frieda looked very tired. Frieda had been busy with more than extra work in the salon while she was gone, of that Anna was certain. Later Anna asked, "*Tante Frieda* can you tell us how to find old Mitza?"

"Of course, Mitza still practices her arts, but she is hidden away. If you intend to see her, you must be very discreet," cautioned Frieda. The women nodded in unison. They knew that spies were everywhere and did not want to endanger Mitza.

Two days later they stepped off the tram close to the center of the city. The three friends walked with purpose and chatted about daily concerns until they reached the brick building that Frieda had described to them. They waited at the corner to ensure that no one was watching them and then slipped around the building but could see no doorway along the side. They rounded the back and there beside a garbage bin was a crooked old doorway, exactly where Frieda said it would be.

Anna knocked three times on the door and waited impatiently. Did Mitza remember their appointment? Had she been apprehended by the Nazis? She knocked again, three times. Mitza slowly opened the door a crack and peered out. With a nod, she opened the door wider and motioned them to enter. She quickly closed the door and locked it securely behind her, motioning them to sit in a small waiting area.

Mitza was a tiny 4'11" woman with dark skin. When she smiled, her eyes twinkled in her heavily-lined face. Mitza wore a brightly colored handkerchief in the style of the gypsies and a dark dress belted at the waist. Hunched over, she shuffled painfully into the inner sanctum.

When it was Anna's turn to have her fortune told, she entered an area that Mitza had cordoned off from her living quarters with black velvet curtains. The area was dimly lit by a lamp that had mystical symbols outlined in the shade. A patterned shawl covered the top of the table.

After several minutes, Mitza asked, "May I see your right palm." She turned it slowly from side to side. Then Mitza gathered Tarot cards. Beautiful images of the moon, sun, camels, and male and female figures flashed by on long narrow cards. "So, my dear, let us pause for a moment. Close your eyes and think about the question you wish to have answered. Are you ready?" Anna nodded but Mitza held the stack of cards in her hands for several minutes with her eyes closed and then began to lay them out in a distinct pattern around the table.

Mitza's eyes darted from card to card as she studied the position and relationships of the symbols. She spoke of Anna's temperament and her work at the salon. She described key events influencing the question and then stopped. "Ahhh, this is what you seek. You will meet a man soon, but he will go far away and you will follow later. You will live happily enough. You will have few tears and you will be far across the ocean."

Chapter Nine
Violence Unleashed

As Bruno raised his zipper and drew in his belt, he asked Katia, "Do you have the money?" She wrapped a pink robe around herself and opened the drawer of her dresser to retrieve Bruno's payment. He counted it slowly and then his eyes travelled over her body with a proprietorial look. Katia turned away and moved to the window to feel the autumn sunlight on her face. "*Auf Wiedersehen,*" Bruno said with sarcastic cheerfulness. The door slammed.

Her eyes filled with tears and for a moment she stood frozen in the warmth of the sun; blinking she rushed to the bathroom for the ablution that water provided. She scrubbed, scrubbed, and scrubbed her flesh clean.

Meanwhile Bruno happily saluted his brethren as he passed them, feeling quite self-assured as he sauntered down the street enjoying the afternoon; and then, he saw Ada. "There she is with her son again. Look how she moves. Isn't she a nice piece—not like that filthy whore I just had my cock in." He had seen sexier women, but something about Ada's regal carriage and her classic beauty transfixed him.

"The little bastard is so happy walking with her. His face shows it all. She is wrapping her arm around his shoulders. What are they laughing about?" Bruno wondered as he stared, racked with shameless jealousy. He knew this was more than the average bond between mother and child. It was one of mutual respect and understanding, a friendship. Without realizing why, Bruno's guts twisted with desire.

"*Heil Hitler! Hallo, gnadige Frau.*" Bruno accosted the mother and son. Ada, unflappable, returned the salute and continued to walk with Oskar, but Bruno introduced himself, "I am *Herr Kaufer*, the block warden." Ada nodded but did not introduce herself. "And you are?" he pressed.

"I am *Frau Brandt* and this is my son, Oskar. Oskar was bright and polite as usual, not sensing the menacing presence in front of him."

"How old is your son, *Frau Brandt*?"

"He is eleven years old now," Ada replied cautiously and then added quickly. "Oskar very much enjoys the Hitler Youth athletic program. In fact, I must leave to make his meal so he can return for evening training."

"Very good, very good, *Frau Brandt.* I will see you again."

Ada managed an obligatory smile which vanished when they were finally able to continue down the street. She felt uneasy.

Bruno didn't like the way his afternoon had changed. He felt inferior, worthless again. Ada had been polite but at the same time aloof, and she oozed class. He could detect an educated German accent. His instincts knew she was an aristocratic person beyond his reach. He couldn't leave it alone.

Fuming Bruno thought, "Maybe she is one of those high and mighty Prussians. Their time is over. We live in a new world where the Third Reich is supreme. I am a Nazi! I will teach her to respect me!"

"Katia, what can I do for you this fine morning?" asked Frieda as she wrapped the cape around Katia's shoulders.

"Oh God, bleach my hair. My adulterous customers feel less immoral if they fuck an ARYAN prostitute!" she laughed ruefully.

"Won't Bruno beat you again if he sees that?" asked Frieda with concern.

"He will beat me anyway, the *blodes Schwein*! He really believes he is a little Hitler, I swear. We should all be such model Aryans, yes? Blonde like Hitler, tall like Goebbels…" Frieda laughed.

Anna was between customers so she joined Katia and Frieda. "Have you ever been to the *Libella,* Katia? My father used to perform there."

"Yes I have. It is VERY elegant. The clientele has changed but even now the women wear furs and gold. Men wear the uniforms of officers. They take the girls for dinner in the restaurant attached to the night club. Anna, the dance floor in the night club is GLASS with lights underneath. I have not been there often—more for high class whores. They even own homes. The men buy them champagne and gifts… Just like my lover, Bruno," Katia added sarcastically. The three women broke up laughing.

Anna's smile faded as she thought with affection, "Katia always has a joke and a smile and is one of the few customers that never complains and yet her life…"

"Could I see you in private before I leave, Frieda?" asked Katia. When they were in the apartment, Katia took money from her purse and gave it to Frieda. "Would you put this with the rest, please? I can't keep much money in my room. I don't have a pimp, but I still pay…extortion at the hands of Bruno—keeps me out of the work camps," she shrugged humorously. Then her face darkened.

"One day I will have enough to leave this life."

Frieda nodded in solemn hope.

At dusk the November air had turned cold and the skies oppressively grey when Anna stepped onto the trolley car to return home for the weekend. She was anxious to spend time with her mother and the children. She chose a window seat so she could look at the streets or doze and not have to talk with other passengers. She was not particularly cheery after her day spent with demanding customers. Anna had a few treats for the children and a new comb for her mother and was imagining their reactions when suddenly her reverie was shattered by glass flying out of a shop window less than a block ahead. The trolley car continued down the track.

It was happening farther down the street outside a furrier's shop as well. Window panes were being broken and the brown shirts were beating people in the streets. She could hear the wails and shouting from inside the trolley car as it continued unwaveringly on its course.

Anna stared open-mouthed as they passed homes being looted and trashed, families crying in the street, children dressed in only their night clothes. The uniformed men had mounds of their loot already loaded into trucks and the people, the hated Jews, were being corralled.

Anna stared with disbelief at the scene in a graveyard they passed. Graves were being dug up and headstones broken, the synagogue was burning. The contorted faces of soldiers were revealed by the flames like images conjured up from hell.

Only this was really happening.

As the streetcar took her closer to home, Anna saw more broken windows and destroyed homes. The violence was incomprehensible. Now she fully grasped why Frieda fought injustice at all levels.

The trolley car finally reached her stop and once on the street, Anna ran home. When she made it to the kitchen and saw Mari's face and warm smile, she hugged her and wept uncontrollably. In between gasps Anna explained what she had just witnessed. Mari was alarmed to see her daughter so upset. Anna had always controlled her emotions.

"How horrifying for you! What is happening? The shops were owned by Jews so all of the families you saw were probably Jewish too. Why are they doing this? Where will they go now?" Mari asked with concern.

Mari immediately telephoned Mr. Wolfe but no one answered. She called Frieda. No answer. Slowly Mari eased herself into her chair in the kitchen. One arm extended out on the table; she dropped her head onto her arm. Anna touched Mari's shoulder and then left to make a pot of coffee.

Finally the women realized that they must get some sleep and walked upstairs arm-in-arm. Yet Anna could not sleep with the images plaguing her mind—soldiers breaking windows with unbridled fury, wielding axes, hatchets, daggers and revolvers—German soldiers wearing masks of hatred toward German citizens.

The next morning Frieda telephoned, "Anna, are you all right? Hell broke loose not long after you left. Stay home until I let you know it is safe. You need to be with your family."

"I could not believe what I saw from the trolley car… We are all safe here and you, *Tante Frieda*?"

"They won't touch my shop. I am a non-Jew," Frieda reassured her. "Now let me speak to your mother, darling…Mari, they took *Herr Wolfe* and Lisel and the children—everyone, gone."

"Oh God, I telephoned last night hoping to bring them here but no answer. I was too late…" Mari said in anguish.

"The looting and beatings became worse during the night. No one seems to know the extent of the damage; and whether or not, this happened anywhere else in Germany," Frieda stated.

"I don't understand how the average Jew is such a threat? Where will they be taken? Work camps?"

Frieda didn't tell Mari that she had gone to the train station before dawn and through the chaos of people jostling for position in the queue found a train of closed box cars. She could hear the cries of children and women and muffled shouts through the cracks in the wooden doors. She ran down the length of cars calling out for *Herr Wolfe*, Lisel, and the children but she heard no response.

She returned home feeling defeated and lost, her thoughts scattered. "What will I do without the wisdom and guidance of *Herr Wolfe*? He has been my main underground contact and leader for all these years? We were undetected even by the Mullers. *Herr Wolfe* is the mastermind behind our entire operation in Leipzig. I cannot possibly manage. Who will lead? Where are they being taken? What can I do?" She was inconsolable. She had the unsettling sensation that nothing was real. All seemed an illusion.

This surreal atmosphere was still evident when two days later Frieda was walking to the Catholic Church to meet Father Engel. She was alarmed to see the SS dragging two men and a woman out of an office building. They forced the bewildered Jews to clean up the mess in the streets.

"I want to see this all gone, or you will stay here until it is completely removed." A large, loud man commanded as he pushed the woman. It wasn't long before a crowd of jeering citizens had gathered to further humiliate the persecuted Germans.

Frieda became ill when she realized that children were among the onlookers, casting rocks and humiliating taunts at the harmless office workers. But Frieda remained mute and took no action. It was too dangerous to speak out against this atrocity at this moment. She could be taken away. Her battle would remain hidden from their eyes. They would not see the next ambush from her!

The next day when Frieda arrived at the Catholic Church, she made straight for the confessional. "Bless me Father for I have sinned. It has been four months and one week since my last confession. And these are my sins…"

He slipped a piece of paper through the blind. She placed it in the heart of her prayer book.

"Your sins are forgiven. Go in peace," said Father Engel, but Frieda had already vanished.

Her search for the Wolfe family continued with the help of Father Engel. He had assisted her on countless occasions. His network through Germany and into Rome was intact despite the efforts of the Nazis to destroy the influence of the church in the daily lives of Germans.

The Nazi goal was to divert the people's devotion from the pope to the *Fuhrer*. The struggle to preserve their rights as Germans had been effectively repressed but the underground, unrelenting, were at war.

Frieda thought, "Father Engel's assistance yielded no trace of the Wolfes—only the horrifying information that Jews had been transported by the thousands to a ghetto in Poland to await transport God knows where."

When Anna returned to work, she could see that Frieda was very troubled. The black shadows around her eyes were visible through her makeup and her hair was untidy. Previously Frieda's appearance had never been compromised.

She worked quietly and was polite to the customers but in a mechanical way. In the evening, Anna talked about her sister and brothers to amuse Frieda but received only a wan smile. Anna knew better than to pry and thought that time would heal whatever was corroding Frieda's heart.

Over the weeks, Frieda looked less tired and she was impeccably groomed again, but Anna could tell she was still troubled.

One evening Anna attempted another tactic to lift her spirits. "Frieda, would you like to join Klara, Nat and I at the movies?"

"I am too old and tired to go out."

"Please, we are celebrating," said Anna, "Nat has been accepted into medical research!"

When Klara and Nathalie arrived, they too pleaded with Frieda, but she declined, "You go. Have fun. Congratulations Nat, my darling!" Finally accepting her decision, the young women left in a flurry of chatter and laughter.

Alone and lost in thought, Frieda sat for some time slowly sipping a cup of coffee. She jumped when she heard the back door open. By the time she crossed the kitchen, a tall man in the black uniform of the Gestapo was standing before her.

"They have found me. What now, the camps?" she thought in terror. Frieda looked up into the man's face in disbelief. "Come in! My God, *Herr Wolfe*, it is you!" They clung to one another as though they had found–something precious they thought was lost forever.

"Sit down and I'll get us a drink," Frieda whispered composing herself.

Mr. Wolfe slumped into a chair and waited quietly… "I lost them, Frieda. They separated us…men together and women and children in other cars… I think they took them east to Poland or further. I hear about reservations for Jews.

I escaped before the border and have been trying to find my family these past weeks… I should have moved them out of the country long ago. I let my pride and the Cause cloud my judgment. They would be safe now if I had only…" groaned Mr. Wolfe. He gulped the drink Frieda placed in front of him and shook his head in despair.

"We couldn't foresee that the situation would escalate to this. It is the 20th century. How could such barbarism have occurred unchecked in Europe? Since that night, I have heard no one mention November 9 or where the people were taken. It is as though nothing happened—a nightmare to be forgotten in the light of day."

"Unbelievable…" he sighed. "Can you hide me for a day or two? I need to rest."

"Of course. Anna will return after the cinema tonight and will be here tomorrow, but she will take the trolley car home for the weekend."

"We can talk more freely then about the network and our priorities," Mr. Wolfe said in his deep voice.

Frieda nodded and placed a plate of bread, cheese and smoked pork on the table. "I will take supplies into the dugout for you. It will be very cold so take an extra woolen blanket and a candle." That night Frieda slept soundly, something she hadn't done since November 9.

The Third Reich had passed a milestone. They had met no significant resistance during the sanctioned pogrom, Reich Crystal Night of November 9, 1938.

Whether people had become calloused by five years of incessant anti-Semitism propaganda or whether they were silenced by the threat of violence to themselves, the result was the same. The Nazis knew that they could proceed with their plan for racial cleansing and no one was going to stop them.

Chapter Ten
Luminal Moments

Anna wore her black and white polka dot dress with the wide, black belt and black, leather shoes. She had painted her nails a bright pink and Frieda had done her hair up in a French roll. Although she was only 18 years old, Anna looked mature enough to blend with the crowd at the *Libelle,* a popular dine and dance club.

The musicians all knew and liked Anna so she felt important when she was welcomed at the club or allowed in ahead of others waiting patiently in the queue. The mere mention of her father's name impressed people. He was a popular performer in the orchestra at the *Libelle* when he had been on leave from the military so no one suspected her of spying for Frieda. Anna enjoyed working at this venue, absorbing the music, fashion, and lively conversations.

Her eyes had become trained to see details in a glance. She memorized the faces and often the names of Nazi officers and wealthy industrialists that frequented the club.

To profit, the businessmen were forced to work indirectly, inviting key Nazis to lavish dinners, buying rounds of drinks, and giving goods or services that were currently in short supply. Favors bought and given were important to personal success in the Third Reich.

Anna observed exchanges of money and papers through the grey, smoky haze of the club. She overheard conversations in spite of the music, laughter and shouting. She remembered the preferred drink of noteworthy regulars and the mood or personality traits of an identified target she was instructed to watch.

Was the individual nervous or cocky, deceptive or transparent? She picked up clues from habits, eye movements, stance, clothing and so on. She gathered information almost subconsciously now—rarely had to concentrate.

Anna was sipping a drink with no alcohol when a very well-dressed and very drunk woman brushed by her and, in the packed club, accidentally dropped her fur coat. Knowing the value of the coat, Anna grabbed it quickly. Anna walked over to where the woman, who was unaware of her lost fur, was standing with friends.

Excuse me, *Fraulein*, but is this your coat?"

"*Gott sei Dank*! Yes, it is my beautiful ermine that *Vati* gave me when I turned…21 years old," the grateful woman blurted as her companion held her arm to steady her. "I must reward you, my darling girl. Fritz, buy her as much champagne as she wants tonight and forever. What a virtuous young thing you are," she praised as she draped her arm around Anna's shoulders and then slurring a bit asked Fritz, "Light my cigarette, darling, and one for my new friend as well."

Anna, who did not smoke, accepted the cigarette and tried not to inhale. She chose to stay with these wealthy, carefree people and *sich anlfreunden* for awhile. Anna was about to have a second cigarette and another glass of champagne when she caught herself. She remembered Frieda's lessons.

"Thank you for your kindness, Amelia, but it was my pleasure, *gute nacht freund!*"

Turning away with a smile, Anna looked directly into the eyes of a striking officer in the uniform of the German army. He had been watching her. She had never seen him in the *Libelle* previously, and yet for a moment they shared a connection that sent a rush of energy through her entire being. Shocked by her attraction to him she turned away rather suddenly and walked over to the bar. He followed.

"Would you permit me to buy you a drink?" he asked courteously in a clear deep voice.

Anna paused before accepting, "Yes, but only one, and then I must leave." Her heart was pounding in her ears.

"It must be a memorable one then… *Fraulein*?" he asked good-naturedly.

"Anna Muller and your name, *mein Herr*?"

"Reiner Lange, Anna. I am pleased to meet you, but I suspect most men are," he complimented with a sparkle in his eyes and a smile that threw her off balance.

However, she was composed when she asked, "I have not seen you in *Libelle* before."

"I suspect that a young woman like you has not been a patron of this club for very long."

"Were you in Czechoslovakia?" Anna asked to change the topic.

"Yes, the campaign was a success. No bloodshed," Reiner asserted.

True. With precision, the Reich had seized mineral resources and glass, textile, and armament industries. They took aircraft, artillery, and tanks. Jewish firms were expropriated and assets transferred to German industry; and of course, the Czech gold reserves funded the Nazi war effort. And yes, little bloodshed.

"In fact, by March, the Czech Republic was part of the Third Reich and Czech labor was conscripted to work here in Germany," answered Reiner.

"Now we have Austrians and Czechs working for Germany. Could we have had a more peaceful outcome for all concerned, Reiner?"

In reality workers who resisted conscription to Germany were threatened with custody in work camps.

"Are you employed, Anna?"

"I am training to be a beautician. I live with my aunt at her salon. She is both teacher and friend to me. How long will you be in Leipzig, Reiner?" Anna asked to deflect further questions. She was thinking he must be more than thirty years old.

"I don't know yet, but I do know I want to dance with you," Reiner stated confidently as he extended his hand to her. They walked toward the dance floor. Holding his hand felt natural and familiar to Anna. She felt inexplicably certain that she would walk anywhere with him. The magnetism between them was making her uncharacteristically reckless.

The orchestra played a waltz. Their eyes remained fixed on each other while they danced. Anna was no longer intimidated by his age or status. She had never met anyone like Reiner before, never felt this way before.

"*Leh tanze mit dir in den Himmel hinein*, I'll dance you into heaven," he murmured the lyrics in her ear as he held her close. Anna was acutely aware of his scent. They reluctantly separated when the music changed to a Charleston.

"I must leave now, Reiner."

"Let me drive you home then," he offered.

"I would like that," she answered against all of the training Frieda had given her.

When they arrived at the salon, Reiner opened the passenger door and extended his hand to help Anna from her seat.

"Can I persuade you to have dinner with me tomorrow at 8:00?"

"Yes, I will have dinner with you. Before dinner, please join us for a drink. I would like *Tante Frieda* to meet you."

Anna held his eyes before she went inside.

Frieda was sitting at the kitchen table waiting for Anna who was much later than expected.

"You are flushed. What happened to you, my darling? Trouble at the *Libelle*?"

"I am fine. I had no problems. But…I met an officer at the *Libelle* tonight. We are going out to dinner tomorrow evening. Would you mind if I invite him in to meet you before we go out?" Anna explained trying to control her excitement.

"Yes, I want to meet him," replied Frieda a bit surprised but clearly not pleased. She resented Anna for placing her operation at risk.

Also Frieda had not anticipated a man in Anna's life yet and was already guarded about this officer's intentions. Frieda did not want Anna to make a mistake she would regret for years to come.

"*Tante Frieda*, he is so good-looking and even though he is older we get along. Oddly, I feel that I have always known him. You have trained me to look for signs of treachery in people. I detect none in him. In fact, he seems honorable," Anna began excitedly, but her story was truncated.

"Do you have any other news for me?" asked Frieda in an icy tone. Anna was shocked and embarrassed by the abrupt dismissal of her important and intimate news but was able to reply curtly, "No, our concern was not present tonight."

She rose and walked toward her room. "*Gute Nacht*," Anna said flatly as she closed the door.

Anna's thoughts and emotions collided. Embarrassment turned to anger. "*Tante Frieda*! Huh! She is using me—she doesn't care about me at all. She has to be in control always. I will never disclose my feelings with her again… No one walks over me! I know the only thing that really matters to her. The Cause! I have been so naive!" Anna made a firm decision to continue some of her work, accept the gifts and privileges that Frieda offered in payment but vowed to never completely trust her again.

"She has crossed the line," Anna swore, uncharacteristically blind to the fact she was endangering their lives and jeopardizing missions in the underground.

The next evening when Anna entered the kitchen to join Frieda, Frieda nodded approvingly. "You look beautiful. Sit down and talk with me please, Anna." Frieda decided to deal with this new obstacle very carefully.

"My apprentice," Frieda said in a low voice, "Are you certain that this man is worthy of you? Are you certain that he is not manipulating you?…Or… worse yet, could he be a spy? Do you think he suspects you of working for the underground?"

"I don't really know anything. I do whatever you say and no more… I will know more about him after tonight," replied Anna in an offhanded manner. She was still very angry, but her mood shifted immediately when she heard a knock at the door.

"Reiner, come in. I would like to introduce you to *Fraulein Frieda Portner.*"

"Anna holds you in the highest regard. It is a pleasure to meet you," said Reiner as he shook Frieda's hand. "Please accept this gift."

"How kind of you," Frieda responded warily.

"Look Frieda," interrupted Anna who was clearly pleased. Reiner presented coffee, chocolate, and smoked pork.

"We are very grateful. The food shortages these past months have been taxing. However, we all must endure deprivation for now to achieve the vision of a united and strong Germany. But please, sit down and join us for a cognac," invited Frieda in a somber tone.

"I agree with you Frieda. And, the campaign should not last much longer. When we regain our lands, Germans will prosper again," added Reiner seriously.

"*Vater* was in WW1 and told me how Germans were devastated by the loss of their lands," said Anna. Her level voice belied her emotions. Frieda's small kitchen seemed to vibrate with the energy of this man. Her senses were highly attuned to the tone of his voice, his movements, his intelligent eyes. Yet Anna asked calmly, "Did you have family in WW1, Reiner?"

"Sadly, my father was killed, but Grandfather survived and ensured that Mother had the support she needed to raise our family. And you Frieda?" Reiner inquired.

"I try not to think of the past Reiner. I have a good life here at the salon; that is apart from having to endure the antics of one young apprentice," she replied in an attempt to trivialize her own life.

"Do you have a problem with the apprentice, as well Anna?" Reiner asked looking again at Anna.

"Hmm, I think I am the problem to which she refers," Anna said flashing him a smile.

They all laughed as Reiner refilled their glasses. "When I was a boy in Bavaria I was, admittedly, a considerable source of trouble for Mother, and at those times I would retreat to let things cool down at home."

"Where did you retreat, Reiner?" asked Anna. "Maybe I should find such a place."

"Into the branches of an enormous beech tree. The tree was surrounded by spruce and oak so discovery was unlikely."

"Actually Reiner, Anna is no trouble to me or her mother so I do not think she will need a retreat just yet. She has been a remarkable learner and wonderful companion to me," Frieda confessed with such sincerity Anna was touched and willing to forgive Frieda's insensitivity of the previous night. Anna would forgive but never forget.

Anna excused herself and went to the bathroom to check her makeup and hair. Before returning to the kitchen she took several deep breaths to maintain her composure.

When Anna returned, she overheard their voices. Frieda appeared to be amused with Reiner's story, "...by the time we left the forest, the boar was behind us. Grandfather always reminded us about our ludicrous hunting trip—the hunters became the hunted."

As Anna emerged, Reiner stood and suggested, "Our reservation is for eight o'clock so we should be on our way. Frieda, thank you for welcoming me to your home!"

Frieda was inclined to agree with Anna that Reiner did not seem dangerous; but still, he was confident and mature and far too charming. "She will be hurt badly if he considers their relationship a fling and abandons her. What would Mari think? She has entrusted her daughter into my care. What if Anna becomes pregnant?" Frieda wrestled with these questions based on her assumptions and the fact that she had never experienced love at first sight. Never been with a man. She decided upon a course of action.

Meanwhile the relationship between Anna and Reiner was igniting. Dinner was interplay on two levels – polite conversation on the surface and an undertone of sexual desire. Finally, the tension unbearable, Reiner asked, "Will you come to my room tonight?"

Anna nodded, "Let's leave now."

The room was elegant with heavy curtains, warm lighting, and fresh soft linens on an enormous four poster bed. Reiner gently laid Anna on the bed as he kissed her mouth. Then he undressed her, kissing her breasts and belly. Licking and then touching her with his fingers, Reiner brought her to climax. She relaxed and fell back kissing him deeply.

When he entered her, Anna was overcome with the concentration of his strength and energy between her legs, of Reiner's weight, his strong thighs. They lay in one another's arms until Anna reached for him again.

During the following weeks Anna and Reiner spent all of their free time together, mostly in bed. They talked for hours and made love in their own world, his hotel room.

Her longing for him was all consuming. She had experienced communication through their physical love that defied description. Their relationship became more intimate than most lifelong relationships. It was as though he flowed through her veins.

Conversations with customers and Frieda seemed superficial. Anna was conscious of Reiner even when they were apart. She could sense him.

Frieda observed Anna's appearance and behavior with concern. "She is so radiantly detached—this can only mean one thing… She will suffer in the end. I know it. He will leave her." But her concerns were unfounded.

On a Sunday in May, the couple rode a motorcycle into the mountains east of Leipzig. They left behind the soldiers, the threat of war, and daily struggles for food and supplies; their hearts were carefree.

Reiner pulled over and pointed to a sprawling and towering beech tree alone in a small clearing. The grass and leaves had the impossible new green of late spring. As they crossed the clearing with their picnic, Anna turned to Reiner and said, "I can think of no other place I want to be. I love you too much!" Holding hands, they walked together to the shade of the towering beech and laid out a blanket.

The light that penetrated the spring leaves dappled their naked skin as they rolled from one position to another, insatiably touching and kissing one another. Finally, they dressed and leaned back against the tree trunk.

"Are you hungry, *meine guteliebe*?" asked Reiner as he took sandwiches wrapped in waxed paper from the basket. They ate in a comfortable silence.

"Will you marry me, Anna," asked Reiner suddenly. Without speaking, she nodded seriously—not the youthful, ecstatic, response Reiner expected.

Anna understood the magnitude of the question and was committing herself, as a mature woman, to a future with this man. After a few moments, they smiled and clung to one another.

"I leave in a few days but will return within two months. We can write to each other and on my next leave we will make arrangements."

"You can meet my family. I have told you so many stories about my sister and the boys. *Mutter* will love you. I know it."

"Yes, well why don't we marry in two months? We don't need an elaborate wedding do we?"

They discussed their plans and dreams, but eventually Reiner had to leave with the promise that he would write.

Anna was sustained by Reiner's letters. She ached for him. Love had given her an unfamiliar vulnerability. She projected herself into the future. So many issues to consider, "Where will we live? He wants to start a family right away. I will finish my apprenticeship. I do not want to lose him to the war. *Vati* is gone for years at a time. If only Reiner and I could immigrate.

My family has not even met him! How can I tell *Mutti* I will marry someone she has never met and a man so much older than I? I will talk to her next time I am home."

Anna had not seen her family in weeks. When Reiner left she went home with the gift of coffee from Reiner. She bought sweets from Becker's Bakery for the children. She could not wait to see her mother, the boys and Rita.

With a hot cup of coffee in front of them, Mari and Anna chatted about the family, but Anna said nothing of Reiner.

Actually Anna never discussed her life outside of the salon with her mother. She did not want to taint her home or make Mari worry unnecessarily. Her history with the Lenz women, the work she did for Frieda and now her relationship with Reiner were known to Frieda, but not her mother. She decided to wait for the right time to tell her mother about Reiner.

It was during Anna's absence from the salon that Reiner was sent to Munich for a top level meeting and was able to stop over in Leipzig. He knocked on the back door of the salon with the vigor of a man anxious to be with his woman. The door was opened by Frieda who seized the moment to save Anna from future heartache.

"Hello Reiner. This is a surprise." She did not invite him to sit down.

"I was called away to Munich and took the opportunity to see Anna. Is she in?"

"I am so sorry Reiner, but Anna left a few days ago for Berlin."

"Berlin? Why? She never mentioned anything in her letters."

"Well, I am afraid she met a young soldier and fell madly in love. You know how girls can be. I suppose she thought you would never come back for her.

I am furious. She has left me with more work than I can handle. Now I must find a suitable replacement." Frieda's lies were convincing.

Reiner assumed his military bearing as he dealt with the shock and pain he felt inside. With a clear, cold voice he asked, "If by chance she returns to Leipzig, would you have her telephone this number?... Or, perhaps I should talk with her mother."

"Regrettably, her mother knows nothing about your relationship with Anna, and I doubt that she would approve. It would be unwise for you to make any contact with the family." Frieda had taken control.

His mind raced as he tried to find a reasonable explanation or a possible course of action. This was not the greeting he had anticipated. After a moment he said formally, "Very well, then, goodbye *Fraulein Portner*." Reiner turned sharply and left. His jaw was set firmly and his eyes were devoid of emotion as he slammed the door of the military automobile.

Later he found himself at the *Libelle* ordering a drink and looking around the club for a familiar face. He turned to the bartender, "Have you seen Anna, lately? Anna Muller?"

"No, sir, she has not been here for some time," replied the bartender apologetically.

"When you saw her, was she with anyone," Reiner inquired.

"No, just the usual admirers but I am not always here, sir."

Reiner imagined Anna loving another man and was crazed with a helpless jealousy. She belonged to him. He was her first lover. They were to marry... She had made a fool of him. It had been too good to be true. Frustrated, he took a table in a darkened corner and drank solemnly until a voice made him raise his head.

"Would you like some company, officer? You look unhappy, *liebling*. I might be able to make you feel better..." Reiner looked at the whore blankly but nodded slowly. "Sit down. May I buy you some champagne?"

When Anna returned from visiting her family, work continued as usual, but no letters arrived from Reiner. She became worried as the time they had planned to see each other approached. "Frieda, have any letters been delivered for me?"

"No Anna darling; has Reiner stopped writing?" asked Frieda deceptively. She thought, "You will thank me one day. I have saved you from certain heartache at the hands of that officer. What could he possibly want with a young woman apart from sex? He would have left you as soon as he became bored or saw another pretty face at the *Libelle*."

As summer ended so did Anna's hope for Reiner's return. Pride had made her stop writing letters, but she never stopped thinking of him. Thoughts of their time together kept her awake until late into the night. She wept in silent agony for him. Her eyes were dim and her face pale as she worked through her days. "How could I have been so misled? Why didn't I see signs of his duplicity?"

Reiner disciplined his mind to forget and move on. Regrettably, he had made a fool of himself over a young woman and would now resume his military responsibilities. His attention turned to the important matter of the imminent invasion of Poland.

During a quiet meal with Anna one evening, Frieda asked, "Will you go to the *Libelle* tonight. I have work for you." But there was no response. "Or the track on Sunday. Perhaps you would enjoy seeing the horses again?"

"No, Frieda, I will never go to the *Libelle* or the race track for you again," Anna replied firmly... "However... I do not want to wait in the queue to get costly supplies to take to my mother. Teach me about the black market. I know that you make deals."

Anna had turned a corner in herself. "Neither Frieda nor Reiner will walk over me again. I have much to do," she thought.

Frieda respected Anna's decision. For a moment she felt remorse for her role in destroying Anna's ephemeral happiness, but also recognized on a more disturbing level that Anna's refusal meant that she was no longer malleable. Anna had changed.

"I will introduce you to some people in the black market here in Leipzig and will also take you to the country and introduce you to my friends, the Baumanns. They deal in black market food."

The Baumann farm was an idyllic, pastoral scene in the August sunlight as the truck pulled down the driveway. Two hefty, menacing Rottweilers charged to intercept them until they recognized the neighbor's truck, at which point they began wagging their cropped tails. Anna and Frieda thanked the neighbor for the ride, and then Anna quickly turned her attention to the dogs. She stroked their sleek, black backs and scratched behind their velvety ears.

"Frieda!" greeted *Herr Thomas Baumann* and *Frau Else Baumann* as they emerged from the steps of their home. Frieda embraced the couple with an open affection that Anna had never seen Frieda express. Frieda turned happily to introduce Anna.

*"*This is *Fraulein Anna Muller*," announced Frieda with pride.

"*Hallo, Herr Baumann and Frau Baumann,*" smiled Anna.

"We have not seen you since you were about four or five years old, child. Your mother brought you to visit us many years ago. My, how you have grown into a beauty!

These are our children Guner and Vilma. You must be hungry after your trip from the city. Come in. How are *Mutter* and *Vater* and the children, Anna?" asked Else cheerfully. Else was inclined to talk constantly in an effort to make people feel at ease in her home.

"Mother works long hours as a tailor and is somehow able to keep my three unruly brothers, Leo, Ralfie and Otto in line. My young sister Rita, who is a little angel, is a big help around the house though…

Vater writes regularly, but we have not seen him for over a year. He will be on leave soon, and when he returns, the house will be full of music again," Anna explained hopefully despite the concern she harbored for her father.

"We had several lively evenings here at the farm after your mother married Olav. We sang and danced to your father's wonderful American music. Those were happier years to be sure…" Thomas's sentence faded into his memory.

Anna interjected with, "I remember your grand horses. They were enormous with the long, silky hair around their hooves and flaxen manes and tails. King and Queen? Are they still alive or do you have other draft horses now?"

"They are very old but, yes, still alive. We have younger stock working the farm now. We find our horses the most affordable and reliable way to till the fields and harvest crops. Adolf's new tractors break down and fuel is prohibitively expensive. If only they would just leave us alone to manage our farms the way we have for generations," complained Thomas passionately.

"Thomas, please not now. Anna, perhaps you would like to see the horses? Guner, Vilma why don't you show Anna around the farm while we talk with Frieda," urged Else.

As Anna and Guner crossed the yard to the barn, the scent of sage filled the air in the afternoon heat. Anna drank in the clear air of the country. Fields stretched to the horizon, the hay already cut and stacked. Dozens of crows circled and then landed and were feeding, black against the golden stubble.

They passed the hen house before reaching the barn. Anna stopped. "What is it, Anna? You like chickens? " teased Guner.

In truth, the cooing chatter among the chickens soothed Anna. "You are right; let's move on to the horses," she agreed reluctantly.

The cattle had been turned out to graze on the lush green pasture, but the horses were in their stalls. They were peacefully eating the remaining hay in their mangers. Anna leaned over the stall rail to watch a young gelding twitching his muzzle back and forth to pick up some scattered pieces of hay. She didn't flinch when he stomped his front leg suddenly, trying to rid himself of a persistent fly. Anna watched the horses as Guner disappeared on some agricultural chore unknown to her.

In the kitchen, the conversation had turned to intelligence recently acquired from the underground. The Baumanns had heard of Hitler's plans for the invasion of Poland and that officers in the German army opposed the Nazi decision. They doubted the stability of Hitler as leader of Germany.

Anna, however, was oblivious to these serious matters. She left the barn for the tree line where she lay in the grass and let the sun warm her body. Gone were the roar of tanks and trucks, the shouts and songs of soldiers, and the aggressive monotony of the marching cadence in the streets.

She looked up at cumulus clouds that had just appeared in the afternoon sky but could not see any imaginary figures. She saw only clouds. Closing her eyes, Anna listened to the crows and felt the earth beneath her. For the first time in many weeks she did not think of Reiner. She had found her own serenity.

Thomas shook his head, "As if we don't have enough challenges! Weather alone is unpredictable. Now we have to contend with Nazis who think they are farmers. They want to control us but have no idea about agriculture.

And Frieda, you will remember how hectic it is at harvest time. The Nazis tried to make work for students and other jobless louts by sending them to our farms to work during harvest. Those inexperienced or lazy people have only been another burden, a hindrance to our farm production.

Government is of little interest to us. The party in power may try to control us, but our village solidarity survives! Our customs, common rights for wood collecting, and of course, sharing labor at harvest time has been around for centuries…"

"Guner and Vilma must be of great assistance to you," ventured Frieda.

"Yes, they are, but Guner is listening to the constant propaganda about the great jobs and exciting careers open to him with the Nazis. You know that before Adolf, doors opened to only the privileged sons of Prussians. Now a private can become an officer in Adolf's army.

The posters make war seem so glorious—no lost limbs—no blood—no death. Many of our youth are attracted to the image. It seems like an exciting alternative to what they experience on the farms. The Nazis have created a restlessness that does not help us. We farmers have always struggled to keep our sons and daughters interested in staying on the farm."

Else interjected, "Did you know the Reich Food Estate has tried to take over the distribution of farm produce from us?" Frieda shook her head in reply.

"Say, we sold directly to our customers for 10 *pfennigs,* Frieda. The Reich Food Estate sells the same for 16 to 20 instead."

"We sell directly to the Black Market and circumvent the Food Estate!" Thomas pounded the table with his fist.

"Anna, Anna!" called Vilma from the barn door. "Let us go in for dinner."

Anna awoke with a chill. Jumping to her feet she shouted, "I'll be right there." After the best meal Anna had eaten in weeks, she asked if the family would like haircuts. "I brought my scissors with me. It would be no trouble."

"Yes Guner has needed a haircut all summer. He will be the first. Don't look like that young man. She won't hurt you," teased his mother. The big, muscular young man turned crimson as Anna began trimming his thick, unruly hair.

"Tomorrow we will take you to the train bound for Leipzig," said Thomas as they all retired for the evening. Anna slept a deep, dreamless sleep and wakened refreshed and hungry.

Breakfast was already served in the kitchen. As Anna took the last bite of homemade bread and strawberry jam and drained the last drop of coffee from her cup, Else approached her with a bag. "Take this to your mother, Anna. It contains food she may not have readily available in the city, especially the butter."

Already Anna considered the Baumanns her extended family. She was lifted from her depression and felt restored.

Once back at the salon, the rhythmic routine of her daily work gave her time to think. Sometimes she would allow herself to remember Reiner, but she would never permit herself to imagine a future with him; that was too painful. She knew she had to move on.

Unknown to both Anna and Reiner their future had been irrevocably altered by Frieda.

Chapter Eleven
Madness

Adolf Hitler slammed down his fist as he shouted at his generals:

"Close your hearts to pity. Act brutally! The stronger man is right! Eighty million people must obtain what is their right. Their existence must be made secure. The greatest harshness!"

In September, 1939 Germany invaded Poland. Russia had agreed to take Eastern Poland and Germany the West. This was not to be a war of fronts and trenches as in WWI, but rather, lightning warfare or *Blitzkrieg.* Hitler wanted to avoid a long drawn out war that would result in severe deprivation at home. Instead, he wanted life to appear almost normal to most Germans.

Warsaw was bombed. In one month, the Polish army was defeated and as Christmas passed the rest of the world did not seem to care.

And yet, a sense of apprehension hung in the streets of Leipzig. People wondered whether or not the war would actually end with the acquisition of Poland. Many had experienced the trauma of bombings and the long-term, damages of WWI and were legitimately concerned about where the campaign would lead them. Others were able to convincingly deny the threat of world war. In any case, most people had learned to keep their opinions to themselves.

Even customers in the salon were oddly quiet. Weeks earlier the room had been full of friendly chatter and laughter as women took a break from their daily routines to be pampered by a beautician.

Ironically, the block warden, Bruno, incited discussion in the salon because he was pressuring families to prepare for air raids.

"*Herr Kaufer* keeps pestering us to take air raid precautions. I sewed sand bags to put in front of our windows," complained one woman.

"We have cleaned out a spot in our root cellar and taken a supply of water down in case we are forced to remain under for hours," said another in a hushed tone.

"I have block-out blinds so at least we can have light inside when it is night time. The enemy won't see our lights."

Anna's next customer was unfamiliar to her. She was clearly a career woman working for the Party. Anna instantly disliked her, but she greeted her pleasantly anyway, "How may I help you today, *Fraulein*?"

"A manicure and my hair washed, set, and styled," she demanded brusquely as she glanced around at the other women with a disapproving glare.

Unfazed, Anna continued, "Let's do your nails first. What color would you like? Here are the shades available. This new one, Peachy Delight has lipstick to match that would complement your complexion."

"No, that won't do. I will take Crimson Rose and please do not presume to know what becomes me."

The woman's aggressive and condescending attitude gave Anna a visceral reaction. "You, *blode madehen!*" she thought, but asked softly, "Do you work here in Leipzig, *Fraulein*?"

"Yes. However, I often travel to where the Fuhrer needs me."

"I see...Some of the other customers were discussing preparations for air raids. What do you think about the threat of an air strike?"

"I believe the *Fuhrer* will protect us. He is supreme. Even his enemies dismally failed in the assassination attempt last November. *Mein Fuhrer* is unscathed. We are unstoppable in the acquisition of our lands.

We have already taken Poland, and Britain and France have not shot a bullet yet. Our *Wehrmacht* and the *Luftwaffe* stop at nothing and act with speed and effectiveness. The *Kriegsmarine* dominates the sea. So, do I believe that we must fear an air strike from Britain? No, absolutely not. The war will soon be over. Does that help you understand, dear?"

Seething inside, Anna nodded in reply and thought, "So it is not possible for a beautician to be smart. You have no idea who I am."

"Be careful. Spill any of your chemicals on my blouse or suit collar, and you will pay!" The Nazi clerk threatened irritably.

"You need not worry, *Fraulein*. I'll use an extra towel. Your suit is made of such lovely fabric," Anna said kindly to flatter her, demonstrating only the best manners.

"Yes, it is Italian. My shoes are from Italy, as well. Real leather," the woman bragged. Leather shoes were rare since most of Germany's leather was on the feet of the military.

The woman turned her head from side to side and looked in the mirror that Anna held so she could see the back of the hairstyle. "No, that is not what I asked for. Change my wave. Blend it better with the hair that sweeps up into the roll."

"Certainly, *Fraulein*," Anna countered cheerfully, "How is your hair now, better?"

"That will do. I must hurry back to the office for a meeting," she said importantly as she stood and made for the cash register. Although the arrogant customer did not even tip, Anna continued to smile after she was gone.

"*Blode madehen,* I just charged you three times the price," Anna laughed to herself as she placed the "Closed" sign in the window and began cleaning up. "Ada and Oskar will soon be here."

When Ada arrived at the salon she was soothed by the scents of chemicals and soaps, nail polish and lotions, "My dear friends, always well-groomed and calm despite the unspoken tyranny everywhere. In this place I can speak my mind without fear of reprisal."

Anna thought Ada lacked her customary poise as she entered the salon. She seemed anxious to escape whatever was outside.

"How are you Ada?" asked Frieda as she motioned to a chair by the sink.

"I have had an unpleasant encounter with *Herr Kaufer*, the block warden. I don't quite know what to do." Anna stopped sweeping the floor when she heard that name. He had already caused harm to another customer, Katia. Surely Ada was not in danger too.

"Are you all right? Would you like a drink of brandy?" asked Frieda, but Anna had already disappeared into the apartment. When Anna returned with three drinks, Frieda looked up and nodded her approval.

"He pounded on my apartment door this afternoon. I opened the door and stepped into the hallway to talk so he would not come into my home. He is so repulsive and malevolent," uttered Ada with a distraught look on her face.

"We know the block warden, Ada; we understand," assured Frieda.

"Ostensibly he was to determine whether or not my apartment was prepared for air raids. He pushed past me and marched into my home. I left the door open so I could leave quickly if necessary, but he slammed it. Then he said he had been looking into my past and knew about my husband. I demanded to know why and that is when…" Ada could not finish her sentence. Anna stopped cleaning and sat beside Ada. Frieda stopped combing out Ada's hair. Out of respect, they waited for Ada to continue.

"*Mein Gott,* if it wasn't for *Herr Kramer* from across the hall pounding on the door incessantly, I could not possibly have escaped the warden's grip.

You see, *Herr and Frau Kramer* had invited Oskar and me to their apartment to show us a short-wave radio in their possession. He knew I was at home and had seen Bruno enter the building. I think *Herr Kramer* suspects the warden of multiple crimes.

Do you know what was especially disturbing? When Bruno left, he gave me a malicious look as if to say, 'This is not over yet.' I feel cold all over thinking about him even now," Ada shuddered.

"My neighbors have agreed to watch my apartment, and I now have a weapon concealed in the kitchen."

"Have you heard from Franz recently?" interrupted Frieda with what seemed a completely irrelevant question. Anna wondered why on earth Frieda would be asking about Franz at a time like this.

"Yes… I have. We write to one another regularly and he often telephones from the United Press office in Berlin. He plans to visit me here since I cannot leave Leipzig until Oskar has completed his school year.

Franz is adamant about my joining him when he leaves for the United States. He says he must publish his book so the West will know what is looming here in Europe. However, the papers must be arranged and I must be certain that my decision will not jeopardize Oskar's future," Ada said hesitantly.

"Listen to me, now," said Frieda firmly. "Marry Franz and the passage for both you and Oskar will be secure."

"He hasn't formally proposed yet, Frieda and…"

Frieda in a bold move took her by the shoulders and insisted, "You can make him propose. You can make him think it was his idea. Do you know what I am talking about, Ada? Do you understand how important this is for you and Oskar? Your family cannot help you right now. Get out of Germany!"

Frieda sat down, but she continued to stare intently at Ada. "Will you do it?" asked Frieda plainly. Anna was surprised that Frieda would speak to an aristocrat so boldly about personal matters.

Ada did not reply so Frieda resumed cutting and styling her hair and Anna began mopping the floor. The silence was broken when Oskar knocked his special code at the door so they would know it was him and not a spy.

As Ada and her son were about to leave the salon, Ada turned to Frieda and said, "I will do it. Thank you. I am in indebted to you."

In Poland, Olav had become very successful in the military. He was a natural leader of men. He demonstrated tactical savvy and was also capable of practical decisions when it came to the training and mobilization of his men. His Nazi superiors, however, also knew the value of Olav's temper and the ruthless cunning which were deployed whenever his principles were challenged.

The Nazi strategy was to racially cleanse areas in the newly occupied countries where Germans would settle when the war was over. They apprehended Jews and delivered them by rail transport to ghettos in Warsaw. From there they would wait until transportation was provided to reservations in the East. Hitler did not want ghettos in Germany where they would be visible to the German people.

With the takeover of Poland complete, Olav was ordered to select a special unit to take care of a problem of "undesirables" at a site east of Warsaw. When he arrived at the assigned location, he was given specific orders to execute the prisoners as they came off the train. When he surveyed the prisoners, he realized they were clearly not all criminals; but rather, men, women, and children whose only crime was that they were Jews. Others included Polish officers and academics who were not Jewish but could potentially be a problem to the Nazis.

The unsuspecting people were herded to the edge of a pit and then shot in the back by Olav's soldiers. The victims collapsed into a common grave. After executing hundreds of people each day, many of the soldiers questioned their orders. Was this the battle they were supposed to fight?

Many soldiers were sick with remorse over the slaughter. They couldn't bear the odor of corpses rotting and the tortured cries of the condemned. Many of the unit had to be drunk all day to complete the assignment of mass murder and later to forget their macabre job. They had all been trained to follow orders unquestioningly for the Third Reich, but this?

Even Olav faced conflicting thoughts. He believed that death is a necessary sacrifice to defend against threats to freedom, justice, and survival, but he could not accept and certainly not approve of killing citizens who appeared to be no threat—this was no battle field? He was tormented every night about the orders he was forced to give.

Faces formed a collage on his eyelids the moment he closed his eyes—innocent toddlers, naive women, and proud men—their expressions shifting from confusion to terror when they realized their fate and then to anguish when shot. Finally, he saw their death masks in his hallucinations. He couldn't sleep most nights.

Olav could not rationalize his mission. In addition, his men were losing control. Some were falling down drunk overcome by the atrocities, while the sociopaths in the firing squad were abusing prisoners prior to killing them. He could no longer manage the situation.

And then one sunny morning he opened his eyes but was unable to see the sun. Too many faces obscured the light—mouths forming words without sound, grimaces, eyes of the insane and depraved, eyes of innocence. They wouldn't go away. He was taken away discreetly and given an ample dose of tranquilizer.

Mental breakdowns had become a problem among officers of the firing squads so Hitler's inner circle set funds aside for rest cures. Olav was sent back to Leipzig on a rest cure before being reassigned.

When Anna picked up the telephone at the salon, she scarcely recognized her mother's frightened voice. "You must come home as soon as possible, Anna. Father has a gun and has been drinking all day. I cannot understand what he is shouting. He can't even see me when I am standing in front of him. Rita is hiding in her room and Otto is sobbing hysterically; he is so afraid. Leo and Ralfie will be home soon, and I do not want them hurt if they try to approach Father. What should I do?"

"Keep everyone away from him, *Mutti*. Do nothing, say nothing to upset him. I will leave immediately," Anna ordered.

No music or laughter reached her ears this time as she entered her family's home, only the incoherent ranting of Olav. He was in the living room sitting in his chair, a vodka bottle empty on the floor beside him. He was waving a revolver about his head and then in front of him as if he was attempting to take aim at villains standing in front of him. Without hesitation or concern for her own safety, Anna entered the living room, closing the door behind her.

"Father it is me, Anna, I am so glad you have come home!" she said softly.

"You are not Anna. Anna is my little *lochen*. What have you done with her?"

"You have been gone a long time, and I have grown up. I work at the salon. I finished my apprenticeship," She explained trying to help him remember. "*Vater*?"

Olav didn't hear her. He shook his head back and forth scowling, "They made us kill them. Polish officers…and *Mein Gott* the women were so afraid for their children. The stench of fear is still in my nose." Wincing, Olav rubbed his nose frantically. Then suddenly his mood shifted and he again waved the revolver at a menacing presence somewhere in front of him. "Stop, or I will kill you," he roared.

Anna changed her tack, seeing that her father was disappearing into his nightmare and may not be able to surface again. She stood in front of him and barked, "*Oberleutnant Olav Muller*, listen to me! You were only following orders. YOU did not kill them! You are a Nazi, but you would never do such a thing. You had no choice. You only followed THEIR orders!"

"I was only following orders. Yes, I was only following orders. How could I have saved them?" He agreed trancelike.

"Now you must not think about this anymore. You must survive. You must survive for your family. You must come back to Mari, Leo, Ralfie, Otto, little Rita and me. Stop this now! Sit up like the officer you are! We must survive. Nothing can ruin us. Look at me, *Vater*," Anna said with authority.

Olav looked into her eyes and she knew he saw her this time. His shoulders lowered and his head drooped. The arm holding the gun fell to his side.

"Give me the gun," Anna said calmly as she moved toward her father. She took the gun slowly from his hand and removed the bullets.

She then pulled up a chair beside Olav and lit two of his cigarettes, one for him and one for herself. They sat for some time smoking without conversation, and then:

"I was ordered to follow procedures or else *sippenhaft*—they would send the *Gestapo* to murder all of you. This war is run by criminals capable of the most heinous crimes. The atrocities are beyond forgiveness. Germany will never be the same…never," Olav uttered gravely.

They sat in the living room as the evening light faded to darkness. Anna saw that Olav was sober and subdued. "Come. Let's go into the kitchen for coffee. *Mutti* will be worried."

"Yes, my Mari will be waiting," Olav agreed.

Mari turned around a bit wild-eyed as Olav approached. She pushed back loose hair from her brow and then reached out to hold him. "I do not deserve you," he whispered in her ear.

Anna left her parents alone and looked in on the boys. Ralfie was reading, Otto was asleep and Leo was playing tricks with a small ball. Ralfie immediately dropped his book and Leo his ball. "What is wrong with *Vati,*" asked Leo with a worried look.

"He has been fighting in the war and has had to be brave. Today he had what is like a nightmare," explained Anna. "But now he is awake and feels much better. He will stay home with us for awhile to get some rest and then return to his job at the airplane factory. He will help the engineers build more airplanes for the *Luftwaffe*. Won't that be nice to have *Vati* back? Now it is time for sleep."

Both boys looked relieved at the prospect of having their father at home. Anna kissed each of them before closing the door.

Rita was still awake in her room when Anna entered. She was sitting cross-legged on the floor drawing, but when she saw her older sister, she jumped up to hug Anna. With Rita clinging to her neck, Anna sat down on the bed and smoothed Rita's hair. "We will be fine. *Vati* is all right now. He was having a bad dream from too much war and too much vodka." Anna rocked her little sister back and forth until her eye caught a glimpse of paintings stacked in the corner. "Rita, will you show me your paintings."

Rita laid out the pictures along the wall for Anna to see. Anna studied each one closely. They resembled mosaics, but instead of tiles, Rita used her paints. "These tell the story of Hansel and Gretel! What beautiful, jewel colors you have used. And the figures—my, that is a frightening witch," Anna chuckled.

"Will you tell me the story again, Anna," pleaded Rita.

"Yes, may I see what you are sketching first? Your pictures are wonderful!"

Rita shyly brought the charcoal sketch to Anna. The drawing was a portrait of their mother, Mari's face and shoulders with her arms on the kitchen table holding a cup. Her shoulders were slouched and head tilted to one side. Her face had an expression of sadness, dark shading under the eyes. Fine lines were etched around her mouth and eyes. Anna was speechless. Rita had insightfully depicted the exhaustion and suffering of their mother.

"Come, I will tell you the story," said Anna gently. Rita cuddled close to Anna with her arms around her knees and one hand holding her doll. It wasn't long before both were asleep, the story unfinished.

Hitler portrayed and promoted mythical status. The remarkable success of his invasions was undeniable. By April of 1940, German troops had invaded Norway and Denmark. May saw the Netherlands and Belgium occupied by the Germans. The British were defeated at Dunkirk, and in June the Germans marched on to Paris. In one month, France's army collapsed.

It seemed as though Hitler's *Wehrmacht* was invincible. Optimism filled most German homes due to the success of the war and the prevailing myth that Hitler could not be stopped.

Optimism filled the Muller home not because of Hitler's magical powers but because music had returned. Music had been the best medicine for Olav's recovery and a means to communicate with his sons. Leo had a tenor singing voice and played several instruments. Ralfie didn't sing but was quickly excelling at the piano and violin under the tutelage of Olav.

One summer evening after Leo returned from Hitler Youth, he announced to everyone, "We will be having a performance tomorrow at 7:00 p.m. in the living room. Our family, as well as, our neighbors *Herr and Frau* Hoffman, Axel and Rosa will be in attendance."

The next evening Mari traded her apron and house dress for a fresh cotton blouse and skirt in honor of the special occasion. They all greeted the Hoffmans at the door and brought them into the living room. Anna had set up several kitchen chairs for extra seating.

Axel and Rita were side-by-side with Anna next to them smoking a cigarette in her perfectly manicured fingers.

Leo, his dark eyes on fire, entered the room and took his position by the piano. Taking an important stance he introduced the musicians. "I would like to welcome all of you here this evening for the debut of the Muller Trio. I think you will be surprised and delighted by our first selection. Accompanying me will be Herr Olav Muller, violin virtuoso, and Ralph Muller, pianist." As Olav and Ralfie entered the living room, the others clapped enthusiastically.

Anna was proud of her brothers and was relieved to see her father coming back to life in the music. Everyone sang along with the chorus and when the performance was over they all had a rare treat of chocolate cake with their coffee. It was a good day.

That night when Olav and Mari were in bed, Mari changed the mood when she whispered, "When I was standing in the queue last week, I thought I heard Mr. Wolfe's deep voice. I looked around but only saw women and children in line, an old man on a bicycle, and a few soldiers. I felt unsettled, Olav. Often I think of him, Lisel, the children. Where could they be? Are they still alive?"

Olav's face darkened in despair as he held Mari close, "They may be in the Warsaw ghetto waiting to be moved somewhere in the East. We must try to forget and instead look to the future. We all have a price to pay in this war. Let us try and get some sleep. I must be at the factory early tomorrow."

The next day, the hot summer weather drew the children outdoors. Mari and Anna sat on the back porch steps watching the boys and Rita. Anna noticed grey hairs mixed with dark blonde in the braids that encircled the nape of her mother's neck. Despite the strain of recent years, she was still lovely, her face golden in the summer sun.

"*Mutti*, look at Leo. He has grown so big this past year. The training with the Hitler Youth has given him quite a strong build for a boy 12 years old."

"I know, and he is clever," added Mari.

"I can think of many women at the salon that would die for a head of thick dark curls like his."

Ralfie and Leo were playing with the neighborhood boys—a war game, of course, with handmade wooden rifles. Otto was by the porch playing with his tin soldiers. Rita was hanging the laundry on the clothesline by the washhouse.

As Anna drew on her cigarette, Mari regarded her children with affection and sympathy. Her thoughts wandered from the backyard, "They have only known this culture of war. Of course my Leo's heroes are soldiers. Who do they see constantly marching and working in the streets? The school books, the posters everywhere—always the tanned, confident, handsome young men.

Role models at Hitler Youth always encouraging:

Health

Fitness

Fight

Role models who teach the morality of violence.

My own husband is now more military than musical. Maybe Otto will know another Germany."

Anna noticed the change in her mother. "Would you like me to make us a coffee, Mutti?"

"No, I will go inside. I want to put the pork on to cook slowly for dinner. Will you keep an eye on the battle for a while?"

"Yes, and I will dig up some carrots and potatoes for supper."

Over the din of children's laughter and squeals, Anna set about thinning the carrots and finding potatoes large enough to take from the hills. She looked up when the boys were suspiciously quiet and saw Leo threatening Axel.

The young neighbor, Axel, who represented "the enemy," was cringing beside Leo. Leo began kicking him, "Jew, swine! You came here at your own peril and now you must bow to the greatest of the Aryans, Leo. Get on your knees."

Anna shouted for Leo to stop but her brother continued kicking and then punching Axel, disregarding her commands. Axel, a big boy for his age, had already begun defending himself.

"Stop this immediately!" she cried as she yanked Leo away from Axel and pushed him hard toward the house. "Wait for me in your room." Leo had never heard Anna speak in that tone of voice or felt her painful grip. He obeyed without argument or hesitation.

Axel's tear made a track through the dirt on his cheek. Ralfie was already offering a hand up, but Axel stood up quickly, rejecting his help. He brushed the dirt from his pants and then wiped his face quickly. Rita stood beside him and reached gently for his hand.

"I am fine. Please do not tell my parents, Anna."

"I am sorry, Axel! Leo took the game too far. He was wrong," Anna apologized softly.

"I am fine. Come Rosa. Let's go home."

Anna waved good-bye to the children and told Rita and the boys to go inside. Anna brought the vegetables to her mother and said, "I will talk to Leo, *Mutti*."

After a while Mari thought, as Leo's mother, she should be reprimanding him, but when she put her hand on the doorknob to the bedroom, she overheard, "We were only pretending to be soldiers and Jews, Anna. They told us Jews are subhuman at Hitler Youth!"

"Was Sid Wolfe not your best friend? He was German and Jewish. Was he subhuman?"

"No," Leo admitted.

"Axel is our neighbor and friend? You must apologize to him…"

Mari removed her hand from the door and went back downstairs. "I could not handle it better," she thought. "I will miss Anna when she leaves again for the salon…

And how will I handle Olav? He has been talking about Beatrice lately; how she should live with us since she is too old to take care of herself. I won't have Beatrice back in my house. I must be more vocal and fight against his decision.

Olav likely feels guilty that we never invite her for holidays or music nights but he knows as well as I do that she would not approve of our music choices. He knows how she upsets the household too. The children are afraid of her and dislike her harsh discipline. Surely he won't ask her to move in.

Our home is too small, and actually; if he were honest about it, he finds her as disagreeable as the rest of us. And Rita! I don't want Beatrice near my angel." Mari's fears eventually subsided since Olav never mentioned his mother again for weeks.

Olav knew how his family felt about his mother so he decided to visit his mother alone to see if she really needed his help. He was in good spirits on that day. "Even she will like the chocolate, cheese and fresh bread I have brought. Such decadent treats," he smiled to himself proudly as he climbed the stairs to his mother's apartment.

"Come in, Son. Why are you in Leipzig? On LEAVE?" Beatrice queried without affection.

"I have brought you these, Mother. Shall we have some bread while it is fresh?" suggested Olav.

"I suppose, but I have more than enough. The block warden, *Herr Kaufer*, ensures that I have the best. Coffee, chocolate, beautiful smoked pork, butter—oh, I tell you. Look at my leather shoes," boasted Beatrice as she begrudgingly laid out her table for a lunch.

"When will you be going back to the front, Olav? *Mein Fuhrer* is waging the war of the century and here you are having a rest!"

"I am back at the airplane factory temporarily. You know the *Luftwaffe* is essential to winning this war too, Mother, so we must continue to produce more planes." Olav defended himself but he felt diminished by his mother and was already planning to exit at the first opportunity.

He decided to flatter her so she would stop criticizing. "You still keep a spotless home. Everything is so clean and neat, exactly as I remember growing up."

"Of course, it is our German way. Your WIFE could do better in that regard," Beatrice sighed. "You are NOT in charge of your own home, Olav. And YOU an officer!" The venom she could not contain escaped from her tongue.

"Mein Fuhrer is cleaning this country," Beatrice's voice was becoming shrill. "Soon all of the human filth will be gone and our country will be home to Aryans alone. No more criminals, prostitutes, sick people, racially impure— no more Jews! Clean, clean! Do you understand what that means for Germany?"

"Oh I understand," Olav replied with a clenched jaw. "Perhaps I should leave. As you reminded me, I have work to do. Good-bye *Mutter*."

"You haven't eaten, Olav. Sit down and keep me company until we have finished our lunch! You NEVER visit me! If only your father were alive! Where are you going that is so important?" Olav heard his mother blithering as he closed her door. He burst into the street and never looked back.

"It was a mercy that *Vater* died in the war," he thought.

"Do not leave, Olav!" shouted Beatrice as she opened the door to the landing. "How DARE you turn your back on ME!" Her face was flushed as she made for the top step to call out once more so her son would hear. Beatrice raised her arm admonishing him with her finger pointed forward in an absurd version of the Hitler salute. "Olav, you come back here at once!" she screamed.

In her rage, the elderly woman miscalculated her footing and caught her shoe on the top step. Losing her balance, Beatrice toppled down the stairs where she landed legs wide apart, skirt high on her thighs, head slumped to one side. A comb had loosened itself from her hair releasing long strands of grey hair to fall across her face. When a neighbor entered the apartment building, she was shocked to see the austere and proper *Frau Muller* in such an undignified position on the floor – dead.

A grotesque puppet abandoned by her puppeteer.

Father Engel officiated the funeral for Beatrice. Only Olav, Mari and the children attended since Olav's father had died in WW1, his aunt and uncle were gone, and the whereabouts of his cousins unknown. He had been an only child and Beatrice had no close friendships. Mari and Anna's faces were impassive as they sat motionless in the pew. Leo, Ralfie and Otto were restlessly sitting as still as they could, doing their best to behave in church. Rita was the only one in the Muller family who shed a tear.

When they returned home for a late lunch, Rita sat on Anna's knee. "Are you all right *lochen?*" Anna whispered in Rita's ear.

"It is sad. *Grossmutter* was never happy. I remember she had nightmares. Maybe God is hugging her now," Rita replied.

Chapter Twelve
Karl

By autumn 1940, Anna had received word that she must work at an airplane factory like so many other women who replaced the men conscripted to the military. The salon had been her home for five eventful years. She packed her personal things in a bag and stood looking around the small apartment reminiscing when suddenly Frieda appeared from the salon.

She approached Anna with a sincere and gentle smile, "Anna, you have become a gifted beautician. You came to me as a young girl and I see before me a mature and competent woman. I am sure our customers will miss you... I will miss you."

"Thank you. I hate to leave. We won't be apart for long, Frieda. Come home and visit. Leo and Ralfie will perform for you and *Mutti* is craving adult conversation." After a cursory embrace, Anna was gone.

Change came quickly and soon Anna was adjusting to work in a large munitions factory where she assembled parts. She took her place on the line all the while surveying the situation. The skills she had developed spying for Frieda at the race track and the *Libelle* helped her perceive what others didn't see. It wasn't long before she understood the chain of command. She saw exchanges between the men in authority and among employees.

Even though Anna worked as a laborer, she was well-groomed with her nails polished and hair styled. She saw the Nazi bosses assessing her and responded directly as an equal with a friendly but respectful *Heil Hitler*. Anna was slowly making herself known.

Many of her coworkers on the line looked at her with envy. Oddly, others were anxious to befriend her. Anna didn't really care whether the women liked or hated her. She was courteous but essentially preferred to be left alone. That wasn't always possible.

"Anna, *Herr Schulz* likes me. He tells me I will soon have a promotion to supervise a line," boasted Gerda.

"Won't that be nice for you," replied Anna but she thought, "*Blode madehen!* You are a whore. You will not get a promotion. They don't respect you. You are a pathetic sycophant."

On the other side of Anna was another young woman that also annoyed her. She chattered on, "*Mein Fuhrer* will defeat any evil country that threatens to harm us…." Believing every word, she simply parroted the propaganda that barraged Germans every day.

While Anna smiled pleasantly enough, she did not join in conversation with her co-workers, and eventually they stopped talking to her. The factory was deadly boring so Anna often let her mind wander to past experiences working at the salon and wondered how the women were faring.

Despite the drastic changes in her life, Anna adapted well. She was grateful to go home to her family each day. Harmony had returned to the Muller home and they enjoyed a reprieve amidst the uncertainty of the times. Add to that an occasional visit with her best friend, Klara, and Anna was content for many months.

There is an ease in friendships that have lasted since childhood that is inimitable with new friends later in life. Perhaps it involves sharing a time of innocence or the varied experiences of maturing; at any rate, Anna trusted Klara's reassuring voice and took comfort in their mutual acceptance.

After weeks apart, Klara telephoned. "Anna let's go to the movies or a dance tonight."

"Yes, let's go to the cinema. I will meet you there at 7:00."

"Have you heard from Nat at all?" asked Anna as they buried their chins into their fur collars. The raw January wind was freezing their faces.

"Yes, she has joined the Party and can now be paid well to conduct medical research. She says that over two thirds of physicians in Germany are Party members. They enjoy unimaginable privileges and amenities.

I suppose Nat was pressured by her peers as well as the Reich to join the Party, but, in any case, she deserves a prosperous life after everything she went through with Lena.

I think she was recently moved to a facility north of Berlin. I am happy for her. All her immediate needs are met so she can devote herself to her work," explained Klara.

"Hmm…. And how have you been, Klara? Will you be staying in Leipzig, or will they be moving you to a field hospital?"

"I will remain in Leipzig to be close to Mother and Father at the butcher shop. By the way, they tell me you have not stopped by for some time," said Klara.

"We are working ten and twelve hour shifts at the factory so I am usually too late or tired," Anna explained.

"And your father?" asked Klara.

"He is at the airplane factory and in his spare time is teaching Leo and Ralfie to read music and play instruments. They are wonderful. Why didn't I inherit their musical talent, Klara? Leo even sings!" remarked Anna in mock despair.

"Look at him," nudged Klara as they entered the cinema. Ahead of them was a particularly attractive man in uniform.

"You will never change, Klara," said Anna smiling.

After the movie, Anna whispered her objections, "The movie was fine. You know, the hero won the girl but just when we thought the movie had ended, their Aryan son pops up out of nowhere and greets them in a Hitler Youth uniform. He snaps to attention and shouts, *Heil Hitler!* Did we even know she was pregnant?" The friends laughed into the winter wind as they left the cinema.

"It's no wonder people talk about the *Fuhrer* constantly these days. It is all we see and hear. And, look how many countries he has taken in just forty-five days! To tell you the truth, I am proud to be a German. Only when will the war end?" asked Klara. "We can't go on like this forever."

"Father says the *Luftwaffe* and *Wehrmacht* are mobilizing to advance east," replied Anna. "The munitions we make at our factory alone tells me the war isn't over yet."

"Here is my stop. See you soon?"

Anna nodded and waved good-bye.

It was an evening in March and no light shone from street lamps or the moon. Anna was returning home from work on the trolley car. When she stepped onto the sidewalk, she heard a familiar laugh. "Klara where are you. What are you doing?"

"Anna, I want you to meet my friends," was Klara's reply from out of the darkness.

"I am going home. It is late," Anna objected. Three shapes appeared beside her.

"*Guten Abend Fraulein Muller*. How are you tonight?" asked one of the men. She liked his voice instantly.

"Please call me Anna. I am fine, and you."

"Anna this is *Herr Karl Lowe* from Poland, conscripted here to work in one of the munitions factories. And, this is Josef."

"Good Evening," said the voice coming from the taller shape. Anna recognized his Czech accent.

Karl asked, "May I give you my arm? It is dark. We will walk with you the rest of the way to your home."

"Anna, we are all going to a dance on Saturday. Would you like to join us?" asked Klara hopefully.

Anna agreed but when Karl offered to pick her up at home, Anna hastily refused, "No, no you can't! I will meet you at the corner under the street lamp." She could not predict the reaction of her father.

"All right then," chuckled Karl good-naturedly. "I will be there under the street lamp."

On Saturday Anna was indifferent about her date with Karl, but was in a pleasant frame of mind because she always enjoyed an evening with Klara. When Anna arrived at the street lamp at the agreed time, she was quite taken aback by Karl.

She had not guessed when they met in the dark that he would be so attractive. He was dark-haired with kind, brown eyes. He was almost six feet tall with a barrel chest and strong arms and legs. He nodded and smiled steadily at her.

"*Hallo liebling*. Let's go," Anna said as she smiled at him and took his arm.

When they arrived at the dance, Klara and Josef were already dancing. Klara pointed to a table and later joined them. Karl and Anna had a drink and then Anna lit a cigarette shifting her weight to her hip.

"Do you have family in Poland, Karl?"

"My parents live in Warsaw, with my younger sister now. Actually, I grew up on the river. We ran a tug on the Oder River. Lived on the boat. I know the Baltic Sea too. We brought the ships from the sea down the river to the cities to unload supplies."

"Do you miss that life?" asked Anna. "You must have been rocked to sleep by the water." She watched him roll up his sleeves. She liked the hair on his forearms and something about the way he lit and held his cigarette was sexy. He looked at her with an unwavering eye and warm smile. She was surprised that she was attracted to this man. "I did not think I would ever be able to look at anyone else after Reiner," she thought, "and here I am wondering what he will be like in bed."

"Yes I miss the water, but the fumes from the coal-fired engine on the boat damaged my father's lungs. You know my family never really had friends until we settled in Warsaw. A gypsy life… I will tell you about Poland later. Let's dance," suggested Karl.

He slid back her chair and took her by the hand. Klara was sitting on Josef's lap kissing him but looked up as Anna passed. Anna wagged her finger at Klara who raised her eye brows and lifted her shoulder into her neck as if to say, "I can't help it," and returned eagerly to her Czech boyfriend.

It turned out that Karl could dance. They stayed on the dance floor for the foxtrot, Charleston, and polka, and then sat down perspiring and laughing. In a moment, Karl had a drink in front of her. "Let's step outside and cool off." As soon as they were outside, Karl offered Anna a cigarette and then leaned against the building. She followed. They smoked in silence and then Karl asked, "Would you like to see me again?" Anna nodded.

After curfew the two couples walked to the tram laughing in the dark streets. Klara and Josef were a bit wobbly and vocal but drew no unwanted attention from locals. Before Karl and Anna parted, she invited him to meet her family before their next date. Permission was not forthcoming….

"What do you mean I cannot go out with Karl. Why won't you even consider meeting him, *Vater*," challenged Anna in a level voice. She was convinced her father had read too much hate literature in *Die Woche*, the Nazi newspaper.

"He is an *auslander*. He is not good enough for you. I won't hear of this!" shouted her father. He shook his head and then with a dismissive sweep of his arm sat down heavily in his armchair in the living room. His daughter would not be dismissed. She stood her ground.

"Karl's mother is German. How can you be so inhospitable? I have never asked to bring a man home to meet my family. Do you not trust my judgment?

I want him to meet you. I am proud of you. My family is everything to me. Please *Vater*. I ask once more."

"All right, I will meet him and if I think him worthy of you, you may introduce him to *Mutti* and the children," Olav conceded.

The following Saturday they were all sitting around the table talking and laughing. Evidently Karl had been accepted by the Muller household.

That spring of 1941 Olav was called back to the Eastern Front. Mari had mixed emotions after he left. On the one hand, she was sick with worry about Olav. "Was our embrace the last I will have with him? Will he be injured or have a nervous breakdown again? Can I cope with the growing boys alone?"

On the other hand, she was relieved. Olav's moods were difficult to understand and an undercurrent of tension and anger often filled the space around him. The floor, the air, the chair in which he sat deflected any personal contact.

"Everything will be fine now that Anna lives at home and Karl visits often. And, Wolfgang Hoffman will not be going to battle because of his limitations from polio," she thought. "We will all help one another. And…someday Olav will come home."

Olav felt guilty that he was relieved to be away from his family. Oftentimes, he felt out of place at home. He didn't always know how to help with raising the boys and Rita was so unusual.

"Actually," Olav thought, "I have to admit that I am only completely comfortable with Anna. She is emotionally mature and forthright in her opinions. I always know where I stand with her. What a girl!"

At times he was burdened by a feeling of inadequacy because of his nervous breakdown. His thoughts rambled, "Mari has to take on any sewing jobs she can find. The house is too small with the boys growing so fast…

I couldn't have worked at that plant much longer anyway. It has become impossible to produce the quality they want within our timelines and the Cretans with whom I must deal!"

Olav was glad to be back in the barracks among men. The job of war demanded different layers of his personality, ones that were less vulnerable. War required him to focus on the present.

Feeling optimistic and confident when speaking with his commander, he said, "Sir, I expect the campaign will not take long. The Russians are weak from the revolution and poorly equipped and trained compared to our *Wehrmacht*."

Olav was shocked by the response, "Russia, unlike Germany, is not neat or orderly. But don't be fooled, *Oberleutnant*. We must not make the fatal mistake of underestimating the ferocity and tenacity of the Russians. They overtook a collapsing feudal society, and united, the people are rebuilding. Russians are wild and tough. You think we cannot be beaten?" Much later Olav would remember his words.

In June of 1941, Operation Barbarossa began – the invasion of Russia. As Olav scanned the sea of men, he was filled with a rush of pride. "Look at the organization—years of preparation and training," he thought. The power of thousands of men intent on a common goal set every molecule of his being on fire. His senses were heightened. They were ready like a tidal wave sweeping across the Russian terrain.

Anna missed her father, but she did not allow herself to dwell on what could happen to him. She would not allow horrid images of him in battle take over her thoughts. She made the most of her time with her family and Karl. On most Saturday nights Klara, Josef, Karl and Anna went out dancing.

Despite the bombings that had become more frequent and closer, a live band performed to a crowd of young people gathered to have fun—forget their problems for a while.

It was a sultry evening in July when after dancing until they were wet with perspiration, Karl and Anna decided to take a walk through the forest beyond the dance hall. When they had reached a secluded area, they stopped under a tree. Karl held Anna against the trunk and they began kissing. He pulled her dress up and quickly entered her. Anna moaned, first because of the sensation of Karl inside her and then because her bare back was rubbing against the bark. She whispered in his ear and he pulled her from the tree and squatted with her on his thighs. She loved his strength as he lifted her up and down until he came.

They walked slowly toward the hall. Karl stopped and turned to face Anna. Her features were clearly visible in the shaft of moonlight breaking through the trees. "I love you,'' he said as a matter-of-fact. Anna kissed his mouth deeply as they turned back towards the hall.

"Where have you been? They played that new song from the United States, 'In the Mood'," greeted Klara.

"It was too hot in here and we needed fresh air." A thick, smoky haze filled the hall. "Now let's have one more dance before I must leave," said Anna standing up enthusiastically, but the dance was pre-empted by a piercing siren, warning them of an air-raid.

The orchestra and all of the occupants of the hall moved swiftly down to the air-raid cellar and waited. A few couples kissed seemingly without a care while others were clearly frightened. One of the musicians began playing a cheerful tune on his ukulele and before long others were singing along. Anna could hear the distant, hollow sound of a bomb striking. After a period of silence, they heard the screaming all-clear signal and climbed the stairs to the hall. The orchestra started playing, drinks were poured, conversations increased in volume, and the dancing resumed. This had become standard protocol when out dancing on a Saturday night. Regardless, Anna was relieved to have Karl close by.

It was also reassuring for Mari and Anna to have a man around that they could trust. When he wasn't working, Karl helped the family with certain jobs and his solid confidence was calming. His presence became especially important to them when they were informed that they were moving to a subdivision where new homes had been built for favored SS officers.

"Come everyone and gather around the table; we have something important to tell you. Because *Vati* is an important officer in the SS, he has been rewarded for his service to Germany. We have been given a new, larger home. We will be packing our things soon and moving. Won't that be wonderful?" Mari announced with as much enthusiasm as she could muster. The boys did not respond at first, but Rita was already reacting, hugging her doll and rocking back and forth.

"No, no, no, no," she repeated as she shook her head. Anna said, "Come with me Rita, *mein liebe*." She took Rita by the hand and led her to the living room. "No, no, no," Rita continued raising her voice.

"Rita, you and I will share a room and we will hang your beautiful paintings around the house to make it our home—to make it beautiful. All of us will be together and that is what really matters." Anna put her arm around her sister's shoulders to steady her, but the troubled young girl would not stop rocking. Anna tried to imagine the source of her sister's distress.

"Is something else troubling you? Are you nervous about attending another school?" Anna attempted.

Rita's eyes were full of tears when she looked up at Anna, "Axel. I don't want to leave Axel—and Rosa. What will happen to them? Will they have a new house too?"

"No they will stay here but can visit us sometimes at our new house." Rita was inconsolable. She rocked faster, shaking her head and crying.

"I will tell you your favorite story." The rocking slowed and the crying was replaced by sniffing. "Once upon a time not long ago or far away there lived a woodcutter and his wife and their two children. The boy's name was Leo—I mean Hansel and the girl's name was Rita—no, no, not Rita, Gretel…"

In the kitchen, Otto asked, "Will *Vati* be able to find us?"

"He surely will, my son. You don't have to worry about that." Otto took tin soldiers from his pocket and began playing with them on the kitchen table.

Leo was more distraught. "I don't want to go to a new school. I want to stay with my friends… I want to stay with the same Hitler Youth group. I am a leader there!"

Mari said, "You will make new friends easily, Leo, and you will see your friends at Hitler Youth camping trips and competitions."

"It won't be the same! I won't leave!" he shouted angrily.

Karl stopped the outburst firmly. "Leo, stop shouting NOW! You are the oldest of the boys. *Vater* needs you to be the man of the family when he is away. He suffers when he is away. It is difficult for all of us, but we must be strong.

You are twelve years old now. You MUST behave like a man and help your family. You must be tough like Vater."

Leo thought for a moment about Karl's words and then nodded. His face was a mask of determination as he walked from the kitchen with long strides as though rehearsing a manly walk.

Later that evening, when the family was asleep, Mari allowed herself to be honest. So many memories were in this old home, in the very woodwork. She had misgivings about the move. What would be the real price of the new home and special privileges?

Chapter Thirteen
Retribution

At first, Ada couldn't imagine moving to the United States. With Frieda's prompting, however, she decided that immigration was her best shot at a future. War-ravaged, occupied Europe was no place to raise a family.

Her son, Oskar, was enthusiastic to immigrate and Franz was desperate to leave Germany. His stories about the States created a bright picture of the future – a future together.

The first stage in their plan was for Ada and Oskar to move immediately to Berlin and live with Franz until preparations were complete. While she packed, Ada let Oskar participate in a camping trip with the Hitler Youth.

At fourteen years of age Oskar was tall and lean with excellent posture like his parents. He walked with confidence not only because of his noble heritage, but also his ability to defend himself against most Hitler Youth bullies. He was now leader of a Hitler Youth division and took his job seriously.

At the camp, tents had been set up across a field and maneuvers organized for every moment of each day. Oskar was making his rounds before returning to his tent for the night when he heard a skirmish behind one of the tents. The strangeness of the nervous, muffled laughter made him look behind the tent. Three teenage boys were standing in a circle. One was pulling up his pants. Another was stepping on the neck of a much smaller boy who was gagged and lying face down in the grass. A fourth boy was sodomizing him.

At first Oskar could not comprehend what he was seeing. Oskar had heard jokes about men who liked other men in the army, but this was an act of violence. Even though he was shocked and frightened, he commanded in a low, authoritative voice. "You there, STOP immediately!"

One of the boys who were standing stepped forward holding a knife out in front of him. He was smirking as he stared at Oskar, "What will you do about it? This Jew boy deserved what he got." He swayed from side to side with the knife outstretched carving the air, his eyes narrowed.

"Get the hell back to your camp, or I will report you to the Reich Commissioner," ordered Oskar.

The four remained where they were standing for a moment and then the leader assessed the situation and decided it was too risky to fight this camp leader without being heard by someone else. They slowly moved away and strutted out of sight in the cocky manner of thugs.

The younger boy had removed the gag and was painfully getting to his feet. As Oskar approached him he saw the blood, "Come with me to the barracks so you can clean up. In the morning you can go home. Believe me, they will be punished."

Sleepless, Oskar was distraught and confused by what he had seen. He inwardly raged against the violent sex offence. He wanted justice, wanted to set things right. He decided to report the offenders to the coach and let parents know what had happened at Hitler Youth camp. Other boys could be in danger.

The following day before breakfast, Oskar approached the coach. "Sir, I have a violation to report."

Herr Schulz listened carefully to the story and nodded silently. "You have demonstrated great courage for your age. Leave this with me. I will see that they are punished."

Oskar returned to his camp and continued with the day's activities thinking that he had done the right thing. That afternoon a messenger told Oskar that the *Reich Commissioner* wanted to see him. *Reich Commissioner Keller* told him that he would be taken to a leadership camp where he could tell his story to the authorities and receive the credit he deserved. But Keller engaged the assistance of a monster familiar with Oskar and his mother.

"Oskar Brandt!" rejoiced Bruno. He could not believe his good fortune. "The Reich Commissioner wants ME to take care of the problem? He said that the incident at Hitler Youth camp cannot be made public. The reputation of the Nazi training program cannot be jeopardized. Two of the little bastards are sons of prominent SS officers. They will all be in debt to me."

Oskar was escorted into the back of a covered truck. Benches lined the sides. Several young people were already seated. Even when the door was locked and the truck drove away, Oskar suspected nothing. As the gas encircled them, the last thing Oskar saw before he was dead was his mother's face.

"No one can accuse me of killing Oskar without sufficient cause, or say that the penalty was too severe," Bruno reassured himself. "I was told to take care of the problem so that the incident could not be made public. Well, the virtuous son won't talk now. That whore will know PAIN! She will fear me. She will respect me!"

Meanwhile Ada kept looking up from her packing to check the time on the clock. "Where is Oskar? This isn't like him. He is such a conscientious boy. I must telephone *Reich Commissioner Keller.*"

"Do not worry *Frau Brandt*. He has been taken to a leadership camp for further training and awards."

"Oskar never mentioned that to me. Why was I not contacted? You did not receive my permission to take my son anywhere. He is supposed to be at the field camp. I want him home now!" Ada commanded.

"Now *Frau Brandt* you do not want to deprive your son of advancement and privilege in our *Fuhrer's* training camp do you?" continued the *Reich Commissioner.*

"I want him home!" demanded Ada.

Then his tone changed from conciliatory to shrill. "He will NOT be coming home yet. I will inform you when the training is complete." The conversation had been terminated.

Two days later Ada heard a knock at the door. It was the golden pheasant, Bruno. "I have an official letter for you *Frau Brandt*. May I come in?" Bruno sneered as he pushed her aside.

Ada was sick with concern about the contents of the letter but outwardly displayed no weakness. As Ada reached for the letter, Bruno withdrew his hand in a controlling way.

"Give me the letter and get out of my home immediately, or I will call for help," yelled Ada outraged.

"No one will come to your aid this time." He produced a knife and when Ada attempted to reach the door, Bruno grabbed her quickly and turned her around with her back facing his belly. He grunted, "You will listen to me *hure nude*. You will do as I say."

He pushed her face over the sofa, holding the knife to her neck and roughly pulled up her skirt. He raped her with force from behind. She screamed out in pain, but no one heard. It was over quickly. He kneed her hard in her lower back as he pulled away.

Bruno stood up, shook his head and squared his shoulders. He straightened his uniform and slipped the knife back in his trouser pocket. Slowly scratching his chin, he leered at Ada, who was now standing.

He reached into his jacket pocket for the letter and then threw it on the floor. "Is this what you want?" he scoffed and then turned sharply and left.

Ada's hands were trembling as she opened the envelope. It was one of the many falsified letters that parents received about children who were designated undesirable by the Nazis. It said that Oskar had died of pneumonia that had spread through the leadership school.

Ada sat down shaking and looked about anxiously. "Pneumonia? So quickly? How can this be? Not Oskar! There must be some mistake! Where is he? I want my son back!"

It was the stench of onions and old cigarettes mixed with Bruno's body odor that made her mind snap to attention. She needed to clean the air and her body of his filth. As she stood up to open the window, Ada was nauseated by the sticky wetness of Bruno's semen running down her inner thighs. She hurried to the bathroom and washed every trace of him from her body frenetically.

That night Ada oscillated between weeping, sitting on the sofa trancelike, and pacing. She clapped her hand over her mouth to stifle guttural screams of anguish. By morning, she collapsed and slept. When she awoke the confusing storm inside her had stopped, and rage propelled her forward in a straight trajectory. She knew where to go and what to do.

Ada knocked on the back door of Frieda's apartment. Surprised, Frieda cautiously opened the door. When she saw Ada's ghostly face and puffy eyes, she quickly took her by the arm and led her to a chair.

"You are the only one I can trust, Frieda!"

Frieda sat down across from her and asked, "What is it Ada? What has happened?" There was no reply. Ada placed the letter in front of Frieda and motioned for her to read. Frieda did not look up at first. She stared at the paper trying to grasp the meaning of the words. Slowly she raised her eyes and then stood painfully. Silently she found the cognac and poured each of them a drink.

The liquor thawed the icy reality that had seeped into Ada's body. Frieda sat with her forehead in her hand, her mind racing. She could not say anything to Ada. Words of consolation seemed trite.

"When Bruno delivered this letter he raped me, Frieda."

"Bruno is behind this!" Frieda exclaimed... Do you want me to find out what happened to Oskar?

"Yes," Ada responded grimly. "And..." Ada was attempting to marshal her emotions. "Bruno must die." Ada knew she was taking a risk to suggest such a thing but she was desperate for revenge and justice.

Frieda didn't flinch. "Leave this with me and come back in two days after working hours to discuss a plan. For now you must have some hot broth and bread."

Frieda's network revealed that Oskar had been gassed in the back of the truck transporting youths to a burial site. Frieda thought about Katia and all the others Bruno had abused and extorted. She developed a plan to murder him but needed help.

When Anna received the telephone call from Frieda requesting morphine, she responded without hesitation. Klara was able to call in a favor to get the drug for Anna. Within days Anna delivered the morphine to the salon.

The familiar scents of shampoos and chemicals and the soup on the stove of Frieda's apartment filled Anna's nostrils. She hadn't realized how much she missed her life there.

Anna asked no questions and Frieda only nodded her thanks as she took the morphine. They talked about salon gossip until Anna left to catch the tram.

Frieda was unwilling to involve Anna in the murder of Bruno. At times she had felt guilty about some of the work Anna had done for her. Also, Frieda guessed that Anna would likely refuse to participate in such a crime. Regardless, Frieda would not expose her to such danger. This was not Anna's fight. But it was Katia's.

Frieda had called Ada and Katia to finalize the plan to murder Bruno. "He is very strong. What if we cannot overpower him?" worried Ada.

"Maybe we need a gun," added Katia.

"That will take too much time. Ada must leave Leipzig as soon as possible. I will handle it."

The next night, the three women were ready. At the salon, Frieda telephoned Bruno, "*Herr Kauser*, these times are becoming very dangerous for women in business. I am wondering if there is something I could do for you to guarantee my protection from the eyes of the Gestapo."

"I can think of something. When should I come over?"

"I will come to you, since I have an apprentice living with me, and we will want our privacy don't you think?"

"Oh yes, oh yes," Bruno replied eagerly.

"I will be over at 10:00 when it is dark."

The block-out blinds and curtains darkened the homes and the streetlamps were off when the women arrived at Bruno's lair. The others hid while Frieda knocked at the door.

Frieda had chosen her makeup and undergarment with care to achieve the desired effect on Bruno. "Good evening Bruno, darling," Frieda greeted in a sexy tone. She walked in and turned to face Bruno as he closed the door. Before he could lock it, she had opened her coat and taken his hand to draw him close to her body. When he saw her almost naked body, his moist, red lips hungrily attacked her face. He lowered his head intent on her breasts. He didn't see her reach into her coat pocket to withdraw the syringe. Frieda drove it deep into his neck and then pushed him away with all her strength. She rushed to the door and let Ada and Katia inside.

Together they stripped Bruno and hung the uniform of the pheasant neatly on a hanger in clear view. Ada placed the noose firmly around his neck and then checked to ensure that no one was in the street. The three women dragged him to the curb. Frieda threw the rope over the bar behind the streetlamp and the three women hoisted the fleshy body four feet off the ground. Once the rope was tied off securely, the conspirators disappeared in different directions—Ada took the tram to her apartment to visit her neighbors and thus guarantee an alibi while Katia and Frieda walked back to the salon.

At Frieda's apartment, the two women breathed deeply as they closed the door on their crime. Frieda retrieved Katia's savings from the hiding place.

"He is gone Frieda, he won't be able to touch me again!" gasped Katia in disbelief.

"With your savings you can begin a life of your choosing. You must move quickly though Katia. It is becoming increasingly difficult to cross the border.

I will probably never see you again. Good luck my friend. I will truly miss you!"

"Oh Frieda," Katia's eyes filled with tears. "I could never have survived without you. My dearest of friends, thank you!"

They embraced each other and then Frieda urged, "Leave now Katia and never look back." On the following morning:

Katia crossed the border to Holland

Ada boarded the train for Berlin

Frieda opened the salon

A cluster of neighbors and Gestapo stared at the glaringly naked, flaccid body of *Herr Bruno Kauser* hanging from the streetlamp in the brilliant morning sun.

Ada was ashamed to feel exhilarated as the train left Leipzig heading north to Berlin. The three of them had done the unthinkable. She had avenged the murder of her son. Bruno was dead! But soon the fear of being apprehended by the Gestapo replaced her elation. Her palms were moist and perspiration was forming on her brow.

She thought, "Surely the others will not be discovered. Unwittingly, I have put my dearest of friends at risk. Frieda remains in Leipzig while I escape safely to the United States. Perhaps I have made the biggest mistake of my life."

The murder of the block warden would have to remain a secret forever she had decided. She would never jeopardize her life with Franz or the lives of Frieda and Katia by confessing to Franz. "I must only tell him that Oskar died suddenly of pneumonia as officially described in the letter."

Ada felt duplicitous. "How can we possibly have an enduring marriage when I withhold such deep secrets from Franz? Yet is a German alive today that does not hold secrets?"

By the time the train pulled into Berlin, Ada had vowed to herself that the truth and her suffering would have to be locked deep within; where the pain that is beyond tears resides.

Franz was at the railway station, his eyes searching the crowds to catch a glimpse of her. She saw him first and waved. After a brief embrace, Franz put his arm around her and guided her through the crowds in haste. He whispered in her ear, "Berlin has changed since the Russian war began. We must wait to talk."

During the taxi ride, Ada noticed the anti-aircraft cannons mounted on buildings. An enormous cement tower about one hundred feet high was armed with long guns mounted in each corner to fire at aggression from the sky.

Franz explained, "They are fired by remote control from another tower where a large receiver detects enemy planes. My apartment is half a mile away but it sounds as though the guns are leveled straight at my windows. My windows rattle until it sounds as though they will shatter, and the floor vibrates. The guns are fired in unison, and it is terribly hard on the nerves and ears even in the air-raid cellar."

Ada did not want to talk so she encouraged Franz to continue, "What is the green material I am seeing even on the lampposts?"

"It is the most gigantic camouflage scheme ever known – five miles from Brandenburg gate to Adolf Hitler Platz where my office is located in the radio studio. The whole thing is covered with a canopy of green netting. The idea is to make the area look like a forest to prevent detection by enemy pilots.

I have stood on top of the tall Columbus House on Potsdamer Platz on clear nights and watched the British aircraft approaching. As they came closer more and more searchlights scanned the sky. I counted seventy-five beams piercing the air, and then hundreds of guns opened fire. But trust me, darlin'; we will be out of here soon. You won't have to put up with anymore of this frightening war. Let's think about our honeymoon instead," Ada agreed with her smile.

When they were behind doors, Franz began gently, "Do you want to talk about Oskar now?"

"I know you loved him, Franz, and we were becoming a family, but I don't think I can speak about what happened… And…it is unlikely that I will be able to speak of him in the future. It is simply too difficult."

"I won't pressure you. You need to grieve.

I should have taken you both away sooner and maybe this would not have happened. I hate this damn war! …So sorry, Ada!… I miss him."

After a moment Ada said with resolve, "My son is gone…but you and I must not blame ourselves… We can't let his death destroy us. We must make a new life together."

That night Franz held Ada in bed and let the conversation drift away. He touched her face, outlining her features gently with his fingertips. He kissed her hand as he held it, and let her curl up at his side, her head on his chest. She had not felt safe for a long while. Ada slept soundly, a respite from sorrow.

Their plans to immigrate to the States did not move forward as quickly as hoped. Franz required an exit permit that was delayed. No valid reason was offered whenever he inquired about the delay. Their home in the United States seemed to be drifting out of reach.

Over the weeks to follow Franz and Ada watched Berlin deteriorate around them. Ada became increasingly nervous. Franz was also tense since he had observed firsthand the change in attitude toward Americans.

No longer did American correspondents enjoy the privileges and respect received during the previous years. For that reason, he had taken to speaking German at all times instead of English.

Franz complained to Ada, "Degeneration is everywhere—no maintenance of buildings, there is little food or clothing. Even transportation suffers! After the invasion of Norway and France in 1940, many civilians benefited from the spoils of war—women in the streets wearing silver fox furs and silk stockings—Hell! We had decent cigarettes and French cognac.

Then the High Command orders that the food, leather, beer, wine and other treats be sent to Russia to feed, clothe and entertain the German troops. The High Command have their share of luxuries. The working people suffer!"

"I suppose the old, aristocratic families are still comfortable?" asked Ada, praying that her family fortune was intact.

"Most aristocratic families have made their bucks on guns and chemicals.

This new aristocracy, though, are the higher up Nazis who didn't have a *pfennig* ten years ago. Look at Ley, the contraceptive king and Goering, the steel king, for instance," Franz explained. Ada's question remained unanswered.

"Perhaps we could see a movie to take our minds off this purgatory in which we find ourselves," suggested Ada.

"Sure, a comedy is playing at the *Gloria Palast*. I warn you though; it may be mediocre at best. We will undoubtedly be mistreated by a lengthy news-reel before the feature. Our other options are mainly war films, terrible productions!"

"A comedy is what we need. Later we could have a drink at a dance club."

"Let me tell you about some of the popular night spots. You should find this funny. One of my personal favorites is the Golden Horse Shoe," Franz began sarcastically. He hoped to cheer Ada a bit. Her face was so pale and drawn and she seemed frail.

"In the center of the floor of this tavern is a ring. The only Negress in Berlin brings out a horse. Yes, a horse! Customers, mostly ladies, pay to ride around the ring with their skirts up on their thighs exposing enough leg to make the men shout their approval and offer money. Fifty *pfennigs* buys a slow trot and seventy-five a good gallop. Can I interest you in a bit of equestrian delight tonight? I would like to see your legs," teased Franz.

"Oh how vulgar!" Ada replied in exaggerated disdain. Inside she was sick at how these women had to demean themselves in order to eat.

"I thought not… So then, we have *Walterchen der Seelensorger*. This is a small dance hall near the *Stetiner Station* area where *Herr Walterchen* matches middle-aged bachelors with spinsters and widows with widowers. I don't think I dare take you there especially before we are married."

"Oh Franz," Ada laughed. "Is there no place we might go?"

"Yah, as long as we carry our identification cards. I was in a place once called the *Die Neue Welt*—sometimes they are out of brew though. One time Gestapo cornered me and made me produce my passport to prove I was not a parachute trooper."

Anna winced.

"Okay, okay; I know a place that plays jazz and blues and the owner stashes a private bottle of Johnnie Walker under the sink."

"I am beginning to think your apartment is where I should like to go after the movie," said Ada and then humming a popular waltz she moved close to Franz. They danced cheek-to-cheek.

The movie distracted her from the fact that she felt dead inside. Time seemed to have stopped. She was in a bustling city, but inside she was still; she couldn't feel anything. Berlin, the war, nothing mattered anymore.

After the movie they didn't bother with the clubs but returned, instead, to the apartment as Ada had suggested. Their lovemaking was tender and unhurried. Soon Franz fell into a satisfied sleep. Ada was alone to think of Oskar.

While Franz was at work, Ada walked about the city streets for a distraction, anything to stop the reoccurring thoughts that plagued her mind. She was frantic to leave Germany. She longed for freedom from the threat of death at the hands of the Gestapo.

One day, Ada took the subway to the United Press office, where Franz was working to surprise him and to keep herself moving. As if she were an objective observer from another country, Ada looked into the faces of the working men and women. Their faces were pale, red rings around lifeless eyes. Without exception they were an unhealthy thin—too many hours worked in shops and factories and too little nutrition.

The human stench on the subway made the reality of life for the working Germans even more dismal. The pungent smell of body odors and sour clothing was overwhelming in the improperly vented subway car. Most Germans were rationed only one small cube of soap for the month. Of course the soap was insufficient for hard-working people with so few clothes to wear. Ada controlled the urge to vomit.

When she arrived at her stop, she was happy to walk the remaining blocks to the United Press Office. She inhaled clean air, and then suddenly, she couldn't breathe.

Driving down the street was a long, black Mercedes followed by a military truck. They stopped in front of the United Press building and a man in long coat and felt hat got out and made for the door. Several large men followed.

"Gestapo! Are they arresting Franz? What if he is taken to a work camp? Or, are they looking for me?" She knew it would be foolhardy to attempt reaching Franz. Two of the men were posted on the street and would ask her questions. She looked at her watch, feigning a commitment to be somewhere, and then turned and retraced her steps quickly.

At the apartment, Ada paced, "Will we never reach the United States. Will we never be able to start a new life? Perhaps I should telephone my uncle for protection in Prussia… the telephone might be tapped! No, I have already ruined lives. I cannot put the rest of my family in danger over my actions."

The hours passed slowly and still no word from Franz. Finally, she dozed, but was awakened violently by her own screams. The nightmare was about Bruno. She washed her face with cold water and made a pot of tea to help restore her balance.

Ada felt trapped. Waiting seemed endless. Then she heard the inevitable key in the lock. She leapt up quickly but stood motionless beside the table. "Have they come for me?" The door swung open and Franz entered. "Oh God Franz, are you all right?" Ada cried as she rushed to him.

"Yes I am, but I was detained by the Gestapo. We will be okay. I tell you; it won't be too soon to be out of this damned country for good." As Ada set out some bread and cheese, Franz told her what had happened.

"They did a search of desks belonging to certain journalists. I was plenty scared since in my desk drawer is a sheaf of notes a foot high of facts, mostly about economics and quotations from interviews—names and details." In addition, I have exhaustive information on air raids, the locations of anti-aircraft guns and a lot of unpublished material about the German army. I have gathered the information for journalistic purposes, of course, but it could easily be misconstrued to represent political and military espionage.

He paused as he took a sip of Mosel and then shaking his head went on, "The leader, a thick-set man in a long overcoat began asking me direct questions. He knew about my education, my family…and he knew you are my wife. The whole lot of them were threatening. The boss then received a call, presumably about something more important, and suddenly they all left. I am not sure what the hell this is about, but I am sending another cable to the States to apply some pressure for our exit papers. We must get out of here while we still can."

After this incident, Ada thought it best to sequester herself in their suite until Franz had the papers for their departure. The grim reality of Berlin and fear of the Gestapo were overwhelming. Finally, the day did arrive when Franz came through the door holding papers high in his hands.

"We are leaving!"

Crossing the border into Switzerland, the couple found another world. They left grey, lifeless doom for the vibrant colors of normal. Ordinary life appeared exciting—health tinting the faces of the locals—friendly greetings. Berne was a charming city. Houses were clean and neat with brightly painted walls. Shops had real products for sale not just props in the windows. Ada and Franz devoured the goods displayed with their eyes—rich red meat, coils of sausages, apples, oranges. Ada closed her eyes in appreciation while taking in the fragrance of a bar of soap.

Restaurants were open and selling sumptuous meals. Clothing hung in shops and real leather shoes were in stock! After a seemingly decadent meal the couple took a room at the *Schweizer Hof* across from the station. They did not want to miss their train to the coast.

On December 7, 1941, as Franz and Ada gazed with gratitude at the Statue of Liberty rising from the waters of the New York harbor, the Japanese bombed Pearl Harbor. A few days later on December 11, Adolf Hitler declared war against the United States. The devastating news could not subdue their optimistic steps as the couple walked down Main Street on American soil.

Chapter Fourteen
A Different Time and Place

Anna didn't entertain the usual summer guests after Erich and Niels left in July. She needed the solitude at her home in Northern Ontario. It was the end of September, one of Anna's favorite months in the North. She typically stayed at her home until the leaves had fallen and then, like the Canada geese, headed south.

Every year her neighbors, Jim and Gail, winterized her log home and opened it again in April before she returned from West Palm Beach, Florida. Anna thought, "Without their help, I would probably be forced to move in with one of the boys, or worse yet, into one of those confining apartments in the city."

Gail invited Anna for lunch to make arrangements, and afterwards Jim lit a fire for a sauna. Although Anna's sore knee would have felt much better after the heat and steam, she declined in favor of a quiet afternoon alone.

As she walked home, Anna used her diamond willow walking stick to steady herself. The cane was embedded with an amethyst stone near the handle and was an eighty-fifth birthday gift from her neighbors. She treasured the effort they had put into finding, carving, and polishing the wood into a work of art.

Anna breathed in the autumn air. The poplar leaves were like amber coins on the damp road. A gust of wind arose and swept leaves up into a miniature golden tornado in front of her and then danced them off the road into the trees. Most of the trees were now in full color and the lower bushes burned a deep red.

Once home she lit a fire with birch wood and put on a pot of coffee. She sunk into a leather armchair by the fire and sipped her coffee, gazing out at the mist on the lake. A red squirrel leapt from the bird feeder to the window ledge in one fluid motion. Standing on its hind legs, the squirrel clasped its tiny hands on its chest. It froze and stared straight ahead like a tiny priest—contemplative, listening, concerned.

The chickadees, finches, and grosbeaks shared the sunflower seeds until a bold blue jay swept in to fill its gullet. The tropical colors of the birds against a background of golden birch leaves and deep evergreens held her in a peaceful reverie. She was reluctant to leave the lake this year.

Then she remembered how the month of November can be in Northern Ontario. The wind's voice would change from a gentle whisper in the aspen leaves to a roar deep in the white pine crowns and dense spruce bows. The fresh fall air would turn bitterly cold and the earth would freeze solid.

With that thought in mind Anna phoned her travel agent to book her flight south. Erich and Niels had convinced her to visit with their families on the way to Florida so the first leg of her journey was to Toronto.

The day she left Thunder Bay was overcast. When she looked out from the airplane window the landscape seemed bleak and lonely. Anna knew the time had come to visit her family and then friends in West Palm Beach.

As the aircraft descended over Lake Ontario, she saw the striking Toronto cityscape rising up from the shoreline. The CN Tower, a signature architectural structure for the city, pierced the bright, cool sky.

Niels was there to meet her. "*Mutti,* here is your throne," he teased. She refused his offer of a wheelchair to make the short passage on the ferry to the mainland.

"I will manage with my cane, Son." Niels knew better than to argue with his mother. "Erich will meet us at the restaurant," he said as he hailed a cab. The tradition was for Erich, Niels and Anna to catch up over a drink before driving home to the families.

Niels watched his mother with admiration. She was wearing a camel hair coat, black gloves and purse, and black pants. Her soft cream scarf set off her pale hair and gold jewelry. She extended her hand as Erich walked over to greet her and then settle her in a chair.

"People look at *Mutti* even at eighty-seven years old. The server has respect for her and she hasn't opened her mouth yet. You wait, man," Niels thought.

And then Anna turned to the server and with her low voice and heavy German accent said, "Dawling, please get me a Riesling and, oh, you have such a nice smile young man. What is your name?"

"My name is Don, ma'am."

"Please call me Anna; and after you take my sons' orders, please add a drink for yourself and put it on my tab. Anything you like, dawling, anything at all."

"Thank you, Anna," the waiter said grinning.

Before long the conversation was lively. Anna made eye contact with Don and raised her manicured finger, making a circle in the air. He nodded and disappeared quickly. Soon he was back with another round of drinks and the appetizers. The table beside them would have to wait.

Erich's smile vanished when he said, "We should be leaving for Oakville before rush hour, or we'll be very late for dinner. Diane is making dinner for everyone. Our girls as well as Nathan and Cheryl will already be there."

Of course, Son, and let's pick up a bouquet of fall flowers for Diane on the way," suggested Anna.

Soon they pulled up to a large split-level home with a carefully manicured lawn. Baskets of asters adorned the steps and an autumn wreath hung on the front door. Erich opened the door to a noisy welcome.

"Diane, how are you? How nice to see you. Oh my darlings! You have changed so much since last Christmas," said Anna as the two families greeted her enthusiastically.

They enjoyed a meal of pork roast and gravy, roasted potatoes, salads, buttered carrots and parsnips, and a sweet potato casserole. Then while everyone sat back to talk and await the chocolate soufflé, Diane asked the oldest of the girls, "Meghan, would you help me collect the dishes and put them in the dishwasher?" Meghan continued to sit in her chair.

"Your mother asked you to give her a hand, honey," said Erich coming to the rescue.

Meghan's face was red as she glared down at her napkin. Suddenly, she stood up throwing the napkin on her plate. She stomped out of the dining room and ran upstairs.

"Teenage girls are so much fun to be around," said Diane apologetically.

"She is twenty," Anna stated.

No one addressed Meghan's behavior, so apparently these outbursts were not uncommon. Anna looked disapprovingly at Meghan's plate. She had left her plate half covered in food. Anna never could get over wastefulness.

"I'm going downstairs; are you in Nathan?" asked Stephanie, the younger sister by two years. As they made their hasty retreat, Nathan pulled up his jeans that had been dropping dangerously close to his knees. His boxer shorts managed to stay in place though, the startling primary colors drawing attention to his backside.

Anna looked at the young adults, puzzled, but said graciously, "I will clean the counters and load the dishwasher if Cheryl will bring the dishes to me. You make the coffee, okay Diane?"

The next morning Anna was having breakfast with Diane and Erich when screams interrupted their morning conversation. "Good Lord, what are they fighting about now?" exclaimed Erich clearly annoyed. "Do something, Diane!" Diane rushed upstairs to investigate the crisis.

"Well fuck you!" shouted Meghan. A door slammed. Diane and Stephanie came downstairs. Stephanie was sobbing and shouting something about her sister. Diane was hugging her and consoling her as though she were a child instead of an eighteen year old woman.

"I know sweetie, Meghan will get over it. We will go shopping after lunch. All we need is some retail therapy." She smiled effusively and hugged her daughter's shoulders; however, Stephanie carried on.

Erich was clearly embarrassed and angered by the histrionics in front of his mother but said nothing.

Finally, Anna, unable to bear what she considered complete nonsense ordered firmly, "Stephanie, stop this NOW. You are behaving like an imbecile. You are no longer a child. Go upstairs and take a shower to calm yourself and then get dressed to go out with us."

Stephanie began to argue but Anna cut her off with a raised finger before she could speak, "No! Not another word, get moving—upstairs." Stephanie left dramatically, marching out of the room with her fists clenched at her sides.

"I am sorry that you have to see this, *Mutti,*" said Erich, "Raising girls is not easy. It must be the hormones."

Diane's back tensed as she walked away to the sink with the breakfast dishes.

Anna saw and suggested, "Diane would you like me to talk to Meghan or do you want to do the honors?"

"She probably wants to email her friends on the computer. Maybe we should just leave her alone. She will want to stay in her room this afternoon no doubt."

"I am visiting and would like to spend this day with my granddaughter before I leave for Niels' house. I will go to her room," Anna persisted. Diane shrugged her shoulders and nodded. Erich buried his face in the "Globe and Mail" newspaper.

Not long after Anna and Meghan entered the dining area. "And the university did nothing about it? Well, later we will discuss a few options, my darling," Anna was saying. Meghan was dressed and ready to go out. Then Stephanie appeared.

"I'm sorry, Steph," said Meghan.

"No worries," Stephanie replied as she grabbed her cell phone off the kitchen island. "Let's go!"

The family took an autumn stroll at the Gairloch Gardens enjoying the ducks, geese and swans that had made the lake's shore their home. They took in an art exhibit at the Oakville Gallery and then lunch at the Paradiso. The day had been salvaged.

The following morning Niels came for Anna in his BMW. As she waved good-bye to Erich's family, Anna breathed a sigh of relief. "Is there somewhere in this city where I can have a cigarette," Anna laughed.

"I know just the place—our patio," said Niels as he navigated down the QEW heading for Queen Street West. "Cheryl took Nathan to a football game and won't be home to guilt us until later this afternoon."

They drove past the bistros and shops of the area and then on to Niels' downtown home. Anna liked the renovations he had made to their old brick house. Niels had gutted the kitchen and bathrooms but the original woodwork and brick in the kitchen and dining room area gave the home character.

Niels was also a gardener and had transformed their tiny backyard into a stunning sanctuary. An eight foot fence protected the yard and apart from the small patio with its pergola, the entire space consisted of flower beds linked by a meandering path of slate.

Niels carried a tray with Riesling in an ice bucket, blue cheese, a fresh baguette and an ashtray. He placed the tray on the glass table between them.

"There you are, Niels. Oh thank you, dawling. My favorite!"

"Now where are those nasty cigarettes, *Mutti*?"

"Will you be able to get away to West Palm Beach in March this year?" asked Anna as she passed her son a lit cigarette. "I know you are busy with the financial crisis we are in."

"I will be there for sure."

"Fabulous!" said Anna genuinely pleased at the prospect.

"As long as you promise me a dinner party with that cast of characters you call friends," Niels teased.

"Of course," Anna smiled as she inhaled the last of her cigarette. "Before Cheryl and Nathan arrive, I want to talk to you about Erich."

Anna had raised her sons as if both were her own but they were, in fact, half-brothers. Anna was not Erich's biological mother. She had acknowledged many years ago that she would never be as close to Erich as Niels. Growing up, Erich had a temper and was socially remote. As an adult, he tended to agonize and analyze the life out of living.

Raising her son, Niels, had been easier. They had an open relationship, understood one another. She knew she should talk to Erich directly about her concerns instead of Niels, but the risk was that Erich would probably never speak to her again.

"Diane and Erich are working parents, and yes, they have a long commute… I am sure they are exhausted by the time they arrive home in the evening, but they have not dedicated enough of their lives to raising those girls. They walk all over Diane, and Erich ignores the problems. Maybe he can't reach them or discipline them, but it is sad to see what is happening. The girls are so insensitive and the language!"

Niels listened and sipped his wine. His mother continued to rant.

"The girls' rooms are filthy. Clothes, dishes—*Mein Gott*—it is terrible! And in such a beautiful home! They have a television and computer in each of their rooms…leading separate lives under one roof. Is this the way a family should live together—apart?" Anna vented. She lit a cigarette and then went on.

"We have not talked about last Christmas either. Diane and Erich gave the girls expensive gifts and in return they gave their parents nothing, nothing at all. They did not even help with Christmas dinner or clean up. They lay around as though they were bored and putting in time. I will never spend another Christmas with Erich's family. It upsets me too much.

Somehow those girls always have the money to go out with friends or spend money on their hair, manicures, pedicures, tanning sessions, and clothes but give nothing to another soul! They are so selfish! They don't even have a part-time job!" Anna paused.

She looked at Niels. In a soft voice she asked, "Have I been too harsh, Son? …What do you think?"

Niels deadheaded a few of the nasturtiums still flowering in the patio pots. Anna waited for him to respond. She knew he was loyal to his brother and would choose his words carefully.

"Well…the kids are part of a generation with similar traits…and the computer has changed everything…It is complicated, *Mutti*…"

"It seems straightforward to me; parents aren't taking the time to teach their children values and ways to cope with life. Instead, they buy them off with material things or mindless recreational activities!" She retorted frankly.

"*Mutti?*" Niels waited and then explained calmly, "…Erich and Diane are having marital problems."

"How bad is it?"

"Who knows for sure, but I don't think their marriage can last much longer."

"Oh no!… I should have known… I have said enough for now…yes? Let's go inside and cook," Anna replied with a heavy heart.

The mother and son began taking vegetables and meat out of the fridge onto the stainless steel surface of the kitchen island. They had often cooked together. "Hey stop *Mutti*! Today let's put this back in the fridge and go out to Terroni's. It's a great restaurant not five minutes away."

Cheryl and Nathan were already there, talking excitedly about the football game. Anna smiled at their enthusiasm. She also liked the clientele of the restaurant that were from a range of age groups. The place was full of conversation and laughter as well as music from a lone musician in the back. This, combined with the tantalizing aroma of garlic and herbs, distracted Anna from Erich and Dianne's marital problems.

"Nathan, tell me all about college and your new job, but first; I see you have a new pierced earring," observed Anna.

"Grandma, I know you probably think earrings are for girls but they are cool for guys too," said Nathan defensively.

Anna laughed. "I know that, but did YOU know your great grandfather, *Herr Olav Muller*, wore an earring in each ear."

"No way!" responded Nathan.

"Oh yes, and his pants stayed up instead of falling down to his knees. Should I buy you a belt?" offered Anna.

Nathan could take the teasing from his grandmother. He knew she loved him, and he cherished the conversations they had in private. She had always treated him like a person not just a kid.

Anna fascinated him with her German accent and stories about the North—meeting people in Canada for the first time—his dad and uncle and their respective dogs and teachers over the years—fishing trips they took with friends from the reservation. "She always tries new things and takes no crap people," Nathan thought proudly.

"Do you want me to start bugging you about smoking, Grandma? You know it is not good for your health…" poked Nathan.

Anna playfully slapped his wrist. "I will be the one doing the nagging around this table. It is the God-given right of old women."

Too soon Anna's visit in Toronto ended and Niels was driving her to Pearson Airport. Before she checked through security, Niels winked as he said, "Call me once in a while if you can spare the time *Mutti*."

"I love you, Son," she said as she hugged Niels. "I will see you in the spring."

Niels watched as his mother walked through the archway of the metal detector and began talking with a very large African American man in uniform. He saw the man smile and speak into his radio. Anna was flying first class and asked him to help her reach the gate. Niels had no doubt that she would reach her gate in comfort. "She is a 'femme fatale' to be sure," he thought.

He was surprised at how profoundly lonely he felt when she was out of sight. Once in his car, though, he shifted his mind to the business of making money with money—on the stock market. In 2008, that was a challenge indeed.

When Anna entered the Fort Lauderdale airport in Florida, she stopped for a moment to smell the sea air and feel the humidity on her face—85 degrees Fahrenheit with a breeze. Royal Palms replaced spruce trees—red and pink bougainvillea replaced the dogwood and mountain ash of Ontario.

The limousine took her down Poinciana Way along the ocean, passing Jaguars and Mercedes—homes with roofs of red Spanish tile—colorful awnings—walls painted pastel yellow, salmon, or pale blue. Soon she saw St. Edward's church and knew she was close to her condo.

She couldn't wait to settle in and desperately needed a swim to loosen her joints which had stiffened during the flight. Despite the maintenance of her housekeeper, the condo had the dank smell of a home abandoned by its owners, devoid of life. The air conditioning was working, but Anna opened the windows and sliding doors while she unpacked her groceries. Then she changed into her swim suit and snapped on a bathing cap.

With a glass of lemonade on ice and her cigarettes she slowly made for the pool. When she took off her sandals, she realized the decking was too hot for bare feet. Anna moved as quickly as her body would allow and then…she was floating in the water. She swam her customary lengths, feeling so much stronger in the water than walking on land.

Anna was beginning to feel much better with the swim and the heat; however, as she was changing for dinner she caught her reflection in the mirror. "You need to pay a visit to Ted tomorrow."

The next morning, Anna left for "Aloha," her favorite salon. The exterior of Ted's salon was covered with a colorful mural of water, fish, flowers and birds. Over the entrance was a large sun with rays extending onto a wall of indigo sky and palm trees with lime green leaves stretching from the sidewalk to the eaves. Once inside, a plastic palm tree covered in twinkle lights lit the entrance near the computer.

Ted greeted her by name. "Anna, where have you been all my life," said her gay hairstylist. He was not only skilled at his job but a warm host. "What would you like this afternoon—a coffee, Perrier, a glass of wine?"

"I'll have water but you need to get busy; you have a challenge today."

"Sit down, honey, and let's take a look. Your hair isn't too bad."

"I was waiting for you Ted, dawling. Look at my nails and now that I will be barefoot, we need to do something about these," she laughed as she stretched out her legs to show him her feet.

"Not a problem! We will Floridize you in no time." As music played in the background, Anna relaxed while Ted began to dye, cut and then set and style her hair. The other hairstylists took care of customers while the friends caught up.

"How long has it been since you have been spending winters in West Palm Beach?"

"About thirty years, the first ten with my husband. I have known you for at least twelve years."

"Time flies. I had just opened the salon when I met you, right?"

"Yes, you only had a couple of chairs back then. You have done so well, Ted."

"Thanks, it's good to have you back!... Did you visit family in Germany this past summer?"

"I saw them in the spring. We went to Vienna to hear a Strauss symphony and went on to Italy for two weeks. Then I spent most of the summer alone at the lake in Ontario," explained Anna.

"Isn't it dangerous to be alone? Don't you have bears and wolves up north? They could attack you, honey," teased the hairstylist.

"The animals don't care for human company much. It is a rare thrill to see the bears and wolves."

"What about the snow?"

"I don't live in Banff, Ted. You won't see snow in July."

"Don't you get lonely at the lake without a city close by?"

"Thunder Bay is close enough... No, I am never lonely or afraid. You know something? I am happy wherever I am. But! If you came to visit, dawling, I would be even happier!"

"Maybe one of these summers, I will surprise you... West Palm Beach is perfect for me though. I have to tell you, I prefer people around me and the action of the beach... I like the fashion, bars, dancing. Everything is colorful here, from the ocean to the flowers and our clothes."

"And your salon murals!" added Anna in appreciation.

"Exactly. The action and color make me happy. I think I would be depressed living anywhere else. And then there is the warm weather."

"Yes, I understand. I enjoy living here during the winter."

"May I ask you a question, Anna?"

"Of course."

"Why didn't you ever move back to Germany? You still have family there. You seem to have such a great time on your trips."

"Too many rules in Germany! They know exactly where you are all of the time. Cameras everywhere! I don't like that much control. Nobody bothers me where I live in the wilderness. It is perfect!" Anna replied emphatically.

"Remember the kid's toy that looks like a scope, but when you peek through it and twist the other end, multiple colors and shapes appear?" asked Ted. Anna nodded.

"That's it—your life is a kaleidoscope of experiences!" Ted announced waving his sheers in a grand gesture.

"Maybe you are right, Ted."

"Change your life for new, colorful experiences and see how they all fit together in a pattern," he continued.

"But tell me, how have YOU been? Are you still with Jerry?"

"Gawd no, we split up two months ago. He is so possessive. Our relationship reminds me of a song on the radio and Ted sang:

"Your love is like a straitjacket baby

And I can't breathe

Loosen your grip

Just a little bit

And maybe baby I won't leave

Just maybe baby I won't leave

Only I did leave don't you know." Ted chuckled. "And then, of course, I was the one who had to find another apartment! Not so smart? I guess I need to twist the kaleidoscope."

They laughed and then continued chatting until Ted said, "It is done. Look at you!"

Anna touched his arm affectionately as she gave him a generous tip. When she left the exclusive salon, she began thinking about a dark time in Germany when homosexuality was illegal under the Third Reich. Gay men were sometimes shot in the street or sent to concentration camps, isolated from society. They didn't survive the brutality in the camps for long. They did not see much in the way of beauty or fun, only gray sorrow. Anna was grateful that today in 2008 she had Ted to color her life with humor and friendship at the Aloha salon.

Anna had finished her afternoon swim and was reclining on a beach chair under a sprawling apple green umbrella.

"Hello there gorgeous," called a familiar baritone voice.

"Max, dawling, how wonderful to see you!"

The big, pear-shaped man joined her with a rum and coke in one hand and glass of white wine in the other. "Cocktail hour, Anna. It's been a bit boring around this complex. The MacLeods next door to me sold their condo to a rich widow from the Midwest. I haven't had anyone around for company to fill the gap after you snowbirds headed back up north. I need some conversation. I know you can remedy that!"

Max could somehow keep a large Cuban cigar lit and in his mouth while talking. On occasion that could be a long time.

The old friends were laughing loudly, "Stop Max, stop. My side is killing me!" Anna screamed. They did not see the widow approaching their table.

"Drunk already," she stated superciliously.

"Pardon?" Max said turning around sharply. "Oh, it's you."

"I heard there is a party over here."

"Anna, this is my new neighbor, Evelyn."

"Hello, Evelyn, would you like to join us?"

"I might as well. There isn't much to do here. God, it's so hot I can hardly breathe. You know I suffer a bit from asthma. The humidity kills me. I have no energy when it is this hot and humid. No energy at all."

"That is unfortunate." Anna sympathized.

"I see that lazy man who cleans the pool did a lousy job again. How can anyone swim in that?"

"I had a lovely swim. All I saw were some petals floating in the corner where the bougainvillea shrub is."

"What is your name again, dear?" asked the fifty year old widow.

"My name is Anna."

"Well, Anna, your hair is very stylish for someone your age. Where do you have it done?"

Anna ignored the barbed compliment and replied, "I go to Ted's. He's…"

"I won't pay those prices. Besides he's a homosexual. Well, I guess they are everywhere these days. What is the world coming to?"

Max and Anna were speechless, but the widow wasn't.

"You have a strong accent. Where are you from?"

"I was born in Germany," Anna answered curtly.

"German…hmm. I have a joke you're going to love… What do you call an angry German?" Neither Max nor Anna responded.

"Sour Kraut!" she laughed wryly. "Get it? Sauerkraut like in a Reuben sandwich—Kraut, the name for a German? Get it?" she carried on hysterically—a bitterness behind the laugh.

Anna got it all right. She knew the widow was deliberately trying to insult her perhaps because of her friendship with Max, perhaps because of the war, perhaps because she was rude.

"*Blode madehen!* She underestimates me. That woman does not know who I am. I have lived a life beyond anything she could imagine," Anna thought.

In a way, Anna was inwardly amused by the plebeian woman. "Money cannot buy class. Look at those frightening eyebrows. She should have gone to the Aloha salon." Evelyn's eyebrows had been plucked in such a way that they arced in permanent surprise.

Anna couldn't believe her ears. Evelyn was in the midst of a character assassination of her friend who was scheduled to arrive the following week. As Evelyn droned on criticizing and judging her unsuspecting friend, Anna thought, "How could she say such things about a friend? What would she have left for an enemy?"

Anna quickly decided to leave. "Thank you for the drink, Max. I must be on my way. I have another commitment. Enjoy your evening," said Anna as she rose from her comfortable chair. Max stood with her in the manner in which men of his generation showed respect for a woman.

"We will, dear. Are you going in for a nap?" Evelyn asked in a condescending tone.

"No, I am going shopping with Ted," Anna replied cheerfully over her shoulder.

Ted was cocoa tanned and handsome as he waved from his white, convertible Volkswagen bug. He wore Elton John, large, white sunglasses with rhinestones framing each side, a loose-fitting Hawaiian shirt with jeans and expensive flip flops. His silver hair was cropped short and his big smile revealed beautifully whitened teeth. Anna thought he was visibly, happily, gorgeously gay.

He helped Anna into the cream leather seat and drew a drink for her from the glove box where it had been chilling. Before leaving he reached around to ruffle the necks of two purebred Corgies enjoying the view, safe in their respective seat belts in the back seat. They drove into the sun with the top down, classical music playing.

"Max, will you come for dinner Thursday evening? Ingrid will be arriving then to stay for the winter and I am making a traditional German meal she loves. I want to surprise her."

"I will be there for sure." How about I bring a pie for dessert? Max offered.

"No, you don't have to bring a thing. Besides pie is an American treat. Germans don't make pies. I will have a chocolate pudding with a vanilla sauce."

Anna relished the thought of cooking for her friends, especially Max. He had as much appetite for food as he did for life—always a welcome guest.

Anna knew a small deli owned by two southern characters she liked. They sold quality meats and special imported foods. She left that afternoon to buy her ingredients for the dinner—eight pork hocks and two pounds of pork neck, seven jars of sauerkraut along with onions and allspice—bay leaf and peppercorns for seasoning.

"Anna, how y'all doing? Looks like you're fixin' to have quite a spread. You havin' red beans and rice along with them pork hocks?" boomed Earl the proprietor and butcher.

"No, sauerkraut, and on the side, some grated potato. Where is Lily today?"

"She's been too long in harness—done worked her hind legs off! Needed a day to rest some." Earl smiled.

"Please say hello to her. I must show her the plants she gave me. They are beautiful. Your wife has been very kind to me."

"Yes, ma'am, she so sweet she fattening," Earl exclaimed good-naturedly as he packed the last of the groceries. "Now you have a fine meal darlin' and come back to see us real soon."

While the cab driver was bringing her groceries into the condo, Anna heard a voice calling from behind, "How is my new Kraut friend today?"

"Hello Evelyn, can you hear me all right?"

"Yes dear. Nothing wrong with MY hearing."

"Kraut?…Friend? Don't EVER call me Kraut or dear again, and I am NOT your friend… Excuse me while I finish unpacking my groceries."

Anna's recipe took time to prepare – two days to simmer and later mince. But, Anna new the surprise dinner for Ingrid would be worth the effort. Thursday afternoon Anna set her dining room table with linens, china, and candles. She stocked the bar and chose a selection of music that all would appreciate.

When her friends arrived, they spoiled the surprise for Ingrid by talking loudly and incessantly from the moment they arrived. Ingrid heard them from the parking lot.

"I am here! Finally some life! How wonderful see you!" They exchanged hugs and warm greetings.

"What is that I smell, Anna? Did you really…?"

"Yes, and it won't be long until it is ready."

While having dinner, conversations crossed the table and overlapped. Some rousing stories were cut off before the speaker could finish. It seemed that the loudest voice won!

"I don't see why you and Ingrid are going to an art gallery. The work in your condo is top," said one of the neighbors. He pointed, "That one of the woman. Deliberately black and white with the exception of the emerald necklace and earrings in brilliant color or the musician with only his violin in color." What do you think it means, Ingrid. "I find them both fascinating!"

"I believe the color represents where love is or maybe the soul," replied Ingrid philosophically. Ask Anna, though. Her sister painted them years ago.

And from across the table, "There's a big difference between tightening your belt and eating your belt. We fat Americans have no idea what it was like," boomed Max, the history buff.

"I don't WANT to know," said Ted laughing.

"Anna, this is delicious," remarked one of the guests. "Let's toast the chef." They all raised their fine crystal glasses to Anna.

"I like this red wine," someone commented. "It is like velvet on my tongue."

The conversation at the other end of the table had shifted to Hitler and the war. "Did you know the bastard called himself a wolf—Adelwolfe means noble wolf in old German. Ironically he was a vegetarian. A Prussian general's account says he would place his left hand on his knee, like this, and his right hand by the plate. Then he would lower his head, like so, to plate level and with his hand scoop up veggies into his mouth…"

Anna turned to Ted and asked, "A cruise leaves Miami next week for the islands. Let's go, Ted!"

"Sure, I could get away for few days. Who else is interested?…"

A couple was lamenting the decline in their fortune. "What about the drop in our investments over the past six months? It will take some time to recover from this one. Hey, you Canadians will be able to buy up some pretty cheap Florida real estate. Have you talked to Niels about the stock market lately, Anna?"

"A bit but you can discuss it with him when he visits in March."

Someone asked, "What do you think of our neighbor, Evelyn. Have you met her, Ingrid?"

"No I haven't yet, but I am sure she will be by the pool tomorrow."

Max jumped in, "That aggressively boring widow had the gall to tell that old Kraut joke. You know—the one that goes…what do you call a pissed off German…a sour kraut. Normally, who cares, right? A harmless play on words. We can all laugh at ourselves. BUT, that woman was clearly attempting to offend Anna."

"What an idiot! She has no idea how incredible Anna is—what she has accomplished in her life; the people she has helped; what a friend she is!" exclaimed Ingrid.

Anna did not hear the kind words as she sat contentedly observing the faces illumined by the candlelight:
laughter from the gut
thoughts expressed openly
food eaten with gusto

Chapter Fifteen
Home

Olav had the constant struggle of maintaining the morale of his men. Although the Russian prairies were magnificent in their vastness and bountiful with crops ripening, without mountains the monotony made the soldiers melancholy. Any villages were already destroyed by the retreating Russians. The Russians deliberately left no food supply for the advancing German army.

To make matters worse, the High Command did not foresee the effects the Russian rainy season would have on the troops. They did not have adequate winter clothing or equipment essential for survival in the North. An early snowfall on October 10 melted, turning the roads to quagmire. More rain dragged tanks and motorcycles into at least 2 ft. of heavy red mud. The soldiers made little headway and were exhausted with the struggle of walking. Horses labored to haul the heavy guns out of the deep mud.

Supplies could not get through, and if the threat of starvation was not enough, they all knew that the Russian winter was coming. The High Command had arrogantly assumed the invasion would be over quickly as in the case of all of the other invasions—a fatal error. A *Blitzkrieg* had not been feasible under these conditions.

Despite these setbacks, by October 14 two million Russian civilians had left Moscow as the German army surrounded the city. It appeared that a German victory was at hand.

However, the Russians were on the move. By December the Russian counter attack stabilized their position and stopped the German advance near Moscow. Alongside tanks designed to travel in Russian conditions was the Russian cavalry thundering down snowy roads on hundreds of horses. They were agile. They were fast. They understood winter.

Troops from Siberia arrived armed, dressed in white camouflage and on skis, flying across the snow-covered terrain. They cut off supplies using guerrilla tactics.

Meanwhile, the German troops to the south were carrying out their orders. Olav buttoned up his overcoat and wrapped a scarf, which Mari had made, around his head. The men under his command were now a brotherhood, and he felt obliged to protect and encourage them to the best of his ability. He straightened his shoulders and clasped his hands behind his back as he marched down the line.

With every joke he made about the weather or words of praise for their courage, the men would rally, but the situation was too bleak to sustain optimism for very long.

The soldiers constantly suffered from dysentery and combined with extreme subzero temperatures another challenge presented itself.

The men had the choice of relieving themselves on the side of the road and risk freezing when they pulled down their trousers, or filling their pants with excrement and risk infection and disease. The men had to endure these indignities along with the constant itching from lice and scabies.

To mobilize the men suffering under these extreme conditions, Olav would often sing in his clear, tenor voice and soon his men would join in as together they marched against despair and insanity.

Spirits plummeted further when the Commander-in-Chief resigned his post in protest against Hitler's decision to continue the war on the Eastern Front. Then on December 6 the Russians attacked with shattering force.

After advancing 2,000 kilometers, the great German *Wehrmacht* was in full retreat. Hitler blamed his Prussian generals and appointed himself Commander-in-Chief.

The Muller family had adjusted to their new home supplied by the Nazis. Located in a subdivision on the outskirts of Leipzig, the house had modern conveniences and more space for the growing boys. The dining area had wooden paneling enriching the walls and built in wooden benches encircling three sides of the table. The living room had modern wall-to-wall carpeting, a sofa and oak table, and was the home of the family piano and an assortment of other instruments. Mari was thrilled with the refrigerator, as well as, the other appliances. Jobs, such as laundry, could be completed so much quicker and with less strain.

The family had also accepted their daily routine. The children were settled in school with new teachers and unfamiliar students. The factory where Anna worked was not far from the subdivision so she was able to commute to her job in less time.

When Anna arrived home from work at the factory one evening, she found her mother reading a letter at the kitchen table. Mari looked up, "I have a letter from *Vater*."

My Dearest Mari,   *December 15, 1941*

I awakened from a dream of you this morning. I could feel your presence all day. How I miss you, my darling. You must be very busy raising our children. I can't tell you how much I enjoy your letters about them. I regret that I cannot be there to see them grow up and to help you.

Who would have believed this war would last so long? The men have been struggling. Thousands have been taken, not just by the Russians but by severe frostbite, starvation, and dysentery.

The fuel freezes because there is no antifreeze so we light fires under the tanks to start them. Our machine guns won't fire and the telescopic sights are useless. I am sure help will come soon so please do not be concerned.

Perhaps I will be home by spring. Until then I will hold you in my dreams.

Yours always,
Olav

"How can this go on? Your father's account is very different from the news broadcast. I don't believe anything I hear on the radio anymore."

"I know… I wish we could do something… It may be a small thing, but perhaps we could send a bit of Christmas cheer. The children can make Christmas cards for *Vater* and Nat and the others."

"Rita, Christmas is coming! Let's make cards," Anna called as she found her box of cherished waste—bits of colorful wrap, wool, ribbon and paper she had stored over the years. We need cards for *Vati,* Nat, Karl, Klara, the Hoffmans, and *Tante Frieda* "What ideas do you have for Nat's card?"

Rita was looking over their materials in earnest. "I will make a card with a Christmas angel and a candle on the front," Rita replied. Anna watched as Rita's soft, white ten-year old hands fashioned beauty out of scraps.

Mari's red and calloused hands had made bread and cookies. They were covered in flour so she wiped them on her apron and came over to the table to see Rita's creation. "My *lochen,* Nathalie will love your card!" Rita sat back in her seat and lowered her head shyly. "I drew pictures of each of us inside so she would not be alone," Rita replied.

"We could all sign the card under each of our pictures inside the card. " Anna suggested. "Leo, Ralfie, Otto, come to the kitchen. We are making Christmas cards," Anna called.

"Look what Rita made for Nat. Let's sign in our neatest handwriting or printing," Anna said as she herded them around the table.

Soon the children were absorbed in constructing cards—quietly sharing materials, scissors, and ideas. Then Leo began to first hum and then sing *Kling Glockchen,* and they all joined in. It was a serene afternoon to be remembered or preserved like a scene inside a snow globe; an experience out of reach to Olav fighting on the Eastern Front.

Karl watched over the family as much as he could. He was able to spend more time with them since his apartment was closer to the Mullers now that they had moved to the new house. He would find whatever they were lacking in the black market—chiefly food items and Anna's *Kamel* cigarettes—and bring them to their house.

Also, since they had moved, Mari received double the ration slips, which was another benefit of being the wife of an SS officer. Compared with the majority of people in Leipzig, they were well-fed and Mari kept them well-dressed.

On Christmas Eve the Mullers awaited the arrival of their former neighbors, *Herr Wolfgang Hoffman, Frau Bertha Hoffman* and their children, Axel and Rosa. *Tante* Frieda was unable to join them and Klara was spending Christmas with her family at the Kalbfleisch Butcher shop. The Kalbfleisch's had given the Mullers a goose which was in the oven. Karl was already settled in with *Asbach Uralt* brandy and Anna sat with him smoking a cigarette.

When Mari, who had been in the kitchen cooking and baking most of the day, took off her apron, she looked radiant. Her face was flushed to a healthy pink and her eyes were dancing with spirit. She wore a mauve pullover sweater and grey and black check straight skirt for the special occasion.

She placed the *Weihnachtsengel* on the piano. The wooden Christmas angels playing instruments had been a gift from her parents. The Advent Wreath, made of cones and holding four candles, was in the center of the round oak table. Mari had made a special red Christmas table cloth for underneath the wreath. "Everyone come into the living room. Dim the lights now. Ralfie will be lighting the candles this year."

"The Hoffmans are here," Mari called out. "*Frohlich Weihnachten*! Wolfgang, Bertha! *Frohlich Weihnachten* Axel and Rosie!"

As soon as Axel had his winter outer wear off, Rita took him excitedly by the hand, "Come see the Advent Wreath and the boughs, Axel. I made you something for Christmas but you cannot have it yet. *Mutti* baked *Lebkuchen* and *Platzchen*. Do you want the gingerbread and a shortbread star or the moon cookie. Which one would you like?"

"I would like a star," replied Axel. Axel had just undergone a growth spurt and was a big-boned boy. He seemed much older than his years especially when compared with tiny Rita who was his own age.

"I will have the same as you. Sit beside me at the table, Axel." He followed Rita as she skipped in front of him.

Anna suggested, "While the goose is roasting, why don't we sing carols? Leo you can play the violin and Ralfie the piano. Sing the special one you have been practicing."

*"Even though we do not have a tree this year, I would like to sing a song to the trees of our past. On this snowy eve, we give you *O Tannenbaum,*"* Leo announced formally, as though he were conducting an orchestra in front of an audience of hundreds of people.

Olav would have been proud of their performance.

"And now, join us in Silent Night. I ask *Frau Hoffman* to lead us since I will be accompanying my brother on the flute."

The candles lit the faces gathered around as they all sang the familiar carol. The air was laden with the scent of food—apple and sausage stuffing, ginger from the *lebkuchen* cookies. Mari wiped a tear from the corner of her eye.

At that moment, outside of Berlin, Nathalie leafed quickly through the mail that had arrived at the lab, and stopped immediately when she recognized Anna's handwriting on an envelope. She sat down at her desk and carefully opened the Christmas card. "That must be Rita's work. What beautiful angels! The talent she possesses! And the family…there is my little Ralfie. His writing has improved. He added 'I love you Nattie.' Of course, no signature is below the figure of *Herr Muller*.

Like me, he is not home with the family either. Perhaps he too didn't realize it is Christmas. Superstition anyway," thought Nathalie. She couldn't admit to herself that the festive season brought back painful memories of Lena. Nathalie held the card, her smile lingering until she lovingly tucked it away in a box of treasures that included the portrait of Lena – away from prying eyes.

Abruptly, she returned to her research with zeal, forgetting the sentimental Christmas card, oblivious to the outside world. In truth, she had cut herself off from the outside world. She ignored the events of World War II and the machinations of the Nazis. In her lab she had found stability and purpose, a place where she was comfortable, at home.

Mari called from the back door, the snowstorm muffling her words, "Leo, stop teasing Otto or you will all have to come inside." Otto had quit playing snowball warfare and was making a snow angel. Rita had joined him. They could feel the cool dampness as large snowflakes landed on their faces. Otto closed his eyes and stuck out his tongue to capture snowflakes as they fell. Rita's thick eyelashes and braids were adorned with the white crystals.

Later that evening after the children had gone to bed, Mari, Karl, and Anna played cards. As Anna dealt the first three cards of *Skat,* she began talking about theatre news. "I cannot believe that we will never see another film with Joachim Gottschalk. His were my favorite films." *Mutti,* remember *Ein Leben Lang* with Paula Wessely. It was the biggest box office hit of the first year of the war.

"I liked *Das Maedchen von Fanoe* and *Die Schwedische Nachtigall*. We didn't have to put up with propaganda in those movies," added Karl as he picked up four more cards and thought about his trump.

"He was not a Jew. Why couldn't they have left him alone," protested Mari.

"The Propaganda Ministry harassed him for a long time because like the other *Artistenwelt* in the film industry, he would not conform, and also, the matter of his wife was a thorny problem. She was Jewish…He became famous despite the fact that Goebbels deprived him of any publicity in magazines and newspapers. Goebbels obsessively threatened him. He was told to divorce his wife and renounce his child or be banned from the movie industry forever. He would not succumb."

"How brave and such a story of love! What happened after he refused?"

"The Nazis arrived to take his wife and child to the East to be resettled. The entire *Gottschalk* family was waiting for them. Dead… They had chosen to remain forever together in their home."

Chapter Sixteen
Shell Shocked

"*Bombenlose Nacht*," greeted Karl as he saw one of Josef's Czech friends in the street. It was a cloudy day in the spring of 1942.

"*Bolona*," he nodded with a smile. The greeting for many Germans had shifted from "*auf Wiederseshen*" to "*Bolona*," short for Bombless Night. On such nights, they could actually get some sleep in their own beds instead of spending a large portion of the night in cellars and bomb shelters. People were often in a miserable mood from lack of sleep and hunger.

Karl could hear the train whistle in the distance and the sound of brakes as the trains made their way through the train station. The steam rose in the air and people milled about without much commotion. As a pressure valve released a high-pitched squeal, Karl turned off the main street and made his way to a less respectable part of the city. He stopped in front of an unobtrusive house by a brothel. After looking both ways, he walked around the corner and entered by a side door.

Karl was alert. The black market trade was volatile and Karl knew that should he ever let his guard down someone would smell an opportunity to exploit him. He did not care for the weasel-like Czech behind the counter. The man did not barter fairly.

"No! That is worth two packages of cigarettes and the chocolate," Karl insisted. The Czech shook his head. Karl stood firmly and stared at the man. The Czech shook his head again. Karl grabbed him by his thin throat and pulled him roughly to his face. "I said two packages of cigarettes and the chocolate! I haven't time for your games." Karl released the man's collar and pushed him roughly away.

The Czech then shrugged his shoulders and placed the cigarettes and chocolate on the counter. He squinted a bit and made an exaggerated apology,

"I guess I made a miss…take. The rate changed today. *Ja*, two packs and the chocolate is a fair exchange," the man sneered.

Karl backed up slowly, tucked the hard-won goods in his jacket, turned abruptly and left. It had begun to rain so he pulled his collar up and the rim of his cap down. He had walked maybe a block when a man almost bumped into him saying, "Hello friend, do you happen to have a light?"

As Karl reached in his jacket pocket, the assailant punched him in the gut. Karl buckled but stood up swiftly to head butt the man and then knee him in the groin. Karl heard a boot slide behind him and shifted to the side, but not before the club hit his neck and upper back. As the second man raised the club to swing again, Karl kicked him hard in the knee cap and then punched him in the head. When the man was on the sidewalk, Karl kicked him several times until the man lay still.

Karl quickly emptied their pockets and continued walking down the street. As soon as he could, he caught a tram. Out of the rain and away from the thugs, he sat with his arms across his chest and head lowered. Under his wool cap his face was hardly visible. "I should have waited until the evening to make deals with the others outside. These bastards don't know what they're doing." Karl was annoyed with the assault because his shoulder was sore, but was by no means disturbed in any other way. In fact, the scuffle had been a welcome outlet for his emotions.

Karl was raised on a tug that transported ships from the Baltic Sea down the Oder River to towns and cities. From the time he was a boy he had learned from his father about defending himself against the rough dock workers and thieves that often lived around the ports. Most of the boys he had met in his youth were tough as well, so he had his share of fighting long before he was in the Polish military.

Saturday night he would be playing cards with Anna and Mari. "I want Anna to have these cigarettes to persuade her Nazi bosses to promote her. She is too fine to be working alongside those other common girls on the line," he thought. "The chocolate will be a treat for Anna and her mother."

Sure enough, that evening, his gift was very much appreciated.

"Thank you, Karl! Chocolate! Come sit down, and I will fix you a drink," said Mari. Anna gave Karl a kiss that expressed her gratitude.

"Should we play cards?" asked Anna.

"Of course," responded Mari.

"*Skat?*"

"Is there another card game?" laughed Karl. A comfortable warmth filled his chest and belly, but it wasn't just the brandy. He liked taking care of these women. He felt manly. They treated him with respect and love. They smelled clean and lovely, delicious—a welcome break from his friends at the apartment.

"How are Josef and Klara?" asked Anna. "I have not heard from Klara for awhile."

"Klara has been working long hours at the hospital so they don't see one another as often...

Josef has told me some important news. I do not know if you have heard." He ended on a solemn note. The women put their cards down.

"The Czech underground has killed Reinhard Heydrich. Two Czech men trained by the British were the leaders in the assassination."

"My God," exclaimed Mari. "How on earth did they get to him? Heydrich was in the High Command."

"The details are unclear but Josef said that Heydrich was riding in an open automobile with only his driver. No bodyguards or military escort. One of the assassins attempted to shoot him and failed and the second threw a grenade which landed in the automobile and hit Heydrich. He did not die immediately and the underground thought their mission had failed, but he eventually died in Prague a few days later from the shrapnel."

"What will Adolf do in retaliation?" Anna interjected.

"Well, this will not go unpunished. The Nazis are outraged that one of their own leaders could be killed by a small band of disorganized Czechs. Josef is ecstatic about the victory, says the bastard, Heydrich, underestimated his people, thought he had mastered them and that they were now loyal subjects. He says this hit was sanctioned by the Czech government not just the Resistance."

"*Obergruppenfuhrer Reinhard Heydrich* dead. I do not believe it! He was Himmler's right hand," said Mari. "And the assassins?"

"Josef does not know for sure but thinks they are still in hiding."

In the Muller kitchen they had no knowledge of the scope of Reinhard Heydrich's atrocities delivered upon the German people and the rest of Europe. They had no knowledge of his plan for the Final Solution to exterminate all

Jews in Europe. They could not know that this plan was moving forward without him.

"No one has ever succeeded in previous attempts to kill the Fuhrer or High Command," remarked Mari.

"Let's play another hand," Anna suggested. "Brandy, Karl?"

On Monday morning heading to work, Anna lit a cigarette and thought about securing a promotion at the factory. "I have a package of cigarettes from Karl. I will use the cigarettes to persuade *Herr Kramer* and *Herr Grob* that I am capable of managing the floor."

As she took her place on the assembly line, *Herr Grob* approached her with a swagger to his step. She was immediately on edge from his body cue.

"I hear you are going with a Pollack," he stated accusingly.

"No," Anna angrily retorted, "He is half and half. His mother is German." The Nazi took another menacing step closer. Anna hissed, "Give me the phone and I'll call my father in Russia. He is *Oberleutnant* in the 6th. He can talk to you about this matter."

Herr Grob became red in the face. After a pause he hissed, "All right we'll leave it." He spun around and marched away to bully another woman.

Anna turned to her job and seethed with each of her movements. "How could I lose my temper again and over remarks made by such a stupid man? Frieda trained me better than that. I must learn to control myself or one of these days they will send me away to a work camp.

Where are the camps and why do they even have such things especially when we are in a world war?" she asked herself. Her mind then wandered to Olav, "And *Vater*, oh *Vater* where are you; how are you? Ahh, I cannot concentrate on my bosses right now… They will be here tomorrow."

Mari was discouraged by her circumstances, as well. She stood in line for food rations and later sewed what she could while the house was quiet. "I have so very little business since my wealthy Jewish customers have been moved east to reservations or work camps.

The others have no money to spare for new clothing. I am reduced to mending or altering garments so they can be worn again. Little Gunther was thrilled with his older brother's hand-me-down trousers that I altered. I patched his vest so no one would see where the hole was. He was such a proud boy in his new clothes," she smiled to herself. All her work was for the few food, household items, or favors that she could barter.

Mari was exhausted but hid her vulnerability from her children. She must remain steadfast for them. She could not control the escalating chaos in Germany, but she controlled what occurred in her home. "My family and I will live with dignity regardless of how others choose to live, what Adolf makes us endure, makes us become," she said out loud, and then thought:

"Today I cannot even cry
I must clean my home
I am too calm
Somewhere beyond sad
Somewhere beyond fear
Somewhere beyond hope
But I am still open"

That evening Mari knew she needed help. She left Anna with the children and sought the solace of the church and the words of the priest to quell her fears. As she entered Saint Thomas church, Mari breathed in the peace and calm emanating from the wood, the stained glass, the cross, and the statue of the Virgin Mary. The very air seemed to create a protective shield around her.

After blessing herself with the holy water and genuflecting before the cross, Mari lit votive candles for her parents and older brother and then prayed for their souls. Slowly rising, she sought her quiet pew in front of a stained glass window. On the kneeler she began reciting Hail Mary's on her rosary beads. The repetition drove away confusing thoughts and helped her focus.

She then disappeared into prayer. The priest's voice was melodic as he recited Latin and the organ music was Beethoven, Mari's favorite. Communion that day elevated her soul to a place she had not been for many months.

At home Anna prepared a simple meal while her mother was at church, and Rita played hopscotch on the sidewalk. She had no chalk but had easily sketched the squares for the game with a rock. She hummed sweetly while she tossed her flat stone and hopped on one foot being careful not to step on the lines. "Is no one around to play with you?" called Anna from the front door.

"The boys are playing guns, and I didn't want to call on anyone. Besides I only like to play hopscotch with Axel. He doesn't cheat," Rita answered as a matter-of-fact.

Anna knew how sad Rita was to be apart from Axel so she asked, "Would you like me to play with you? And then we will go inside for supper." The sisters sang as they played hopscotch. Anna let Rita win. Smiling they rounded up the boys to come inside the house.

Otto now seven years of age was allowed to stay outside under the supervision of his older brothers, Leo and Ralfie. With Olav away, Leo, now thirteen, was the eldest man in the family. He took his role seriously since Karl set him straight.

Although Anna checked on the boys frequently, she trusted them to stay out of trouble. Lately, the war had made them all more insular.

The children were in bed when Mari returned from evening mass. Anna was relieved to see serenity replacing the taut, expressionless look on her mother's face. She knew the recent letter from Olav saying he would be delayed had affected Mari deeply.

"Would you like coffee, *Mutti*, if we can call this concoction coffee."

"Yes, *mein lieb*," replied Mari as she slid onto the bench at the kitchen table. "When was the last time you were able to go to mass? You always have so much to do. You scarcely have time to see your Karl."

"I am fine, *Mutti*," Anna tried to reassure her mother. "As long as we are all safe. I am fine. It is much worse for others."

Mari and Anna were scarcely asleep when they heard the siren at 1:00 a.m. They met in the hallway and like a trained response team moved efficiently to awaken the children, wrap them in coats, and retreat quickly to the cellar. Mari brought some water and blankets while Anna carried Otto. He was crying softly, half asleep and scared. "Will the bomb kill us tonight, Anna," he asked.

"You will stay on my lap so I can hug you. You won't be alone." Anna soothed. She could never lie to quell fear in another. She did not know if they would be bombed or if they would survive the night, but she did know she could make her brother feel safe and loved at that moment.

Rita leaned on her shoulder and Ralfie and Leo were on either side of Mari. Sometimes when the bomb scare was earlier in the night, Leo or Ralfie would play an instrument or they would sing or hum a song to buoy their spirits and pass the time. Anna would sometimes read a book out loud or tell a story.

However, everyone was always aware of the unmistakable thunder of the bombs despite the well intentioned distractions. Tonight the family was quiet, dozing periodically until the signal screamed at 4:00 a.m. Sleepy they returned to their beds until it was time for school and work.

The strain of attack was constant but somehow the summer weather soothed troubled minds and broken hearts. Karl said to Anna one evening after supper, "Why, don't we get away from the factory at lunch time and have a picnic at the park? We could have a refreshing swim in the midday heat. We will have a break from our horrid jobs."

"But Karl, we don't have the same lunch break, and besides, we won't have enough time will we?" questioned Anna.

"Now that you are the boss of the factory floor, I am sure that you can switch your lunch break with someone. I have your father's motorcycle to use so I am confident I can get us back to work on schedule. We will have fun, Anna," insisted Karl.

"You are right. I would love to swim this week. The weather has been so hot," she acquiesced.

Karl packed some bread and cheese and a bit of smoked pork for their picnic. When he pulled up to the large airplane parts and munitions plant, Anna was waiting. Her face was beaming with anticipation. He was overcome with love for her and yet also felt the weight of sadness. The war was depressing everyone. He realized he had not seen Anna look so happy for a very long time.

When they reached the park, they raced each other into the pool. "Ahh," Anna thought, "I am back." They floated together and kissed and then Karl said, "Hungry, Anna? I will set up our picnic spot behind the beech tree over there so we can have some shade."

"Sure. I will be along in a minute." Anna dove under the water to the silence. She swam until she thought her lungs would burst and then shot up for air. Karl watched her emerge from the water and walk to shore. She smiled and waved; and when she reached him, dripped cold water over him.

"My shirt is wet! You..." He grabbed her and wrapped her in the blanket. Come here and eat. Anna sat down laughing and reached hungrily for the food. As she accepted the bread and cheese, she kissed Karl on his lips and then his shoulder.

After they had changed back into their work clothes, Anna said, "Let's go over to our tree and sit in the shade for a few more minutes."

"Sure, you know I can get us back to work on time as long as you aren't afraid of a little speed," he teased.

The summer heat and the break from her worries made her crave sex with Karl. She pulled him to her and then turned around with her elbows on the large branch in front, facing the park. She dropped her panties so he could enter her from behind, but to an onlooker he was only hugging her. His large hands stroked her smooth bottom. She was ready.

When he entered her, the sensation travelled up her spine and into the back of her head. She slowly ground her hips back and forth against his groin. He reached under her blouse for her breast. "Oh God, Anna!" he growled as he dropped his head and closed his eyes.

Anna turned around and they kissed, but an air raid siren interrupted what she wanted to say. "We need to get out of here NOW!" shouted Karl as he grabbed Anna's hand and their bag and made for the motorcycle.

They saw the plane in the distance and then the bomb strike over the vicinity of Anna's factory. It all happened so fast. As they drew closer to the factory, they saw the black clouds of dust and flames and heard the hollow roar of wood and concrete breaking apart. Karl stopped the motorcycle and they robotically got off and stood together looking at the specter in front of them. Neither spoke. The plant was annihilated, rubble scattered everywhere.

Anna continued to stare and then shook her head over and over. "We should look for survivors."

When he saw how shaken she was, Karl immediately slipped his arm around her waist and guided her to the motorcycle.

"I am taking you home now."

Mari knew something was wrong when she heard the motorcycle pull up. They were supposed to be at work. Also, she had heard an air raid siren which was rare during the day. Running to meet them she cried, "Anna, are you all right, *mein lieb*? What has happened?"

Karl helped her off the motorcycle and Mari wrapped her arm around Anna's waist. Together they entered the house and made for the kitchen.

The couple sat speechless at the table while Mari fixed them all a shot of brandy. Finally, Karl said, "They hit the factory. It appears to be completely destroyed. There was nothing we could do. Hundreds of people!"

"If you hadn't asked me to go for a picnic and swim; if I hadn't changed my lunch hour to be the same as yours, I would be among the dead. Karl you have saved my life." Anna dropped her head into her hands and closed her eyes. Her mind repeated, "Timing is everything…timing is everything."

Chapter Seventeen
Concealment

Anna found a job at Karl's place of employment, *Erla Werke,* another aircraft manufacturing plant outside of Leipzig. Years before, Anna's father had worked at the factories when they were being established. They had provided much needed employment for Germans.

Now the workers were primarily German women and forced labor from occupied countries. The *auslanders* were housed in barracks beside the plants, private apartments, schools or hotels. They received standard wages and rations.

However, an echelon existed according to race, with the Jews holding the lowest position. They seldom received the promised payment or rations and were guaranteed the most uncomfortable accommodations.

Because Karl was half German and had received valuable training in mechanics, he was able to stay in an apartment with his Czech friend who also had specializations. Regardless of their status, all employees worked twelve-hour shifts. Karl and Anna were able to take a break together. Probably the only thing they enjoyed during their day.

Anna was placed in finishing and Karl was in another section of the plant in parts. Karl accepted his position and deliberately avoided attention of any kind, while Anna, on the other hand, had no intention of blending in with the hundreds of other workers on the lines.

She immediately began observing the interactions among the Nazi supervisors to understand how to best manipulate them. The worst among them and the top of the food chain was *Herr Weiss*. He had a reputation for gratuitous cruelty. Anna's attention and black market gifts were targeted at him.

Weiss' imperious finger was constantly in the face of the labor, as well as, other supervisors. It was a common sight to see him whip slow workers with his crop.

Herr Weiss was pedantic, swelling with authority and conviction when he identified an individual breaking a rule, regardless of how slight the infraction. He was full of criticism and insults and empty of praise, neither friendly nor even civil to anyone. Anna continued her watch.

On her way to the washroom one morning, she chose a route that took her past *Herr Weiss'* office. He was talking to another supervisor. "Look at how straight he sits in his chair with his face impassive, and yet under the desk his leg is moving in a rapid jiggling motion. Ahh, inwardly, he is irritated, impatient, maybe insecure," Anna thought. "He lit a cigarette! Good."

The next day, Anna decided to pay *Herr Weiss* a visit in his office. "Excuse me *Herr Weiss,* I am *Frauline Anna Muller* and have been recently transferred to your factory because I am the only known survivor of a recent bombing." Anna noted the man's tiny, precise printing.

"And what is it that you want, special survivor, *Frauline Muller?*" he answered superciliously. "You are away from your bench. Do not waste my time," ordered *Herr Weiss*.

"Clearly you are the man in charge of this factory." Anna's voice was loaded with respect and admiration. "Because this is a new job for me, I want to be certain that I am following the rules and completing my job properly.

My father is an *Oberleutnant* in Russia and my brothers are proud Hitler Youth. I too want to do my part for *Mein Fuhrer* with the utmost efficiency."

"Of course… *Frauline?"* he asked raising his voice.

"Anna Muller, *mein Herr. Heil Hitler*." Anna smiled formally as she left. Her manner revealed confidence and poise. "I will make sure he remembers my name," Anna thought as she returned to her work bench.

On the way home, Anna thought about the Nazi, *Herr Weiss*, "I will watch and wait for an opportunity to approach him again."

Anna was tired as she sat at the kitchen table with her mother. Mari said, "Would you like to read the letter from *Vater*? It sounds hopeful."

My Dearest Mari,   *August 17, 1942*

We are finally on the move once more. The horses are strong enough to pull the carts of supplies. Today the countryside appears quite peaceful. The fields are lush green and the sky as clear a blue as you could hope for. After our long stationary period, the men have recovered somewhat both in spirit and health. We are marching south to the oil fields while another wing of the 6th heads east to take Stalingrad. We have had no encounters with the Red Army.

We expect to take over the much needed oil supply for our navy, air force and army so we can see this war to its conclusion. I am confident that the siege of Stalingrad will be over by September since we have met with little resistance.

You mentioned in your last letter that Karl is of some assistance to you and Anna. This brings me great relief. He is a good man.

I cannot quite take in the magnitude of the simple lunch date Karl and Anna had in July. The factory was bombed! Thanks be to God for sparing our child.

I knew Leo and Ralfie would continue to do well in their studies but how does Otto fare? Tell Leo to practice his violin concertos and Ralfie needs to keep up with his etudes on the piano. I miss you all so very much, my darling.

Olav

"I miss him, *Mutti*. I pray he returns before another year passes."

"Let's send him another parcel. Do you think Rita could paint a picture he might like?"

"I will talk to her about it and perhaps she will have an idea for *Vater*. Most of her pictures are realistic sketches of people in Leipzig—everyday scenes. Here she is."

Rita now twelve years of age had remained petite. She would never reach five feet eight inches tall like her older sister. Rita's long, brown hair fell to the base of her back and was generally plaited in two braids. Her large soft brown eyes reflected her gentle, shy personality.

"Let me brush your hair, Rita." Anna loosened the braids and began brushing the thick hair. With her left hand she held the hair at the scalp and brushed with her right hand the full length of Rita's hair. With smooth rhythmic strokes she brushed until the hair shone.

"*Mutti* would like to send a parcel to *Vati*. Will you paint a picture to cheer him?" Anna began.

Rita's eyes were closed while she enjoyed the brushing. Without opening her eyes, she replied, "I will make a picture of Leo playing the violin."

"He would like that very much, my little one!" said Mari. Rita's insights always shocked and touched Mari deeply.

When it was time for bed, Anna followed Rita, and together they said prayers. Before tucking Rita in for the night, Anna asked, "Will you show me any of your pictures Rita?"

Without hesitation Rita got up and reached under the bed where her sketches and paintings were hidden from view. She gave the sheaf of paper and canvases to Anna and sat beside her. Slowly and carefully Anna studied each picture. She saw black and white sketches of soldiers. Another picture showed only a face and helmet. A canvas depicted women in a ration line with baby carriages, holding toddlers in their arms. The nature of the subjects and composition of the artwork was far beyond the level of any twelve-year old girl. Rita was most certainly a gifted artist.

"I hardly know what to say… We have become numb to these images in our lives. You remind us to see and feel. Do you sketch at school, Rita?" asked Anna suddenly very concerned.

Rita looked down and paused. "Sometimes I draw but hide the picture in the back of my notebook."

"Your teacher might not approve of your pictures. She may harm you."

"But why would she do that? I am a good girl," Rita asked ingenuously.

"She might think your paintings portray a bad side of the Third Reich. Teachers would rather see pictures of smiling children and soldiers marching. Think of a parade. They would like to see the happy faces of children waving pennants with the swastika on them."

"I do not go to many parades. This is what I see," insisted Rita.

"Listen to me, *lochen*," Anna cautioned firmly as she put her arm around Rita's shoulders. "The teacher could call the Gestapo, and then they would come dressed in their black uniforms and take you away from us. They could take you away to another family or to a work camp."

"What is that?"

"It is a place where people are punished. They live together in large cold buildings and work all day. They have very little food or water and they are beaten often. You do not want to go to a work camp do you?

You must speak of this to no one at school—no one anywhere but *Mutti*. Do you understand?" Anna said desperately.

"I'm scared, Anna!" Rita cried with a trembling voice and tears running down her face.

"Now you know to be very careful. Keep your remarkable pictures hidden from view at home and only draw happy pictures of children and pets to please your teacher when you are at school. Draw a pretty picture of your teacher maybe?"

"She is not pretty," Rita said with a sly smile and a giggle as she wiped the tears from her face.

"I love you so much *lochen!*"

During the autumn of 1942, radio broadcasts again reported a successful Russian campaign at Stalingrad to mask the truth from German civilians. In fact, Hitler denied the requests for food, medical supplies, and of course, assistance from the rest of the army; and instead, urged the army to make the ultimate sacrifice for the Third Reich.

Hitler had underestimated the Russian savvy in defending their country. Stalin had no intention of letting his namesake city, Stalingrad, go to the Germans. The Russians brought in recruits and supplies from the East and ferried troops across the Volga. They took over bombed buildings as strongholds and hid from the Germans, using guerrilla or gangster tactics.

But all Anna and Mari heard was the propaganda on the radio and newspapers saying, "The war is coming to an end. We will be victorious." Life continued in the Muller home.

"Rita, please read to me while I am ironing and later we will work on your arithmetic," said Anna. "And Leo, you and Ralfie practice your music in the living room."

Anna listened to Rita stumble with each word she read, but was convinced that by reading from her primer daily, Rita could reach the standards required to pass her year.

Mari prepared the evening meal while she listened to the boys' music. Otto played with his soldiers nearby in the kitchen. Mari was warmed by the harmony among her children and consciously looked at them around the table to imprint their faces at that moment into her memory.

Karl arrived after the children were in bed and asked if he could talk with Mari. "*Frau Muller,* I would like to take Anna to meet my mother in Warsaw. She works for the mayor and he has arranged a New Year's celebration that we are invited to attend. Do I have your permission?"

The previous calm left Mari as she inwardly panicked at the idea of Anna crossing the border. She did not want her daughter to go to Warsaw. "My God," she thought, "Anna has never been far from home. What if they make trouble for her at the border? I know they will marry soon and Karl is anxious to introduce her to his mother. I suppose they need some happiness… I will hide my concern."

She agreed, "Yes, Karl, you and Anna deserve a holiday and I should think your mother misses her son terribly. I know I would certainly miss you."

"All right then we will make arrangements, Anna. I will let Mother know," Karl ended the conversation with a nod and hint of a smile.

The next day at the factory Anna put the plan into motion, "*Herr Weiss, Heil Hitler!*" greeted Anna as she approached her superior. "May I have a moment to discuss a personal matter?"

He looked importantly at his pocket watch and then nodded and motioned to his office. When they were settled, Anna began, "I have disciplined Christa as you requested and would like to be certain that my actions meet with your approval." *Herr Weiss* nodded.

Anna went on, "I have assigned her to clean the lavatory on her break for one week. Do you think the time is sufficient for her to reflect on her lazy habits?"

"Yes, *Frauline Muller,*" he replied. "You have not made me regret promoting you. Keep it that way."

"Thank you. Would you care for a cigarette, *mein Herr*?" Anna passed him a package of cigarettes. He took one and motioned to return the package. "Please keep them. I must return to work, *Heil Hitler?*"

Three months had passed since Anna had received her promotion, and she was already enjoying the benefits of manipulating the authorities. Soon she intended to broach the subject of her trip to Poland with her now malleable boss. To authorize the trip, she required his approval and signature on formal papers.

In the meantime, Anna pretended to be pregnant and bribed the midwife, who had delivered all of the Muller children, to sign the forms stating that she was pregnant. Anna figured that pregnancy was the best insurance for a safe and unimpeded border crossing. "Yes, young, blonde, German and pregnant— the ideal woman," she smiled.

On their lunch break Anna asked Karl, "Why can't you travel to Warsaw with me?" He had told her that he would be entering Poland illegally with a friend of his. Apparently, it was the only way he could avoid problems. "I have not even met this friend Sigmund. How do we know he can be trusted?" she persisted.

Karl was intractable, "Anna, the border guards will not permit me to leave Germany. I am forced labor in Germany. If I defy them I could be sent east to the work camps. Weiss would never sign my papers. I am forced labor. Do you understand? I will tell him I was off with pneumonia when we return." The conversation ended sharply when an employee rounded the corner. No one could be trusted. They returned to work.

"*Herr Weiss* may we talk today, when convenient for you?" Anna asked politely.

"Yes, at 2:15 you may come to my office," was his brusque reply.

At 2:13 Anna knocked on his door. "I have good news to share with you, *Herr Weiss*. I want you to know that I am pregnant with my first child. I want to do my part for our Aryan race."

"Congratulations!" he said neither pleased nor shocked about her announcement. Marriage was not a moral issue for the Nazis. Children were the priority.

"With your permission I would like to visit relatives in Poland in the *Sudetanland*. Is it possible to take some time around New Year's to make the trip? Do I require papers from you *mein Herr*?... I have papers here to prove that I am pregnant. Would you like to examine them?" Anna requested courteously as she passed him the forms.

"This appears to be in order. I will give you permission," he agreed coldly and signed the papers with a flourish.

"I am most grateful," Anna smiled as she rose to leave.

"You have four days," Herr Weiss stated as he looked down at a stack of charts he was updating. He had purposefully made her trip impossible.

And then it happened inside Anna again. "Four days?" She replied angrily. "That is not enough time. I would have to turn around and return to Leipzig as soon as I arrived. I will be too exhausted from travelling and would be at risk at this time in my pregnancy. I do not wish to lose my baby! Do you want to be responsible for killing my unborn child?" Anna protested vehemently.

"Take it or leave it!" *Herr Weiss* barked.

"I will be back when I am ready!" Anna stormed out of the office.

Her heart was pounding as she returned to her bench. "What have I done?" And yet no reprimand ensued, no Weiss beating her with his crop. No work camp.

"We are going to Warsaw for New Years, Karl! I have my papers."

"I will leave first and meet you there. Mother and I will pick you up at the station. I must send word to her soon. She will be very pleased."

Before they knew it Christmas had arrived, and it was Karl's turn to leave for Warsaw. Anna and Karl took the trolley car to the train station. It was hectic with travelers returning home for Christmas. Karl knew the train master and had already bribed him for the train schedules on that night. He and Sigmund would meet a couple of hundred feet outside the station in the darkness and then cross the tracks to a train of box cars eastbound that night.

Karl turned to Anna and held her tightly. "I will come for you, Anna. You know I will." He kissed her lips, and she clung to his neck.

He gently pushed her away and swung his knapsack over his shoulder. He was moving in the direction of the industrial outskirts of the station. Suddenly, Anna called, "Karl?" He quickly turned to face her and she mouthed, "I love you."

Karl winked and then disappeared into the shadows. "Anna has rarely said that to me," He thought with warmth before he focused on the night ahead.

He saw a shape in the darkness where the men were to meet. Sigmund's face became illuminated when he struck a match and held it to the end of his cigarette. Sigmund's shoulders were hunched against the cold night air. Karl swiftly reached him, "Put that out. Don't you know how to shield the end of your cigarette with your hand! Let's move. Be quiet because even though it is winter, our boots will be heard on the heavy ballast. We have no wind tonight. Sound will travel."

They crossed the rail yard about 150 yards from the station and slipped around a car in the mid-section of their train. Karl opened his jacket so that his belt was free. Attached to his belt was a hook he had milled for the purpose of latching himself to the undercarriage of the car. Sigmund followed. Karl hoisted himself up by grasping the brake pipe and then attached the hook securely to the pipe. He quickly placed his feet and elbows onto the base of the I-beam supports.

As he was adjusting the position of his knapsack, Sigmund tripped on the rail and made a scuffing sound on the ballast. Alarmed he recovered as quickly as he could and was beside Karl. "Make no sound. Someone may have heard," Karl whispered.

The heavy sound of footsteps in the snow and gravel was nearing their position. The young men controlled their breathing when they heard the guard stop beside their boxcar. "What the hell is he doing?" thought Karl, his heart pounding. Soon he smelled the match and cigarette. The guard seemed to take an inordinate amount of time to smoke and relieve himself. Eventually, he was summoned and marched away at once. Karl and Sigmund breathed a sigh of relief.

The side sill on the boxcar dropped low enough that the guard was not able to see their bodies tucked up underneath. He would have to squat down and crane his neck from side to side to see. Most guards were too lazy to squat but some would sweep under the cars with semi-automatic rifles. This form of travel was always dangerous.

Although Karl had made the trip to Warsaw before, he had checked with the train master to ascertain the number of stops before they reached the yard in Warsaw. However, he also knew that when at war, German trains could be stopped at any time within the German borders. No guarantees. Karl's senses were heightened to detect any signs of danger. The train continued on schedule though, creating a hypnotic, metallic rhythm as it rolled along the tracks to Poland.

The train whistle broke the night air and the brakes squealed alerting the young men as they approached Warsaw. Karl tapped Sigmund's shoulder so he would be ready to drop when the train stopped on the outskirts of the city to switch tracks. This was long enough for the men to swiftly disappear into the night. They had arrived safely and eluded the guards. A surge of adrenalin took them to a backstreet bar.

The next day in Leipzig, Anna left her concerned family. Rita was weeping in the doorway reaching out her hand to Anna. "Don't go, Anna, please don't go."

"My darling, Rita," Anna consoled as she hugged her sister tightly. "I will be home soon… Guess what. I will bring back a gift for each of you," Anna promised as she left for the station. When she boarded the train for Poland, her heart was heavy. She had never been far from Leipzig and her family.

Once the train was moving, however, she forced thoughts of Rita and Mari aside and instead imagined the excitement of the mayor's New Year's party. She drifted into a deep sleep and wasn't disturbed until the train arrived in Warsaw.

Karl and his mother were waiting at the station as promised.

"*Frau Lowe* what a pleasure to finally meet you," Anna said in German. "I must confess that Karl speaks German well, and so I have been only very slowly learning to speak Polish."

"Welcome to Warsaw, Anna," responded *Frau Lowe*. "Karl has told me so much about you, and I can see he was not exaggerating."

Anna appreciated that while austere in her dress and mannerisms, Karl's mother could express warmth in her beautiful brown eyes. Her grey hair was pulled straight back into a bun at the nape of her neck and she wore no makeup. This made a pair of high quality gold teardrop earrings with rubies against a dark ermine collar even more striking.

As they drove through Warsaw in a sleek black car, Anna alternated between listening to their conversation and staring quietly out of the window. Karl and his mother spoke German primarily but often switched to Polish words and phrases.

Anna interrupted them courteously, "Excuse me, but who…are…all of those…people and why…are they behind the fence?" she asked transfixed by the sight.

"This is the Jewish ghetto," answered *Frau Lowe* gravely, "They are awaiting transportation east for resettlement. The Nazis moved 250,000 people last summer."

Anna was stone quiet for the rest of the drive as she remembered the pogrom in Germany, in November of 1938. She thought of Mr. Wolfe and his family. Were they brought here?

Frau Lowe's apartment contrasted sharply with the ghetto. It was elegant with a high ceilings, traditional wooden furniture and heavy brocade fabric on the sofa and window coverings. The art, china, glassware, lace and linens all gave a formality to the rooms.

Karl's sister, Roksana lived with her mother and worked as a secretary at the city office. Their lives clearly did not resemble their former life on the Oder River.

"Karl, this is the last letter I received from your father," *Frau Lowe* said in Polish as she passed a note to her son. "I have not heard from him since."

After Karl read the note, he held it in his hand for a few minutes before returning it to his mother. "I don't understand. Where is he…?" he asked in Polish. His mother shook her head and stood up quickly turning to look at Anna.

"Let us have some food and a drink to celebrate your arrival, Anna," *Frau Lowe* said in German.

Anna smiled politely, "Thank you. I am very happy to meet you and be welcomed into your home." Anna realized that she was now the *auslander*. There was much that she did not know about Karl's family and his previous life.

The mayor's party was on New Year's Eve. Six grand rooms were decorated for the holiday season. Tables were covered with food in quantities Anna had never seen before—chocolates, dark rye breads, blocks of cheese, roasted geese, hams, fruits. She was most impressed by a torte with 20 layers.

Karl and she danced and sang together. Then, Karl danced with his mother and Roksana while Anna danced with the mayor. She was introduced to various politicians and business people and exchanged pleasantries with poise. She had been educated very well in Frieda's charm school.

Late that night when Karl and she were alone, Anna asked, "How long has your father been missing?"

"About two years."

"What do you believe has happened to him? Was he conscripted?" probed Anna.

"He is an officer in the Polish army. I am sure we will receive an explanation soon," Karl mollified Anna.

"Your sister doesn't say very much. Is she shy?"

"Yes, very."

"I noticed blue and black blotches on your mother's skin. What happened to her?"

"Frostbite. She escaped from a Russian camp following WWI and walked across country during the winter with her sister and brother," was Karl's terse reply.

"Karl! *Mein Gott*! You never told me," Anna whispered. "Why was she in a camp?"

"It is over. I do not want to talk about it now, *putchen*."

"I understand," said Anna. She knew it was a personal affront to pry and she had pushed him too far.

The remaining days of the holiday included secretive conversations among the Lowes of which she was not a part; however, they entertained her in elegant settings. Anna instinctively knew how to adapt to Karl's family culture.

On the train returning to Leipzig, Anna reflected on her visit in Warsaw, "*Frau Lowe* is a mystery, Roksana a wooden figure, and *Herr Lowe* most certainly a ghost. Karl is so different from them; so different when he is with them.

He is an approachable, large personality, strong, and capable. And…he knows how to take care of others. Yes, he always knows the right thing to do." Suddenly, Anna was overwhelmed with love for Karl. She missed him terribly and worried about him travelling uncomfortably in the cold suspended under a train.

Anna didn't know that *Frau Lowe* needed more time with Karl to complete her mission. She gave Karl an envelope.

"Wait at the station in Leipzig for one hour after your arrival. A man will approach you."

"How will I know him, Mother?"

"He will find you, Son. He will say, 'We all pray that 1943 will be a good year.' If he does not show within the hour, leave and destroy the envelope."

Having arrived in Leipzig, Karl shouldered his knapsack and lit a cigarette. He did not have to wait long. A shadowy man stopped not far from him and set down his package of belongings. Karl nodded in recognition of the code phrase and shook the man's hand while slipping him the envelope.

"*Auf Wiederschen*," Karl turned and left the station with a steady, purposeful walk, cap pulled down on his forehead. Although his head was lowered slightly, his eyes darted back and forth surreptitiously to catch any sign of danger.

Meanwhile, Anna had returned to her job after her lengthy holiday. She fabricated a convincing story about losing the baby while on her trip, and so *Herr Weiss* did not reprimand her when she returned late from Warsaw.

Karl produced medical papers indicating that he had been ill with pneumonia and unable to work. No repercussions. They returned to their winter routine of daily survival.

It was Mr. Wolfe's shadowy figure that had left the train station at the same time as Karl in possession of the envelope. He boarded a tram bound for Frieda's salon with information to decode.

"They need more weapons and explosives in the Warsaw ghetto, Frieda. They have plans for an uprising this month. Bunkers have been built and they are training.

Also, I have news of the *Wehrmacht* in Stalingrad. A Russian victory is imminent. The German soldiers have no more supplies. They have run out of munitions and food, eating raw horse meat to survive. They are succumbing to malnutrition, typhoid; and, of course, frostbite.

And there's more. Another assassination attempt on Adolf is in the works."

Frieda shook her head wide-eyed.

However, once more Adolf Hitler survived an attempt on his life unscathed. It was March, 1943 when Operation Flash was attempted. Hitler was flying to Russia to speak to the troops. The conspirators, Prussian officers known to Hitler, intended to bomb his aircraft in the air so it would look like an accident. This would clear the way for a coup.

Determined, the conspirators placed a bomb concealed in a brandy box aboard the aircraft. The charge in the bomb was sufficient to blow up the entire plane, but it malfunctioned and did not fire. At least the bomb was retrieved before the conspirators were discovered. Undaunted, the conspirators decided to try again.

Major Rudolf-Christoph von Gersdoriff volunteered for the honor of conducting a suicide mission. Two bombs were hidden in his overcoat. He planned to lead Hitler, Goering, Himmler and the rest of the entourage through an exhibit of Russian weaponry in Berlin, and then assassinate them all when the bombs exploded. All he required was ten minutes for the bombs to detonate.

Although Hitler had allowed half an hour for the briefing, he suddenly cut the meeting short and disappeared from the building by a side door into the street. In the end, only the conspirators, many of whom were clergy, were the only ones shattered by the outcome of the Overcoat Bombs mission.

Like so many others in Germany, who fought against the ideology of the Third Reich, Mr. Wolfe and Frieda were beleaguered. They were discouraged by the failed assassination attempts and were devastated by news of the Warsaw ghetto rebellion.

Although the remaining Jewish people had fought bravely, their rebellion had ended in flames. *SS Brigadefuhrer Jurgen Stroop* ordered the burning of the ghetto block by block, resulting in thousands of people being burned alive or suffocated. Mr. Wolfe and Frieda sat in despair for a long while after hearing about the tragedy.

"I can imagine their screams mixed with the roar of the fire. When will this agony stop, Frieda?"

In Warsaw *Frau Lowe* wept.

Chapter Eighteen
Ultimatums

Anna was late again. This time she was, in fact, pregnant. Her thoughts collided, "How can Karl and I possibly have a child during the war? We barely have enough food for the family anymore, even on *Vater's* pension. I need to barter on the black market to feed them. *Mutti* needs my help. How would we manage with the burden of another child? What should I do?

Karl would be such a good husband and father. I long for a family with him someday. I must talk to Klara."

Later as Anna sat in the tram en route to meet Klara, she remembered an incident at school. A sparrow had hit the window and sat stunned, its head drooping dangerously to one side. Klara quickly picked up the tiny bird and held it inside her cupped hands with her thumbs covering the bird's back. Encircled by Klara's protective fingers, only the head peeked out.

Anna said to leave it, but Klara insisted that the warmth of her hands would help revive the stunned bird. After about five minutes, Klara lifted her arms and the bird flew away. "And now, she cares for the sick and injured at the hospital," Anna thought with pride.

In the meantime, Klara was finishing her shift at the hospital and thought, "I haven't seen Anna for weeks. I wonder what is on her mind. It will be good to see her. These last few shifts have been difficult with the head nurse tailing me constantly."

Regardless of the head nurse, though, Klara enjoyed her occupation as a nurse. She liked her crisp, starched uniform that embodied professionalism and a clear sense of purpose—to ease the suffering of her patients. When at the hospital, she could forget about Germany crumbling and the constant demands of the war. She could do something of value within the walls of the hospital.

The ward smelled of disinfectant mixed with the odor of urine and excrement. One of her patients had soiled the bed, and Klara immediately saw the shame on his proud face. He had been a heroic pilot before he was shot down by the British and did not feel particularly fortunate to be alive. Without flinching she smiled and said, "This will only take a minute. Bear with me, though, I can be a little rough, wearing these gloves."

Periodically, she looked him directly in the eyes with kindness, not pity. "You know, I think the food is better in here than outside these days, and you don't have to wait in a ration queue," she said light-heartedly. No reaction. Only misery.

Soon she had cleaned him and replaced his hospital gown. The scent of freshly laundered white cotton sheets replaced the stench. Dignity had been restored. "Here is the bed pan so you can reach it easily. I will be back in a moment with morphine to make you more comfortable."

Klara prepared a tray with the morphine and antibiotics for her patient. She administered the drugs and was gathering up her supplies to leave, for her next patient, when the pilot said sincerely, "Thank you, nurse!"

"Don't mention it," She responded flirtatiously as she looked back over her shoulder. He smiled.

Her next patient couldn't have been twenty years old. "This young man will have such a struggle ahead," she thought, "with both legs amputated above the knees… Maybe he would enjoy a breath of spring air."

She fetched a wheelchair and blanket and approached his bed. "You and I should get out of this place Martin. Let's go outside," Klara said whispering as though they were hatching a secret plan.

"Yes *frauline*," he agreed, but his eyes showed no enthusiasm.

The sky was free of clouds and wailing bombers and sirens. The light breeze brought with it the fragrance of new growth. Klara pushed the chair beside a rose bush in full bloom and sat beside her patient. They watched the antics of a pair of squirrels. "Where is your home, Martin?"

He talked about his village until Klara realized she had to return to the ward. As Klara wheeled Martin back toward the door of the hospital, she glanced at him. His face was upturned to the sun and his eyes were closed. A tear ran down his cheek.

As they entered the building, her officious head nurse barked, "*Nein, nein, nein*! I told you not to take patients off the ward without my approval. NEVER do this again! I must ALWAYS correct your dreadful habits and complete disregard for ALL protocols."

"Yes, *Frau Schmidt.* Never again. I will take my patient to his bed immediately." It was enough to appease her superior so Klara could catch the tram to meet Anna.

Anna was waiting patiently outside the cafe smoking a cigarette. She guessed that Klara had been delayed because a patient needed her care.

"Thanks for coming. How was the ward today?"

Klara shrugged, "I will tell you about it later, but first let me know what is on your mind. Klara stood with her muscular legs slightly apart. She always looked people straight in the eye as though braced for any storm that might ensue.

She lit a cigarette and then cupped her left hand under her right elbow. Her right hand lifted a cigarette to her mouth for a puff and then another. She lowered her arm and butted the ash and then held the cigarette close to her face before she began." So, Anna, what is it?

"I am pregnant," she whispered in Klara's ear as the trolley car passed. "I cannot decide whether to keep the baby or have an abortion. I know we are Catholic, and besides, abortions are illegal; and yet, I do not want to have a baby born now—during the war."

Klara showed no surprise as she took another puff of her cigarette and dropped it to the sidewalk. Without judgment Klara said, "You must make the choice, but here are your options as I see it. You already know a midwife if you choose to keep the baby, and I will give you the name of a doctor at the hospital that will perform an abortion for cash if you choose to end the pregnancy… His name is Dr. Huber… Have you told Karl?"

"No, I haven't told him yet. I wanted to think it through…with you."

"Tell him as soon as you can. It may become more difficult the longer you leave it. His feelings must be considered too. I don't like to interfere, but that is my suggestion."

"You are right," replied Anna gratefully, "I will call him tomorrow. Now let's go into the cafe and sit down." The young women linked arms as they walked toward the door. Anna already felt better.

"How is Josef?"

"We are not going together anymore. We broke up about a month ago. Didn't Karl tell you?"

"No, he didn't. He doesn't talk about people much. Actually he can be too discreet at times. And, I can't press him for information or he becomes angry. The strong, silent type I guess! What happened with you and Josef?"

"Josef was fun for a while, but we have no future. I have nothing in common with him."

"You would have more in common with a German doctor?"

Klara shrugged, "Maybe. I almost live at the hospital don't I?"

The friends were refreshed by conversation and mutual support. When they parted both were filled with a feeling of well-being that belied the dark times in which they lived.

After seeing Klara, Anna had made arrangements to talk to Karl at his apartment. That evening as she dashed to the trolley car, Anna was anticipating Karl's reaction to her pregnancy, "Will he be happy? Will he want to keep the baby? Will he blame me?" When she stepped onto the street in front of his building she paused nervously, even though it was pouring rain.

"What a deluge!" Anna gasped as Karl let her into his apartment.

"Well, allow me to help you with your coat." He drew the coat off her shoulders and hung it up. "Let me help you with your blouse too. And your skirt…"

By then Anna was reaching for the buttons on his shirt. They couldn't stop kissing while he lifted her legs up around his hips and walked over to his bed. They tore off what was left of their clothes and made love while the rain ran down the window panes in torrents. Lightning flashed periodically to reveal Anna's lithe body rising and sinking slowly over Karl's muscular frame, her back and head arced, Karl's hands on her breasts.

Later when they curled up together, Anna whispered almost painfully, "I have missed you, missed you so much!" He held her tighter, "I love you, *putchen*!" After resting in the peace of their love, Karl asked, "Are you hungry?"

"What do you mean? Of course, I am always hungry." Anna poked him gently in the stomach. "Are you?"

Karl lit a candle by the bed and retrieved his knapsack. "Look what I have, cheese, bread and vodka." They sat up in bed and ate and drank and talked about the factory and the black market until Anna knew she could not delay telling Karl about her pregnancy any longer.

"Karl, I have something to tell you. It can't wait." Her tone had changed so Karl turned to her listening carefully.

"I am pregnant… Just under two months…"

Karl paused to fully grasp what she was saying before answering such an important question, "I am excited… I want to have a family with you, Anna, more than anything, but I want us to marry first and have our own home. I cannot do that right now in Germany. If we move in with your family, we will be a burden to your mother…"

"I know…. So adoption? I don't think I could bear to give our baby away… No, maybe an abortion is the only way." Anna felt like crying.

They laid back and held each other without talking. Anna let her tears run down Karl's chest. He was saddened but soon became enraged and bitter about the war—the loss, the pain, the hunger—suffering.

A warrior's resolve began to build in his gut and then his groin. He thought angrily, "Anna will be my wife and we will raise our children where they can be safe and free."

Karl moved on top of her and took her with forceful passion. She understood what couldn't be expressed in words. Afterwards they held each other unable to speak. Finally, Anna rose from the bed saying only, "I will make the appointment."

"I love you, Anna!" Karl said as he hugged her.

She closed the door quietly behind her. The air was purified by the June rain.

It was mid July in 1943 when Karl and Anna entered the hospital for the abortion. Karl said reassuringly, "I will be waiting here, Anna."

Dr. Huber performed the abortions in his office, which at that point was hot and stuffy. Anna could scarcely breathe. Her tension and doubts grew until she wanted to run out the door.

The doctor said, "There now young lady, relax. Open your legs." Anna was nauseated and her entire being was repulsed at the thought of opening her thighs for this hideous man to invade her body. "I'll give you something now to make this a bit easier for you," he said coldly.

His metal-rimmed glasses and reptilian eyes were the last thing she saw. Then it was over and she awakened alone. "Life and death," she kept repeating in her head as she dressed.

Anna already felt unbalanced and slightly ill when suddenly the shock of an earthquake hit. Time was suspended as she felt the tremor and heard the roar. Instead of falling apart, her brain snapped into clear focus. "What is happening?" She opened the door. "Where is everyone?" Then she saw Karl running down the hall towards her.

Karl placed his hands on Anna's shoulders to steady her. "Can you walk?" She nodded.

"Listen to me carefully. We have been bombed and will have to walk to the closest tram." Karl could see that Anna was weakened and trembling. "I will help you."

"Where is Klara? We must find her first!" Anna cried.

A steady stream of humanity flowed into the hospital. People were being pushed on stretchers, some were carrying the injured or leading those who were blinded and deafened by the blast. Children were crying and clinging to their mothers' necks.

"I must find Klara," Anna said wretchedly. They turned and headed to the ward, but they didn't have to walk far. Klara was running toward them dodging the incoming patients. The women clung to each other for a moment and then Klara said, "Can you make it home with Karl?"

Anna quickly nodded in reply. "And you?"

"I must stay and help. Please contact my parents when you can."

Karl said, "Come Anna, we must go." Anna took his arm without hesitation.

Everything about the scene outside the hospital was wrong. How could this be happening on a hot, sunny, summer day? The trolley car was standing on end with cables dangling. Buildings were burning, dark clouds of dust settling around the rubble. Dismembered bodies lay in unnatural, broken positions. Anna was numb. The blood. The smell.

A man walked slowly down the street beside a horse pulling a cart. "Oh no, no!" she thought, "The wagon is full of bodies. Oh God, NOOO! A baby!" Anna vomited.

Karl grabbed Anna around her waist and gently pulled her forward. Their faces were set, eyes fixed somewhere ahead, their pace steady as they navigated in shock through the wreckage. It was as though they were in some macabre, slow-motion, horror film.

"Keep moving, *putchen*, one step at a time," Karl urged, "one step at a time."

Over the following months, the bombing was unrelenting. In the early hours before dawn on the fourth of December, the British Royal Air Force targeted the city center of Leipzig. "*Mutti,* we have been hit again! The downtown is gone—the conservatory, university, library, museum, the old marketplace, all gone. What will *Vater* say?" Anna exclaimed to Mari.

"Father will be devastated. Do we know how far the bombing reached? I must call Frieda. I hope the line isn't down!" said Mari urgently.

Anna fed the children while her mother tried to reach Frieda. The evening meal was bean soup with bits of bacon for flavor and a slice of rye bread each. It was barely enough for the three growing boys. Leo was now fourteen years old, Ralfie nine, and Otto eight.

Mari entered the kitchen with relief on her face. As she sat down at the table she nodded and said, "Frieda is fine and the salon undamaged. She said the bombing didn't reach her area."

Anna's mind was filled with images from her apprenticeship. The salon had been a sanctuary to so many women. She said a prayer of thanks that it had been spared and that Frieda was safe.

Anna placed a bowl of hot soup in front of her mother. "Thank you, *mein lieb,*" Mari said. Anna gently touched her shoulder but sat down angrily.

"Why do they have to destroy our culture? Aren't the factories enough? Why don't they just fire on the army instead?" Anna raged.

Leo joined in, "We have to go down to the cellars three times a day now! Our bags are always packed! I want to join the army and stop all this."

"Shhh, shhh. You are only fourteen, Son. War is difficult for us all. We must endure this together. Soon it will be behind us," Mari soothed in her calm, gentle voice… "I think we all need to hear some music tonight, boys. Will you play us some songs?"

"Yes *Mutti,*" her sons obediently replied in unison.

Life had indeed become drudgery and even Christmas arrived without much celebration in the Muller family. Olav sent a letter to Mari that briefly conveyed the situation in Russia and, once again, the hope that he would be home soon.

"How much longer can this go on?" Anna asked exasperated.

"There is no official that we can ask. What can we do, my child? We wait and we wait. We persevere. Let's eat our pretend food. Call the children, please."

Somehow Mari could make her pretend food edible. She mixed water and flour with fat and then blended in the spices used in sausages. This they ate on bread. Tonight they ate quietly. Not even Leo could cheer them on that bitter winter night.

By February of 1944, the Americans were bombing in the daylight and British at night. Klara was overworked with all of the resulting casualties. Although she could barely keep up with emergency cases, she checked in on a particular soldier whom she liked. He had demonstrated courage despite the serious injuries he had sustained. Klara observed a change in him, and knew it was his time.

She placed a stool beside his bed and sat down quietly. His face was gaunt with a yellow tinge to his skin tone. Charcoal blue flesh surrounded his sunken eyes. She placed her hand on his arm.

He knew she was there, "Look Klara—the pigeons at the window. Do you think they found a warm place against this winter cold?" His smile held such love for the birds, their feathers iridescent in the sunlight.

"Ahh yes," she said softly, "They are beautiful." When she looked at him, he was gone. She felt his energy leave. Unable to move, she fought the emotions rising in her chest and stayed beside her friend to say good-bye from her heart.

Then Klara respectfully closed his eyelids and covered him with the blanket. She was still reeling from the poignancy of the moment, when she was forced to stand and listen to *Frau Schmidt* bark orders.

The workload continued to escalate through the month as did the aerial bombings. Klara was working a night shift when the British and Americans hit with the force of 700 bombers. It was one of the worse strikes, but Klara would not know the extent until she arrived at home.

The Kableisch Butcher Shop was a pile of rubble and her brother and parents were dead.

The neighbors that were still alive and strong enough were helping each other gather and identify the corpses and important belongings that were still intact. She worked tirelessly most of the day with them, having been conditioned to cope with crisis. She also knew subconsciously that she could not face the terror of the truth. Not yet.

Someone drove Klara to the Muller home. Mari answered the door.

"May I stay with you? My family is dead and the butcher shop is rubble," stated Klara matter-of-factly.

"Oh *mein Gott*, of course! Come in." Mari's warmth wrapped around Klara who was now in severe shock.

During the following weeks Klara became part of the Muller family. She had the understanding of her best friend and soothing motherly attention from Mari. Leo and Ralfie had a new audience to impress with their physical prowess and musical talent. Rita was pleased to be moved to her mother's bedroom so that Klara and Anna could share a room. Young Otto seemed happily oblivious to the family dynamics. They all adjusted to the situation about which nobody spoke.

Klara's grief was mute when distracted during the day, but had a voice during the night.

"Shh, shhh, what was it this time?" Anna whispered as she held Klara around her shoulders. Klara had sat up in bed suddenly, moaning incoherently. She was drenched in sweat and was now breathing heavily.

"I will be fine. I just need a minute," she reassured Anna. Anna lay back against the pillow and waited.

"It was the hospital again. I saw Martin in his wheelchair unable to move as walls caved in and others were reaching out for me from their beds. I tried to save them but couldn't move. They appealed to me with their eyes as they were being covered with rubble. It was so real."

"Yes the horror is all too real," Anna agreed sardonically. "Can you sleep? Maybe we should turn on the light for a while."

"No, I can sleep. It is past now."

The Muller home had adopted a quiet, subdued daily routine, in contrast with the rampant chaos outside. They all looked forward to visits from Karl, who always managed to cheer them in some way.

"Karl is here," Mari sang out loud enough for the family to hear. Anna and Klara and the boys came to the kitchen immediately, but Rita stayed in the bedroom sketching a picture.

Karl carried a box tied up with string. "Look what we are having for supper." To create suspense Karl slowly opened the box. "First, we will have some fresh rye bread," he said lifting the prize for all to see, "with some cheese. But that is not all. We have ten pounds of REAL sausages!" he finished to the applause of everyone in the room.

A celebratory air filled the house during the preparation and eating of the meal. Leo brought out his father's ukulele and led them in a folk song that lengthened the happy moment into the evening.

As Karl was leaving the next day, Anna asked, "Where is your coat? Officially it may be spring, but the wind is raw today. It looks like rain."

"I don't need it, *putchen*. I like the way you worry about me though," Karl said as he kissed her good-bye.

After he left, Anna realized what had happened to his coat. Karl had traded his leather jacket for the food.

"Good morning, Klara," Anna greeted. "Would you care for some pretend coffee?"

Klara nodded and reached in her pocket for her cigarettes and matches and then remembered she didn't have any.

"At least it will warm you against this cold, damp morning," Anna went on cheerfully as she gave her a cup.

"*Danke schon.* Yes, I go to work this morning... You know, over fifty hospitals have been bombed, so I am fortunate..."

That night when everyone was in bed, Klara said to Anna, "I am grateful to be in your home. You share music, laughter and love. Our home was never as happy. My father did not allow displays of emotion. None of us are musical either. Were musical I should say... You have all made me feel welcome and have kept me sane."

"Let's get some sleep. Good night," said Anna warmly as she closed her eyes. She knew Klara's nightmare would soon follow. It did.

Klara was gasping for air and her body was rigid when Anna turned on the lamp. She placed her hand on her friend's arm to steady her.

"I was searching for my family on our street before it was bombed. I knocked at each house but malignant strangers came to each door. I began to run from them until I reached the butcher shop and went into the back, but again, *auslanders*. I asked about my family, and they only shook their heads not comprehending what I was saying. I was lost in my own home. I attempted to call Mother but had no voice."

Anna wiped the tears from her friend's cheek and sat up with her until Klara seemed calmer.

On D-Day, the sixth of June, 1944, the Western Allies invaded Normandy and liberated France and then Holland and Belgium. Meanwhile, the Red Army unleashed a strong offensive attack that took them to Poland.

The war was coming to an end, but incredibly, Hitler and his elite maintained the facade of power, of certain victory.

On the twentieth of July another assassination attempt on Hitler's life failed at Valkery. Hitler broadcasted a speech:

"…The bomb, which was planted by Colonel Count von Stauffenberg, burst two yards from my right side. It injured several of my colleagues, one of them died. I myself am wholly unhurt… The clique of usurpers is an extremely small band of criminal elements who are now being mercilessly exterminated… This time an accounting will be given such as we National Socialists are wont to give… I see this as another sign from Providence that I must and therefore shall continue my work."

While propaganda was broadcasted to the German people that victory remained a possibility, Olav dealt with the reality. They had lost the war against the Russians. The Russian army had entered Poland.

He sent word to Mari that arrangements were made for Karl and Anna, *Frau Lowe* and Roksana to travel by military train to Belgium.

Mari read between the lines that the Lowes had to get out before they were killed. She struggled with the idea of Anna leaving, while recognizing simultaneously that Anna was a grown woman who had to lead her own life with Karl.

She showed the letter to Anna and Karl. They all agreed half-heartedly that it was for the best.

However, when Karl and Anna were alone in Karl's apartment, they attempted to come to terms with the information from Olav. They lay opposite one another on their sides talking.

Karl began, "I have informed Mother and she and Roksana will arrive in two days. Later you and I will board the train with them here in Leipzig.

Marry me, putchen," Karl finished in his deep voice. He traced her outline—breast, waist, hip and thigh with his calloused hand.

Anna kneeled on the bed beside him and took his hand. "No, I cannot leave my family now. Not until *Vater* is home. Not until the war is over. I cannot leave them."

Karl jumped to his feet and paced across the room grasping his head in his hands. "You may not have another chance. The Russians are coming, Anna!"

"I cannot go," Anna whispered through her tears, "I will not leave them."

Karl continued to pace frantically.

When he finally returned to the bed, his mood had changed. He held Anna firmly. "I understand… You are an honorable woman…I will prepare for us to immigrate after I settle in Belgium."

"Yes, Karl! After the war is over…" They held each other as the cold truth that they would be separated flooded their bodies. Suddenly, Anna pulled away from Karl. The tension was unbearable. "I love you with all of my heart, Karl! You are the one I trust." They parted reluctantly, both heavily burdened by Anna's decision.

Once home, Anna observed Klara and thought about all of the changes in her friend. She had lost her vibrancy and sense of humor. Only a rare, cynical joke was shared between them. Anna knew what to do. She must convince Klara to take her seat on the train to freedom, just as Klara had freed the small sparrow. She broached the subject with her friend that night.

"What have you got to lose, Klara? I will join you as soon as I can. We can all make a new start," Anna insisted.

"The hospital needs me, and besides, I have never been away from Leipzig. It is my home."

Anna's voice was raised as she implored, "Hospitals anywhere in the world would be fortunate to have a nurse like you, Klara. Listen to me. Leipzig has been destroyed. The city center is unrecognizable. Your street and its occupants no longer exist. Your family is dead! You are collapsing in front of me.

Take this opportunity to make a fresh start. The borders have been closed and who knows what will follow. There is no time to waste. Please, please my friend! Go!" Anna's intensity and rational arguments finally convinced Klara.

"I would never have dreamed of such a thing, but, yes, I will go. I will be ready to board the train tomorrow." Klara nodded.

"This will be for the best. You will have Karl and the others to help you make the preparations to immigrate.

You can carry only a few items with you, Klara. Let's pack them and then…your nails, darling! I am giving you a manicure, and I'll set your hair. You must escape looking beautiful!" The friends laughed and were relieved to be doing something frivolous at such a poignant time in their lives.

Only Anna could accompany Klara and the Lowes to the train station. Not much was said since they were all struggling to mask their fears. Also, soldiers were everywhere. They did not want to attract attention. Anna gave a formal handshake to both *Frau Lowe* and Roksana before they walked over to the military train.

When she turned to Klara, Anna lit a cigarette which they shared. She reached in her purse, "I want you to have this, Klara." It was a photograph Mari had taken of Klara, Nathalie and Anna when they were girls. Anna hugged Klara and whispered. "You will be fine. I will miss you!"

As a reminder of happier times, Klara joked, "Check out that guard by the train. Maybe he is single!" They both smiled and tossed back their heads, but when Klara looked back at Anna before stepping onto the train, her face was contorted with emotion.

Karl was waiting for her. Anna began to tremble and her eyes filled with panic when she looked into his eyes. He stepped forward and wrapped his arms around her. "We can do this, *putchen.* We will be together," Karl whispered in her ear reassuringly. He took her shoulders firmly, "*Auf Wiedersehen…*" he said with a wink and boarded the train.

The train begrudgingly chugged forward. Karl waved out the window. Anna's arm shot high into the air waving, reaching. She did not take her eyes off him as he slowly disappeared from her view.

When he was out of sight, Anna stood motionless like a rock in a stream. Soldiers, guards, and civilians walked around her. The cacophony of voices and trains filled the air. An SS guard told her to move on. She took in a deep breath and straightened her back and shoulders. "I must go home," she thought, but when she turned, she faltered. Her center of gravity was gone.

Chapter Nineteen
Under Siege

"Keep your head down," shouted Anna, but her words were lost in the explosion. Anna covered Otto with most of her body and shielded Rita's head with her arms. Following each sharp crack and crash they flinched and then held one another more tightly.

When the din had abated Anna called out, "*Mutti*, Leo, Ralfie! Are you all right?" But they were temporarily deafened by the blast. She crawled to where Mari held onto Leo on one side and Ralfie on the other. Anna lifted each of their heads in turn. The boys were in shock but seemed uninjured. Mari's foot was covered in blood. Anna soon realized that the floor beam above their heads had broken, and a piece of it had fallen on Mari's ankle.

Anna tapped Leo's arm and motioned for him to join her, and to the others she indicated that they must stay. Part of the stairwell was covered with debris, but Anna could see predawn light at the top of the stairs. Leo and she removed enough of the debris to clear a path up the stairs, and then she returned to her mother to assess the damage to her foot. Mari couldn't move her foot without wincing but managed to get to her feet with the help of Anna and Leo.

Once out of the basement and into the early morning light, the family stood in a row silhouetted. Leo and Ralfie supported their mother, and Anna held the hands of Otto and Rita. They were motionless, staring at the lurid colors of their burning neighborhood against the shades of pink and mauve in the dawn sky. Their subdivision was in ruin.

Before they all surrendered to despair, Anna made a quick decision. She said loudly and firmly, "We will walk to the Hoffmans. Leo and Ralfie, you help Mutti for her ankle is sprained. We have a long walk ahead of us so let's move. Did you hear me?" In answer the family took their first steps forward.

They scarcely reached what had been the street when Ralfie wailed, "The piano!" In front of them was roughly a foot of piano keys sprawled on broken concrete. He began to cry, but Anna stifled his cries sharply, "Stop this instant. It is only a piano. One of us could have been killed. We can replace the piano. Keep walking Ralfie."

On the four-kilometer walk to the Hoffmans' other homeless people were stumbling through the streets in shock. Some carried cherished belongings, others an injured loved one.

When she saw fear taking shape on her brothers' faces, Anna used Karl's words, "We can do this one step at a time, one step at a time… Leo let us sing." Leo led them in songs while they trudged bravely to what remained of their old neighborhood.

To the stragglers, the Hoffman house was a beacon, untarnished in the autumn morning sun. When they knocked, Wolfgang Hoffman opened the door. His eyes widened in astonishment as he recognized his friends huddled in front of him. "Come in, come in! What has happened?" Soon they were surrounded by Bertha and the children, Axel and Rosa.

Rita released her grip on Anna's hand and immediately ran to Axel. The Mullers had lost everything but found what they needed—restorative water, food, and friendship.

The next day, Wolfgang Hoffman took Anna and Leo back to the wreckage in search of anything salvageable. Disappointed, Anna had found none of their furniture or paintings. "Anything of value has been stolen, Anna," said Wolfgang.

"Look over here, *Herr Hoffman.* I think I have found *Vater's*…" Anna had spotted something shiny. "Yes, it is his saxophone!" She clutched it to her chest. "Leo, look, look!"

"Permit me to play you a tune," Leo bowed seriously as he took the treasured instrument from his sister. The music drifted over the remains of their former life with a beauty that made the people rummaging in the area stop and raise their dirt-streaked faces to listen to the sound of hope.

Leo lowered the saxophone solemnly and returned it to Anna. Memories of music continued to play in his mind.

Nathalie had always relished mail received from Anna. Often notes and pictures from the children were enclosed. A recent letter had a question from Ralfie, "When are you coming home, Nattie?"

She never answered his mail. It never occurred to her that she might write or telephone once in awhile or abandon her research for a visit; that is, until she read the letter in her hand about the bombing.

Nathalie immediately approached her superiors to request time to visit her family, and to her surprise, she was granted a leave without question; after all, she had not taken a vacation for five years. Research had been her priority.

Being a Party member, she was given preferential treatment and so made the trip to Leipzig effortlessly. When she arrived at the Hoffman home in a military car, a uniformed SS soldier carried her luggage. "Hello *Herr Hoffman*. May I come in?" They were expecting her.

"*Frauline Lenz*, of course, what a pleasure to see you again!" Wolfgang greeted formally. After the imposing car drove away, and they all knew no search would be conducted, the household flocked together noisily to welcome Nathalie.

"*Hallo, hallo!* You have all grown so much!" Nathalie exclaimed as she embraced everyone. "Leo your voice has changed! Can you still sing?"

"Of course," Leo boasted, "I will sing for you later and play the ukulele."

"Where is Ralfie?" He was waiting in the hallway shyly, but Nathalie rushed over smiling. "Oh my dear Ralfie," she said as she hugged him tightly. Let me see your blue eyes." As she held his face in her hands, she wiped the tears out of the corner of his eyes with her thumbs.

"Nat, we don't have a piano anymore. It blew apart in the explosion."

"Someday you will have another. I know it," Nathalie reassured Ralfie.

Then she took his hand and brought him into the dining room to join the others.

"I have brought some gifts for all of you," she said as she released the clasps on her suitcases. She had chocolates and cheeses, smoked pork, coffee and canned goods, soap and cigarettes. Both cases were full of now rare items that had once been common place in Germany.

"Rita, look what I have for you!" Nathalie took a box of paints and art paper from her suitcase and presented them to Rita. She stared in disbelief and then as though the art supplies were extremely fragile she carried them carefully into the bedroom for safe-keeping. She hurried back and hugged Nathalie, "*Danke schon, danke schon, Nat!*"

After the children had gone to bed, the adults discussed their current situation. Nathalie sympathized, "Leipzig is not the city we once knew. I feel lost here. Our reference points are gone—the regal medieval buildings are mountains of rubble. This must have been very difficult for all of you to witness. And now even the Muller home. Thank God you all survived!" Nathalie exclaimed lowering her eyes when she thought of Klara's family.

She looked at the changes in the faces of Bertha and Mari. Although they were still attractive women, their faces at forty-four years of age were haggard and edgy from the strain of protecting their families from starvation and unrelenting strafing and bombing by enemy aircraft. She noticed that Wolfgang's shoulders were stooped and he leaned forward from the waist which made him appear more disabled.

"I have seen little of the outside world these past five years. My life is my research," Nathalie explained.

Anna guessed that Nathalie seldom saw anyone. Her appearance reflected her reclusive nature. Nathalie had always down-played her beauty but now even her long auburn hair was pulled back straight and tied in a bun. Anna supposed it was partly about efficiency—comfortable, neat, easy to arrange. Ironically, the effect only accented her fragile beauty—clear, white skin, small features, and crystal eyes. Her dark austere suit was of fine wool and her flat leather shoes were for comfort only. Despite her drab clothing, she wore silk stockings which confirmed her privileged position in the Nazi Party.

They all talked late into the evening but when the young women were alone, they discussed more personal matters. Anna talked softly about meeting Karl and some of their experiences, especially their impromptu lunch that had saved her life…

Then true to Nathalie's character she stated succinctly, "I have never been with a man and I don't think I ever will."

"Yes, you will. You simply haven't met the right one. Most men would feel awkward with you. You are a genius!"

"Thank you for the compliment, Anna; but after watching Lena, I can't be bothered with relationships. She was constantly preening, seeking attention from any man in close proximity of her. She would do anything to please a man. I cannot waste my valuable time…"

The conversation paused as Nathalie admitted to herself, "Most men are so banal. Actually, sex is repugnant to me. I don't want their attention OR love." To Anna she said, "I don't need men. I have my family and you are all I need. Speaking of my family, when will *Tante Frieda* be here?"

"Tomorrow," answered Anna as she squeezed Nathalie's arm. "It is good to see you, Nat!"

They reminisced about their school days with Klara. "She could never see anything in the clouds. It used to make her so frustrated, remember? I wonder where she is now," said Nathalie.

"So do I... Maybe we should get some sleep," said Anna sadly.

The following morning they were sitting together on the front steps when Frieda arrived. Nathalie sprang up and stared at Frieda for a moment before she rushed to her. Frieda held her tightly as Nathalie wept convulsively.

To respect this uncharacteristic display of emotion, Anna turned aside and lit a cigarette. She didn't hear Frieda when she said, "So, my darling, you can finally cry. It is good. Get it out. There, there; it is good."

Too soon it was time for Nathalie to leave. She departed amidst the warm farewells of the Hoffmans and Mullers. However, it was impossible for Anna to say good-bye. Instead she hugged Nathalie, and then waved until the military car was out of sight.

Through the window of the train, Nathalie witnessed Germany in ruins. The distressing scenery and faces on the train contrasted sharply with the serenity Nathalie was experiencing. Inside she was sustained by the richness of love given so freely by her surrogate family.

When she was back at the research center outside of Berlin, she entered her living quarters like stepping into a comfortable pair of slippers. Soon she would be alone with the elegance of science and the thrill of discovery, removed from the escalating events leading to Germany's defeat.

During December of 1944 and January 1945, the Germans fought a remarkable counteroffensive, but ultimately failed to halt the advance of the Western Allies. The Allies crossed the Rhine and began to spread through western Germany. By April, the Russians had reached Berlin from the East.

On the thirtieth of April, Adolf Hitler committed suicide. Many of the Nazi supporters careened off one another on the way to the abyss, following their *Fuhrer* and his love, Eva Braun.

The inevitable defeat of the Third Reich on May 2, 1945 was hailed as a victory of good over evil. Celebrations took to the streets in the allied countries.

However, the German people had little to celebrate. They were defeated, a culture with no war heroes to celebrate. Foreign victors occupied the cities and rural areas, replacing the Nazi terror with their own brand.

The war was over, but Germany was under siege.

"Are you Nathalie Lenz?" said the uniformed American who barged into her lab. She nodded at the sound of her name. "Ma'am, we would like you to come with us immediately. You are being relocated in the United States of America. My men will take care of the contents of this lab." The interpreter didn't really clarify the information.

In any case, she had no choice but to cooperate. "Take only your personal belongings." Nathalie was uprooted and deposited in the back of a military jeep with a small suitcase on her lap containing a few clothes and her box of memories.

An American military escort drove her out of the country. Rail lines had been destroyed. Chaos seemed to be everywhere she looked. As they drove through Berlin streets, she gazed out the window like a tourist sight-seeing in hell—miles of corpses strewn about—hundreds of orphans wandering aimlessly, crying or standing helpless and terrified—dust, debris, and fire.

Nathalie's inner dialogue with her long-dead mother staved off the panic that was consuming her as the images of mayhem passed by. "Where am I? How could this be Berlin, Lena? I am glad you cannot see this. Remember the theatre and the restaurants? How beautiful you were, Lena." She closed her eyes for the remainder of her ride away from her family and Germany to where? Freedom?

Anna had no knowledge of what was happening to Nathalie and that she would never see Nat again. Instead, Anna had laundry to do.

"*Mutti*, I will do the laundry now and hang it on the line this morning. The weather is warm so the clothes will dry in no time," Anna suggested. Later Rita helped her carry the laundry outside. Anna put down the hamper and turned back to close the door. She didn't see Leo, but Rita did. She flung her clothes basket on the ground and ran toward him.

Leo had a rifle propped on the fence and was aiming at an American soldier on the street. But Rita had also seen a group of American soldiers coming around the corner at the end of the block, and one of them had his rifle leveled at Leo.

"Leo, no!" Rita shouted as she jumped up and grabbed his shoulders from behind, pulling him backwards. They fell clumsily to the ground. The bullet from the American's rifle missed. Leo's rifle fell to the side without firing.

Anna hurried to her sister and brother and dragged Leo with difficulty into the house. He was now sixteen years old and taller than she. And…he was in a rage.

"The Americans bombed our house. They took everything from us. They deserve to die. We must fight back. *Vater* would not stand for this! He would fight!" Leo yelled.

"What has happened? We heard shots," Mari cried. Anna was peeking through the curtain to see if any soldiers were approaching the house. Fortunately, something else had demanded their immediate attention and so they were continuing down the street. Relieved she turned back to the others.

"Our soldiers gave me a loaded rifle and told me to shoot the Americans. I want to fight like *Vater*! I want to protect all of you!" Leo exclaimed passionately.

"The war is over, Leo. *Der Fuhrer* is dead. Germany has lost the war," Mari confirmed slowly with resignation.

"No, never! We must fight!" Leo cried desperately.

Wolfgang entered the room and in an authoritative voice reiterated, "Germany has lost the war, Leo. Those German soldiers should never have enlisted your help. Now give me the rifle," ordered Wolfgang.

Leo relinquished the weapon, but his teeth remained clenched and he breathed loudly through his nostrils.

"The Americans would have killed you, Leo, if Rita had not acted swiftly," added Anna. "Promise us you will never do such a thing again."

"I cannot!" said Leo with the conviction of Olav.

After the household calmed down, Leo and Axel were allowed to go outside. They made for the garden shed where they could talk privately. Although Axel was two years younger than Leo, he was already taller and of a huskier build. He was also mature for his age. The boys were equals.

The friends had become close conspirators. They listened to the rumors in the street and stole and bartered for food together. They had agreed that it was their responsibility to defend and feed their families.

"Father moves slowly now," said Axel. "We must take charge, protect the women. You know what the German soldiers said…The Russians are coming."

"The Russians are coming," repeated Leo grimly. The teenagers had two rifles and ammunition hidden in the shed.

Chapter Twenty
The Spoils of War

Wolfgang and Bertha asked Mari to sit down with them. "Mari, my sister's family needs shelter. They too have lost their home. Wolfgang and I will not have room for everyone," explained Bertha dismally.

"Oh... I am sure we can move to the Baumann farm. They will have room. You have been so very kind these past months. Perhaps we can find a way to send food to you from the farm. I will discuss this with Thomas and Else. Is it possible for Anna and Rita to remain? They will be safer in the city," Mari suggested erroneously.

"Anna and Rita can stay in the garden shed until winter, and then we'll see..." said Wolfgang. "I will talk to a friend about transport into the hills for you and the boys."

Later Mari rationalized, that all things considered, the move was for the best. Leo was a malcontent rapidly becoming out of control. She wanted him away from the turmoil and violence in the streets. Otherwise, she knew he would come to harm. Also, the younger boys might follow in their older brother's footsteps. At least on the farm they would all be kept busy working with Thomas, Guner and Vilma.

Awakening before dawn, Mari left Leipzig with her portion of the severed Muller family. They crept into a wagon covered with a canvas tarp. An impoverished man and his old horse, ostensibly removing only rubble and body parts from the city transported them to their sanctuary in the hills. For the occupants of the wagon, the horror of the cargo was accompanied by profound regret and the pain of separation. The journey seemed endless.

"No one stopped us!" exclaimed Mari when they finally arrived. "Thomas... Else... I am so grateful to you," she cried as she embraced the

Baumanns. Looking miserable and shaken, the boys stood in a row while they awaited instructions.

"These are my sons, Leo, Ralfie, and Otto. They have no experience with farming but are quick to learn." Each of the boys shook hands with the Baumann family politely and then slowly began to survey their new surroundings. Their forlorn expressions conveyed interest when they saw the animals and forest.

"Please, come into the house for a meal. Mari, it looks like you need a hot cup of herbal tea," invited Else warmly.

They all sat around the large country kitchen table to a meal of meat and vegetables the Mullers had not seen in a very long time. The three Muller boys were trying their best to have table manners, but somehow their heads crept close to their plates; they were almost shoveling the food into their mouths without chewing. The boys did not appear to be listening to the conversation and did not even look up so intent were they on the delicious meal. Mari let it go.

"Have more to eat boys," urged Else and we have sweet preserves and pudding for dessert.

"*Frau Baumann, danke schon.* Your cooking is very good," praised Leo in sincere gratitude. The boys were contented and ready for sleep when they went to bed shortly after supper. After the women cleaned up and washed the dishes, the adults had some privacy to discuss the situation on the farm.

Thomas began, "The Russians occupy this entire area and once a week a patrol will come here for our food. This has become routine—working to feed the enemy—huh! If that isn't bad enough, sometimes a nasty lot will prowl around looking for potato snapps and women. We never know when these types will appear.

I have told them over and over again—no women here! My wife lives in Leipzig to care for elderly relatives… They do not know about Vilma – God forbid! You would not be safe if discovered, Mari. Guner and I would be unable to protect you against all of the soldiers and their weapons."

Mari was terrified. She struggled to remain calm but was nauseous.

"I have built a cave behind an outbuilding where you will hide on the routine visits from the soldiers. When someone unexpected comes, we will raise our secret alarm—a cowbell. When you hear the sound, the three of you must hurry to the cave. Stop for nothing. You will be quite comfortable in there. We have supplies, food, and blankets stored at all times. We will practice tomorrow so you will recognize the sounds of the cowbell and understand the protocol for these unwelcome visits.

Mari, I don't know if you recall that I speak some Russian. Anyway, I picked it up during WWI. If soldiers show up, I speak loudly in Russian and attempt to distract them," explained Thomas. "This will also help to warn you if we can't reach the bell in time."

Else cautioned, "Vilma and I usually don't stray far from the house. Our gardening is done in the early morning beginning before dawn—same with the chickens. We don't stay out in the open.

If you ever want to take a walk in the forest, you should ask us first… These precautions are not so bad once you are used to them. Ah, and we are forced to be good housekeepers because we can leave nothing feminine lying around for the roving eyes of Russian prowlers to detect."

During the weeks ahead, Thomas and the boys deceived the soldiers when unwanted questions were asked. Leo was particularly adept and usually covered for his younger brothers. Mari followed the necessary precautions and after the first few visits by the Russians, was less edgy.

When alone with her thoughts at night, Mari wondered why Olav had not returned. Was he alive, injured, dead? With the telephone and mail service down, she was entirely cut off from him. Before leaving Leipzig, she had gone to the missing persons' bureau but had no luck. Though hopeless, Mari did not shed a tear. She chuckled bitterly to herself, "If I start crying now, I may never stop."

Mari also prayed for her daughters each night. She thought, "Anna is competent and wise. She will make the right choices for Rita and herself. The Hoffmans will also do what they can for my daughters… *Mein Gott*, how I wish we were all together again."

While Mari and the boys began looking healthier on the farm with food and fresh air, the city people were starving. They were gaunt and gray.

The Americans gave food rations, but troops had been deployed to fight in the Pacific so supplies were spread thin. In addition, the ruling Russian military administration that would eventually take over Leipzig received very few supplies from Russia. Their rations were sparse.

Wherever they could find some earth in the yard and boulevard, Anna and Rita planted potatoes as well as onions and cabbage. With Bertha's sister and her seven children living in the house, they were becoming frantic for more food. Then in August, Thomas smuggled food to the Hoffman home in the false bottom of the old man's wagon.

Relief also came in another form. The street was no longer plagued by as many tanks and soldiers at all hours of the day because the soldiers began concentrating their efforts in the center of the city. They could relax a bit.

Anna would often see Axel and Rita outside together in the late summer sun. "They sit as though they are one," thought Anna. "They don't even talk for the longest while. When they move, they are in unison—he is so big and she tiny." She smiled to herself. "Rita and Axel have been close since they were toddlers."

Anna looked fondly at Rita. At fifteen years old, she was lovely. "At least I don't have to worry about Axel's intentions. He loves Rita's pure heart too," Anna thought. "He guards her and actually doesn't even like anyone else around her. Huh, especially the four other boys living in his house! Young love in these dark times is like a rose blooming on a battlefield. Can it survive?"

Anna and Rita had made the garden shed, quite cozy. They made a bed out of a combination of materials and it was quite comfortable. Rita sketched pictures on the walls of the shed and painted pictures using her gift from Nathalie. She preferred to read or draw in the shed unless she was with Axel or Anna.

Anna was clamping a clothes peg on the corner of a carpet she was hanging on the line when she realized Rita hadn't been around. "I will check the shed," Anna thought beginning to feel sick. "Where would those two have gone?"

"Has anyone seen Rita?"

"She is probably with Axel," answered Rosa.

"No, Axel went out early this morning."

Axel had explained to Rita that he would be gone for a couple of hours in the morning. He had heard about a military base not far away that had supplies and food for the soldiers. He was checking out the security at the base with a friend. He left at 7:00 a.m. on his bicycle.

When Axel had not returned by noon, Rita began to worry and ventured out to look for him. Anna had given Rita strict instructions to never leave the house without her or Axel—even for a short distance. She forgot. She had always had difficulty remembering simple instructions and could not comprehend the notion of consequences. All she understood was that she must find Axel. He could be in trouble.

She walked rapidly down the street, but soon broke into a run. Her thoughts became muddled as she thought of being separated from Axel. "What if he is hurt? What if he never comes home like *Vati*," Rita said out loud. Her panic made her heart pound and breathing come fast. Tears were running down her cheeks as she ran an erratic course, crying, "Axel, Axel, Axel!"

Rita came around the shell of a building to where four Russian soldiers were smoking cigarettes.

"What have we here?" said one of them malignantly speaking in Russian. In two strides he was beside her.

"Have you seen Axel?" she asked innocently with tears running down her cheeks. There was no reply.

He threw Rita to the ground and lifted her dress while he pulled his pants down to his knees. At first Rita was shocked and hurt from the fall; then unemotionally she stared at the man on top of her, not understanding what was happening. He looked like no one she had ever seen—narrow eyes, dark-skin, heavily-lined face.

The soldier reeked of body odor and urine. With the disgusting stench of ancient cigarettes, yesterday's alcohol and the morning's onions, he panted heavily over Rita's luminous face; and then struck her head to the side so he could not see her innocent, now terrified eyes. He savagely raped her with the intense hatred he held for all Germans.

When he was finished, he looked up grinning at the other three soldiers who had shuffled over to join in the fun. As one of them prepared to take his turn, the soldiers heard a call from another soldier announcing that he had located a barrel of potato snapps not far away. They hurried off in anticipation of a night of oblivion without another glance at the child, lying helpless in the dirt, desecrated.

Rita's head was turned to one side. No life formed in her eyes. Her body twitched and then was still. Blood covered her thighs.

Axel was riding home on his bicycle as Anna was hurrying off on foot to find Rita. "Axel, we can't find Rita! I think she may have wandered away in search of you. Come with me. We must find her!" she shouted.

He spun around on his bicycle and was gone.

Anna marched in the direction she felt Rita might have taken and then began running. "If anything has happened to my Rita…!" And then she saw them. Axel was carrying Rita in his arms; her limbs hung lifeless.

"Is she alive, Axel?" Anna cried as she reached them.

"Yes, she is breathing, but she doesn't seem to be conscious. She can't move."

Anna would not allow the icy truth to paralyze her. She focused and moved quickly. In a tub of hot water, she bathed her younger sister gently and then cleaned the wound on the side of her face with sterilized salted water. That evening in the garden shed, Anna wrapped Rita in a warm blanket and shawl and fed her a thin, hot broth.

Rita closed her eyes while Anna brushed and brushed her long hair slowly. She retold the fairy tale of Hansel and Gretel. "Rita…it wasn't that long ago you saved Leo. Like Gretel saved Hansel! You are very brave, little sister," Anna praised.

When it was time to sleep, Rita curled up in Anna's arm like a small child. Anna covered them both with the blanket and gently stroked Rita's forehead, humming a children's folksong until Rita sunk into sleep.

Anna held her all night while anguish ripped her apart. For her entire life she tried to protect her younger sister. "Rita is so delicate, so precious. The thought of her being raped…" Anna's face contorted in silent agony.

When Anna opened the shed door in the morning, Axel was waiting. Anna's first observation was how much older than his years he looked. His eyes almost frightened her. Suffering had been replaced with revenge overnight. She didn't know that he had rifles hidden and had used them on Rita's assailants. She did not know to what extent he and Leo had become violent young men in the streets.

Anna told Axel, "Rita is sleeping. I will be spending my time with her until I'm confident that she is stronger. She hasn't spoken yet…shock. You may visit in the shed or sit outside with her anytime you want though. She will be anxious to see you."

Wolfgang and Bertha found a man in the neighborhood who had once been a doctor. He gave Rita a new drug called penicillin. Later, he examined her.

Rita was not pregnant.

By September food arrived from the Baumann farm and Rita seemed a bit healthier. Anna kept to as safe a routine for her as possible. Every morning

Axel checked in on them. "Axel, come in." Rita moved over to sit beside Axel, her eyes full of affection and trust.

"I have brought you something, Rita." Axel had stolen a stack of typing paper from the base supply cupboard. He gave it to Rita. She held it to her chest. "You can sketch pictures." She kissed his cheek and put the paper in the corner with what remained of her paint box.

"Why not draw something now," asked Axel. Rita shook her head and resumed her seat beside him. Rita had not spoken a word or done any art since the trauma. Instead, they played cards quietly for the rest of the afternoon.

The autumn rains settled in. One evening after eating their meal in the house, Anna and Rita hurried for the shed but were already soaked by the time they closed the door. They hung their damp woolen sweaters and socks over the chair to dry and crawled under the blanket for warmth.

"Do you hear that, Rita?" A cat was howling outside in the storm. Anna couldn't bear it so she let in the wet, gray cat. Although she wasn't sure if befriending a cat was a good idea, she was soon proven wrong. Stormy provided companionship and a distraction that the sisters needed.

Anna and Rita loved to have him on their laps. He was warm and comforting. He made them laugh. Rita was even inspired to sketch again— Stormy sitting, curled up, his face…

Anna sang softly as Rita petted Stormy. When she stopped singing, they listened to the rain; and then Anna told family stories hoping that Rita would say something. They stayed close together in the days ahead with the sound of water dripping and the smell of damp wool.

By the end of October the weather turned cold. Axel had brought them more woolen blankets, socks, hats and gloves. Anna was concerned about their living situation. Where would they go? Soon they would have to move out of the shed.

"Stormy, come in! It is cold and windy outside." The cat shot in with his ears lying flat and made directly for Rita's lap. After circling a couple of times and kneading her with his claws, he eased down in just the right spot and purred.

That night they couldn't sleep for the wind. The wind in the old window panes made a variety of whistling sounds.

"Anna listen! Can you hear the wind music?" Rita whispered.

"Yes, yes I can, Rita!"

Anna closed her eyes and smiled thankfully. Rita had finally spoken. For a moment the weight of sadness lifted.

Anna, Rita and Stormy moved into the cellar of the Hoffman house for the winter of 1946. Anna despised the dark and the dampness and longed to be above ground where windows let in the light. She helped Rita recover, tried to be encouraging to everyone in the house, but over the weeks eventually capitulated to the language of cold and hunger and chaos—of separation and loss.

More frequently she dwelt in her mind, recalling memories of security in her parents' home, familiar sounds, smells, and sights, her job at the salon, Nat and Klara, and always Karl.

She thought, "The war was quite distant for the most part, but now that it is over, Leipzig is worse, our street is a war zone—unrecognizable—as are the starving Germans and the foreigners. When will this end?"

She had no coordinates to guide her into the future. Her only consolation was her sister and a stray, gray cat.

On her way for rations one miserable day, Anna trudged through the snow, mourning into the winter wind. She waited for two hours and only received half of the expected rations. Her hope froze into disappointment and resignation.

She walked past the end of the queue and looked up suddenly when she heard a woman's hysterical voice.

"If I wrap him better he will be fine. He will be warm soon. He just needs some food," she said breathlessly while her hands, moving sporadically, wrapped the baby and then rewrapped him differently. Anna moved closer to help.

The woman continued as she rocked the baby in her arms. "I just need another blanket. He needs a little warm food. It is my fault. He will be fine. He just needs to stay warm. He will be fine." She rewrapped him again and again.

Anna began to speak, but when she looked into the woman's sunken eyes she saw insanity, and in the blanket a dead baby boy.

"Take these rations," Anna soothed. "Your son is beautiful." For a moment the woman smiled, and then she snatched the rations like a feral creature and disappeared into the snow.

Anna took a moment to square her shoulders and hold her head high. On the way home her inner steel began to elevate her. She would not augur into the perilous muck of self-pity. That inevitably leads to destruction.

"Rita, we will not let this destroy us!" Anna screamed into the blizzard.

Chapter Twenty-One
Returning

As Anna and Rita rode their bicycles by an area of brick and debris in a heavily bombed area of the city, Rita pointed to the women bent to the task of clearing and searching.

"That will be the day!" exclaimed Anna. "I will not be one of the *trummerfrauen*—rubble women... dirty work," she told Rita. "I will find a job that will give us some benefits."

So Anna found a job as a nanny with a Russian family. They were kind to her and fed her well. She made the best of it—took food home to Rita and the others when she could and seized the opportunity to learn a bit of the Russian language. Being a realist, she had arrived at the conclusion that since the Russians were the new authorities, it would be advantageous to speak their language and understand their customs.

However, after almost a year with the family, she wanted more than her job as a nanny that paid little more than room and board. Also, Anna was desperate to leave the isolation caused by separation from her family and culture and the inability to communicate by telephone or mail.

Finally, unable to take it any longer, she sought the help of the last remaining constant in her life. Frieda. She hoped a visit with her would shed some light on the current situation in Leipzig. Anna knew Frieda would have information about current politics and social changes. Frieda would know what to do next.

When Anna opened the door of the salon, she immediately felt like she belonged. The past two years were so momentous that it seemed like decades had passed since she had experienced the familiar smells and sounds. All were comforting.

When Frieda walked in from the apartment at the back, Anna couldn't move. There was her *Tante Frieda*, whom she had loved and admired as a child and who trained her. Frieda hurried over and led her by the arm to the apartment.

Anna had not seen her mother or brothers for almost two years or her father for six years. She had to carry the rape of her sister in her heart – war and postwar trauma. Suddenly, Anna began to tremble and weep with the relief of seeing Frieda.

Frieda hugged her tightly, wiped away her tears and then told her firmly, "Now, get yourself a bowl of soup, and I will be back in a moment. I'll tell the girls to take the last of the customers."

"How wonderful to see you, my darling! Let me look at you," Frieda said as she took Anna's face in her hands. After Frieda heard about Anna's situation, she suggested, "Why don't you work for me again?"

"Do you have enough business to hire me? Who can afford a beautician these days? Most German women are wearing those dreadful scarves for weeks on end to protect their hair from the rubble filth."

"We have a new clientele, Anna—Russian soldiers and German prostitutes. You will see," Frieda reassured.

"Thank you, of course I accept. Will I be able to return to the Hoffmans' for the weekends? I need to check in on Rita. I am confident the Hoffmans will take care of Rita during the week and… she will be in school again with Axel. Axel takes odd jobs and barters on the black market. I believe he is only attending school to keep Rita safe," Anna explained in confidence. She was unable to talk about the rape, though, even with Frieda—too painful, another secret to lock away.

"Of course you can check on her, but it may not be every weekend."

Shortly after, Anna moved back to the salon. She and Frieda resumed their former working rhythm. They knew what had to be done and covered for one another. It wasn't long before Frieda let her other girls go.

"Frieda, I feel bad for them."

"Don't. They were too slow and too forward with the customers. Actually, I didn't really trust them either. I know one of them was stealing from me. People are so desperate these days. They will do anything to survive."

A Russian officer entered the salon. Anna greeted him at the counter. He was smoking a cigarette that stayed in the corner of his mouth as he spoke.

"I need my hair cut. I can pay you in canned food," he said. He grasped the cigarette between his thumb and finger and inhaled deeply as though he were sucking in life itself. Then he butted it decisively in the ash tray.

He was a sergeant posted at the power station down the street. He came in regularly for a haircut and spoke German fluently.

"I have not seen you in here before. Frieda normally gives me a shave and haircut. Do I need to be concerned? Will you slit my throat or scalp me?" he asked good-naturedly.

"Not if you behave yourself," she quipped in Russian. "My name is Anna Muller and I am pleased to meet you. Frieda taught me everything I know, so rest assured, I can cut your hair. No bloodshed."

As Sergeant Kuznetsov was leaving, he took Frieda aside and spoke in a secretive manner.

Later Frieda explained to Anna, "Our Russian friend would like us to make a meal next week. He acquires beef and pork from the urban farms. Sometimes he brings milk, sugar, and noodles too. We can make them a large pot of soup and they will eat here. I usually keep some of their bread and canned meat and hide it for myself."

Although Anna agreed without hesitation, she was inwardly wary. She knew that many of the Russian soldiers had taken over German homes. Women, some of whom were the former home owners, were forced into prostitution between the hours of two to eight a.m.

The women prostituted themselves for a roof over their heads, food or small items such as soap. Beatings at the hands of the Russians were common and harsh. She trusted that Frieda knew what she was doing and had assessed the sergeant accurately.

Anna's fears were allayed. The men drank and ate heartily and were courteous. "*Nastrovye!*" they toasted. Then the singing began.

Later as Frieda and she cleaned away the dishes, Frieda said with relief, "We have food for next week."

Not long after, six of the guards at the station were drinking the strong alcohol made in the forest. An instigator said, "Let's have some fun, comrades. I was entertained by two gorgeous women down at the hair salon. I know the blonde one was looking at me. She liked what she was seeing." They all laughed. "The sergeant treats the dark one like a queen. He should share don't you think? Let's wander over for some more of their hospitality."

"Those are Russian soldiers yelling outside. Oh God! They are pounding on the front door of the salon," Frieda whispered to Anna. They barricaded the apartment door with furniture.

"Anna, leave at once for the police station! Climb out your window in case someone comes to the back door."

As Anna escaped through the back window, onto the wash house, then to the ground, she could hear the men shouting incoherently at the front of the salon. She ran down the street to the German police station. Out of breath, her heart pounding, Anna rushed into the building, telling the police only the bare facts.

"We can't help you. We are only German policemen. We have no jurisdiction over the Russian military."

"Then give me the telephone please. I will make one call. Quickly! They will harm her!" Anna ordered impatiently.

"Operator, please connect me immediately with Sergeant Kuznetsov at the NKWB—the power station."

"It is Anna, Sergeant Kuznetsov. Your men are breaking into the salon. Frieda needs your help. Now!"

"Understood."

Anna ran back to the salon shaken by thoughts of what might have happened to Frieda. The sergeant was already at the salon. All six men were lying down in a row on the street. Sergeant Kuznetsov was beating each of them with a leather bat. One of the soldier's arms was bleeding because he had punched a hole through the glass in the salon door, but the sergeant struck him too without mercy. "Bring the truck around," Sergeant Kuznetsov commanded the soldiers standing at his side.

He knocked at the salon door. When Frieda answered, he apologized formally and then turned on his heel, motioning to the guards to throw the men in the truck. The next day the drunken men had been replaced.

Impervious, Frieda and Anna resumed haircuts and civil meals with the sergeant and select guards and continued to stockpile what food they could from the Russian's supplies.

"I need some fresh air, Anna. I will ride the bicycle downtown to buy more solution," said Frieda. "Summer is my favorite season."

Anna was pleased to see Frieda take a break. Her face was drawn and her body moved stiffly.

"Yes, what a sunny day! Take your time. I will manage."

Anna had anticipated that Frieda would appear rejuvenated when she walked back through the door of the salon; but instead, her eyes were swollen and red and her face twisted in discomfort.

"She threw pepper in my face and the other spit on me!" Frieda exclaimed as she stumbled past Anna to her apartment. "I can hardly see!"

Anna joined her as soon as she could. "What happened?"

"Two of the women in our neighborhood approached me as I arrived here on my bicycle. They pretended that they urgently needed to talk to me. When I turned toward them, they called me a Russian whore. So much disdain from our own German neighbors!"

"*Blode* women! Their actions are unforgiveable! We can rely on only a few people in this world, Frieda."

"Yes," Frieda agreed as she washed the spit off her face and dabbed at her eyes… I have been meaning to tell you…one of those reliable people will be home soon."

Anna tilted her head in an inquiring way.

"Mr. Wolfe will be here soon, Anna."

"What do you mean? He and his family disappeared on *Kristallnacht*, November of 1938."

"He survived, Anna, and has been fighting for justice ever since."

"Anna was speechless. With the memories of the Wolfe family, she suddenly missed her father, missed the music. Her chest was racked with pain."

"Mr. Wolfe is alive? Father will be so happy to be reunited with him." Anna refused to consider the thought that Olav would not return even though it was 1947. The war had been over for two years.

That weekend as Anna was leaving for the Hoffmans' to see Rita, she met a group of neighborhood women boarding the tram car at the same time. She extended the usual casual greeting. Two turned their heads but immediately looked away when they recognized her. The other, who had been a former customer, reviled Anna with her eyes.

After being shunned, Anna burned with embarrassment and shame until she acknowledged how asinine the women were. Later she considered a deeper reason for their behavior, "The women directed their anger at Frieda and me because they feel helpless against the forces that have controlled their lives for the past ten years. They can't strike out at the real source of their problems so they delivered it squarely at us, the closest scapegoats."

It was a minor incident when compared to the other experiences in Anna's life but a turning point none-the-less. "German against German. Unfair treatment by a neighbor after all we Germans have been through."

A plan began to formulate in her mind that required something in short supply. Money. She decided to trade more aggressively on the black market to not only make money for her family and the Hoffmans; but also, to immigrate when the timing was right.

Frieda and Anna had traded in the black market zone close to the train station for years so Anna began with the familiar—the three houses near the train station.

As she was leaving one of the houses with her bag full of incriminating goods, a German police car was driving slowly down the street in her direction. Anna saw the car, but also saw a young Russian soldier walking in front of her.

She took his arm gently saying in Russian, "Hello darling, are you busy?" She strolled slowly beside him, smiling up into his bewildered face. Anna whispered an explanation, "The police."

"I can make some time for you," he replied and then in her ear, "They haven't passed yet." She pulled him by the collar to her face and kissed him. The strangers stood kissing until the police car disappeared around the block.

Anna and her new Russian accomplice laughed for a moment. "Thank you for your help," Anna said pulling away from him. "May I offer you a cigarette?"

"No thank you, but may I take you to a cafe to celebrate your narrow escape?"

Anna agreed as she linked her arm back in his. On the way, they stopped by a shop and he bought her a pretty hat and matching gloves. Laughing as they muddled through a conversation that alternated between broken German and broken Russian, they had a drink and parted, greatly cheered by their time together. They both enjoyed a moment in life that should have been quite common for young people.

Before she returned to the salon, she had bartered away the hat and gloves and was exhilarated by the day's successes. No mess, no strings. She was on the move, regaining some control over her life.

Frieda had given her permission to store her contraband in the small attic near Anna's bedroom. Anna lay in bed estimating what she would need to begin trading with a man called Shapiro, a surviving Jew who ran his own operation—beyond the black market zone. She slept soundly holding onto her goal tightly—her goal to immigrate even if she never heard from Karl again.

The next morning when Anna entered the kitchen, Mr. Wolfe was seated beside Frieda at the table. He stood and grasped her hand in both of his. "Anna, how good it is to see you! Frieda cushioned the shock for you I am told."

"Yes, I am so glad that you are alive, *Herr Wolfe*. My mother often wondered about you. On one occasion, she thought she heard your voice in the street. This haunted her for some time. She never really believed you were gone. And…here you are… We mourned the loss of all of your family."

"Thank you. It has tortured me ever since I lost them…but…we must somehow continue to live. Do you agree?"

"I do. I can't dwell on suffering. People go mad that way," Anna replied somberly. She had seen the darkness of despair.

Anna noticed that Frieda wasn't participating in their conversation. In a glance she saw the difference in Frieda. A relaxed contentment softened her features. Her previously sallow cheeks were pink and her lips rosy. Life had returned to her eyes and her apartment with the return of Mr. Wolfe.

Anna had never seen Frieda with a man and never imagined that she would ever be with anyone. She was always the solitary, impeccable, indomitable *Tante Frieda*. With warmth, Anna embraced the reality that Mr. Wolfe and Frieda were lovers.

"Yes, we must continue to live," Anna said as she excused herself to open the salon.

The streets of Leipzig were crowded with people walking or cycling. Most motor vehicles belonged to the military or police. Trams were packed. To avoid prying eyes, Anna knew she must be out early in the morning to do business. She had gained the respect of two men that she met quite regularly on a quiet street corner to share news and make deals.

When she approached, they offered her a piece of thick rye bread smothered in onions accompanied by a shot of forest alcohol from a hidden flask. "We have knowledge of a card game with the stakes you have been looking for. The problem is that you would be playing with eight men."

"Give me the time and address," Anna replied confidently.

On the following Saturday night, Anna took the tram to a stop near the address her contacts had given. The area was rough. She hesitated before turning the doorknob. Standing straight, Anna put on a smile and walked in to greet the stranger in the hallway. From her peripheral vision, she noted a telephone in the foyer and a water closet further down the hallway.

"We are in the back. Come with me," the man said curtly—all business.

Anna tossed her hair and followed confidently.

"Sit there. We are waiting on one other. Would you like a drink?"

The game was twenty-one. Eight other gamblers were at the table while two men supervised the game and freshened drinks. As arranged, a leak had informed them that a wealthy woman, who was unknown in most gambling circles, would be joining them. Anna's emerald necklace and earrings confirmed her status. They assumed she would be an easy mark.

Anna learned to bluff when she began her apprenticeship with Frieda and simply adapted her skills to this new scenario. Soon she was winning. Acting the part of a novice, she made an overly optimistic bet. She won again and again. Looks were exchanged around the table.

Anna knew the other gamblers would demand a chance to win back their money. Always able to think fast when in danger, she said, "Would you get me another drink, darling while I go to the water closet?" She picked up her winnings into her purse. "I like this game. I will be back as soon as I call my husband to tell him I will be home late tonight."

Anna rushed to the telephone and called the police station. She said she was in danger and gave her location. She said she didn't know what would happen if they did not come for her immediately. If her plan succeeded, she would have a ride home and protection from the gamblers. The voice on the other end of the line said they were on the way.

She had to get out soon. How long would she have to wait for the police? She held the receiver in case the dealer came looking for her, and he did.

He walked down the hallway and raised both hands in a gesture of annoyance as if to say. "Come on! What the hell are you doing? We are waiting!"

Anna placed her hand over the receiver and whispered. "Give me five minutes, and then I can stay for a few more hours. Thank you, darling." She brushed him away with her manicured hand, but he wasn't going anywhere. He took a firm stance, his arms across his chest.

She then turned away ostensibly for privacy but allowed him to listen. Her performance of a spousal disagreement with a nonexistent, irate and suspicious husband convinced the dealer who shuffled angrily back to the card room.

The police were already parked outside. The performance continued as Anna ran for the police car and then told them a remarkable story. Sympathetic, the two men on duty willingly drove Anna and her $30,000 *reichsmark* in winnings to safety.

Anna would not disclose the events of the evening with Frieda and Mr. Wolfe, but instead, discussed news of reconstruction projects beginning in Leipzig. Soon she apologized for being exhausted and retired to her room.

Actually she was full of adrenalin and hope from her winnings. Her thoughts were racing. Now she would have enough money to help the family, as well as, buy her way into the fur market.

By the autumn of 1947, her success had increased her confidence to trade deeper in the black market. Anna was driven by her desire to immigrate. She never missed an opportunity to make a deal and thrived on the challenge of doing business with a more elite network of people; and yet, above all, she still needed to be anchored in the routines of the salon and the security of Frieda's home.

One day Anna was removing the cape routinely from a customer when her father, *Oberleutnant Olav Muller*, walked in the salon door and stood motionless looking at his daughter.

Anna dropped the cape, and walked slowly toward her father holding his gaze. She couldn't believe her eyes. "*Vater, Vater* is this really you?" The salon chatter ceased as they watched Anna rush into her father's arms and hold him tightly. She trembled as she wept into his shoulder. His eyes were closed to dam the flow of emotion that leapt from his chest.

Frieda discreetly broke in with, "Olav and Anna, come in, this way." She kissed Olav's cheek and then led them into her apartment where they could have some privacy.

"I will join you as soon as I close the salon."

"*Vater*, it has been six years since we have seen you. We have missed you so very much. Mutti and the boys are at the Baumann farm and Rita is with the Hoffmans." Anna carried the conversation, explaining the significant events that had occurred while her father slowly nodded his head, his eyes unfathomable. She could discern that he had not had any conversations for some time and had to concentrate to follow what she was saying.

Anna poured each of them a drink and then sat beside her father, pausing to absorb the magnitude of this long-awaited moment. Olav had a different air about him like a traveler returning from exotic places; only instead of the scent of the sea or spices and sunlight, Olav smelled of leather, exhaustion and suffering. His face was lined by battles and his eyes deepened by experience. His hair had turned steel gray. Anna was struck by her father's unassuming dignity. The war had changed but not beaten him.

"I knew you would return. Where have you been since the war ended?"

Olav gulped the drink in one shot and then slowly began, "They bombed a building beside us…filled me with shrapnel. I was shell shocked, awoke one day in a sanatorium after surgery where I slowly recovered with the help of a new antibiotic…and time. No telephone…. No memory." He poured himself another drink. "Sometimes I can't control my temper. For no reason I will explode. They tell me I will improve—that I should stay away from difficult situations that might provoke me."

"*Vater*, it should be easy to avoid trouble these days," Anna joked.

With a hint of a smile he nodded in agreement.

"I have employment as a police officer when I am ready… No trouble in that job." They both shook their heads and laughed sardonically.

"Even your smile is sad, Anna! You too have suffered my child… You have been strong."

"Thank you *Vater*, but I am certainly not the only one. Women everywhere have had to shoulder responsibilities alone. It has destroyed some and made others tough. *Mutti* and *Tante Frieda* have been good examples and a source of strength for me," Anna added modestly.

"And your Karl. Any word?"

Anna shook her head, "You know, the borders have been closed and most telephone lines and mail services are still down."

"Perhaps word will get through soon. The allies are sorting out how our country will be divided and have been involved in reconstruction… An American business is rebuilding our subdivision…soon we will all be together again in a new home… I can work as police officer or maybe help Thomas on the farm until our house is completed," Olav stammered as though he did not know how to pronounce the words.

Frieda flung open the door, her demeanor charged in anticipation. "Olav look." Mr. Wolfe came forward with his hand extended. Olav stood immediately when he recognized his old friend—back from the dead.

They shook hands firmly. Neither spoke. Words seemed inadequate. They had both seen too much since last they played music together in the serenity of the Muller home. On the surface they had fought on opposing sides—*Herr Wolfe* in the resistance and Olav in the SS. At a deeper level, though, both had fought for the Germany they remembered and loved.

Rather than trivialize their experiences with small talk, Mr. Wolfe said, "Excuse me for a moment." He appeared with his violin and played a sonata. Olav sat forward with his arms on his knees looking down at the floor and listening intently; but when the music reached a climax, he sat up letting his head fall back from his shoulders, his eyes closed in ecstasy.

After Mr. Wolfe laid his violin on his lap, a long period of silence followed. Not understanding and slightly uncomfortable, he apologized, "Forgive me. I may have made a mistake…"

Olav began chuckling from deep in his stomach and before long all of them were roaring with laughter. Tears rolled down Anna's cheeks.

"Believe me there was no mistake. *Danke schon*!" Olav reassured him gratefully.

"You played superbly," said Frieda.

"Beautiful, beautiful!" praised Anna.

Later Anna disappeared to her room and carefully drew her father's saxophone from under the bed. Cradling the instrument in her arms she walked up to Olav and offered it as one would a newborn.

Leo rang the cowbell as soon as he heard the engine. The women dropped what they were doing and made directly for the cave. Thomas marched out to the driveway to address the situation. The engine didn't sound like a Russian army vehicle. "A German police car—what on earth?" he thought.

Olav stepped out of the passenger side and motioned for the driver to leave. Thomas squinted and then recognized the seasoned man walking toward him.

"Well, well. Olav Muller, you have returned to us alive!"

"Thomas, my friend, will you take in another member of the Muller family. I can still pull my weight."

"Of, course I will. Welcome. Let me call the others. Quickly everyone. Olav is back! Olav is back!"

Leo raced to the cave. "*Mutti, Vater* has returned! He is here! Come."

Incredulous, Mari paused trying to fully accept what her son was saying. Could it be true? Leo grabbed his mother's hand and pulled her forward. Mari broke into a run and met Olav as he was rounding the farmhouse in search of her. They stood close together facing one another.

The years apart melted away, and they recognized each other—the young people they once were… "I know you.. I remember," Olav thought.

Mari began to weep. Olav took her in his arms and kissed her hair and then her cheek and lips. Their kiss was long and filled with relief, regret and rejoicing. Mari held her husband's face in her hands, tears streaming down her face.

"My love," he said from the depths of his being.

Ralfie came running toward them, "*Vati, Vati*!" Leo was waiting respectfully beside his parents, but Ralfie pushed past him to embrace his father.

"My son, oh my son!" he hugged him and reached to shake hands with Leo.

"You have become a man, Leo. Come here." Tears formed in Olav's eyes as he embraced his oldest son.

Otto arrived but was unsure as he hugged this stranger he had heard so much about.

They walked toward the house in a mass of excitement. Then the boys broke away from their parents and began clowning around in reaction to the intensity of the reunion.

Surprisingly, once in the kitchen with the Baumanns, Olav felt awkward and was quiet. He had stored images of his sons from the last time he saw them six years previously. They had been small children and now they were grown, almost unfamiliar. The kindness of the Baumanns, their home, and Mari's beautiful face overwhelmed him.

And then Leo began telling funny stories about what had been happening on the farm. Soon the other boys were talking and enacting situations that had occurred with the Russians. Later Olav played a song on his saxophone and then everyone danced to folk songs Leo played on the ukulele.

Once again they were reunited and enlivened through music.

The Mullers were able to move into their new home before Christmas. For the first time, Olav spent time with Rita and was astonished by her artistic talent. He also observed the bond between Axel and her and approved wholeheartedly. He even approved of a gray cat that always seemed to be underfoot.

When Christmas arrived the Hoffmans, Frieda, and Mr. Wolfe joined the Mullers. They were all very grateful to be together again. Mari thought:

"This year carols are sung from the very heart of Christmas

The snow thick on the branches stops my breath

This beauty makes me silent as winter."

Chapter Twenty-Two
Head West

"You will get a better price in West Germany, Anna," Shapiro stated matter-of-factly.

"How do I cross the border? Of course, I have no papers," Anna asked unfazed by the suggestion of such a perilous venture.

"There are ways. I know someone who might accompany you for a price. He trades on the other side, knows how to cross Checkpoint Charlie."

"Thank you for this information. I will consider it. Now, I wish to purchase a few gold coins…"

Anna had worked tirelessly buying and selling fabric, furs and now gold coins. She had a network of informants and key contacts established. Anna may have lacked her family's musical talent, but she could certainly orchestrate business on the street with acumen and finesse.

She kept her activities to herself. It was not just the fear of discovery by the authorities, but also disapproval from her parents. Anna would not be a burden to her parents. She only wanted reprieve and happiness for them. Frieda knew about her clandestine activity, but even she did not know to what extent Anna was involved.

In June of 1948, Anna and Frieda received a welcome visit from Father Engel. With his usual grace he sat at the table and shared a drink with the women. Anna thought, "He took care of the burial of Lena Lenz, the funeral for *Grosmutter Beatrice*, and all of the baptisms in our family. He was a balm to my mother's soul and a comfort to Karl and me over the years. I wonder how many others he has helped or saved. He looks weary, but the lines on his face are from forbearance and compassion. He reassures me somehow that life will be all right."

Frieda saw another side of Father Engel, a warrior. He had been a key figure in the Leipzig underground movement to overthrow Adolf Hitler and his High Command. For centuries the Roman Catholic Church operated secret networks, tunnels, codes. He worked in a small part of that global system.

"Here, my child, I have a message for you from Belgium." Father Engel passed Anna a letter.

Anna had always believed this day would come. Her eyes raced through the letter, "It is from Karl. Thank God, he is alive! Thank you for delivering this to me, Father. I have not heard from Karl since he left three years ago. He is still in Belgium…Would you be able to send a letter back to him?"

Father Engel was hesitant, "I can begin the exchange, but cannot predict how long the letter will take to reach Karl, or if it will even reach him intact."

Anna rushed to her room for a few minutes and returned with a letter to send back to Karl. "Thank you, Father."

"God bless you," the priest said warmly as he took the letter and rose to leave.

Later Anna's mind raced, "Karl finally has papers to immigrate to Canada. He can wait for two months for me to reach Belgium before the ship sails. I knew he wouldn't fail me. I have enough money to leave, but I will never get legal papers to leave East Germany here. I'll make arrangements to travel with Shapiro's man and escape secretly across the border."

Anna was intent on reaching Karl without interference from anyone so she did not consult others about her plans. She knew her father would never allow her to cross Checkpoint Charlie illegally. Olav knew very well that the Russians would shoot to kill anyone trying to cross along the two kilometer-wide strip of land that ran the length of the nation north to south—dividing the country into East and West Germany.

And so, because of her suspicions that they would block her departure, Anna ignored the tactical knowledge, and connections of those close to her—Frieda, Mr. Wolfe, Father Engel and Olav. She would undertake the crossing alone.

The following Sunday when Anna was home with her family, she tried to burn each moment with them into her memory to savor in the future.

Leo at 18 years of age was a popular, handsome young man, quite muscular after working on the Baumann farm, but she noted a smoldering rage within his brown eyes that disturbed her. They would be full of charm one moment and then shift to anger the next.

Like Leo, Ralfie was strong from physical labor. He walked with a bit of a slouch and his movements were more fluid than Leo. His blue eyes twinkled with a quick wit. Otto at aged 12 was clearly shaping up to be the big-boned boy of the Muller family. "Who wouldn't love his easy-going open personality?" Anna thought.

Anna's heart ached when she looked at Mari in her apron. "How will I live without her wisdom and love. Forgive me!" Anna wept inside.

"*Mutti*, here is some fabric a friend traded for haircuts and shaves. Perhaps you could make a new dress for yourself."

"*Lochen*, it is stunning! I have not seen fabric like this in years. Thank you!" Mari said as she stroked the material.

Anna watched Rita and Axel sitting beside one another and smiled. Axel lived with the Mullers now since the Hoffman house was still full of relatives. Rita helped with housework and continued with her art, and Axel had begun a mechanical apprenticeship. Anna could bear separation from Rita knowing she had Axel.

When she was preparing to leave, Rita came to her side and said softly. "You are always in my heart, Anna." She placed Anna's palm over her heart. "I love you."

"It is as though she senses that I am leaving," thought Anna. Anna slipped her emerald necklace and earrings into Rita's hand and whispered, "I want you to have these. Don't say anything right now." Rita slipped the jewelry into her pocket.

Later Anna approached her father, "*Vater*, I am glad you have the job playing music at the dinner club instead of working for the police. You have spent enough of your life in a uniform."

Olav agreed as he kissed his daughter's cheek. "I am ready to hang up the uniform. The saxophone is great company."

When Anna was leaving, she looked back and waved before reaching the street. Then dragging herself away from her family, she forced herself to concentrate on what lay ahead and the details of her departure. Soon she was back at the salon.

When Frieda and Anna were alone, Anna began, "I would like to say something to you, Frieda."

"Of course, what is it?"

"I admire what you did during the war even though I knew very little of your work with Mr. Wolfe. And now the orphanage! The two of you will continue to save lives. I want you to know that… I love and respect you, *Tante Frieda!* You have taught me so much over the years."

"What is this, *liebling*?"

"I want you to know how I feel, that is all."

Frieda nodded and held both of Anna's hands with her own. "My Anna, you have been like a daughter to me. I love you so very much…Sleep well." Frieda guessed that Anna was leaving soon, and this time, chose not to interfere in her life.

Shapiro's man appeared at the meeting place as arranged. When he smiled at Anna, his eyes squinted so tightly not a bit of his eyes showed. It was impossible for Anna to read him. Anna sensed something menacing about him, but he distracted her with the plans for their crossing before her suspicions had a chance to take hold.

"We will cross Checkpoint Charlie on a night without much moonlight. We will have roughly a kilometer of farmland to cross before the actual borderline to the West. Run hunched over, close to the ground so our silhouettes are not spotted as easily.

You must not speak. We might encounter a patrol. They usually carry flashlights and sometimes have dogs if they are anticipating trouble. We have the weight of our packages to carry and about two kilometers to cover before we are across.

The searchlight from the watchtower scans the surrounding land at the border in timed intervals. We will count the length of the intervals. We will count in our minds so we hit the ground before the glaring searchlight exposes us. If you panic and lose count, we will be cut down by the automatic rifles of the Russian guards. It is imperative that you are punctual, or, I will leave without you." Undaunted, Anna made preparations.

Although Anna estimated that she had sufficient money for bribes, food, transportation, and lodging, she intended to move additional black market goods in West Germany to cover unforeseen expenses as she awaited her travel permit to cross into Belgium. Anna had stitched gold coins in the hem of her skirt.

On a cloudy night in August, Anna and her guide gathered up their parcels containing fabric and furs to smuggle across the border. They crouched behind the barbed wire allowing their eyes to adjust to the night. He tapped Anna's shoulder to begin moving. Suddenly, she felt a flood of regret and was about to run back, but she saw Karl in her mind. She snapped to attention, her mind completely alert.

Accustomed to the night sky, she was now able to follow the dark shape of her guide across what seemed an endless expanse of field. Her leg muscles were burning.

A sound. Her eyes probed ahead but she couldn't see the guide. Simultaneously, she caught a glimpse of a silhouette of soldiers and heard a gruff chuckle. "Please, no dogs!" Anna appealed mentally.

She couldn't see her guide anywhere. Taking a few steps to her left, Anna found a depression in the field. It seemed to be a shallow ditch running for some length. Anna quietly crept into the ditch and lay on her stomach craning her neck to look around. He was already there lying on his belly behind her.

The guards were close, talking in low tones. She held her breath as they walked alongside the ditch. "Boots! I see their boots!" A cigarette butt landed not far from her head. "Keep walking, please, keep walking!" Anna screamed in her mind.

The guide did not move for at least fifteen minutes after the guards had passed. Then crouching close to the ground, he tapped her on the shoulder as he passed her. They began the last stretch to the border, to the watch tower with its probing light that never slept.

Suddenly his arm shot out from his side, his hand motioning Anna to stop. They crouched and when he raised his finger they began to count in their minds. He then motioned to be at the ready. Go.

The field was uneven and Anna tripped but caught herself. "Count. The light is sweeping around." Anna's heart was pounding in her ears like a tribal drum. "Count!" The light was almost upon them. "Down!" She fell to the ground, breathing heavily. He was still there in front of her. "Count. Run. Don't fall. Don't drop the parcels. Here is the light. Hit the ground. Count. Run."

They made it!

He helped her over the fence and grabbed her arm to direct her away from the actual border station and its prying light. "I will take you to an affordable hotel where you can pay me for my services."

Anna was elated from the rise in adrenalin after the perilous crossing of Checkpoint Charlie. She thought, "The worst is over now. I made it! I am in West Germany. I will be with Karl and Klara soon!"

Anna paid her guide and received directions from him to the black market zone. She then checked into the hotel at five *reichsmark* per week. Her tiny room had one wooden chair and a narrow bed frame covered with a thin, filthy mattress—no sheets or bedding, only a pillow slip.

Anna suddenly felt deflated by her grim surroundings and the fact that she was completely alone in an unfamiliar place. Exhausted, she covered the mattress with fabric from her store of black market goods and collapsed into a deep sleep, heedless of her dirty clothing or the mud on her hands.

The next morning, Anna washed quickly and changed into a clean dress. She left the muddy skirt in the corner to be washed later and hurried to the black market zone for food. Returning with some canned food, she settled in the chair and ate hungrily.

"The first task today is to apply for my papers," she thought, but her attention quickly shifted. She stopped eating when she noticed the fabric that had been covering the mattress was gone. She jumped up and kicked the bed over. To her horror the packages were gone. Her skirt was no longer in the corner. "My gold!"

Anna was livid. She marched in circles around the tiny room with her palm to her forehead, "He robbed me. He must have been watching the hotel waiting for me to leave. I was set up—careless….Shapiro?" She slumped down in the chair.

Once her fury and fears subsided, Anna took inventory, assessing her situation. "I have my savings in my purse. If I apply for my papers now, I should still have enough money to reach Karl in Belgium before he leaves."

But the papers were delayed. Her money didn't last for very long with the high inflation in West Germany.

By the end of October, she could not afford the hotel; and because of the prohibitive price of food, she had nothing to eat. The Red Cross refugee camp near the border was her only choice.

A kind, tired woman showed her to a bed of straw in one of the many tents and explained the hours the soup kitchen was open. As she lay on her scratchy bed, she looked at the amber ring on her finger, a gift from her father. She looked at her burgundy, Italian leather shoes, also a gift from Olav. She felt the material of the dress that Mari had made and regretted leaving Leipzig.

Two weeks passed in the camp—purgatory, between her home in Leipzig and a life with Karl. Waiting. "Karl will leave for Canada. He cannot wait much longer."

She pleaded with the authorities. No papers. More waiting. She knew the dream was over. "Karl must have left. He probably didn't receive my letter. He is out of reach." She admitted that she had taken a huge gamble. She had miscalculated the risks and lost.

The kind woman at the camp was making rounds and saw how dejected Anna looked. "How are you, dear?"

"I don't know what could be the matter with me. I am so itchy."

"Come with me, " she said and they walked toward the medical tent. "The doctor will take care of you."

Phlegmatic, Anna sat up straight while the doctor shaved her head to treat the lice. Tresses of soft wavy blonde hair drifted to the earth. Then he gently wrapped a turban around her bald head.

When Anna was alone, she looked at her nails. She picked frantically to scratch the remains of the "Rose Petal" polish from her nails and chewed her torn and chipped finger nails with her teeth. "I am hideous and dirty. I am alone. I can't go on. Where is Karl? Why couldn't things have been different?" She felt defeated.

A distant inner voice uttered defiantly, "This is the path of madness! Self-pity! Stop now." Anna silenced her precipitous thoughts and steeled herself to make it through the long, grim days in the camp.

November was a month of chilling wind, rain, and dark passionate clouds. She retreated to her tent and passed the time in her mind, fluctuating between the future and the past.

She remembered how the homes in Leipzig had looked at dawn—interior lights golden in the grey light. Inside their family home, she had found peace in the early morning.

She imagined the smell of coffee shared with her mother, sleepy children with tousled hair seeking hugs as they came into the kitchen for breakfast. She remembered an image of the morning sunlight reflected on the wall creating abstract patterns of warmth. "How precious a simple routine becomes when it is gone…"

November also brought about change. Anna's thoughts became more realistic, "My papers are not ready and I have no money. It is too dangerous to return home alone. I cannot continue to wait here. It has been over four weeks. I must go to Hanover and find a job. 'We must somehow continue to live,' Mr. Wolfe had said."

Anna looked for a travelling companion around the camp. She had noticed a young woman who would be attractive to men should the women need to pool all resources. Anna approached her in the soup line, and coincidentally, the woman mentioned Hanover. Good enough.

It was a cold winter day when Anna and her female companion, who seemed suspiciously friendly, arrived in Hanover. They wore only light coats over their dresses and men's socks in open sandals. Anna had sold her Italian shoes but could not bear to sell the amber ring. She slipped it into her pocket away from criminal eyes.

The women hurried into a restaurant, rubbing their hands and stamping their feet. They ordered coffee and were sipping their hot beverages slowly when the door of the restaurant opened and two men entered. The blonde one tripped and then recovered like a performer in a circus act awaiting applause, a wide smile across his florid face.

When Anna and her new acquaintance laughed appreciatively, the men walked over to their table. The blonde, husky man was Peter, a Ukrainian. His friend soon left the group, but Peter stayed and bought the women food. Anna explained their situation to Peter, and he subsequently offered the women a place to stay for the night.

They were relieved to find shelter with a man who did not seem violent or dangerous in any way, but Anna was concerned about her companion's talent for pick pocketing. She did not want to jeopardize their arrangements with Peter.

That night Anna confronted the woman, "Do not even think about robbing Peter. I have seen you looking around… He is our only hope right now." Her warning did not go unheeded. Nothing was stolen from Peter, but the following morning she had vanished and Anna could not find her amber ring. Anna felt numb.

With her friend gone, Anna acknowledged that staying with Peter was her best and only option. Her world had toppled and Peter offered protection from starvation, the cold of winter, or worse. He worked for the English as a clerk, moving supplies in canvas covered trucks. His job had pilfered benefits.

Sometimes Peter and Anna got along well enough—telling anecdotes and laughing with one another. Peter played the clown. His disheveled blonde hair and facial contortions made Anna laugh at times.

Too often, though, he was dense and vulgar. She hid her disgust and performed compulsory sex in exchange for a place to live and protection. She made the best of her situation knowing the alternative.

"Let's escape to Venezuela, Anna. We would be free there. We could live like rich people in a country like that. One of the drivers was telling me about lots of Germans escaping to Brazil and Venezuela. Marry me, and we will run away to a jungle and live like Adam and Eve—fuck all day. Have beautiful blonde babies."

"No, never!" thought Anna, but her reply was noncommittal, "We'll see what happens."

Anna had accepted the fact that duplicity was a prerequisite for her survival. She now believed that starvation made morality superfluous—A luxury of the well-fed, safe, and free.

Chapter Twenty-Three
Cataclysm

In the spring of 1949, Anna was finally able to gain employment. *Frau Klein*, a widow who lived not far from Peter, asked Anna to be a nanny to her two young children. The payment was room and board. Anna accepted immediately.

Frau Klein soon realized that Anna was a reliable nanny. The household was organized, and she had established a rapport with the children. Anna had the ability to teach in a way the children enjoyed, but also, disciplined them appropriately. *Frau Klein* was free to operate her catering business knowing her children were in good hands.

"My oldest son, Kurt, will be here this evening. He is more like an uncle to the children because of the age difference…works in the downtown area of Hanover selling motorcycles and automobiles. Between his job and a girlfriend, who occupies most of his spare time, we don't see him much. It is always a treat to have him back home."

"I will make something nice for our evening meal then?"

"Yes. I already wonder how I have managed without you."

Anna had settled the children to their arithmetic exercises at the kitchen table and was stirring a pot of chicken stew. She was about to add dumplings when she heard footsteps. The door opened letting in a breath of spring air. She turned expecting to see *Frau Klein*, but it was her son, Kurt.

"Kurt!" the children cried in unison, jumping from their chairs. Kurt swooped his sister up into his arms and gave her a kiss and then ruffled his little brother's hair. "You aren't *Mutti*." he said when he saw Anna.

"Hello Kurt. I am Anna Muller. Your mother hired me last week to help out with Heinz and Sylvia."

"I am pleased to meet you."

Both were thrown off balance. Anna returned to the stew and Kurt sat down with the children discussing their arithmetic. Anna was shocked by her response. "I thought I was dead inside. It has been five years since Karl left Germany."

The feeling was reciprocated. Kurt was stricken at the sight of Anna. He became keenly aware of all his senses. His body felt ready. "Who is she? None of my girlfriends have ever made me feel like this before."

Frau Klein came home and broke the sexual tension in the kitchen. All of them gathered together, talking comfortably over a hearty meal. Their tired, saddened, winter spirits were lifted.

Anna was drawn to the fire and humor in Kurt's coffee eyes. While he appeared to sit in a relaxed, carefree position, she sensed a restless vitality, like a cat ready to pounce. She listened to every word he spoke.

During the weeks that followed, *Frau Klein* was aware of the growing attraction between Anna and Kurt and approved. She thought Kurt's previous girlfriends had been flighty—not good enough for her son. Here was a woman of substance, melding well with her family.

On a hot Sunday in June, *Frau Klein* suggested that they walk to the river with a picnic lunch. After a swim and lunch, they were ready to pack up when Heinz pleaded, "May we stay longer *Mutti*? Please?"

"Yes son, we will stay. Kurt, why don't you take Anna home, and I'll stay here with the children for another hour."

As soon as they had closed the door, Kurt pulled Anna to him and covered her mouth with his. They kissed passionately while they grasped for flesh. He pushed her against the wall and entered her with all the desperation he had stored from weeks of wanting her. Anna's arms were raised above her head, and he clasped her fingers tightly as he came. Breathing heavily they paused for a moment, their foreheads touching. Then he kissed her tenderly and said, "We have an hour." Taking Anna's hand, he led her into his bedroom where they made love again.

Anna was alive. She was aware of blood coursing through her veins; her skin and hair were sensitive; she felt sexy almost all of the time. *Frau Klein* was pleased to see Anna glowing; and, even happier when only three weeks later, Kurt proposed.

Sleepless in the bedroom she shared with Heinz and Sylvia, Anna wondered, "Is this love disguised as sex, or sex disguised as love? I always saw my future with Karl. This is all so strange. Kurt is eight years younger than I. I do not want to end up like Nathalie's mother, Lena." Heedless, Anna craved his body and did not want to live without him. Kurt had resuscitated her. Finally, she decided.

"Love…is always a gamble, but I do not want to be alone anymore in an unfamiliar city. Adrift by myself. I will marry him."

Kurt found a luxurious apartment in downtown Hanover where they would be closer to his job. He took Anna shopping to select new furniture. She chose a dining room set of heavy, polished dark oak. The living room had a bank of windows facing the street. She placed the round dining table and buffet on one end and a sofa and two chairs at the other. The sofa tables matched the dining set. Upholstery and draperies were in shades of blue, mauve and gray, the carpets lush and tasteful. In the corner was a bird cage with two canaries, a wedding gift from Kurt's aunt.

Anna had been absorbed with her new life and enjoyed preparing her husband's favorite meals in their bright kitchen. One afternoon when Anna was preparing Rolladen, she put her knife down and looked out the window. "What am I doing here? How could I have ever guessed that my life would change so much in less than a year.

I was in the Red Cross camp—bald and broken! Now I have beautiful clothes and manicured finger nails—a husband, a home. And food!" She turned back to her recipe shaking her head and smiling. "Not the husband I imagined, granted, but a better life."

Anna covered each piece of beef with mustard, bits of bacon, carrot, and onion and then rolled and tied each with string. She fried them, turning steadily to brown. Then she added some water and cooked the meat slowly for an hour.

In another pan she cooked finely cut red cabbage in bacon fat with a bay leaf. Later she would add the apple slices to cook. She then prepared potatoes to serve with the beef gravy. Dessert would be chocolate pudding with vanilla sauce. She couldn't wait for Kurt to come home.

Kurt flung the door open, taking off his fedora and long winter coat in one motion. "*Schissen*, I am home. I missed you!" Kurt never seemed to tire. He was energetic after long days of work and only slept about five hours at night.

"Hello Darling! How was your day today?" she asked as they kissed.

"I sold a fortune today. Let's celebrate with some wine." He told Anna some hilarious stories about customers and the owner of the dealership.

"What smells so tasty?"

"Rolladen. Your favorite."

Anna served the dinner, and let Kurt eat his fill. "This is delicious. Why aren't you eating?"

"I want you to feed me."

He paused for a moment to see if she was serious and then carefully fed her small portions from his fork. She did not finish her meal until they were finished having sex.

That winter saw recovery in Hanover. Reconstruction was slowly changing the cityscape. While piles of rubble remained in many sections of the city, food and jobs were becoming more available. The mood of the people was becoming more optimistic.

One afternoon, Kurt arrived home from work early. "Anna, put on your coat and come with me. I have a surprise for you," he said excitedly. Kurt had bought an automobile. "Get in."

"It is sensational, darling!" she said as she stroked the dashboard and the upholstery on the seat. He explained all the special features of the engine and then in mid-sentence said, "We are going out to a restaurant tonight to celebrate."

Anna was thrilled. She had been indoors too much during the winter. Kurt did not want her to have a job, but also, he did not like her leaving their apartment without him. She thought he was being protective.

"Let me get ready. I won't be long."

Anna put her hair up and wore a cream dress with a wide belt that accented her narrow waste. When they arrived at the restaurant, Kurt took Anna's coat and placed his hand lightly on the back of her neck to guide her to their table. He saw the response of several men looking at Anna. As he lit her cigarette, he whispered in her ear, "You look beautiful tonight in that dress, but I can't wait to take it off…very slowly when we are home." He wrapped his long arm around the back of her seat as if to say, "She is mine."

The young couple became popular and continued to prosper. When summer arrived, Kurt bought a motorcycle. During the hot weather in July, they were eager to take a ride into the mountains to their favorite lake for a vacation.

"I know where we can find the most delicious *pfifferling*," claimed Kurt.

"Here? I see moss not mushrooms."

"Ah, but follow me," Kurt said as he raised sections of the moss to expose the delicacies. They carefully gathered enough for a meal and placed them in the shade.

"Let's swim," suggested Anna. They raced each other to the lake and floated on the surface in the hot July sun. For once Kurt was relaxed, not restless to be somewhere else. At one point in the afternoon, he even napped while lying on the beach.

When he awoke, he called out, "Anna, you dive like a mermaid… Are you ready to go to the hotel yet?" Anna had the sensation of time being suspended. Many years had passed since she had been so happy. Reluctantly, she emerged from the water.

When they checked into their hotel in Freiburg, they asked the cook to prepare their truffles with smoked ham. Delicious! Even before the drinks, dancing, and laughter with new acquaintances, Anna had decided she must have Kurt's child. She stopped using birth control on their holiday.

By the end of the summer, Anna knew she was pregnant but had yet to see a doctor to confirm. When she was about to tell Kurt, he explained that his mother was ill and needed help with Sylvia and Heinz. She decided to wait for confirmation from the doctor to tell him the good news.

"Of course, I will go," Anna reassured him. "I will probably stay two weeks to make sure she is back on her feet before I leave."

"Take the car. I can use the motorcycle. I will miss you, darling," Kurt said as he hugged her. "I'll see you in a couple of weeks."

Anna was buoyant, looking forward to a bit of independence and a visit with *Frau Klein*. Anna rolled down the window and let the wind blow on her face and in her hair. On the way, she picked up some food, including treats for the children.

Anna settled in, caring for the children and making soup for her mother-in-law. Although *Frau Klein* had a dreadful flu, once the fever was down, she stopped retching and was left with only a cough. Since her mother-in-law was feeling better, Anna shared her news, "I am going to have a baby!"

"Really! You are pregnant! Anna, I couldn't be happier. I am glad you have come into our lives!"

"I haven't told Kurt yet."

"He will be a wonderful father, Anna. Actually, why don't you go home tomorrow and tell him? I am feeling much better. You don't have to stay any longer."

While Anna was driving into the city, she was filled with anticipation, "This is so exciting! I can't wait to see his face when I tell him."

Anna knew something was wrong the instant she closed the door behind her. The apartment was untidy and she was acutely aware of a noisy silence. The two canaries were dead in the cage. She walked toward the bedroom as though in a trance. First she heard giggling and then saw them naked on her bed.

For the first time in their relationship, Kurt was at a loss for words. In a low tone of voice Anna ordered, "Get-out-NOW!" The drunken girl's hair was a tangled mess. She crawled from the bed with a gasp, struggling with her panties and slip. Anna stood her ground and watched as the girl clumsily buttoned her dress and attempted to pull her left shoe onto her right foot. She was about to say something, but Anna stopped her, "Do not speak to me, *hure nude*! Get out!" The girl rushed awkwardly past Anna.

"Anna. Listen. *Liebe*, she means nothing to me. It was nothing—only a fling. You are my true love. You know that!" Kurt explained in an attempt to placate Anna. He was on his feet and anxious.

"…Yes, I know you love me, but don't ever do this again," Anna fixed herself a drink and sunk into the sofa. Kurt had pulled on his pants and sat across from her, looking worried, but he dared not speak.

"All of us make mistakes… Let's try to forget this. Have a drink and I will tell you about your mother and the children," Anna suggested sadly.

Kurt was shocked and puzzled by his wife's reaction. "Does this mean she doesn't really care about me or she cares so much she is willing to forgive and move on?"

When she was alone the following day, Anna stared into the bird cage. No food or water in sight. Her heart broke for the yellow canaries. Their eyes were closed tight and their little feet and legs were tucked in close to their bodies. Once singing and flying about they now lay in their droppings in the bottom of the cage. Kurt had destroyed the birds and their marriage, and now he had forced her to consider abortion. When he came home from work bearing an extravagant gift for Anna, she was already gone.

After the abortion, Anna eventually found a job as a nanny for an English family that lived a safe distance from the apartment. She adjusted to the formal manner and language in the home well enough; and although the children were unruly, Anna soon earned their affection. On a different level, though, she was uneasy with the undercurrent in the home.

Mrs. Flemming smiled and spoke politely to her in English and again in German so Anna would both understand daily instructions and also learn to speak English. Yet, Anna felt the cold reproach behind her words. After several weeks, Anna had to face the fact that she was an *auslander* again and, even worse, a despised German.

Anna was discouraged and unhappy. She felt out of place in the Flemming home and lost and lonely in Hanover.

Also, she was deeply hurt by Kurt's infidelity. At night the tempest in her mind kept her awake. "He crossed the line! Nobody does that to me! He cheated on me, betrayed me. I have lost my child because of him!… He is mercurial and flashy—immature in the way he boasts."

Then she would vacillate, longing for her comfortable home and loving mother-in-law. "Kurt is eight years younger than I. He was never in the military to mature and has not experienced what I have in life. Maybe I was rash in leaving him. We all make mistakes…

Every choice we make changes us in some way. Maybe my choice to leave was wrong, driven by hurt and pride. Am I ruined again—starting over?… Maybe I don't have to forgive him—just love him."

Meanwhile, desperate with remorse, Kurt sought his mother for advice. "Anna has left me. I want her back, but I don't know where to look."

"Why did she leave?"

"I don't know. I came home from work and she was gone. She never even left a note."

"When?"

"Three months ago."

"What did you do to make her leave, Son?"

"What do you mean? Are you taking her side?" Kurt challenged defensively.

"No… But I know Anna would not leave you without a reason. She loves you."

"I love her too, but she still left me!"

"Kurt, tell me the truth because I know Anna would not leave you. She was pregnant. You must have done something horrible."

"*Mein Gott, Mutter!*" Kurt sobbed. He shook his head and roughly wiped away his tears before he confessed. "I slept with a girl from the store. It meant nothing to me. Anna was away with you and I was lonely… We had a drink after work and then…she was all over me… I know now. I was wrong. What can I do?"

"Well Anna would need a place to stay, so she probably took a job as a nanny again."

Immediately, Kurt enlisted the help of friends to look for Anna and relentlessly patrolled the streets alone in his car searching, asking questions. Eventually he found her.

When Mrs. Flemming came to the door, she was surprised to see a striking young man in a long, loose gray coat, quality suit, and fedora. His shoes, the automobile – all of it screamed style and money.

"Yes?"

"*Guten Morgen*. I want to see my wife?" Kurt demanded.

"To whom do you refer, sir?"

"Anna Klein. I know she is your nanny. Tell her I am here, please."

"That won't be possible. I have to ask you to leave, or I will call my husband, the Colonel."

"That won't be necessary," interrupted Anna from behind her employer. Anna had already made her choice to return to her formidably attractive husband.

Life resumed for the Kleins, but Anna now viewed life quite differently. She had always seen life as a flow of past, present, and future and was fully convinced that she had to do whatever was required in the present to secure her future happiness. Now she thought only of the present, "The past is gone—out of reach. There is no glimmering future—only today."

Not long after the couple was reunited, Kurt raised the issue of the abortion after he had been drinking.

"Let it go, Kurt, I couldn't have a baby with a man who was cheating on me. I couldn't trust you anymore and had no way of taking care of a child on my own."

"You deprived me of a family. Make it up to me. Get pregnant again," Kurt demanded.

Anna longed for a family, but because of his bruising accusations and aggressive demands, she still didn't trust him.

Kurt was drinking more than ever. He often smelled of alcohol after work and regularly went out with friends. His immaturity appalled her. "How can he possibly be a father?" She thought it prudent to use birth control for the time being.

Despite the challenges in their marriage, Anna continued to satisfy her husband in the hope that time would heal their marriage. One evening after dinner, she said to Kurt, "Why not stay home tonight?" She stood beside him at the dining room table and stripped slowly down to her garter belt and silk stockings. He reached between her legs and began touching her gently. She led him by the hand toward the bedroom and kissed him while she took off his clothes. His penis was already erect but as he was pulling her close, she broke away and said, "Not yet, let's take our time."

While she poured a bath, she kneeled down and took him in her mouth and stroked his penis until he was close to coming and then stopped and climbed into the bath. Kurt looked at her with curiosity.

"Will you wash me?"

He knelt down and washed her body everywhere. He touched her between the legs until she pushed him away, and her head fell slightly forward, her eyes closed. "I love you!" she said as they both stood up and embraced. He picked her up in his arms and took her to the bed. He began licking her toes and did not stop until he reached her lips. When he penetrated her she was lusciously wet. Kurt's thrust was hard and passionate and when he eventually came, he uttered a prolonged growl. He lifted himself off of her and collapsed by her side. He stayed home that night.

However, despite Anna's efforts to keep Kurt happy, his corrosive drinking habit worsened. Sometimes he didn't show up for dinner at all and would stagger in late at night, loud and inane. On other nights, he was ugly from the alcohol and had endless strings of caustic remarks to hurl at Anna.

After such nights Anna would leave for walks or a ride on her bicycle, only to be followed by Kurt. He would be sincerely apologetic, spouting promises he could never keep.

During these difficult times with Kurt, Anna thought of Karl. She had always felt they belonged together from the moment they met in Leipzig; when Klara called out in the night and introduced them. She vividly remembered the first time she heard his voice. "*Guten Abend Fraulein Muller*. How are you tonight? May I offer you my arm?"

She yearned for the safety of his broad chest and strong arms. He was steadfast, had always taken care of Anna and her family. Kurt seemed foolish when compared with a capable, mature man like Karl.

The March skies were dark. Winter had not yet released its grip—was reluctant to allow the sound, color, and fragrance of spring to live.

Anna refused to accept that her marriage was over because she was afraid to leave again. She deluded herself into thinking that their marriage would improve over time. Anna was shattered when Kurt was out all night; and yet, if she protested, Kurt would blame her for his debauchery. Discussion was futile.

"What is wrong with you? Don't you want me to touch you?" Kurt slurred accusingly. "What did I do now? Took a break from work with my friends?"

"You go out too often. I need to be able to trust my husband. If you don't want to be with me, why don't you let me go? Then you can do whatever you want."

"Don't I provide for you? You are being cruel! You are my wife. I need you. I will kill myself if you leave…"

Anna looked into his intense eyes and for a moment relented to his passion. Then he made the mistake of adding in a condescending tone.

"You just need a baby to occupy your time. Now come over here, *schissen*."

"Not now, Kurt."

"I said come here."

"Not now!"

Kurt loomed in front of Anna ready to strike and then dropped his fist and stormed out the door. When he returned home drunk later that night, Kurt was in a dangerously calm state.

"Don't think you can run away from me again tomorrow because we had a couple's quarrel. Don't think you can run away ever. I will kill you if you try to leave me again Anna! You and I are married and we WILL have a family. You are the ONLY ONE for me."

Anna knew better than to disagree. She resumed the role of a dutiful wife.

On an afternoon in early May, Anna was preparing chicken in cream sauce for dinner when she heard an unexpected knock at the door. A young woman with a troubled look on her face introduced herself as Loni. Anna, assuming that she was from the apartment building, invited her inside and said, "Please, sit down. Tell me what is wrong, and maybe I can help."

"You don't know who I am?" asked the stranger.

"No, I have never met you. What do you want?"

"…Kurt and I have been lovers for months, and we want to be together. He says that you won't agree to a divorce. I am begging you to let him go. He doesn't love you anymore. You refuse to give him a baby, but I am pregnant with his child. Let him go!" the girl blurted hysterically.

"Get out of my house," Anna said calmly pointing at the door. "Get out of here now! You know nothing, *hure nude*!"

After the door slammed, Anna was reeling from an avalanche of mixed emotions. In her mind she ranted, "How could I have allowed myself to be fooled again! How did I convince myself that our marriage could be salvaged?"

Later that evening when Kurt was home, Anna confronted him with his lies. "A friend of yours came to the apartment today, darling."

Disinterested Kurt asked, "My friends know not to come here. Was it Werner?"

"No, Loni is her name."

Kurt dropped the newspaper he had been reading and with a calculating glare asked, "Loni? And, what did Loni want?"

"To tell me she is pregnant with your baby," Anna replied coldly.

Kurt leapt to his feet and marched over to where Anna was sitting.

"Don't you dare complain to ME! I take good care of you! I don't need to explain myself to you. Besides how do I even know the baby is mine?"

"So you admit that you have been sleeping with her? I can't go on like this!"

As Anna turned, Kurt grabbed her left arm and struck her in the face with his right fist. She slipped and fell to the floor.

"Don't talk about leaving again to me," Kurt shouted as he kicked her in her back. "Loni is a whore. She means nothing to me… If you try to leave, I will KILL you."

As she lay on the floor, tasting her own blood as it dripped into her mouth, she thought, "How did I sink to this level in my life? Frieda taught me the signs. I should have known better. I must get up and clean my face."

It was over this time.

During the weeks that followed, she acquired her travel papers at the consulate in Cologne. She lied to her mother-in-law about her destination and purpose of the trip so *Frau Klein* would cover for her.

Since mail service did not flow between West and East Germany, she sought the assistance of the church to communicate a message. Eventually she found a priest who had the necessary connections to Father Engel in Leipzig, East Germany.

Although the priest accepted her letter, he warned that he could not guarantee its arrival. Anna's letter inquired about Karl and requested that Father Engel inform her family that she was well.

Anna wanted to make one more attempt to reach Karl before she tried to immigrate alone and so…she waited.

In the interim, to avoid suspicion, Anna let Kurt believe that he controlled her completely and that she still loved him regardless of his affairs. With the exception of mass, she rarely left the house without him. She was willing when Kurt wanted sex and pretended to be content in their marriage to avoid suspicion.

Anna was relieved when one evening Kurt asked if she would like to go to their favorite restaurant. She looked forward to getting away from the confinement of their apartment. She deliberately chose a fitted, black dress with a low neckline and a string of pearls with matching pearl drop earrings. She wanted to attract attention.

Anna made sure they had a great time. She was attentive to her husband and charming with his friends. She was poised when introduced to his business associates. Kurt was clearly proud of his wife and suspected nothing.

One older man was particularly captivated by Anna and joined the couple for drinks after dinner. The man inadvertently made Kurt want Anna more when he said, "You will never be able to hang onto a women like Anna."

"I know how to keep a woman happy," Kurt said as he wrapped his arm around the back of Anna's shoulders. She turned and kissed him. He suspected nothing.

At mass that week the priest gave Anna the long-awaited letter. She packed everything she needed and left.

The letter gave the location of Karl's aunt outside of Attendorn. Anna found her with ease despite the chaos caused by the war. *Tante Ava* took her in the moment Anna introduced herself. Ava had already heard much of the story of how Karl and his family had escaped Germany with the help of Olav and Anna.

"He waited for you in Belgium for four years. He never heard from you even though he sent letters over and over again. Then he finally immigrated to Canada. His mother and sister remained here in Belgium—as did your friend, Klara. I don't know where they live now.

Karl has a two-year old son, Erich, who lives with him. Karl does not know where the mother is. She abandoned them when Erich was a baby. They never married, Anna. The relationship was only a very brief affair. The woman was…unstable shall we say? To tell you the truth, I think Karl succumbed to loneliness and she caught him at a weak moment."

Anna was relieved to know the truth. Events had not unfolded the way either of them intended. But Karl was alive and had immigrated to Canada! She wrote to him immediately.

For weeks she had been oscillating between joy and fear. She couldn't wait to be with Karl, but she was afraid that he no longer loved her or that someone would separate them again. She was often startled by the irrational feeling that Kurt was searching for her—that he might show up at *Tante Ava's*. The confidence of her youth had diminished.

Karl sent word as soon as he could that he wanted Anna to leave for Canada and gave clear travel instructions. Anna made the twelve-day voyage from Bremen to Canada—twelve days in anticipation.

"Will he be able to love me knowing I was married to Kurt? Are we both so altered since 1944 that we will be unable to resume our relationship?" She wondered.

He was waiting for her when the ship docked in Montreal. They ran toward each other and buried their faces in a frantic embrace. Karl's kiss spoke from his soul and washed away Anna's doubts.

"At last… What a long road back to you, Karl!"

"I will never leave you again, *putchen*…

Laughing and crying simultaneously, Anna took Karl's arm.

Chapter Twenty-Four
Nocturne

Before leaving for the Palm Beach Airport, Niels insisted on taking a photo of the ocean. "Look at the colors, *Mutti*!"

"Beautiful Son! Deep purple clouds and the sea—pastel green—aqua would you say?"

"Yes, and the pale beach in the foreground—gulls against the dark clouds in the distance."

"Will you make a print for me? On canvas like the photo you printed in Toronto, the one of the CN tower rising out of the fog?" Anna requested.

"Sure, I will bring it with me when Erich and I come up north in July. Are you ready to leave?"

"Yes, I think we have everything. I'm glad we went out for dinner with Ted, Ingrid, and Max last night instead of seeing them here today. I can never say good-bye…"

"Okay, let's go before someone shows up." Niels loaded the luggage into the rental car, and they were on their way.

Once in the air, Niels surprised Anna with his curiosity about the past. "*Mutti*, here I am not that far from retirement, and I know nothing about our relatives. You and Dad rarely talked about Germany. I only know Aunt Rita, Uncle Axel and Wolfgang. They visited us at the lake, and also here at West Palm Beach a few times. Were they the only ones from your family that travelled to Canada to see us?"

"The only ones," Anna replied without elaborating.

"I remember you took trips back to Germany when I was little. Did Dad ever travel with you?" Anna shook her head.

"Why didn't he go? Work?" Niels persisted.

"Yes, sometimes he could not leave his job…but returning to Europe would have been too difficult for your father," Anna paused to think about life with Karl. At times memories of the past would eclipse her husband's ability to enjoy the present. Karl would retreat into himself and be unreachable for hours and sometimes days. She had learned to keep the household calm and not approach him during his troubled bouts of depression.

"Didn't he want to see his mother?"

"Grandmother Lowe and Aunt Roksana visited us once when we still lived in Thunder Bay—before we moved to the lake. Grandmother Lowe was ill for some time and passed away not long after their visit, and of course, your aunt is gone now too. She never married, no kids."

"Did they always live in Belgium?"

"Oh yes, ever since they left Warsaw toward the end of the war."

"Why did they leave?"

Anna responded elusively, "Not safe."

"Tell me about the rest of your side of the family. What happened to Grandmother Mari and Grandfather Olav?"

"After the war, they lived a quiet life and both passed away in the same year…1965. Father was a professional musician in Leipzig and the rest of the time dedicated himself to our family…"

Uncle Leo, the oldest of my brothers, was a remarkable musician until the seventies. He was quite the ladies' man, handsome and charming. Women couldn't resist him. No wife or children…Leo wasted his talent, Niels. I think that he never got over the war years…alcoholic, often depressed.

Your Uncle Ralfie was a piano teacher. He married a friend of the family, Vilma Baumann, and they had two kids. Ralfie met her when he was working on the Baumann farm after the war. Ralfie and Vilma are living with their son and his wife in Leipzig.

"You had a third brother as well?"

"Otto," Anna smiled at the thought of him. "Otto and his wife owned and worked in their restaurant in Hanover."

"Tell me about him."

"He was the youngest. Such a good-natured boy. Always loved food. It was no surprise that he became a chef. We were very proud when he opened his own restaurant in Hanover. I have eaten there on my trips to Europe. Very nice, Niels, I tell you, beautiful food!"

"Did they have any children?"

"One daughter and she and her husband took over the restaurant."

"You were the only one in your family that immigrated. Why? Did you and Dad come over together?... *Mutti?*"

When Niels looked closely at his mother, he noticed that her face seemed veiled or clouded over. He came to the realization quite suddenly that secrecy had been critical to survival for his mother. She would not explain—at least not today.

"It's a long story."

"When Erich and I come to the lake in July, will you tell us the story? I should begin a family tree."

"I don't know how far back you will be able to go. I only knew my *GrosMutter Beatrice.* The other relatives died during WWI or from disease between the wars. Others disappeared elsewhere to start a new life.

My mother's best friend, Frieda Portner, was like an aunt to me though. In fact, we all called her *Tante Frieda.*"

Anna asked for ice water and slowly sipped her drink. Images of the salon flowed through her mind. She felt a pain in her chest when she remembered Ada and Oskar. Frieda said she had received only one letter from Ada with no return address and that Ada, Franz, and their boys lived in New Orleans with an addition to the family, a baby girl named Anna. No one ever heard from her again.

"Are you all right, *Mutti?*"

"Good, my dawling. It was all so long ago... We Germans try to forget the war by whatever means necessary."

"Hmmm."

"You mentioned your *Tante Frieda.* Similar to me calling your best friend, Auntie Klara."

"Exactly. Klara is like a sister to me."

"Will she be able to attend Aunt Rita's exhibition in Leipzig next spring?"

"Oh yes, along with a few of her children. I think three of them are retired now so their schedules are flexible. She will have lots of help to get around. She's in a wheelchair all of the time. I may return to Belgium with them for a longer visit with Klara before going home to the lake."

Anna adjusted her seat so that she could stretch out and rest her head comfortably. She closed her eyes, a cue for Niels that it was time for him to read the newspaper.

As she relaxed her body, a scene appeared in her mind; Klara, Nat and her sneaking around the corner of an old building to see a fortune teller named Mitza. She had told Anna, "You will meet a man, but he will go far away, and you will follow later. You will live happily enough. You will have few tears and you will be far across the ocean."

"Yes, I suppose she was right," Anna mused. "I had few tears living with Karl and the boys. Such a good life." Anna's reverie was awakened by the flight attendant.

"I will have a coffee, thank you," Anna answered.

Niels folded his newspaper, "Did you have any other girlfriends besides Aunt Klara?" Niels was not to be deterred from uncovering more information.

"Yes, Nathalie Lenz. When we were young, the three of us were inseparable. Nat was brilliant in school, and later during the war, she worked in medical research outside of Berlin. We never heard from her again after the war ended.

Chaos was everywhere. She may have been killed by the Russians or taken by the English. Many German scientists were abducted by the allies to give the West a leading edge in science and technology…people just disappeared.

I thought Frieda would hear from her, though, because they were very close and the salon address remained the same for over thirty years. Can you believe it? The salon was never bombed. She could have reached us… I often think of Nat."

"Maybe we can find her on the computer," suggested Niels.

"I tried and so did Klara. Nathalie would be 87 years old now if she was alive. Also, if she survived the chaos after the war ended, she may have changed her name to make a new start. She was, after all, a Nazi…" Anna whispered. "…and…she had some things she needed to forget."

"This is fascinating stuff, *Mutti*! I have so many questions; for instance, I always wondered about Dad."

"What do you mean?"

"He spoke, what, seven languages, or was it nine? Also, when Dad had his swimming trunks on, Erich and I noticed marks on his legs. Dad said he had a bad illness when he was a boy and the sores left permanent marks, but I always believed they were scars from something else—bullet wounds maybe? As kids Erich and I imagined Dad as a spy…outwitting the enemy. *Mutti*, was Dad involved in some sort of espionage?"

"…I will wait until you and Erich are together to tell you more about your father. For now, I can only say that at times your father travelled underneath railway cars." Anna smiled and laughed.

"You aren't really going to do this to me are you?" pleaded Niels in fun.

"Order your mother a chardonnay, please." She could always taste the sunshine captured in a glass of chardonnay.

After their drinks arrived, Niels continued, "I get that Erich should hear about Dad at the same time as I do. Okay then…tell me more about Frieda. Were you close? What happened to her after the war?"

"Frieda trained me to be a beautician. I lived in her apartment behind the salon and worked with her during the day. She helped me mature—so much I learned from Frieda. Yes, we were very close. When Erich is with us remind me to tell you about the time I saved her life from the Russians after the war…" Anna baited her son.

"Right now I will say that Frieda was married late in life to a man who was a dear friend of your Grandfather. His name was Mr. Wolfe. He had a law practice and Frieda the salon, but together they established an orphanage in Leipzig after the war."

"You really have my attention now! Such interesting people…and YOU. Never a victim. Never beaten down. Not you. You are extraordinary, *Mutti*! …more alive than people half your age."

"We did what we could or had to do to survive when our lives and homes were destroyed. I hope you will never experience war," Anna uttered in a deep solemn voice edged with pain.

"…Fasten your seatbelts and raise your trays to the upright position… We will be making our descent into Toronto…" the pilot announced.

"Already? *Mutti*, can't I persuade you to stay with us for a few days? We could take in a symphony at Roy Thompson Hall? Also, Erich, Diane and the girls want to see you." Anna shook her head stubbornly.

"You know the snow won't even be gone at home. We have tulips blooming here in Toronto."

"Thank you, Son. Sounds wonderful but not this time. I will catch my flight in the morning and be home in time to enjoy part of the afternoon at the lake."

Gail and Jim were at the airport in Thunder Bay to greet Anna. Anna took a deep breath of the fresh spring air and freedom.

After picking up some groceries they headed out the highway to the lake. "Is the ice off the lake yet?" asked Anna. The question was as common for northerners as a question about traffic would be for urban people to the south.

"Yes, we have crystal, tinkle ice close to shore and the black ice has been roaring in the middle of the lake. We haven't seen any fisherman or cross country skiers in quite some time needless-to-say." The neighbors chuckled comfortably together.

"Come for dinner tomorrow and let's catch up," suggested Anna.

"Won't you be tired from travelling?" asked Gail.

"No dawling, come." Anna said light-heartedly.

By the middle of May the ice was out of the lake and returning migratory birds were breaking the silence of winter with their song. She heard the resident partridges drumming their mating music—the heartbeat of spring.

Dandelions were springing up overnight and the grass was green in Anna's front yard. The sudden surge of life in the North always moved Anna, "I have been alive for decades, and yet spring is still a miracle for me. Rebirth."

By June Anna had almost finished planting her garden. Each year she grew a large assortment of vegetables despite the challenges of the short growing season. Karl and she had enriched the soil with compost over the years. Anna took her time planting to ensure that the rows were straight and each seed was equal distance apart. She covered the seeds to the correct depth and tamped them down carefully. Later as the vegetables grew she tended them affectionately, removing harmful weeds, watering, thinning plants or hilling rows as necessary.

As she worked, her mind would wander to her mother's gardens. Mari had a "green thumb" and had taught Anna all of the basics – but more than that. She had imparted the importance of growing food for survival. "Survival for sure! Rita and I planted potatoes, cabbage, onions, and carrots anywhere we could find some space at the Hoffmans'. Today it is for pleasure."

She walked stiffly back into the log house that Karl had built and cooked a dinner for herself. Later during the gestation hours of the night, Anna dreamed of Karl and awakened with a painful sense of longing. She went to the closet where she kept his old leather jacket and boots. She took his jacket from the hanger and wrapped it around her shoulders.

At dawn, feeling the weight of the jacket, she got up and traded it for a comfortable robe. She padded into the kitchen and made coffee and toast. The morning was warm enough for Anna to have her breakfast on the deck. She sipped the hot coffee and looked around smiling.

The vigilant cliffs across the lake were reflected clearly on the calm surface of the water. A solitary loon gave an undulating cry. Anna closed her eyes as she listened and then lifted her face to the sun.

References

The following references influenced the writing of Kraut. They provided the historical context for the stories.

Evans, Richard, The Third Reich in Power, Penguin Books, 2005.

Judt, Tony, Postwar: A History of Europe Since 1945, Penguin Books, 2005.

Metaxas, Eric, Bonhoeffer: Pastor, Martyr, Prophet, Spy, Thomas Nelson Inc., 2010.

Smith, Howard, Last Train from Berlin, Knopf, 1942.

The World at War Volumes 1-11, Thames Television Ltd., 1973.

Rebekah Hagglund was an English professor, and later, a business writer. More recently, her life has been enriched through creative writing. She lives on the shores of Lake Superior, in the Canadian wilderness, with her husband.